SCRATCH A THIEF

Eddie Pesak is married now, and he's got a young daughter. But there was a time when he was part of his brother Walter's gang. There was a time when he was the gun man on a series of robberies, like that time he accidentally shot a cop in the belly. They caught him on that last job, and he did his time. Now all he wants is to find a job and keep it before Drago—the cop-with-a-grudge he shot all those years ago—rousts him and gets him fired again. All Eddie wants is to steer clear of his past. But that's when Walter comes back into his life...and Sargatanas, his twitchy right-hand-man. They need him for a job, one last job that will get them all what they need to retire. But you don't retire from being a thief. It's like Drago says, once a thief...

HOUSE OF EVIL

Carey Ledbetter, ex-carny, has the perfect setup. As Zedek Kozma he heads a religious group at The Retreat while dispensing sex and drugs to the Hollywood elite. Trouble is, Carey is beginning to forget where carny ends and crazy devil worship begins—the demons are starting to get too real. So when failing B-actor, Paul Berko, accidentally stumbles his way up to The Retreat, Carey isn't sure but that he might have finally met the devil himself. All Berko wants to do is get to know one of the acolytes, Anne Woodbridge. That and soak up some of the free booze. But if Kozma wants him to be the devil, he can be the devil. It could be the role of a lifetime...

D1500192

JOHN TRINIAN BIBLIOGRAPHY
(1933-2008)

A Game of Flesh (1959)

The Big Grab (1960; reprinted as Any Number Can Win, 1963)

North Beach Girl (1960; reprinted as Strange Lovers, 1967)

The Savage Breast (1961)

Scratch a Thief (1961; also published as
Once a Thief as by Zekial Marko, 1965)

House of Evil (1962)

Scandal on the Sand (1964)

Scratch a Thief
— — —
House of Evil

TWO THRILLERS BY

John Trinian

STARK HOUSE

Stark House Press • Eureka California

SCRATCH A THIEF / HOUSE OF EVIL

Published by Stark House Press
1315 H Street
Eureka, CA 95501
griffinskye3@sbcglobal.net
www.starkhousepress.com

SCRATCH A THIEF

HOUSE OF EVIL

ISBN: 1-933586-99-0   R2003860182
ISBN-13: 978-1-933586-99-1

Book design by Mark Shepard, shepgraphics.com

First Stark House Press Edition: May 2016

FIRST EDITION

Throwing Snowballs
at the Moon
by Ki Longfellow

How Zekial Marko (aka John Trinian, covert pulp fiction writer) found the time to write *House of Evil*, beats me. But one day somewhere in the long ago, he dropped a very thin very new paperback in my lap. "Here, kid. Don't say I never gave you anything."

Writers love their books. They keep copies. Not Marko. So when the day came he needed the damn thing back for some damn reason, he stole mine. It took me years to dig up another and cost me thirty five bucks. I'm not supposed to take it out of its plastic sealer. So I never have.

Before he took it, I read it. Anne Woodbridge was me (a portrait not even close, but it was Marko's vision not mine); Paul Berko was him (a little closer to life, but not much).

I saw *House of Evil* as a goof.

It *was* a goof. It was a joke, a riff on 50's horror movies, a laugh up his sleeve. I did not see it for what it really was.

Zekial Marko had written me a love story in the form of pulp fiction at its sweetest and pulpiest and B-moviest.

But oh, pulp fiction fans, here it is again, all shiny and new. Am I pleased? I melt with pleasure.

Reading it now is very different than how I read it long ago. When it landed in my lap, I was a book snob. I read the Russians, the English, the Germans, the French, the Spanish (which amounted to *Don Quixote* and Federico Garcia Lorca), the Americans if they published before I was born or near enough. I read poetry and philosophy.

Now I read *House of Evil* for its words turning to film in my head. If Roger Corman had only found it, even Ed Wood. But more, I read it to see me as Marko saw me. As he saw himself. Crazy cut-outs, comic book heroes, a damsel in distress, book covers, a dream by flashlight.

If Marko read anything, I don't recall noticing. But he did read. *House of Evil* tells me he read as much as I did. Maybe more since his reading included comic books. I just never caught him at it.

It reminds me of what I already knew. Like me, he was a sucker for the black and white screen of the Forties.

As for writing, he moved too fast to do much of that. He was always chasing muses. San Francisco was a muse in city form.

Frisco. City of writers. Jack London. Dashiell Hammett. Bret Harte. Mark Twain. Ambrose Bierce. Ina Coolbirth. (Who? you no doubt ask. She was female. Females do tend to get forgotten.) And just then, singing their last Beat Song: Lawrence Ferlinghetti, Gary Snyder, Alan Ginsberg. Kerouac when he was in town.

There was Richard Brautigan with no discernable niche, then or now. Alan Watts singing an off-key hymn. And Zekial Marko, pulp fiction writer.

As for me, I was there too, come across the Golden Gate Bridge from Marin County seeking my own destiny. (Horny old Henry Miller once felt the same way about Paris. I didn't know him then, so I didn't know that. But I knew him later. Between slow games of ping-pong and sweet young things giving him afternoon blow jobs on his Pacific Palisades couch, we'd swap tales of that most precious thing: the memory of anticipation.)

In that sweet slice of unnamed time between hipsters and hippies, I was the sole baby bohemian in a world of Marin's swimming pools and cheerleaders; the only one to wear black on black: straight black hair halfway down my back, black tights, black turtleneck sweaters and short black skirts—but always white sneakers. The only one who drove a white 1955 Thunderbird with portholes, and spent high school lunch hours under its red leather tonneau cover reading Kafka and smoking.

Whenever I could, I skipped along Frisco's seasalty streets, crisp and crowded and halo'd with hope, my head bursting with words and the love of words. Literature wailing around in there like English apparitions. I knew Art lived around there somewhere... and I intended to move in on her and raise my family of books and poems, poems and books. Already aware that an artist must begin by theft—but stealing always, of course, from the best. Though not yet aware that literature was dead. (I should have known, haunted even then by its ghost.)

Skipping with me, more often than not, was Marko.

"By Balor and his one-eyed butt!" he yelled, doing a foine Brendan Behan. "Oh, for a spin on the great dog sky, glinty and many armed up there! A courtly night, a generous night this. It's time for a nose dive."

Marko, Richard Brautigan and me, tumbling down Richard's five flights of rickety stairs, boozy and bloated with words, a jumble of arms and feet and well-being. We hit the early evening street, loud and laughing.

Us surprising no one on the North Beach street. So used as they were to drunken hairy folk. Or maybe just Marko.

Richard was elated because he'd finally finished his book about trout and furniture. Marko because he was always either elated or terrified. And I was delirious. Because I was with writers. Three in a little over a week. Two published. Marko and Jack Kerouac. Both famous. Jack in an underground kind of way. Marko in Japan and France.

The French thought Marko was a major American novelist. He said this about that: "A bunch of people who think Jerry Lewis is a genius need their sense of humor examined." But he loved it just the same.

I'd never read a thing by Kerouac until ten or so years later—after he'd gone home to Momma, crawled into bed and died of a fear bigger than Marko's. Marko was afraid of too much meaning; Jack as a confused Catholic Buddhist was afraid there wasn't any. Some few pages into *The Subterraneans* all I remember thinking went like this: I wish Jack were fonder of full stops or periods or maybe less fond of dashes so that in reading him and his hipster shit—perhaps in belated homage I should say "digging" him—all about poor beat Frisco angels flipping out on junk or christlike browneyed sadness or just plain personal madness when they realize Holy Fuckola! God untold eons back grabbed her helmet threw a cosmic leg across the saddle of her Harley and split for a vacation in a black hole that is if she ever worked anymore in the first place and they were left to dig the Beach alone. Or even a comma so I could pause now and again to pop a cork or even for crying out loud draw a goddamn breath.

And although Richard read me what he wrote as he wrote it, I never read him either... even after hearing one perfect Brautigan sentence: The sun broke like a beer bottle on the water. But Marko, I read every word of his I could find. Which wasn't easy. Zekial Marko wrote pulp fiction. His titles: *The Big Grab, Scandal in the Sand, House of Evil, North Beach Girl, Scratch a Thief,* were like Kleenex, on the dime store stands for a month, then gone with a sneeze.

None of them read me. How could they? I hadn't written a thing. I didn't know then I'd have to put the pieces of whoever I was back together like a five thousand piece double-sided jigsaw puzzle and live with the cracks.

What *did* I know? Looking back—nothing. What did I want? Everything. What could I do? Anything. What had I done? Met writers, that's what I'd done.

For this moment on the streets of San Francisco, it was enough.

I swung down Grant Avenue, a bard on either arm, both reciting mouth poetry on the trot. Marko speaking the stronger music for his was surely the gift of off-the-cuff gab. He led us like blind mice through the door of one of the dreariest dives I'd ever seen. On the celluloid screen, or peeking through saloon doors in another attempt to find my mother. Marko forgetting—or not giving a fuck—that I was prohibited by reason of age. The barroom was a long tunnel, painted in dead gunmetal gray, extending back into darkness. Room for maybe two abreast to walk its length. The bartop ran from the front door to the toilet in back, its surface pitted with cigarette burns and glass rings. The place reeked of old smoke, fresh sweat, the bad breath of strangers, and maraschino cherries. It was lit with the blue and rose light from a massive jukebox way towards the back. From which country and western music whinnied.

A heavy row of sullen male faces turned towards us as we danced through the door, Marko calling out happy yahoos.

Two minutes later I was in my first barroom brawl. But that was one long excruciating minute after I found myself ordering my first professional drink in a saloon. It went like this. Bartender: "OK, girlie, whaddayawan'?" Me: "Ummmmmahhh." I'd never been in a bar before. Except to plead my mother out. What did she drink? Couldn't remember, couldn't think, and the bartender stood there chewing bubblegum and smoking a cigar at the same time, wiping a soiled glass with a soiled rag and waiting and waiting and waiting and—then. A bit of hell broke off.

Of course it was all Marko's fault. Something he'd said not only heard, but understood. I missed it, but the man on the barstool next to Richard caught every word. Snorting like a pig, he swung round, picked Marko up bodily, and with one great heave, threw him out the barroom door. This was so interesting, the whole bar came to a complete stop. Evidently Marko had landed on his back, losing a lungful of air. We could hear him out there trying to get it back. And Richard? Richard sat there, his beer halfway to his moustachio'd mouth crammed with potato chips, compliments of the bar and put there by Richard himself in a previous moment of goodwill. He, in a brave readjustment of the situation, carefully set his beer down on the counter, swallowed his gluey mouthful, sighed, and gave the man next to him a terrific wallop on the ear. This was *not* the man who'd tossed Marko out the door. That man had his back to me standing legs aglee and beady eyed, watching the door for signs of a returning Marko.

So I jumped him. Surprised, he spun. Far below, I could see the bar floor, buried under mashed butts, whirling beneath my man's bucking feet. Richard beaned him with the bowl of potato chips.

At that very moment Marko charged back in, tripped over the outstretched leg of the man who still held a surprised hand clapped over his outraged ear, crashed into me and my uneasy ride, and we all came down hard on the distant floor. Me snapping my teeth together in a sickening crunch. To thrash around, Richard, Marko, the beaned man, and me, in beer and butts and the boots of angry men.

Later, sprawled in a Grant Avenue gutter nursing cut lips sprained thumbs bloody noses—Richard, for instance, had a real beauty of an egg on the back of his head—Marko reached out, pinched the muscle of my upper arm with ferocious fingers, and said, "See, kid. I told you you'd never get rid of me."

I screamed. From the unexpected pain of a poet's pinch.

All these writers, writing, gave me an idea. Maybe I could start writing too? (About what would come later; at the time I was blessedly unaware of exactly how much later.) But first I had to get my hands on a typewriter. Trouble was, everybody I knew who had one was using it. Besides, I wanted my machine virginal, innocent, untouched by some earlier perhaps less-ardent suitor. I wanted a machine like me, one that had yet to find its voice. What I was really looking for was something I could exchange molecules with like Flann O'Brien's Irish policemen exchanged molecules with their bicycles, a machine that would become partly me as I became partly it. In this way perhaps me and my typewriter would also be writers. Like everybody else.

I decided to buy one, a brand new one hot out of the typewriter factory. For which I would need cash.

I could steal the money but everyone I knew needed theirs—and I'd feel bad. Stealing from people I didn't know seemed kind of... professional.

I needed a job.

Back then, the usual female job entailed typing, standing all day behind a Macy's counter—or lugging food around in a restaurant.

Of course! Juanita's!

Juanita's Galley was the worst, the best, the wildest all-day all-night ham and eggs joint there ever was. You questioned Juanita's food, you could find it in your face.

Juanita hired the young. Like illegal aliens, they worked for peanuts, she could mistreat them, and there were always more where they came from.

Slinging hash, forking English muffins, dripping gummy egg yolk down the pastel polyester backs of slumming Seekers after Arty Thrills & Spills, I worked there for one busy greasy queasy enchanted month. After that, I was never the same. For one thing I had sea-legs; Juanita's was on the abandoned wreck of an old Frisco Bay ferryboat called the Charles Van Damme and the Charles Van Damme was rotting away in the mad midst of Sausalito's waterfront only a hulk or three along from where I'd been shanghai'd by Marko and Kerouac a few months before.

What was left of the sagging peeling shrieking leaking ferry boat rode the tides of San Francisco Bay, high tide and low. There were tides when she hung too high for her ancient gangplanks, tides when mud—black and stinking as Alameda crude—swept her slanted decks, tides when she shrugged off her moorings to seek the fatal solace of the scouring sea; at these times, no engines... for engines there were none. But plenty of customers ran amok.

"Quitters!" bawled Juanita (Juanita never "said" anything; she snarled it, brawled it, spat it). "You're all chickenshits. This mud, it's artistic mud. That gangplank, Picasso's. Fuck 'em. Tide's high? They can't get off? Charge 'em rent."

Marko loved Juanita's. All things being equal, she didn't give a damn about him. Along with Jack and Richard Brautigan, he spent days on the Charles Van Damme. It never closed and so far as I could see, neither did they. Everybody loved the place: movie stars, crooks and politicians (funny how one thinks of one and the other occurs right after), comics, musicians, the rich slumming, the semi mad taking shelter from the norm.

Juanita herself was hard to even halfway like. Fat, loud, filthy, a flying buttress of a broad, mayhem in a muu-muu, nobody exactly loved Juanita—but nobody forgot her either.

Juanita was another artist and her art was terrifying people. When she died, I hope they plastered her behind a wall of the haunted Winchester House.

I was working at Juanita's the night I met one of Marko's frails. Or maybe his wife. Or one of his wives. I never did get that straight. Thinking back, I knew nothing about Marko before I met Marko. He talked, but seldom mentioned his past. Born as Marvin Leroy Schmoker, he came from somewhere near Salinas. There, he'd met John Steinbeck, or at least run a stick along his fence.

That night the Charles Van Damme was packed to the gunwales. It was after two in the am and practically everyone I'd ever met or would ever meet and loads I'd never know or care to know were coffee-swilling food-dodging world-solving table-hopping Juanita-gawping at the top of their lungs. Juanita, who cooked everything, stood center stage cooking as loud as she could, Jack was squinting at the patrons wondering if anyone knew him, Richard was nodding off over one cold-eyed egg, Marko was tripping me every time I passed him, and I was everywhere running my ass off. Eggs over easy here, scrambled there, porridge out on the port deck, hash browns aft. Christ, talk about wanting a typewriter.

Maybe Mrs. Marvin Schmoker showed up right after Juanita went berserk, scooping up about three pounds of link sausages still sizzling on the grill so she could throw them at a sticky table of suited normals brawling over the work of Ayn Rand.

"Shut up! I won't have folks talking obscene around me or mine! You take those dirty mouths and get outta here!"

At that same moment, on one of my fly-bys, Marko reached out a hand to grab the back of my black turtle neck sweater—irrrrk! Me and my tin tray stopped short but six orders of coffee no longer cupped by mugs kept right on going, splat! All over the Modern Art Show Juanita let some poor modern artist stick up on an empty bulkhead.

"Sit down, you," said Marko. "You're an Indian. Say something in Indian to Jack. He's always pretending he scalped someone."

"I never pretend," said Jack.

Marko reared back. "Lie! You pretend you write your crap in one go on rolls of toilet paper."

"I do."

I said, "Goddammit, Marko. Look at all that coffee hanging there."

"It's you," said Jack, looking me over, but missing my face. "I remember you. You're always on boats, a boat girl, boating."

Marko had hold of my sweater. I still had hold of my tray with the six empty unserved cups.

I said, "Let go!"

He said, "Can't. My ring's stuck in your hair."

I said, "What?"

"Your hair," he said and pulled.

"Ouch!"

"Marvin!" shrilled a voice just above my head. It was so high and so sudden and so close it made me jerk back not only my head but my whole body which yanked Marko up out of his seat by his ring finger and a hank of hair out of my scalp.

At the clatter of tray and empty cups hitting the deck, but more, my scream: long and loud and painful—it seemed like the whole Charles Van Damme shut up.

For one rare unprecedented moment Juanita's was silent. Even Juanita, not one to shut up. I think she was off in the can.

I was clawing at my scalp.

Marko was flopping around like one of Brautigan's trout. He'd landed in my lap. From an outsider's point of view, we looked like two of the Marx Brothers rehearsing.

The over-dressed normals sat there as normals usually do, half a hundred necks craned, whoa, a hot night at Juanita's again. Until Richard dropped a perfect brick into this pool of soundlessness.

"Uh oh," he said. Like rings in water, uh oh uh oh uh oh circled the deck.

"Marvin Schmoker, you sneaky slimy sonofabitch." There was that voice again. "What are you doing with that child!"

Jack gave Marko a smile of perfect beat beatitude. "And this is—Mrs. Marko?"

Maybe Mrs. Schmoker had this chilly smile on her chilly round face, and this chilly light in her black and white eyes, and then, there were the arms. She had her arms behind her back.

"And just when," she said, "do you think you're coming home again?"

"Home?" muffled Marko into my stomach.

"I asked you a question, Marvin."

Marko gave up trying to talk and yanked his hand from my head. Whoa.

"Do you know how long I've been looking for you? I even went to San Bruno."

I said, "San Bruno?"

Richard, enjoying everything immensely, said, "Marko's mommy lives in San Bruno."

"That's my man you've got on you," said Maybe Mrs. Schmoker in a scuffed linoleum clothes-wringer voice. She took her arms from behind her back. In one hand was a trowel.

What had she come to dig?

At that exact moment, something hit the Charles Van Damme hard enough to tilt her.

Getting hit hard enough to tilt a huge ferry boat packed with people is really surprising. I know I was really surprised. And if I was surprised, you should have seen everybody else. Maybe Mrs. Schmoker dropped her trowel.

Juanita, never satisfied till a thing was done right, picked up her favorite

Chinese cleaver and was on her way out on deck to smack whoever smacked her ferry, when, right at that touching moment, the prow of a large tugboat showed up through a brand new hole in the Charles Van Damme.

We all survived. The tugboat broke up in all that highspeed Technicolor confusion and sank to the bottom of the bay. Where she is to this day. Covered in feathery sea scum and ghosts. I think.

Breeched and beached, the Charles Van Damme survived. For awhile.

I never saw Maybe Mrs. Marko again and Juanita's never bought me a typewriter, which is probably a very good thing. Years had to pass away before I found my voice. Make that voices.

Marko gave me himself. He gave me *House of Evil*. He gave me a cowboy. The cowboy gave me my first daughter. I named her Sydney.

It went like this: I was living with Maggie, a weed dealer, somewhere in North Beach, drinking coffee, smoking cigarettes, and reading *Crime and Punishment*. I was so excited drinking coffee and reading *Crime and Punishment*, I read it all through the night, read it until I finished it, a Russian marathon. Just as I was snuggling down into my Murphy bed and dawn was sneaking through the burlap curtains, there came a pounding at the door. It wasn't Raskolnikov. It was Hans, a tall stoop-shouldered lump I'd bumped into a few days before at a coffee house on the corner of Green Street and Grant. Not that I wanted to; he got in the way.

Newly arrived from Amsterdam, Hans was one of Maggie's defined creeps: a lank-haired pimply-faced lantern-jawed Dutchman who sat at the feet of bongo players snapping his fingers and erupting like acne every few seconds with little wet wows. This one attached himself to me, followed me home, then haunted our doorstep until the Italian who ran the restaurant underneath swept the dim Dutch bulb away with a broom. And that, happily thought I, was that.

I opened the door. Hans was on my side as fast as a paradiddle and I was standing there in front of my tousled bed covered in nothing but dismay. He shouted, "Goot gott, Americans girl! id ist I!" all the while unzipping his baggy Dutch pants, reaching deep inside to rummage around, for a minute perplexed, then worried, then brightening, as he came out in triumph with the first uncircumcised willy I'd ever seen.

I threw back my head and screamed, "What!"

Zekial Marko said, "It's a prick, kid. What do you think it is?"

Marko? Where the hell had he come from? It was morning. I rarely saw Marko in the morning.

Marko stood in the still open door. Behind him an arrogant young man leaned up against the wall. They were both grinning like dogs. As for Hans, he ran for it.

Marko, talking like Edward G. Robertson, introduced me to his friend.

A young Harrison Ford in bearing, in color, in the shape of the mouth, the light in the eyes, Marko's friend was mouthwatering. Also a cowboy. Or so I thought. Though he did turn out to be a rider. So I was close.

Thinking about it, I realize now even more than I realized it then the cowboy was a present. From Marko. Because I loved Marko but I didn't want him.

I'd seen the cowboy on one of those Sausalito houseboats I've already mentioned and poked Marko. "Do you know… " My question was stuffed with meaning. "I do," he said.

I knew the cowboy was in the middle of an exciting stint with the blonde half of brunette and blonde twins because Marko'd told me. "Two willowy nitwits whose mother is as white as Moby Dick."

I stared. She *was* as white as Moby Dick, and almost as large.

How Marko pried the cowboy loose by what tall story I never knew. It must have been a doozy.

So there we were: Marko, me, the kid cowboy, Dostoevsky, and Murphy the bed. The cowboy stood solid on his dusty cowboy boots, his cowboy hat with the stained sweatband pushed to the back of his sandy head, his denim blue eyes wide at the sight of Maggie's dope. Following it up hill and down dale 'til he came to me. I couldn't say what he saw, but what I saw was he knew how to stand, how to keep his mouth shut, how to move like he knew where he was going, how to keep his hat on like he knew he wouldn't be staying.

What was I expecting? Me, the last baby beatnik, want to get laid? No. But I would, I sure as hell would, if it promised an introduction in the dark. Or revelations. Or recognition. Or whispered explanations. If it opened cosmic potholes to trip in.

I wish I'd felt that way about Marko. And so did he.

Marko left. He must have. I don't remember seeing him go.

Later, the cowboy asleep beside me, I thought of the three gold specks in his blue eye and his cold blue seed in my bewildered belly. I thought of Marko's eyes. He hid behind eyes the color of moss in a rainforest, behind the silver of his tongue.

For shame, I never thanked Marko for the gift. Of growth. And for my daughter Sydney. I didn't wonder where he went when he left his gift. Or what it cost him.

Before Castro was *The* Castro, before the Summer of Love was a flutter of flower-eyed kids come from everywhere, drug dealers hot on their bare heels, Sydney and I lived on an odd steep street at the far end of Market. Clamped to the side of a crumbling hill, my place looked like the Bates house looming over *that* motel. Inside, the ceilings were dark with dreams, empty of Brautigan furniture but full of people... most of them stoned out of their left minds on acid. Acid was a craze in more ways than one.

Marko didn't touch it. Neither did I. (There's a reason for that. I'll get to it eventually.)

He liked weed and drink and cigarettes and talking. I liked coffee and cigarettes and reading.

His movie, *Once a Thief*, in the can, the last book he'd write written, a TV Batman scriptwriter's job rejected ("They want me to write BAM! and BIFF! and POW! I write crap but it's not that damn crappy."), we were hiding from the maddening crowd in my back yard, a yard of scrub and dirt that jumped up towards the tipping and slipping wood fences of the folks who lived on the street above us. Sydney, now over two, picked all the flowers off the flowering bush we hunkered under, me listening to Marko describe a movie playing in his head.

"So, kid, it opens on Route 1. There's the Pacific Ocean smacking rocks around on one side of the road, there's Big Sur on the other side. Scenic, right? Especially since this is an aerial shot. We see a huge van heading north, one you'd expect to find on a movie set. Cut to a few miles down the road and here comes a Brinks truck."

"On Route 1?"

"Shaddup. You're messing with my flow."

I shaddup. He was making enough flow for both of us. Much more and we'd be found by someone on a tsunami acid trip.

"You gotta see it. The van stops in one of those few places where you can pull over, and a movie crew piles out, the actors, the camera man, the director, the works. You see it?"

"How could I miss?"

"Right! And there's cars passing them, slowing to watch a film being made but they can't stop since there's no room on Route I."

"True."

"The actors are dressed like... hell, like actors making some movie. And here comes the Brinks truck. By now the film crew has blocked the road and a few cars are forced to stop both ways. This includes the truck. So what happens next?"

"The truck gets robbed."

"Fuck! Have you seen this movie?"

"No. Is there one? It's obvious."

"OK. Fine. The actors rob the truck, the director directs them robbing it, the cameraman films the whole thing. The Brinks guys are perfect. All the stopped cars think it's swell. They're out of their cars looking to see if they can spot the stars. It goes without a hitch. So they tie up the Brinks guys, stick 'em in the truck, and the lead guy and his doxie drives the truck away, followed by the big rig, all packed with the crew back inside. People return to their cars happy they got to see a scene from a movie being made."

He does that leaning in close thing he does, all the better to see what I think. "So?"

"So?"

"So, it's a real robbery. The Brinks truck is real and the money is real, but the movie truck is a fake. So they get away with it. Whatcha think?"

"What happens next?"

"Who the hell knows? This is as far as I got. Whatcha think?"

"I think if you had more movie I'd go see it."

"Grab the kid and we'll scram outta here. Your house is about to lift off for Oz."

Talking about a movie is more fun than filming one. Unless you're the director. Or the cinematographer. Or a grip. They always have something to do, unlike everyone else. Everyone else sits around waiting for their moment.

Marko wrote himself a part. He wrote me a part. Which is why we also got to sit around. Scriptwriters are almost always banned from a set. Producers don't want them getting ideas... things like, they might be vital to the film.

Filming *Once a Thief* was tedious. Except for the intrigue that wasn't filmed. Alain Delon, a French hotsie, hated Ann-Margaret. In a scene filmed in the club where Carol Doda was nightly baring her impressive boobs, Alain got to slap Ann-Margaret around. He relished it. By the time they got it right, her face was as red as her shame. She was *not* having a good time. Van Heflin disappeared each day. No one knew where. But he came back on time, if even quieter than when he slipped off. Much later we learned he was ill but too much of a pro to show it. Jack Palance had a huge trailer all to himself. Marko and I hung around in that one with Palance. So did a New York stage actor called Tony Musante. Musante played a heavy and he played him hard and mean. As Tony, he was adorable. Marko would later write whole episodes of *Toma* for him. *Toma* was Tony's TV series.

Ann-Margaret was having a nervous breakdown. Lost in a straight role, no singing or dancing her way out of this one. Alain kept at her, she spent her time alone in her trailer, smaller than Jack's even though she'd just made *Viva Las Vegas*. The producers flew in an old hand at the movie game to soothe her, coach her, coddle her. Everybody was impressed by Jeff Corey. He'd refused to rat out his friends at HUAC, got blackballed for twelve years, been in all sorts of great movies, and coached just about everyone. If they were impressed, he was ten times more impressed. I kept out of his way.

And so it went until they called it a wrap.

I learned a very important lesson. Don't get involved in movies unless you're the director.

Speaking of nervous breakdowns, one sunny afternoon in the basement of a Marin County house containing a decent painter and an indecent adulterer, I took one of my rare tokes of weed. Without so much as a fond adieu, I left my body, and if not my body, my usual mind. It was, and remains, the only REAL moment (or hours, who can tell when time suddenly becomes irrelevant, not to mention non-existent) of my life.

For months after I was AWAKE. Until one night on a Santa Cruz beach, my over-taxed nervous system gave the fuck up and I slid through a Black Hole into a panic attack that lasted for three years.

Panic and six weeks in the same Napa loony bin that birthed Ken Kesey's *One Flew Over the Cuckoo's Nest* did not stop me, but it slowed me down. Marko visited whenever he had a car, or could get someone to drive him. He brought me books I couldn't read because who can read stunned on Thorazine? He talked to me but who can hear when the world's spin has slowed?

He held my hand.

Marko was as lost as I in the land of the herbally dumb. He'd had the same reaction. Sadly, he didn't get the gift of Cosmic Consciousness... all he got was the panic. If he panicked in my loony bin, they'd net him. But he risked it all the same.

I learned that almost everyone but me and Marko could smoke a ton of grass and still remain seated in their nice warm bodies. That they could fill their lungs with magic fumes and still hold on to their nice warm walnetto brains. That they could say things like, "Can you dig it?" "Like wow, man, like far fucking out!" That they could read *Stranger in a Strange Land* and think it was telling them something.

Once I was sprung (unaware that if they'd wanted to, I could have been locked up for life), I bundled up little Sydney, and off we flew to New York City with seven hundred bucks between us.
Not long after that, Marko followed me.
But before New York, came Los Angeles.

Now he'd made a major, if awful, movie in Frisco out of one of his books (the one you hold in your hand: *Scratch a Thief*), Marko knew even more people than he knew when I first met him.
Which is how we hung out in Hoyt Axton's house in Topanga Canyon listening to Hoyt sing what he'd just written: *The Pusher*.
Hoyt's mommy wrote *Heartbreak Hotel*. We learned a lot about Elvis, none of it good.
I'd never been in Los Angeles before and after running around with stars and would-be stars, I knew I wouldn't be running around it again.
But Marko inhaled it like the *Day of the Locust*. Maybe that's why he wrote pulp fiction while Richard wrote metafiction. Los Angeles was the *House of Evil*. The scam of scams and it made him laugh.
He bought shiny suits and Italian shoes. He combed his hair. He dazzled producers and movie stars. They did not dazzle him. Lee Marvin was crude. Lee made him laugh. Kim Novak was... not what you might think. Kim made him laugh. Lenny Bruce was cracking up. Nobody laughed.
We went to a party at John Frankenheimer's Malibu house. Frankenheimer'd just released a movie called *Seconds* with Rock Hudson. For directing that one I forgave him throwing a party for a snotty folksinger called Bob Dylan.
As usual Marko was the most interesting person in the crowded house. He looked like Colombo way before Peter Falk looked like Colombo and he held the whole clot of them enchanted with a story half of them wanted to film, and the other half wanted to star in. Being Marko, he never wrote it down.
As for me, I sat in a corner smoking a cigarette like Bette Davis used to smoke a cigarette: out loud. When he finally threw himself down, I asked him: "What do you believe in?"
"That life is like sleepwalking through a Haunted House."
Hearing this, I thought oh God yes! that's what life is like: lonely in the skin, lost in the eye, a tight rope around the neck and sad searching feet a half inch from the floor. It's why everyone runs around in the dark.

I would have said that but Marlon Brando asked me to take a walk on the beach.

And Marko'd wandered off with a little Arabian vanity who said she'd missed the part Samantha Egger played in *The Collector* by a single day, but who would bear Marko his only son.

Soon after, I took Sydney, flew back to Frisco, *then* to New York City.

"Yes?"

"Get your fanny down here."

"Marko?"

How he found me in Greenwich Village stumped me.

I'd fled to New York City with no friends waiting, and no coat. The coat was the hard part. It was winter. It was freezing. There was cold white wet stuff struggling through the orange air. On the ground it was yellow with dog piss and grey with huddled New Yorkers.

First thing I did was drop on down to McDougall Street to buy coats. The coat store sold hundreds of used fur things. I don't know what Sydney's used to be, but mine was muskrat. Shopping at the same time was a young chap with a young chappess. He slipped a note in the pocket of my new coat. Ordinarily I'd throw such things away, but this was one huge city and I knew no one. So I called the number.

Which is how Sydney and I ended up in an apartment on West Tenth and Greenwich Avenue with a New York University School of Law student. One of the Lovin' Spoonful also lived in the building. The tall one with the face of an Indian brave. I had a choice. Why I didn't choose the Spoonful fella also beats me.

Marko had a room in the Beacon Hotel on the Upper West Side. (Speaking of hotel rooms, Marko spent an entire night talking to Lenny Bruce in an effort to keep Lenny from jumping out of a hotel room across from the Hungry I. It didn't stop Bruce from dying young, but it gave him another year of anger.)

Like everywhere Marko had friends in New York and like everywhere, they were writers. One of 'em was flat broke. Between them they worked out a plan to remedy that—which needed me. It was wonderfully illegal, hurt no one, and remains a treasured memory of a day spent on Fifth Avenue with Marko that I can't describe. How long is the Statute of Limitations on derring-do?

Marko stuck a version of it in one of his TV scripts.

At the end of that day, Marko grabbed my arm and pulled. He kissed me so hard we fell against the plate glass of Brentano's Book Store window.

For once, I was game. "Can we do it again?"

Marko said, "Life is an art lesson, kid, we can do it until we get it right."

Zekial Marko went back to Hollywood. I wound up in London. It wasn't the last of us.

There never was a last of us.

I've read *House of Evil* again, the first time in too many years to count, and I sit here wondering what happened to Paul Berko and Anne Woodbridge. If it were up to who I am now, together we'd have thrown snowballs at a moon that never set.

—February 2016,
England

Ki Longfellow is the author is several noir mysteries including *Shadow Roll, Good Dog, Bad Dog,* and *The Girl in the Next Room,* all featuring P.I. Sam Russo. She has lived in Marin County (California), Hawaii, New York, Europe and Vermont, and is the widow of Vivian Stanshall, founding member of the Bonzo Dog Band. She currently travels and writes.

Scratch a Thief
by John Trinian

For Kenn Davis

1 (SATURDAY, DECEMBER 6th)

There were several planted trees just outside the market, and the brick paved mall was littered with fallen leaves: red and gold and amber. The sky was the color of iced lemon braided with thin gray clouds. The tower clock at the far end of the mall read ten minutes past four.

Inside the market, where Eddie Pesak stood waiting for his wife, the air was warm and smelled of wet vegetables and hot tin. A heating system purred directly over the double glass doors. Eddie leaned on a gumball machine and patiently lit a cigarette. He couldn't see Zara anywhere in the checkout line.

It was Saturday, the one day off from his job that he would have a chance to work on his Model A Ford, but since Zara didn't drive he had to take her to the market for the weekly shopping. Tomorrow, Sunday, he would have to take his wife and little Kathy to Oakland to visit with Zara's aunt and uncle.

It was bitter cold outside. When the shoppers left the market they paused near the green telephone booths, glanced sourly at the sky and adjusted the collars of their winter coats.

Eddie rolled the cigarette in his fingers, watching the line move slowly toward the checkout booth. He was a big lean man, thirty-six years old, with short salt and pepper graying hair, prominent Slavic cheekbones, hard, unsmiling mouth. His eyes were dark, almost black, sensitive, deep-set under thick black brows. His hands were thick, the knuckles showing like hard, white knobs above the wire embroidery of hair. His shoulders were slightly stooped. His movements were athletically spare, knowing; but with it all there was a strange air about him, almost of apology.

He glanced at the mall clock. A fat woman shuffled by, nodded a greeting to him, muttered something in Hungarian. Eddie touched the lip of his cap and replied in the same tongue. A blind man tapped by, winked at him. "Hi, Eddie."

"Hello, Saul."

A little girl broke away from her mother in the line and crawled up onto a mechanical elephant. She looked to be about four years old, the same age as Eddie's Kathy.

"Misser? I wanna ride."

Eddie smiled. "Maybe the elephant'll take you off to Tanganyika," he said.

"Naw. That's too far. Besides, I don't know where that is." She giggled, wrinkled the spray of freckles on her snub nose.

"My name's Barbara and my brother's name is Marlon. Put a dime in the elephant, please."

Eddie pushed a dime into the red slot and the elephant started shuffling off to nowhere, whirring and jiggling and flapping its ears.

He left the little girl and walked to the automatic coffee machine where the blind man was blowing into a steamy plastic cup, his red marked white cane draped over his thin arm.

"How's tricks, Saul?"

"You know, Eddie. It's tough. Getting worse."

"Have you heard any news?"

"Drago got back from his vacation," Saul said. He was an old man, probably seventy, and his face was the color of a grocery bag. His eyes, behind the dark glasses, were milky and wobbly, but his eyesight was perfect as far as Eddie knew. "Have you heard from Drago yet, Eddie?"

"No, not for a year," Eddie said.

Saul nodded and put a wrinkled finger into his coffee, testing it. He smiled, swallowed the coffee in three gulps. "Well, kiddo, back on the route. Tap tap, kiddo."

The old man shuffled out of the market, making a great show of his supposed blindness.

Eddie returned to the gumball machine. The little girl had finished her elephant ride and had left. Eddie spotted Zara midway in the line. He stood watching her.

She was a beautiful woman, a tall, dark blonde, twenty-six years old, with large, dark-blue eyes and full pink mouth. She was wearing a rough green sweater, thonged shoes, white, skin-tight trousers. He had met her five and a half years ago and had married her three months later. What he had felt then he still felt now.

He moved to the checkout booth. His wife saw him and made a small face. He winked. The huge cash register whirred and clicked and he automatically glanced at the open tray. The stacks of currency were thick, gray and green and rumpled, and the glitter of silver coins were piled in the first hand scoops.

The old film memory started, jerkily at first, then gathering speed, shaping into a clear picture. Reluctantly, he found himself tricked into thinking of a night many years ago, long before he had met Zara.

Where had it been? The scene itself was clear but the particular locale was hard in coming; then it came back to him, slowly, almost painfully. He remembered that it had been Christmas, twelve years ago. Salvation Army kettles outside on the cold wet streets. Bells jingling. Trees revolving on the main floor of the large store, lights glittering, odors of cut pine boughs and wet umbrellas. It had been in Byerle's Department Store in the East Bay.

It had been one of the good jobs during the fat post-war years. Eddie's older brother, Walter, had cleaned out the payroll counting benches, while Eddie, as usual, held the sawed off shotgun and forced the glassy-eyed employees to the carpeted floor.

The take had been close to eleven thousand cash....

The eyeless film jerked, dissolved slowly, like smoke in a wind, trailing sparks. He lit another cigarette, felt mildly disgusted. Those days were over and he didn't like to think about them. He was always left with a vague guilty feeling, because those memories came to him with a certain flair for the theatrical, with close attention to commonplace details.

Zara passed the booth and stood at Eddie's side. He forgot the Byerle job. He was Eddie Pesak, working john; it was the way he wanted it. The rest was the punk pipe dream of the thief, and it was dead. Completely.

The clerk packed their groceries into a box, accepted Eddie's personal check for the correct amount, and looked up with a quick boyish grin.

"How've you been, Mr. Pesak?"

"Fine."

"About ready for Christmas, are you?"

"Sure."

Out in the parking lot Eddie put the box in the rumble seat of the Model A. While he drove, Zara sat close at his side, her hand resting on his knee. The traffic was light.

"Tuna was on sale," Zara said. "I bought six cans. You'll be having tuna coming out of your ears for about three days."

He drove slowly along Alemany Boulevard. He turned at Italy Street, south toward the John McClaren Park. In the distance the South San Francisco hills rolled gray and yellow with occasional patches of bright green. The sky was still harsh yellow, the thin clouds still a rumpled gray.

When he turned the car into his street the houses became older, more run-down and in need of paint. Cyclone fences faced the pavement, enclosing small grassless yards. The Pesak house was a narrow two-story affair: dark gray, with tall windows, covered porch at the head of a short flight of stairs, covered garage, and steep peaked roof. In the rundown yard there was a straggly row of bushes, a battered tricycle, and a small pepper tree.

Zara went into the house to pay Marie, the baby sitter, while Eddie parked the car in the driveway and carried the groceries up the rickety back stairs to the kitchen. He set the box down. There were several bottles of beer in the new refrigerator that he had bought with no money down and easy monthly payments. He opened a bottle, settled heavily in a creaking chair by the window, and stared bleakly down at his unfinished stone patio and sagging wooden fences.

Zara's voice, talking to Marie in the front room, sounded muffled and tense. Eddie frowned. Kathy was most likely upstairs, taking her noon nap.

When Zara came into the kitchen he noticed that there was something unusual about her movements, something artificial. When she switched on the overhead light he saw that her dark-blue eyes were troubled, avoiding him.

Marie came into the kitchen and stood by the doorway chewing her lips. She looked embarrassed by something.

"What's the matter, Marie?" Eddie asked. "The TV break down again?"

Marie shook her head, looked to Zara as if for support. Zara turned away. Her knuckles were pale on her clenched fist. Eddie frowned again. He thought of little Kathy. Last Saturday, on market day, the boy from across the street had hit her on the head with his cap pistol. Perhaps something like that had happened again.

"Something go wrong, Marie?" he asked. "Is Kathy all right?"

Marie smiled. "Kathy's fine, Mr. Pesak. An angel. She always is." She shrugged, chewed her lip again. "A man came to see you," she finally said.

Zara interrupted, correcting the baby sitter. "Two men," she said impatiently. "You said that there were two men."

"Well, that's what I meant," Marie said. "There were two men. But only one of them talked to me."

Eddie looked at Marie, then at Zara. He knew what his wife was thinking. He remembered what Saul, the blind man, had told him. Drago was back. Eddie felt suddenly cold. His left thumb twitched. A warning. He lit a cigarette and stood up, the muscles in his back growing tight.

His voice was casual, uncaring. "Did they say who they were, Marie?"

"Gee, no, Mr. Pesak. I asked, but they didn't say."

"What'd you tell them?"

"That you weren't here. I told them I was just the baby sitter. I didn't even open the door for them. They talked to me through the door."

"How long ago was that?"

"I don't know," Marie said. "I've been watching TV. It's been an hour, I guess. About two programs ago."

"They just asked for me? They didn't say anything else?"

Marie nodded. "Honest, Mr. Pesak. I asked. And all they said—the one man that talked to me—was that he wanted to see you. That it was important. That's all."

Eddie nodded. Marie was looking puzzled and Eddie gave her a reassuring smile. "Well, don't worry about it, honey. It's probably a friend of mine." He stabbed out his cigarette. "By the way. Did you happen to see what kind of a car they were driving? If it was this friend of mine I might be able to tell by his car."

"Well, it was kinda like a Lincoln, but it could've been something else. I'm not too good on cars. Anyway, it was a brand-new one. Black and real shiny."

"What did the man look like?" Zara asked.

"The one that talked? He was big, kind of fat, you know what I mean? An old man with an overcoat and white hair."

Eddie ran a hand self-consciously over his own graying hair. To a fifteen year old anyone over thirty was probably thought to be old. So that didn't help much. The description fit Drago, but it fit a hundred others, too.

Marie had a coke, chatted with Zara about how her father hoped to buy a new car, a Chevrolet, then after a few minutes left, saying good-by to Eddie and apologizing for not having found out more about the strangers who had come to the house.

"That's all right," Eddie said absently.

Once Marie was gone Eddie opened another beer. Zara unpacked the groceries. Neither one spoke. It was as if they were afraid to say aloud what they suspected. The clock ticked on the shelf over the big black stove. Outside in the street a truck rumbled by.

"Call me when dinner's ready," he said.

He started for the front room, but Zara's voice stopped him.

He looked at her. "What is it, honey?"

"Do you think that it was—Drago?"

It was out in the open. He felt his shoulders sag, the muscles relax. He shrugged, stared at a spot on the worn hall carpet. "I don't know," he said. "I heard he just came back from vacation. It could have been Drago . . ."

She nodded, said nothing more.

Eddie felt guilty. He was responsible for Zara and Kathy. If Drago was going to hound him again, after an eight month layoff, then it was nobody's fault but his own. No one else's. And what made him feel helpless was the thought that his family would have to suffer again because of a shooting that had happened more than nine years ago.

2 (SUNDAY, DECEMBER 7th)

He tried to busy himself with routine the next morning. While Zara was upstairs getting Kathy ready for the once-a-month visit to Oakland, Eddie hunted in the hall closet for the red and gold packing box that contained most of their Christmas decorations. He checked the three boxes of German ornaments, sorted the tinsel strings and cotton angels, screwed bulbs into the three strings of lights. Three bulbs were dead and he replaced them.

He sat by the mosaic serving table in the front room, surrounded by trimmings and ornaments, sipping hot Russian tea. He couldn't concentrate on the Christmas paraphernalia. His mind was still on Drago.

"Goddam Drago," he said between his teeth.

Last night Marie had said that the car had been a Lincoln, hadn't she? And it was doubtful, now that he thought about it, that the caller had been Drago after all. Who ever heard of a cop riding around in a new Lincoln?

He finished his tea, sat smoking a cigarette. What bothered him most was the fact that a visit from Drago was just about due. It was almost eight months ago to the day that Mihaly Dragoman—or Mike Drago as he was called—had pulled in Eddie for questioning in connection with an armored-car robbery. He had been held in the felony tank downtown for three days under the seventy-two hour investigation law. Drago knew, of course, that Eddie hadn't had anything to do with the job, or with any other job, but that hadn't stopped him. Drago didn't take Eddie's retirement seriously. Even old Carl Handley, Eddie's parole officer, had been doubtful in the beginning. Handley, however, soon learned that Eddie was taking his chance to go straight seriously. But not Mike Drago. The old grudge was too strong.

Eddie was straight and even, the old days gone and buried, the old connections cut completely. He didn't even see his older brother Walter anymore.

Carl Handley had said: "Keep your nose wiped, Pesak. Keep cool, keep your fingers out of the pie. The pie's loaded and you know it. Don't forget it. Work it my way, Pesak, and you'll find that the law cuts both ways."

Sure. Both ways. Old Handley hadn't known how true that was. The law cuts when you're crooked—and it cuts when you're straight. Drago saw to that.

Mike Drago had said: "Once a crook, always a crook. You, Pesak, you're one of the biggest crooks I know. I can smell it on you. Like a guy can smell grass or smoke. And you're a gunnie. I ought to know, punk. I ought to know."

The silence in the littered living room was a strain on his nerves. He turned on the TV, then after a minute, turned it off. Nothing held his attention. There had been a brief glimpse of happy animals on the screen, dancing and singing of the miraculous thrill you get if you eat, smoke, wear, or soak your tough gritty beard with the animals favorite brand.

"Did you have the Big Eye on?"

It was Zara. She had changed her clothes, was now wearing a pale-green skirt and thick, white sweater, her blonde hair pulled back and clipped with dark combs. Her high heels rapped on the bare floor of the living room. She bent and kissed him lightly.

"Are you ready?"

Eddie nodded. "Yeah."

"Don't you feel good, Eddie?"

"Sure." He frowned. "Listen, maybe I'll take you to the key system downtown and you can take a bus over to Oakland. Would you mind that?"

She looked faintly puzzled. "No, I don't suppose I'd mind. But why?"

"I still have to work on the car. I didn't get a chance yesterday."

She rubbed the back of his neck with a gloved hand. He moved his head against her breast, the white sweater warm on his cheek.

"Are you thinking about last night?" Zara asked.

He nodded.

"About Drago?"

"Yes," he said.

Kathy came down the stairs, humming and calling for Eddie. When she came into the room she smiled and stood posing, showing off her new patent leather shoes. She had on her Sunday coat and her legs were covered with bright-red ballet tights. She had her mother's fair hair and coloring but the dark eyes and Slavic facial structure were Eddie's.

She hugged Eddie and kissed his cheek, then giggled when his overnight beard gritted against her lips. "Daddy, you need a shave."

"Sure. I always need a shave."

"Why?"

"Because I'm part Santa Claus. Are you ready? Daddy's going to take you down to the big bus station and let you and Mommy ride the bus."

"Can I sit in the back?"

"Sure."

Zara, still looking troubled but smiling for Kathy's benefit, gathered up her purse and topcoat and joined Eddie at the front door.

When he pulled the Model A out into the street and headed for Alemany Boulevard he adjusted the car blanket for Zara and Kathy and rolled up his side window. It was still cold, the sky still rumpled and gray with December clouds.

He didn't notice the black Lincoln following his car one block behind him.

Later in the afternoon, when he returned from dropping Zara and Kathy at the key system building, he finished with the Christmas decorations. He hung the first string of lights around the door window, tacking small nails to clamp the wire, setting up the wreath, running the extension cord to the TV plug in the living room. He found another box of bulbs and ornaments in the closet and checked them for breakage. He finished up and carried his tool kit down to the small garage, then returned to the kitchen and heated more water for tea. He debated with himself, then decided to have a few shots of vodka with his tea. He got down the bottle from the cupboard and brought it to the garage along with the bronze teapot.

The garage was dark. The work on the car was fairly routine and he found himself thinking more and more of the strangers of the night before. Automatically, he sensed that it was Drago and he cursed mildly under his breath as he worked, bent over the rusted fender of the Model A.

Drago was a lieutenant these days, but when Eddie had first run into him he had been a sergeant; a squadron cop assigned to the downtown Geary District.

That had been a bad night. It had been the only time he had fired a gun during a job, and he felt the panic of his imagination every time he thought of it, thought about what could have been The gas chamber, green, metallic, cold, shaped like a huge diving bell in his nightmarish visions, waiting for Bela Edward Pesak. In his visions he could see the bowed head of the prison chaplain, could hear the solemn pacing of his words.... *through the valley of the dead*.... and he could see the ghastly frightened faces of the witnesses gathered at the viewing windows. Eddie Pesak—cop killer—going to his doom, being strapped into one of the two chairs, sucking in the gas, jerking spasmodically with burning lungs ...

That could have happened. If his bullet had been straighter, or if he had fired with intent to kill. But, as it was, the shooting had been an accident.

That night, nine years ago, had been warm, sultry, charged with sudden electrical flashes and soft thunder grumblings. It had rained earlier and the streets had been wet, reflecting the neon lights like cold fire spilled on the gleaming black tar.

Walter, as usual, planned the job. They cut through the wall of the Graphic Rug Company, working in the basement, prying carefully at the cheap stucco, lath, and finally weak brick. Jimmy Sargatanas covered the cut in the wall, Eddie was assigned to the front door on the main floor of the hit—L'Agneau's Jewelry Store. Walter and Cleve Shoenstein brought up the tanks and masks and bag. They had to wear the gas masks because the safe had a device that triggered off a tear-gas bomb if the gutbox was punched or ruptured. Vic Lenahan, the fifth member of Walter Pesak's group, was the driver that night and was waiting for the burglar alarm while sitting in the green De Soto on Stockton Street just off Geary and across from the Union Square Garage and park.

Once the torch had cut the slide bar and the box was punched, the alarm went off the same time as the bomb. Eddie waited by the door, catching brief foggy glimpses of his brother and Shoenstein, looking like glass-eyed horses or men from Mars with their masks, entering the safe and scooping out the diamonds set in the show trays and filed in the envelopes.

The alarm clanged, echoed through the store, and everyone's nerves were drawn tight. Eddie almost broke when he saw the squadroll squeal to a halt in front of the shop, the tires whirping and jouncing up onto the curb. When he saw that there was only one cop he held his ground, raced for the door just as a bullet shattered the door pane.

He swung at the cop, hoping to down him with the heavy butt of his gun, but the cop leaped back. Eddie fell. His mask slipped and came off, and when his hand slammed against the carpet his gun triggered off and the roar filled his ears. When he scrambled to his feet he saw that the cop had caught the slug in his stomach and had sunk to his knees.

It was then that the cop saw Eddie's face, but only for a second. Eddie turned, pushed his mask back on, disarmed the cop, turned and helped Walter carry the jewel sack down to the basement. It had all taken less than two minutes since the alarm had gone off.

The L'Agneau job hadn't netted them as much as they had planned. The newspapers, naturally, placed the take close to seventy thousand, But, after the fencing, Walter's group split an even thirty-five.

Nearly two years after the L'Agneau job Eddie was captured during a singlehanded heist on a savings and loan company on Haight Street. Once he was booked and routinely lined-up Drago identified Eddie as the L'Agneau gunman. The accusation hadn't stuck and Eddie stood trial for the armed robbery charge. He was found guilty.

In prison his past caught up with him in shapes of nightmares, visions, and black moods of guilt and confusion. He pictured himself for what he was, and he realized that being captured was in the long run the best thing that had ever happened to him. He thought back to the L'Agneau job and realized that he could have sucked gas if his bullet had been a few inches higher. The knowledge terrified him. That wasn't all of it, but it was enough.

He served a portion of his time and was paroled. He met Zara and married her. Since that time his life had been peace—and hell.

There was still Mike Drago. The cop blamed Eddie for his gutshot and for his failures. One, his failure to capture the L'Agneau mob, and two, his failure to make his charges stick with the district attorney when he had named Eddie as the gunman. Drago felt that he had been made a fool of— and by a cheap hoodlum at that.

Ever since his parole Drago had been hounding Eddie. So far he had picked him up four times on bum charges, and because of those times Eddie had lost three legitimate jobs.

He set his socket wrench aside, wiped his hands on a piece of waste, and sat on the running board. He finished his second cup of tea and poured a shot of straight vodka into the cup. He drank, staring moodily at the cracked oil-stained cement floor of the garage. It was cold and damp and he adjusted his scarf about his neck, polished off the vodka and started packing his tools away after cleaning them with the waste.

It was five o'clock and his wife and daughter wouldn't be back at the key system until nearly ten. He closed the garage, turned toward the sidewalk, deciding to walk down to Mission and mooch a free beer from Zara's brother Cody.

Again, as he walked hurriedly down the cold street, the black Lincoln pulled slowly away from the curb half a block up the street and followed him.

3

The Budapest Bar and Grill was situated between the Dniester Ukranian Bakery and the Sobri Joska Theater on Mission Street near Geneva. The glossy photographs in the elaborate gilt frames under the theater marquee advertised a Greek-Dassin film and an old Burt Lancaster picture. Eddie paused, glanced at the pictures, then turned into the Budapest Bar.

It was a long narrow room, brightly lit, with a white tile floor sprinkled with sawdust and small green booths in the rear. There were posters in Russian and Greek near the entrance, pictures of Jayne Mansfield behind the bar.

Cody, Zara's brother, was standing alone behind the dark mahogany bar. Otherwise, the room was empty.

"Hi, Eddie."

"How's tricks, Cody?"

"Yah. So so. It's dead. This's Sunday."

Cody, whose real name was György, in no way resembled his sister. He was a huge fat man with several puffy chins and squinty little eyes that reminded Eddie of a parrot's. His skin was an unhealthy grayish color and the flabby pouches under his eyes looked like raw oysters glued to his cheeks. His arms were fat and hairless and his hands were small, dimpled at the knuckles.

Eddie didn't have to order. Cody set up a shot of vodka and a draft beer, then pulled his own stool up and joined him, leaning his huge arms on the draft cooler.

"Play the *csárdás*, Eddie. It might draw a churchgoer."

"Give me a red quarter, miser."

"I'll go broke. All my money in my own machines." He slid a bar-marked coin and when the old-fashioned jukebox was lit and the heavy chrome arm had picked out the record he poured himself a small drink of American whisky and saluted Eddie.

"To this house."

Eddie finished the vodka, sipped his beer, kept his eye on the green clock behind the bar. The rhythm of the Hungarian *csárdás* played quietly in the background. Rich smoke from Cody's freshly lit cigar created a misty veil between them.

"Did you go for a ride today?" Cody asked casually.

"Yeah. I took Zara and Kathy downtown. They're taking a bus over to see your uncle." He frowned. "Why do you ask?"

Cody squinted. "Someone was here looking for you, brother."

Eddie's thumb twitched against his glass. The warning again. He said, "Do you know who he was, Cody?"

"I don't know," the fat man answered in Hungarian. "He was a small man, thin, very white in the face, with curious eyes like a frog."

"Did this man tell you that I'd gone away in my car?"

"Yes. He said that he had missed you. However, there was no disappointment in his voice."

"I see," Eddie said.

They were hounding him, pushing him, trying to upset him. Hatred for the law flared in him, then died. Not the law, he told himself. But Drago.

"Are you sure that he wasn't with another man?" he asked his brother-in-law. "Wasn't there a big man with him?"

"No," Cody answered. "Just the little guy." He spoke again in Hungarian. "He seemed very cold. He wore a necktie: a bowtie like a butterfly. Very elaborate. But that was the only thing with life about him. Otherwise, he seemed dead, distracted, never looking me straight in the eyes. He was white, as I say, like powdered sugar."

Anytime was a bad time to be picked up, but right now was the worst time of all. He had too much to lose.

In prison he had trained to work as a welder and metal worker, and when he had been paroled Carl Handley had found him a good job with a steel company in Oakland. It was there that he had met Zara. She had been living with her aunt and uncle and, ironically, had been employed in the accounting department at Byerle's Department Store.

Eddie had lost the steel job after being picked up by Drago. After that there had been another steel yard, then a paint and brushmaker's job in San Francisco. He had lost all of them after being picked up by Drago.

None of the companies had wanted a man on the payroll who was liable to be picked up for unexpected periods of time. After all, they had explained, they had a job to do and had to have men they could rely upon.

No, it had absolutely nothing to do with Eddie's being an ex-convict, or with Drago's visit with the shop foremen for a little talk—no, not much.

The job that Eddie now had didn't pay as much as the others but he was at the point where he couldn't be choosy. He was driving a truck for Steffman's Industrial Metals on Bayshore Highway near south San Francisco. It wasn't much, but it was everything for now.

"Another drink, Eddie?"

It was after six o'clock. "Sure. One more."

Cody poured the drinks. "Have you seen the picture next door? It's Greek. The other's American."

A customer came into the bar, ordered a draft beer, and settled in one of the rear booths to read the Sunday newspapers. Cody returned to his stool and poured himself more whisky.

"The American film," he sighed. He spoke in Hungarian. "There's Burt Lancaster in the penitentiary. He is trying to escape."

"Does he make it?"

"No, certainly not. It's a Hollywood film. One of Burt Lancaster's own men, one of those in the cell with him, informs to the captain. Everyone is shot and killed in the end."

"That's tough," Eddie said.

"Yes, I suppose. The other film is very beautiful. Melina Mercouri is in that. A lovely girl. I think of the girl and I ask myself why I've never taken a wife."

"Sure. Why not?"

Cody sighed, made a philosophical gesture. "I think not, brother. A beautiful wife would learn to hate me, to feel disgusted at my touch, and would in the end cheat on me. And an ugly wife, one that I could trust, would in turn disgust me." He shrugged. "So, I feel that it's best to buy and forget."

Another customer came, ordered a straight whisky. Saul, the blind man, came in and sat at the far end of the bar. He waved to Eddie. Cody was busy for a few minutes. Eddie sipped moodily on his beer and stared at his reflection in the back mirror.

Money. It had always been a problem before but it was pretty bad right now. Eddie was deeply in debt. He owed on the house and everything in it. And last month, because of Eddie's lack of seniority at Steffman's, his overtime had been cut back in preparation for the Christmas rush on metals. Things were tight right now. Very tight.

If he lost the Steffman's job everything that he had worked for would collapse—like a house of cards.

Cody came back to his stool, glanced at Eddie. "Something bothering you, Eddie?"

"Huh? No, Cody. I've just been thinking.... about Christmas."

"I've been meaning to ask you. What would Kathy like?"

"I don't know. Ask Zara."

Cody nodded. "Another drink?"

"No. I'd better get home. I haven't had dinner yet."

"All right; I'll see you later, brother."

Out in the street the wind seemed more biting, with a hint of salt to it. The tin-foil lamppost decorations whistled and rattled. Traffic was heavy. A small line was forming at the Sobri Joska boxoffice. Eddie stopped at the Dniester, which was more a delicatessen than a bakery, and waited by the scarred counter. The atmosphere was thick with the spicy odors of sausage and paprika-baked chicken. Mr. Zsolnay, the shop owner, was serving a tough-looking kid with a black leather jacket, and when he was finished he turned toward the counter.

"Ah, Bela. How are you?"

'I'm in good health, Mr. Zsolnay. How are you?"

"Time is a friend of the young. Yes?"

"But you have wisdom, Mr. Zsolnay. Youth, with the time, has turmoil."

Mr. Zsolnay nodded. "*Palacsinta*, Bela?"

"Yes. It's to be a treat for my dinner."

Mr. Zsolnay wrapped the *palacsinta*, which was still warm, and Eddie left the shop. He walked quickly, bent into the bitter wind, his package tucked under his arm. When he started to turn into his yard he noticed the black Lincoln. It had slid to a stop directly opposite the driveway. The window rolled down silently and a familiar voice addressed him in the gathering dark.

"Do we talk in the car, or do we come inside?"

Eddie hesitated, then nodded jerkily. "Come into the house," he said angrily.

It wasn't Drago, but it was just as bad. He went up the steps, opened the door, set the delicatessen package in the kitchen, returned to the hallway in time to see the two men enter the house. His thumb was twitching violently and he shoved his hand in his pocket.

"Hello, Eddie. We had to wait until you were alone...."

"Hello, Jimmy," Eddie said.

Jimmy Sargatanas, the thin, frog-eyed man who had asked about Eddie in the Budapest, stepped into the front room. He sniffed at the air, made a sour face.

Behind him, shutting the front door, was the big white-haired man that had come to the house the night before. It was Walter Pesak, Eddie's older brother.

"Hello, Eddie," Walter said.

"Hello, Walter."

Eddie stood there, not offering them a chair, relieved to know that it wasn't Drago, angered to know that it was Walter and his punk lieutenant.

Sargatanas switched on the small green-shaded lamp by the TV and settled himself without invitation on the sofa. No one spoke for a long moment. Sargatanas gazed about the room, looking disgusted at what he saw—the prints on the walls, the cheap American furniture. Walter removed his hat unbuttoned his overcoat, and stood watching his younger brother. Eddie said nothing.

"This is a dump," Sargatanas finally said.

It didn't take much to trigger Eddie. He turned and narrowed his eyes. "No one invited you, kid," he said flatly

"Relax, Eddie," Sargatanas whispered. "We're all thieves here."

Walter stepped forward. "Am I welcome in your house my son?" he asked in Hungarian.

Eddie answered in English. "Listen, Walter, I told you five years ago that—"

"Am I welcome? In my brother's house?"

Eddie started to say no, then checked himself. What good would it do? Could he say that Walter wasn't welcome? It was strange but, as it had always done, Walter's presences served to remind him that his older brother was all the blood family he had, and that Walter had been almost a father to Eddie.

Eddie nodded, then left the room to bring the bottle of vodka and the blood-red guest glasses on the carved, bronze tray. When he returned he sullenly poured three glasses, and as he served Sargatanas he noted that the left side of the a punk's topcoat was fuller than the rest. Probably an automatic, Eddie thought. And as he served his brother he didn't bother checking him for weapons, knowing that Walter rarely carried one. He had no need to. Sargatanas carried the gun for him. And, many years ago, Eddie had held the same job.

"Sit down, kid," Walter said in English.

Sargatanas, who didn't speak Hungarian, glanced at Eddie, watched him sit in the high-backed chair by the mosaic serving table. Eddie held his glass stiffly, avoided Walter's eyes by staring at the carved, bronze tray.

"It's good to see you, kid," Walter said.

He felt like laughing. He knew that Walter was lying, but he said nothing.

"You're being very quiet," Walter said. "I said that it was good to see you."

"*Govno*," Eddie said.

Walter sighed. "That's not a good attitude, kid."

"It's the only one that I've got." His thumb twitched and pressed it against the glass. "Take it or leave it. You can drink a glass in my house, but don't insult me with crap."

"Still the tough guy," Sargatanas said.

"That's right," Eddie said. "The toughest."

Walter, as if he could sense the resentment brewing in Eddie, interrupted, quick to change the temper of the conversation. "We've come to visit you, kid. We—"

Eddie made an impatient gesture, keeping his eyes and face as expressionless as he could. "I said *govno*, Walter! I meant it. I told you five years ago that I was finished. You made a mistake coming here. You were here last night and you were here this afternoon. I don't like to be hounded or bugged by no one. Especially by you." He swallowed his vodka, poured another. "I don't want to hurt your feelings, Walter, but that's the way I felt five years ago and that's the way I feel now."

"I simply came to visit," Walter insisted.

"Get to the point. Say what you came here to say—and then leave."

Walter glared at him, his eyes like moist, black pebbles, his fleshy skin turning pale. Sargatanas smiled at the ceiling and pursed his thin lips. There wasn't a sound. Anywhere.

4

No one said anything. They sat in a triangle, illuminated by the glow from the green-shaded lamp by the TV. Sargatanas was looking amused, gazing up at the cracked ceiling, his untouched vodka resting on the sagging arm of the sofa.

Walter sat in the big chair, watching Eddie. He hadn't moved since the insult. Outside, a car throbbed slowly down the hill from the park, moving in low gear. Eddie sat on the edge of his chair, watching the color of his brother's skin return to normal. Walter still resembled Eddie, but as Marie had stated the night before, he was turning to fat. His hair was thin and white with only a patch of dark at me crown, his suit was expensive, conservatively cut, and large cuff links glittered at his heavy wrists. His eyes were narrowed now, his lips pursed thoughtfully, as if he were trying to gauge how serious Eddie's insult was.

He said, speaking in slow English. "What makes you think that I came here only to get something from you? What makes you think you can order me from your house? Eh? Is that a nice way to act, kid? Do you think that's being hospitable? In our house, when Mama was still alive, did we ever treat our guests this way? Answer me! Did we?"

It was a long minute before Eddie shook his head, turned his eyes away. The weight of the guilt of the past pressed on him. He felt, in spite of what he knew to be true, that he had abandoned not only the old life but his brother and his blood as well.

Many times in the past Eddie had been left with the feeling of guilt because of Walter. Many times he had wanted to refuse him, but somehow, listening to him, being near him, under the familiar influence, he had in the end always agreed. Until his time in prison Eddie had never been able to assert himself with his older brother. Walter was the only one who made him feel this way. With others he had been tough—had had a reputation for being ruthless—but with Walter he had been weak. Walter had been able to sway him, to make him do things that he had argued against.

Walter was the only family that Eddie had, He hardly remembered his mother. She had died in 1938, leaving Eddie to Walter's care. Their father,

a Czech immigrant, had left the family when the depression had first hit the
West Coast, and Eddie's upbringing had been under the strong Hungarian influence of his mother, and later, under his brother.

Walter had been born in the old country, in *Sztalinvaros* on the Danube.
Eddie had been born in San Francisco in the old Ukranian District near
McAllister Street.

There was a strong father-son relationship between Eddie and his brother,
and, as if to emphasize this point, Walter had a habit of referring to Eddie
as "my son."

Sargatanas sniffed loudly, breaking the silence. "I wouldn't live in a dump
like this if you paid me," he said. "It looks sort of like a cheap harem, does-
n't it, Walter? And take a sniff. It smells. Like chicken, that's what this dump
smells like."

"You can leave," Eddie said.

Walter looked uncomfortable again. "Forget it, Eddie. Jimmy was just—"

"I know," Eddie said. He smiled and said in Hungarian: "There are certain parts of the body necessary for the function of man, and if Sargatanas
continues to ridicule my way of life I'll remove those parts from him with
bullets from his own gun. Do you understand me, Walter?"

Walter started to laugh, wheezing, and he slapped his knee. Sargatanas
narrowed his eyes suspiciously. "What'd he say about me, Walter?"

"Never mind, Jimmy. I'll translate it for you later," he chuckled softly.
"Meanwhile, I think you'd better lay off. Eddie's still the toughest."

Sargatanas shrugged, returned to looking at the ceiling. "You know, you
second-string foreigners give me a pain. You always have. In my oasis, that's
where you give me a pain."

Sargatanas blinked slowly and smiled to himself. His eyes weren't like a
frog's; they didn't bulge; they were large, round, but flat, with sleepy lids.
When he smiled—which was rare—he showed delicately-pointed teeth.
His skin was pale, almost translucent, and when Eddie looked closely he saw
the ghostly network of veins on the drooping lids and at his temples.

"Where're you working?" Walter asked Eddie.

"Why?"

"Simply making conversation, kid."

Eddie doubted that. "I work at a place called Steffman's," he said.

"Is it a pretty good job?"

"Pretty good."

Walter lit a cigar, blew smoke toward the center of the room. "You know,
I haven't even met my sister-in-law yet. Or my little niece. You did have a
little daughter, didn't you?"

"It was a daughter."

"I'd like to meet them one of these days soon."

"You won't."

"What?"

"You heard me. I said that you're not going to meet them."

Walter drew the corners of his mouth down, as if he were pained, but it was obviously play-acting. His voice was soft, almost pleading. "You're hurting me, my son," he said in Hungarian.

"My family isn't a part of you," Eddie said flatly.

Walter tensed and continued in Hungarian, speaking rapidly, voice rising dangerously. "Another insult! *I'm* your family! Do I have to remind you of that? You are ungrateful. We were very close until you were sentenced to the penitentiary. Can you remember how close we were? Can you, my son? How can you forget the past? How can you forget the many years that I attended you as a father? How can you say to me now that a woman and child of your present have taken my place in your heart? Your wife has no Pesak blood. Your daughter has Pesak blood. You refuse me to see her. You break my heart, my son. I am shamed!"

"Listen to me, Walter. I—"

"No! You keep still!" He switched to English. "Here you are, buried in this lousy dump, serving the cheapest vodka, like some dumb working john. It's not like you, kid. You used to drink Scotch. Nothing but the best. So what happened? What makes you think you're so goddam hot sitting here in your rats nest serving *me* peasant juice? Huh? Tell me, kid. I'd really like to hear you tell me how happy you are, how content you are to scratch in the dirt along with the other clucks. Go on! Tell me!"

Eddie shrugged. He had no answer for that. He had a feeling, but he didn't know how to put it into words. So he said nothing.

"Remember the old days, kid? Remember Byerle's, L'Agneau's, the Wellington Furrier's? Remember? Remember during the war, down on the Tenderloin, fleecing the johns? And after that the black-market days? Fat? Jesus, sure you remember how fat things were in those days, kid? We were rolling big." His eyes were glittering now, his cuff links flashing as he gestured. "And later. Remember Lamar? The old polecat himself. Before the polecat got scratched in San Mateo? Remember those times, kid?"

"I forgot them on purpose," Eddie said.

Walter scowled. "And now look at you!"

"I'm getting along."

"Sure! Driving a truck for peanuts!"

"I didn't say that I was driving a truck, Walter. How did you know that?"

Walter smiled. "I've been keeping tabs."

"I can see that."

Sargatanas leaned forward, interrupting. "Hey, Eddie? How old is your kid?"

"Shut up," Eddie said.

"Just thought I'd ask. I like little girls."

"I told you to shut up, punk! One more word and I'll forget about that .45 under your arm."

"How'd you know—"

"I said one more word. And I meant it."

Sargatanas looked at him with hatred in his eyes, then he smiled nervously and looked at the ceiling.

Eddie was fed up. He was through playing with words. For one thing, he wanted them out of the house because he was afraid that if Walter stayed any longer he would have to order him from the place—and, despite what he said, he didn't want to do that.

"All right, Walter," he said. "Tell me the word. Put the meat on the table. Why'd you come here?"

"I wanted to talk to you about—"

"No phony build-ups. Lay it down. Let's see the cards."

Walter thought a moment, then nodded. "I have an offer."

"Make it."

"One hundred thousand dollars in cash. For you."

"You're kidding."

"No. I'm not kidding. I never kid." He turned to Sargatanas. "Am I kidding, Jimmy?"

"Nope, you're not kidding."

Walter nodded. "You see? No *govno*, Eddie. One hundred thousand dollars in cash."

"For doing what," Eddie asked.

"One night's work."

Eddie stood up. "All right. You've made your offer. My answer is no. Now you can leave."

Walter's eyebrows raised and he pursed his lips. "But I haven't even told you the—"

"And I don't want to hear," Eddie said. "You're pipe dreaming and you know it. I'm retired. I've quit. Or don't you remember?"

"You mean to tell me that in your position you're going to turn down a hundred grand?"

"That's right."

Walter stood up. "You're making me laugh, kid."

"Okay. Don't bust a gut," Eddie said angrily. "Not in my house. Do it outside. Go sit in your Lincoln and bust a gut."

"I never thought I'd live to see this day . . ."

"You've lived it," Eddie said.

"Can I tell you—"

"No. I'm through listening. I've told you that."

Walter put on his hat, buttoned his expensive topcoat, paused by the door. "We need you, Eddie," he said.

"You don't need me. You just think you need me. You can hire a gun anywhere. I'm not necessary and you know it."

Walter studied him for a long minute, his dark eyes searching Eddie's face as if waiting for a change in attitude. Then, finding none, he turned and left the house without another word.

Sargatanas stayed by the open door, lingering, showing his finely-pointed teeth in a smile. He gazed out to the street, then looked knowingly at Eddie.

"You'll change your mind, tough mouth," he said.

Sargatanas left, following Walter down to the grassless yard. The cyclone gate clanged shut, and the motor of the Lincoln purred to life. Eddie stood by the door, watching until the taillights had disappeared down the street.

His thumb was twitching again and he felt cold all over. He leaned tiredly against the hallway door and stared at the three glasses still sitting on the bronze tray.

It was over. But he didn't think that it was over for good.

5 (MONDAY, DECEMBER 8th)

He was arrested as he was leaving the main gate at Steffman's Industrial Metals at five o'clock. He nodded his usual salute to Forrest, the company day guard, and turned right on Carlyle Street, walking alone to the parking lot on the other side of the rail yard near the Boehme Warehouse. The black unmarked Ford sedan swung away from the curb opposite the warehouse, pulled into the lot, and braked to a quick stop just as Eddie turned to see what the fast driving was all about.

Drago leaped from the passenger door before the car came to a complete halt. A police special revolver was in his right fist, pointed directly at Eddie's middle.

"Don't move, Pesak!" Eddie froze.

"Patterson! Get that bucket. Squeeze him down."

The second plain-clothes man, the one who had been driving the Ford sedan, stepped cautiously to Eddie's side. He grabbed the empty lunch bucket and made a motion for Eddie to raise his hands and turn around. Eddie turned. When Patterson was finished frisking him he was ordered to turn again.

A crowd of workers from Steffman's were gathering at the mouth of the parking lot, gaping curiously at the action. A few of them, one or two truckers Eddie knew well, had, in fact, been talking with him just a few minutes ago.

"Okay, killer," Drago barked, "get into the car. You try one bad play and I'll give you what you once gave me. But I won't miss."

Eddie moved woodenly to the openback seat and crawled in.

"Put your hands against the bar," Drago snapped.

Eddie did as he was told. Drago fitted his cuffs through the bar and snapped them tightly onto Eddie's wrists. The sound they made—of metal grooves snicking into lock point—was one of painful familiarity. The sound of despair. With the cuffs on, locked against the cuff rail, Eddie had been forced to bend forward.

Patterson slid behind the wheel and Drago piled into the rear, pushing Eddie along the rail to give himself room. The car two-way radio hissed, crackled; and the bored nasal voice of the female dispatcher filled the car.

"Did you check his lunch bucket, Patterson?"

"Yes. It was clean."

"All right. Let's go."

Patterson hit the siren and, as the Ford lurched slowly toward Carlyle Street, the crowd parted to allow its passage. Eddie had a brief, embarrassing glimpse of his co-workers, crouching so they could peer curiously into the back seat at him.

It was like a nightmare. He saw workers lining up on Third Street for the bus, a bit of ragged sky overhead, gulls moving over the tankers and freighters tied along the south docks, the sooty gray skeleton of the Islais Channel drawbridge. There were traffic sounds punctuated with an occasional word from the two-way dispatcher. But none of it made any sense. It was familiar and yet unreal. A minute ago he had been heading for home, to Zara and Kathy, to dinner with the *palacsinta* he had bought from Mr. Zsolnay at the Dnieper the night before. And now he was manacled and arrested for the fifth time since his parole.

He stared bleakly at the manacles, at the dirty rubber floor mat, at Drago's highly-polished pointed shoes. Then he looked at Mike Drago himself.

He was a big man, red-faced and pock-marked, with a thick, lumpy nose, coarse white hair, red fold of fat neck bulging over the tight tab collar of his shirt. His mouth was full, almost sensuous, his eyes a curious shade of green, like frozen lime juice.

Eddie, knowing that Drago spoke Hungarian, addressed him in that tongue. "Explain this, Mihaly. Why do—"

"Shut up with the goofball talk, Pesak," Drago said with a bored voice.

"Okay, no goofball. What's the rap this time? You planning on losing me another job? Is that it?"

Drago smiled, making an ugly twist of his full lips, then he swung with surprising speed and his fist slammed into Eddie's stomach. Air whooshed from his lungs, and a flaming red and green spell of nausea and vertigo swept over him. He bent against his wrists, gasping for air. Drago's voice came to him as if it were muffled in cotton.

"No punk, I'm not planning on taking your job. I'm planning on pushing you into the gas chamber."

"Don't kid yourself," Eddie croaked hoarsely.

"Shut your mouth, killer. I don't even want to hear your stinking voice. You kind makes me want to puke."

Eddie said nothing more. His breathing was returning to normal. Patterson was driving along with the traffic, following Third Street north across Market where it joined lower Kearney. Office workers were pouring along the streets, jamming into streetcars, huddling on the narrow islands. A traffic cop blew his whistle, waved a gloved hand. A few blocks later Eddie saw the grim pile of gray stone that was the San Francisco Hall of Justice.

The Ford slowed, turned right into a slot-like alleyway, then right again into the police van and squadroll garage. They halted beside the elevator cage that led directly up to the booking desk and felony tanks.

Eddie had stopped wondering if this was a railroad job or another one of Drago's bluff and screw jobs; whatever it was, he felt nothing now. He moved like a zombie, seeing his surroundings, but not registering them.

Eddie allowed himself to be pushed into the elevator. Drago and Patterson followed, both watching him for a bad play. He didn't say a word or make a false move.

Upstairs, Drago turned him over to Patterson and a uniformed cop, then disappeared into a side door at the end of the hall. Eddie was taken upstairs, rephotographed and questioned as to his birthplace, criminal record, and draft status; then he was taken downstairs again to be booked. Seventy-two hour investigation.

Patterson and the uniformed cop removed his handcuffs, searched him a second time, then led him to the first door at the felony tank walkway. The cop opened the gate, pushed him in, jerked the slide bar at the gate box, and the nearest cell door slid open. "Number nine," the cop said. Eddie nodded, stepped into number nine, and with a loud echo the slide bar pulled the door shut behind him.

The cell was the usual thing. Two bunks: both wire cots that swung up against the wall and fixed with the chain link jammed into a small pin. A wash basin and toilet were fixed in the right corner. The floor was a hard-rubber check, the walls were faded yellow steel except for the barred opening which faced the turnkey walkway.

One bunk was down, and a thin negro kid about twenty or twenty-one rolled to his side and turned his large dark eyes to Eddie.

"What's happenin'?"

Eddie shrugged tiredly and automatically lowered the other bunk, hoisting the chain from the pin. He sat on the thin mattress and pulled the dark-gray blanket toward him.

The negro jumped down from his bunk and slouched against the far wall. He was a good-looking kid with close-cropped hair, hollow cheeks, a goatee and an Errol Flynn mustache.

"Ah'm J.T., John the Tall."

Eddie shook his hand. "Pesak. Eddie."

"Hey, you got a straight?"

"Half a pack. We'll have to clip them."

"Ah'm wid *you*."

They lit a half a cigarette apiece and J.T. inhaled with obvious pleasure. He slouched further down the wall until he was sitting on the black, waffle floor. His eyes blinked slowly, and he scratched his knee with a peculiar rhythm. He was dressed in faded denim trousers, black sports shirt with silver threading and rough high-topped work boots. A black nylon windbreaker hung from his bunk pin.

"Whad you heah faw?"

"Investigation. Seventy-two hours."

"Yeah." J.T. grinned, showing his teeth. One of them was missing. "Ah'm *in*. Tha's all. Just *in*." He shrugged indifferently. "You done hard time, straight man?"

Eddie nodded.

"In Califawnya?"

"Yeah."

"Yeah, man. Ah'm a Hun'sville man. Tay-xas. Tha's a *bad* place to be from. Real bad. You know that? A knocker, that Hun'sville."

"What're you here for?"

"Violation. Hey, straight man, they got a cat whad come by heah an' sells caife and san'wiches, too."

"I'll spring for some coffee when he comes by," Eddie said.

"Ah'm wid *you*. Ah'm you frien', superman. Ah'm you *real* friend. Too bad they not gonna extra-dite you too."

"Why's that?"

"Cuz Ah'm you *frien'*."

Eddie settled back on his bunk and stared up at J.T.'s black windbreaker. Already, the immediate reality of his life with Zara and Kathy was growing misty in his thoughts. It was amazing how little it took for a man to relearn an entirely different attitude. Already it was hard for him to believe that he had ever crawled out from under the rock. It was as if he had never left this life with its cabalistic vagaries of the helpless, homeless, loveless; the night world of fear and total despair.

There were the odors, familiar to the easy timer, almost reassuring in their consistency: lysol, iron, tobacco, caged humanity. Familiar sights, sounds, voices. Strangely, Eddie found himself relaxing.

He would be out at the end of three days. As for his job, his debts, his responsibilities, he would take care of them the moment they became real again. Meanwhile, he was in jail again, living under the badge and the eye. He surrendered himself to his three day wait.

A booming whining voice shouted. "Hey, Number Nine!"

"Yo!" J.T. answered.

"You got a new man in there. Ask him if he's got a cigarette."

J.T. grinned. "We ain't got no straights, do we, man?"

"No," Eddie said.

J.T. shouted to the unseen fellow prisoner: "No! This cat ain't got nothin'!"

Eddie smiled to himself. J.T. was absolutely correct. This cat ain't got nothing. Nothing at all....

6

They came for him at nine o'clock. The skylights high above the barred roofs of the cells had long since grown dark, and the weak night lights cast huge gloomy shadows along the ceiling beams. The sliding metal door to cell number nine opened with a rumble, and the turnkey called Eddie's name. He stepped out of the cell and went to the walkway gate where Patterson and Drago were waiting for him. Cuffs were snapped onto his wrists and without a word he was led to the elevator opposite the booking desk.

They rode down the elevator and then walked along a dark marble hallway that exaggerated their footsteps. There was only one office door lighted: a rectangle of frosted yellow with "private" painted near the doorknob. Patterson pushed the door open and Eddie was shoved into the room. Drago motioned him into a chair.

The office was small, overly warm, painted a sickly yellow and off-white. The walls were cluttered with framed photographs of police academy graduations, autographed team shots from the San Francisco Giants, a couple of stern-faced men, a few letters of commendation from high politicians, and a formal portrait of the district attorney himself.

Drago and Patterson stood at ease near a filing cabinet and old-fashioned water cooler. Eddie sat on the hard, blondwood chair facing the desk. Behind the desk was the district attorney's assistant: a slight, dark-haired, serious-faced young man with sensitive eyes and the young lawyer three-button, dark-blue suit. He introduced himself as Mr. Wilbur.

Wilbur cleared his throat, pursed his lips thoughtfully, slowly packed a large briar pipe from a plastic pouch, and studied a large open folder before him.

Without taking his eyes from the folder he asked: "Bela Edward Pesak?"

"Yes, sir."

Wilbur glanced up then, the dark sensitive eyes absorbing everything, then he closed the folder and smiled thinly "What do you think of your position?" he asked.

"I don't know," Eddie answered.

"I see," Wilbur said. He made a tent of his fingers. "Carl Handley was your parole officer, wasn't he?"

"Yes, sir." Eddie brought his manacled hands up, drew out a cigarette, and asked if he was allowed to smoke.

"Yes. Go right ahead."

Eddie lit one. He was more than familiar with their routine. They always asked obvious questions, questions that they knew the answers to. It was supposed to disarm you, put you into a question answering mood.

"You're married, aren't you, Eddie?"

"Yes, sir."

"Do you have any children?"

"Yes, sir. A daughter."

"Where are you working now?"

"Steffman's Industrial Metals, sir."

Wilbur nodded. "And how long have you been working there, Bela?"

"Seven months."

"And before that?"

"Cummings Paint Company on Twenty-fifth Street. I was paint and brushmaker's assistant."

"Did you like that job, Bela?"

"Yes, sir."

"Why did you quit?"

"I was fired."

"Oh? Really?" He frowned. "Why was that, Bela?"

"I was arrested by Lieutenant Drago, held for three days, and when I got out I'd lost my job. The Lieutenant also talked to my foreman about my record. That's why I was canned."

Behind him, Drago chuckled.

Wilbur looked serious. "Is that true, Bela? This accusation?"

Eddie shrugged. "Of course it's true. You know that."

"Tough break for you," Wilbur said softly.

"Yes, it is," Eddie said.

"Was that remark intended as sarcasm, Bela?"

"No, sir."

Wilbur looked hostile for a moment, then subsided into his bedside district attorney manner. He puffed leisurely on his pipe and gazed at the ceiling. "Why were you sent to Esque, Bela?"

"Armed robbery."

"The L'Agneau holdup, wasn't it?"

"No. I wasn't in on that job," Eddie said.

Wilbur opened his folder, pretended to read something, then nodded. "My mistake, Bela. It wasn't the L'Agneau job. It was the Quick N Ready Loan Company, wasn't it?"

"Yes, sir."

"Are you any relation to Walter Pesak?"

"He's my brother."

"Do you know James Arthur Sargatanas?"

"I've met him. Years ago."

"What about Victor Lenahan? Cleve Shoenstein? Had you met them years ago, as well?"

"Yes, sir."

"You were all in the same mob together, weren't you?"

"I don't understand—"

Wilbur feigned surprise, then amusement. "You don't? Surely one of the old mob was with you during the Mission-Japan stickup!"

"I don't know what you're talking about," Eddie said.

Drago stepped forward, sat on the corner of the desk, and faced Eddie. His frozen green eyes glittered and his red face was shiny with perspiration. "You're nailed, punkie. The only way you'll beat the gas is by fingering your partner and you know it!"

"You're a swine," Eddie said in Hungarian.

Drago swung and slammed him hard in the face. A flashbulb went off behind Eddie's eyes and he sprawled back in his chair. A warm flow of blood oozed through his teeth. When he righted himself he saw that Drago had broken the skin on his fat knuckles.

"You're through this time, killer. And you know it."

Eddie smiled, wiped his mouth with the edge of his coat sleeve.

"Take that smile off your face, Pesak, or I'll slap it off."

Eddie stopped smiling. He had thought that he had been pulled in on a seventy-two hour screw charge, but now he had a suspicion that they thought they had something on him. He hadn't the vaguest idea what they had in mind, but he knew that no matter what it was he was innocent.

"What's the squeal?" he asked tightly.

Wilbur looked faintly surprised, lifted his dark brows, puffed on his pipe. "It's first-degree murder," he said softly.

Eddie stared at him. "You're kidding! Drago cooked this up!"

Drago grinned. "Not this time, punk. Not this time. You're nailed. We've even got a finger. The one you forgot to silence."

"Who?"

"A john."

"Sure," Eddie said weakly. "A john who works for Drago."

"No, he don't," Drago snapped. "This is legit and you know it. We've got the witness."

"Where were you last night?" Wilbur rapped.

"Home."

"Can you prove it?"

"Sure. Why don't you ask my wife ..."

"We did. She said that she was in Oakland last night."

"She came back at ten o'clock," Eddie said.

"We know that. Where were you at nine?"

"I told you. I was home."

"Can you prove it, Pesak?"

"Look—"

"No. You look. Can you prove your whereabouts during the half hour between eight-thirty and nine last night?"

"No, but—"

"Where were you?"

"Home!" Eddie said.

Drago lifted a sheet from his inner jacket pocket and pushed his hat back on his head. "We know where you were, Pesak. You own a dark-green, 1930 Ford Model A. Last night you drove this car to the corners of Mission and Onendega Streets. Eight-thirty. You wore a faded-brown leather jacket with a sheepskin collar. The very one you have on now, as a matter of fact. An accomplice was with you. He was small, wore a tweed jacket and black hat. A red mask covered his face. The two of you entered the Mission-Japan Market and robbed the proprietor of one hundred and eleven dollars. The proprietor protested, and so you shot him three times in the chest with a .38 revolver.

"The proprietor's brother, Charles McCrea, watched the shooting from the rear of the store. He had a perfect view of the killer. Your partner, at the conclusion of the shooting, said, 'Let's scramble, Eddie.' You both escaped in your car, driving northwest on Onendega toward City College.

"From here on I fill in for myself. You dropped your partner somewhere. Perhaps he took another car. However, we know what you did after that. You drove to the key system terminal at Mission and First Streets to pick up your wife. We have two witnesses to testify to your aggravated condition. The parking lot attendant. And the waitress in the cafeteria who saw you spill half a cup of coffee because you were 'terribly nervous and distracted.'

"And you know why you felt that way, killer. And so do we. Charles Mc-Crea is willing to do his duty as a citizen and shove you into the gas chamber."

Eddie stared at Drago. Then at Wilbur. He could feel the noose. He turned in his chair and looked frantically at Patterson. Their faces were dead serious. He could read it. They weren't joking this time.

His voice was strained, which didn't surprise him. "It didn't happen ..."

"That grocer died? Of course it happened. He was dead on arrival."

"No. I meant—" He didn't finish what he had started to say. Nothing made any sense.

"Would you like to make a statement now?" Wilbur asked.

"No!" he croaked. "Hell no! I don't say nothing." His thoughts raced madly, in jerks, like receiving vocal telegrams. What to do? Say? They're serious. Charles McCrea?

He said, "Put me onto your witness. I want to see the finger."

Drago looked at Wilbur. Wilbur nodded. Patterson and Drago pulled Eddie to his feet, and Wilbur got on the phone to make the arrangements. Apparently, Charles McCrea was still in the building.

"I don't want any little fat men," Eddie said tightly. "No screw job on the line-up."

"Have I ever been unfair to you, Pesak?" Drago asked dryly.

7

When he saw the men chosen for the line-up he realized that Drago and Wilbur felt they must have had a pretty tight identification; the men were neither fat nor small; most were pretty much Eddie's size and two of them had pretty much the same dark coloring. This sort of line-up was unusual for Drago.

Eddie filed into the room with five others, turned right and mounted the flood-lighted ramp. He squinted, checked himself before he put his hands up to shade his eyes. He could hear coughing beyond the lights, then shifting of chairs, feet shuffling along the bare wooden floor. Eddie stood in the number-four spot on the line.

A face emerged a few feet from the deck lights, then two more. One of them was obviously Charles McCrea, the witness. He was a pudgy little man, completely bald, with a big waxy-looking nose and small Charlie Chan mustache. Drago and Wilbur stood at his side.

Placing a heavy friendly hand on the witness' shoulder, Drago spoke almost casually. "Now, Charlie, we'd like you to look carefully at the six men lined on the platform. We want you to take your time, study the faces closely, and then when you see the man who did the shooting kindly point him out to us."

"Do I start now?" Charles McCrea asked timidly.

"If you please," Wilbur said.

McCrea, before starting at the number-one spot, glanced curiously up at Eddie, then frowned. He avoided Eddie, moved to the start of the line with a troubled expression.

Sweat broke out on Eddie's face and he felt it roll down his collar. The backs of his legs were quivering, but outwardly he was calm and collected.

McCrea shook his head at the first man, and like a browser in a museum gallery, moved to the next man and peered up into his face. The man on Eddie's right coughed, cleared his throat, stared into space. McCrea moved to the third man. Eddie could feel the perspiration chilling on his flesh under his worn leather jacket and work shirt. In the backglow beyond the footlights he saw Drago's smile tightening eagerly on his face. McCrea moved to the number-four spot, stared for an eternity into Eddie's face.

Eddie had a brief, horrible urge to kick the witness in the face.

Then, still like the museum browser, McCrea moved to the next man, still staring without expression or recognition. A minute later he left number six and turned questioningly to Drago and Wilbur.

"Which man, Charlie?" Drago asked.

McCrea made a vague gesture with his tweed cap. "Nope."

Impatience and suspicion flashed on Drago's face. "What do you mean 'nope'?"

"No. The guy's not here."

"What? Are you sure? I mean—look again, Mr. McCrea."

"I did," the witness said. "I did. I looked at them. Every one. And I told you—the guy's not here."

"But.... are you sure? Listen—"

"I oughta know," McCrea insisted. "You think I'd forget what a guy looks like when he shoots my own brother? Eh? No, I know what he looked like. And none of these guys is the guy."

"What about four!" Drago shouted.

McCrea glanced at Eddie, shook his bald head. "Nope. It looks kinda like him, but it ain't him."

"Leather jacket!" Drago snapped viciously. "Six foot two or three, hundred seventy to eighty pounds, graying black hair, dark complexion, named Eddie, drives a Model A Ford! Goddammit, McCrea, are you going to stand there and tell me that *that* isn't the man?"

McCrea, during Drago's outburst, had backed up as if he were afraid of being struck; he was flinching, but he still shook his head. "I don't know about what you say, Officer, but that guy up there *ain't* the guy."

"Listen you little sonofa—"

Wilbur stepped quickly in and placed a restraining hand on Drago's arm. "Relax, Mike. Take it easy. I know it's tough, but don't blame the witness."

"All right, Jim, all right." He turned to McCrea. "Get this creep out of my sight."

A uniformed cop ushered McCrea from the room. Drago jammed a cigar into his mouth and stood chewing on it, hands on his hips, a look of disgust on his face.

The uniformed cop returned, started ushering the line-up from the platform.

Wilbur said, "Pesak. Come over here. That's right, get out of the line."

Eddie left the ramp, blinked in the sudden darkness, made his way to Wilbur and Drago. "Can I go now?"

Wilbur shrugged.

"If I don't get back home I'll lose my job. I didn't pull the kill and you know it. The witness had no make. So what's holding me?"

"Your arresting officer," Drago snapped.

Eddie stared at him. He said in Hungarian: "Mihaly, it's important that I keep my job. It's important to my wife and my daughter—"

"Shaddup. You're breaking my heart." Drago lit his cigar, said in Hungarian: "You tried to assassinate me many years ago, Pesak. I'm not going to forget it. It lives with me, here, in my stomach when I eat spiced foods. You're a thief. Thieves should be punished. And I'm going to punish you. I mean what I say. No, don't protest, thief. Don't insult me by speaking your mother's language. Say no more."

Eddie felt like punching him in the mouth, jamming the fat cigar down his throat; if it hadn't been for Zara and Kathy he would have. But that would only give him long time for assault and would, in the end, prove nothing.

Patterson showed up from one of the witness-viewer chairs in the rear and escorted Eddie back to cell number nine in the felony tank. The slide bar rasped, and the heavy iron door clanged shut behind him a second time.

J.T. was asleep, snoring softly, twitching in his troubled dreams. Eddie sank miserably on the thin mattress and stared at the springs over him. Beating the phony murder rap had been a break, but he would still have to sit out his three days and would undoubtedly lose his job because of it. He knew how far Drago's hatred and obsession could be carried. He sighed, closed his eyes, turned to face the wall.

That night, as he had during his prison term, he dreamt of the death cell: an inevitable last place; no escape. No matter how hard he tried to go straight there was Mihaly Dragoman—represented in his dreams by a monstrous beast, half dragon and half man—breathing cyanide fumes from flaring nostrils, lunging at him in a long dark corridor. There were scales made of police badges, thousands of them, writhing and jingling. The corridor was straight, but no matter how hard he tried to follow it, the dragon leapt before him and forced him to walk crookedly.

8 (THURSDAY, DECEMBER 11th)

By the glowing, green hands of the small travel clock on the stand by the green-shaded lamp it was eleven o'clock. Eddie sat in the total dark, smoking one cigarette after another, staring at the green face of the clock. He had been released that evening from the Hall of Justice, had caught a taxi to Carlyle Street, where he had left the Model A in the company lot, then had driven home as though it were just another working day. But there had been a difference; he no longer had a job.

"Look, Pesak," Olden, the foreman at Steffman's had growled, "I can't help you. My hands are tied. It's not me. See? It's the big boss. The reason? Officially it's because you took off for three days without notice."

"My wife called you."

"Yeah, I know, Pesak. So? My hands are still tied. Try and look at it my way."

Sure. Why not? Olden saw it Drago's way and Eddie could only see it Eddie's way. Either way the result was the same—he had lost another job because of Mike Drago. Nothing would change that.

He pulled a cigarette from his shirt pocket, lit it from his butt. It was ten after eleven. He crossed his legs and, as Jimmy Sargatanas had done earlier that week, stared indifferently up at the cracked ceiling. He could hear Zara moving about in the upstairs bedroom. Probably wondering why Eddie wasn't coming to bed. Picking up his cup of tea and vodka, he sat there sipping it.

There was a bitter taste in his mouth as he thought of his cell in the felony tank. Number nine, J.T. John the Tall. Where was he now? Had he been extradited to Texas, back to Huntsville penitentiary? Probably. Eddie felt depressed as he imagined the J.T.s of the world, being framed, pushed, shunned, and jammed into cells to shut them up. And the Pesaks. The Pesaks were given a dirty deal as well.

Certainly, he still intended to walk a straight line, but the germ of resentment had been planted. Now it was increasingly difficult to ignore the tiny growing shoot of rage. After all, how much was he supposed to take? What did he have to do to convince the Dragos that he was keeping his nose clean? Another cigarette. More time registered by the glowing green hand. Time smoked away. More cold tea and vodka and sullen, bitter thoughts. Then, as it had always been since his parole and marriage, more self-re-criminations and twinges of guilt as he thought of Zara and Kathy.

Footsteps on the stairs. Light flashed in the hallway. Zara came into the room, paused by the door to adjust her eyes to the dark. The light behind her outlined her figure under the thin cotton nightdress. Eddie felt a stir inside him of sudden love, of wanting to hold and keep and protect. Zara called his name, softly, and when he answered her she came into the room and settled beside him on the couch. Her hands were cool, soft, comforting against his cheek.

"Howdy, big lover."

"Hello," Eddie said.

"Is that a new hat?"

He smiled, kissed her cheek, finding it in the dark with his fingers.

When he had first met her in Oakland where he had worked for the steel company, he had tried to get her attention for three mornings in a row. They breakfasted in the same cafeteria in downtown Oakland near the Tribune building, and he had noticed her his first day in the place. She usually sat in a corner near the water cooler and silverware boxes. Usually the place was crowded. For three mornings he had joined her table and had breakfasted with her. They had never exchanged a word, not even a greeting. On the fourth morning however she happened to look up at him with a soft smile on her lips and had asked, "Is that a new hat?"

He had, surprisingly, felt the burn of embarrassment on his cheeks. "Yeah. I—I bought it last night. Twelve bucks. You know why I bought it?" She shook her head.

"It's sort of a campaign I had in mind. I was going to wear something new every morning. Like a shirt, or a pair of shoes. Every morning."

"Why?"

He shrugged, self-effacing. "To see if you'd notice."

She smiled again. "Are you shy?"

"No."

"You seem to be."

"I don't talk to many people."

They had dated several times, and when he had found that she was Hungarian and that her brother owned the Budapest Bar in San Francisco, he dated her more often. He didn't know why but he wanted a wife who had a background similar to his own, wanted a woman who understood a language that he found to be beautiful and comforting. Perhaps it was because of the mother that he had never known. Whatever, he married Zara three months after their first meeting in the cafeteria, and a year later they had a daughter.

Zara whispered in the dark, "Did I ever tell you—I mean really tell you—that I love you, Eddie ..."

He pulled her gently to him and kissed her. She settled on his lap, pulled his hand to her breast and held it there. They were silent for a long while. Eddie continued smoking, watching the green clock, feeling the beat of Zara's heart pulsing on his palm. When he moved his hand she stirred.

"Are you worried, Eddie?"

"Yes."

"You'll find another job," she whispered. "You always have."

"I suppose so."

"I don't want you to be worried."

"It's just jailhouse blues, Zara. It takes a while to shake it off."

She snuggled against him, the soft pile of her hair brushing his arm. "Kathy was worried about you, but I told her that you'd gone across the bay to work for a few days."

Eddie thought a moment, then said, "And what'll you tell her ten years from now, when she's fourteen? Can you tell her that I'd gone across the bay then?"

"This won't keep up, Eddie. I mean, it can't go on for as long as that ..."

"That's what I've been thinking about. It's been going on for five years now already. So what's to prevent it from going on for another five years, maybe ten, maybe fifteen? What's to prevent the next witness from making a mistake? The law of averages is on Drago's side. Not mine. Sooner or later, if he keeps on hounding me, one of his charges is going to stick, and then I'll be nailed. Tight. Just the way he wants it.

"I don't understand," Zara said. "I just don't understand a man like that."

"I told you," Eddie said quietly. "The shooting. Drago will never forget it. In a way, I can't blame him. But it's been too damn long. Too many years have gone by. He's got a memory like an elephant. That's not all. He's the stupid kind of cop that thinks there're only two kinds of people. Straight and crooked. I guess he thinks it's like a difference in your blood, or something."

"He's wrong, Eddie."

"Sure. I've known plenty crooked cops and lawyers, business men, big shots—and I've known a couple of crooked district attorneys. But Drago can't see that. Those guys are opportunists. But he calls me a crook." Eddie frowned, trying to sort that out. "I think Drago's a nut, that's what I think."

After a long while, Zara kissed him good night, told him not to worry that everything will be all right, then left and went upstairs to bed. Eddie remained on the couch, brooding, trying to adjust his thoughts. It was after three o'clock before he finally left the room and followed Zara upstairs to bed.

9 (MONDAY, DECEMBER 15th)

Eddie left the California State Employment Office and walked west along Howard Street to where he had his car parked. He jerked the door open, slid behind the wheel, and sat there with the hate raging through him. His thumb was twitching crazily, like a puppet's foot caught on a shoulder string. He lit a cigarette, burned his finger, threw both cigarette and book matches out the window. He cursed between clenched teeth.

He had just about had his fill of the whole mess. The employment office employee who had interviewed him had been a young man with crewcut, insidious smile, artificial apologies, busy little hands that riffled through rules and laws and forms and a hundred other papers designed to do nothing more than confuse and intimidate.

The interviewer had said: "Mr. Pesak, I've told you as much as I can, considering.... This office is here to help those deserving—"

"Listen. I've been steadily employed for five years," Eddie had snapped. "I've been putting money into this stinking organization and now I want some of it back. I'm out of a job, the union tells me jobs are scarce, and I've got my unemployment coming to me."

"I understand that. You've made that quite clear. But, still, I'm sorry. You quit your job, Mr. Pesak. You weren't laid off. You weren't fired. You can file, as I said, but as I explained the delay before your first check is—"

"And I told you, kid, I didn't quit my job. I was fired. Don't you get it? Canned. Booted. Fired. I wasn't laid off and I didn't quit. I was fired. Get that through your head."

The young man had smiled. "But your employer has already stated—" And so on.

His patience worn thin, his rage dangerously close to the demonstrative stage, Eddie had finally stormed out of the office.

He sat now in his car, trying to remain controlled. He drummed his fingers on the wheel. He finally got another cigarette lit without burning himself.

He didn't hear the three-wheeler until the cop pulled beside his window.

"Your meter ran out, chum," the cop said.

Eddie glared at him.

"Didn't you hear me, chum?"

"Yeah I heard," Eddie answered.

The cop's expression grew nasty. "Then either you feed that meter or push off!" he barked.

Eddie said nothing, started the motor, and pulled away from the curb. When he glanced in the rear-view mirror he noticed that the cop was still sitting on his three-wheeler, watching him. Eddie cursed the cop, the parking meter, the employment interviewer, Drago, everything and everybody that he saw as he drove quickly toward Third Street.

The district was industrial, with the jungle of the south docks beyond the yards and sheds and smokestack fingers and rusted, weed-grown railspur's shabby unpainted lunchrooms. There were no sidewalks and the streets were broken here and there. There were trucks and trains and chemical fumes and trash heaps. Smoke hung in the sky. Furnaces roared behind corrugated doors. Machines stamped and punched and sliced, and delivery wagons beetled in and out of stacked yards and dirt-road driveways.

Steffman's Industrial Metals was situated two blocks east of Third Street on Carlyle. A high cyclone fence with barbed wire running at a sharp angle along the top surrounded the entire grounds. In the center of the yard the main building stood like a long flattened out shoe box of red brick. Other sheds were in the rear, with loading platforms, furnaces, storerooms. The yard was a maze of piping and stacked spools for shipping. A guard shed with a peaked red roof was at the right of the main gate. A "keep out" sign was posted there in red letters.

Eddie left the car on Carlyle near the telephone pole by the high brick wall. When he came to the gate he nodded his usual nod at Forrest, the guard, and started through. Forrest shook his head, held up his hand. "You can't go in, Eddie. I got the word."

"I want to see Olden," Eddie said. "Tell him to come out here."

Forrest narrowed his eyes, fingered his Sam Browne belt. "I dunno. Olden's the one what said you shouldn't go in. I don't think he wants to see you."

"He'll see me. Call him on the phone and tell him I'm here."

"You won't give no trouble, will you, Eddie?"

"No. No trouble."

"Awright. But you better be up'n up, Eddie. Olden told me not to let you in. He's got a down on you. I don't want no trouble."

Eddie waited. Forrest went into his shed to make the call. A gull circled lazily overhead, moving in a pillow of chemical smoke, then settled on the high wall by the telephone pole. A few minutes later Olden came striding heavily across the yard. The gull flew away. Eddie felt his back muscles tense, his big hands automatically curling into heavy fists.

Olden was a big man, heavier than Eddie, with a hard weathered face, thick lips, mean little eyes under wispy brows. He walked as if he wanted to draw attention to the fact that his stomach hung over his cowboy belt. His voice was flat, rasping, jerky.

"What you want, Pesak?"

"To talk."

Olden squinted, glanced at the guard shed. Forrest was nowhere in sight. "Yeah. Okay. Talk."

"I want to know why you told the employment people that I'd quit my job."

Olden moved a step closer. His voice dropped. "Listen, you, I ask you kind like to understand my point, but you don't. Not you. You're stubborn. You're a whiner. See? I don't like whiners, Pesak."

"I'm not interested in what you like or don't like, Olden. I'm interested only in knowing why you put the shaft into me."

"Shaft? You quit, dad. That's all I know. Ain't no one shafting you."

"You fired me, Olden."

Olden's face reddened. "You trying to establish prejudice, Pesak? You trying to say that we canned you? You going to say we canned you or laid you off because of your prison record? You trying to raise a big stink with the union or the state?"

"That's why I was shafted? Because you want to protect this lousy company from a prejudice charge? Is that it?"

"Sure. We don't want no union officers coming around her and goofing our shop because of you. We don't want no fuss. See?"

"You knew I wouldn't be eligible for unemployment. You shafted me because a cop named Drago told you to. I didn't know that you were a copper's fink on top of being a stinking company man, Olden."

"Listen, you, I told you before. Don't whine your problems to me. I'm not your daddy, Pesak. I'm not gonna hold your mitt while you whine and—"

Eddie hit him. He could feel the hot jolt clear up into his shoulder. He hit him flat-footed, springing his shoulder, putting his back into it and curling his wrist a second before contact, exactly the way the books say you should.

Olden dropped. His mouth was split, blood splattering and bubbling on his chin. He was almost unconscious, eyes glazed, face slack, but he shook his head like a wet dog, clearing himself, and staggered clumsily to his feet. He spat blood. "You mother—"

Eddie hit him again, charged with the acid juices of five years of pent-up hatred for all the swine that had ever shafted him. Olden staggered back, trying to pull himself together for a bull-charge. Eddie moved in, throwing one punch after another.

Forrest's hand slammed out of nowhere and the butt of a .38 service revolver cracked Eddie's wrist. Eddie stopped. Forrest leveled the gun.

"You'd better hike for home, Eddie. Don't make me bust you. You'd better walk before Olden wakes up."

"Thanks, Forrest."

"Don't thank me for nothing, kid. Just pick up feet and get outa here."

Still shaking, spoiling for more action, he turned and left the gate. The Model A started up with one fire and as he drove along Third his hands started to twitch uncontrollably with the setting in of the reaction. Sure, it didn't help matters any, but the satisfaction was real. He should have punched harder, should have stomped Olden's teeth in.

The girl behind the first desk looked up when Eddie came through the door. She gave him a tired four o'clock smile, lifted non-existent eyebrows, pushed a green pencil into her dull brown hair.

"Yes?"

"I want to see one of the officers," Eddie said.

"Are you a member?"

"Yeah."

She asked him to wait, indicating a reading room to the right, then left the office. Eddie sat in a hard chair and impatiently leafed through a worn copy of *Time*. There were pictures of industrial captains and politicians, snide film reviews, several nonsense columns on communism, and page after page of rocket and missile advertisements. A big clock ticked on the wall. Eddie smoked two cigarettes.

A fat man wearing a shiny black suit waddled into the room, smiled benevolently, waved a pudgy hand. "You wanna see me, brothuh?"

"Yeah."

"What can I do?"

"I'm a member. I want a job."

"So you wanna job, brothuh?" The fat man looked pained. "You were here yesterday, weren't you? Sure, I remember. You came to us from the paint and brushmaker's. About seven months ago. I got four-year brothuhs outa work. You gotta come in the morning. Everyone comes in the morning. It's tight right now. Real tight."

"When does it get loose?"

"Loose? Well, it gets loose maybe by April. Maybe later."

"I'll come by in the morning," Eddie said.

"Sure, brothuh. You do that now. Okay? Anytime you got a problem, you come right to see me."

"Sure. When I get a problem I'll be right over."

"Yeah, that's the way to be."

Eddie left the office. Outside, he stood on a street corner, watched sad faces drift by, listened to shoes shuffle on the gray pavements. He was thinking that he might be able to stagger by for three months if he could swing a loan and double-back. If he borrowed say, a thousand dollars, then he could pay the loan company the first three or four payments out of the thousand and meanwhile live off the rest of it.

Before returning to the car he stopped at a cut-rate drug store and had a hamburger, then looked up the addresses of a few nearby loan offices. When he stepped out into the street again he was feeling better, a little more hopeful, and after his flare-up with Olden earlier, a little calmer.

Another office. This one was painted in muted greens, splashed with split philodendrons and rubber plants. The desks were big, shiny, clear of unnecessary papers. The chairs were unusually comfortable. Eddie sat back, feeling good, smoking one of the English cigarettes that Mr. Wadsworth, the silkysmooth loan official, had given him from a thin, gold case. So far, everything had gone rather smooth. Eddie's assets, even though he owed on everything, seemed sufficient. "More than enough, m'boy," Wadsworth had purred, then had excused himself for a minute—just a formality—to check Eddie's credit rating. "Nothing to hide, eh, m'boy?"

"No trouble, Mr. Wadsworth. I'm A-1."

Wadsworth returned. He looked exactly like his name: worth wads. His suit was expensive, nubby gray silk with narrow cuffs. His hands were white and smooth, the nails glistening as if they had been treated with lacquer. His face was tanned, blue-eyed, white-haired, and he reeked of cologne.

When he slid behind the desk Eddie noticed the no-nonsense air, the cold change, the suspicious, fleeting glance. Wadsworth opened a folder, cleared his throat.

"Sorry, Mr. Pesak, we can't handle a loan for you."

He looked away, avoiding Eddie's questioning stare, pretended to consult a memo pad, making appropriate faces of decision, drumming his lacquered nails on the desk, glancing importantly at his wafer-thin wristwatch.

Eddie stared at him. Why was he thinking what Wadsworth would be worth? Why was he wondering how many people there were in the adjoining office, how quickly he could do it? It was dumb, dumber than dumb. Wadsworth had his name, knew his address, but still ... The disgust he felt for the cold refusal had triggered a long-hidden impulse in him. He felt like belting Wadsworth and taking the dumb office for every stinking penny hidden in every stinking drawer and pocket. Then the brief thought passed, went into a dark closet to crouch in his thoughts, joined the others that had been planted there in the fat days of the post-war years.

"Still here, Pesak? Didn't you hear what I just said? I'm terribly sorry, but this office cannot, under any circum—"

"I heard," Eddie said tightly. "I don't get it."

"You don't. I'm sorry, and I'm very bus—"

"I can see you're sorry. You keep saying it so often it must be true. A minute ago you were calling me 'm'boy.' What happened, Mr. Wadsworth? Aren't I your boy any more?" Eddie's eyes glittered strangely and his brows knitted close together. "How sorry are you? Too sorry to pass the loan? Too sorry to give me the brush? Is that how sorry you are?"

Wadsworth looked chilled now, but there was the gesture of the frightened man as he reopened the folder. "Your credit, Mr. Pesak is—"

"A-1. Just like I told you. I've never missed any payments in my life. Never. So tell me how my credit's bad. Tell me that and I'll file it away in the same drawer with your sorrow!"

"Leave my office, Mr. Pesak. Leave, or—"

"Or what? You'll drown me with your tears?" Eddie rose menacingly. He felt that he had come to the end of the line. No more runaround. No more crap. He said, practically hissing, "You tell me why I'm being shafted again, you crummy bastard, or I'll stretch your fat neck!"

Wadsworth stood up, glared red-faced at Eddie. "You're a thief," he said coldly, then seeing that his words stopped Eddie he continued, gathering speed and confidence, "Almost eight years ago you held up one of our branch offices. The Quick N Ready Loan Company of Haight Street. Do you deny that? Oh yes, we know your record. Our companies have a cross-filing system that would, in a small way, simply amaze you, Mr. Pesak." His blue eyes shone triumphantly. "We don't offer loans to thieves who try to rob us." He cocked an eyebrow, looked smoothly righteous. "Now leave this office before I telephone the authorities and have them escort you out."

Eddie turned, without a word, and left the office. It wouldn't be worth it to strangle Wadsworth. Why go back to the joint simply to satisfy a one-second urge? Eddie was straight, intended to stay straight. So what if he thought about crime now and then? It was natural wasn't it? Sure, why not. He had been a thief every day of his teen-age and adult life until five years ago. No one said that he had to blot out his past. All he had to do was stay straight now. It's now that counts. Still, why didn't *they* forget about it, why didn't *they* leave him alone and let him live in peace!

Anguish, rage, despair, boiled through him. When he stepped out onto the windy, paper-littered street he saw the sadness of the hour—the time of dark and light, of crowded buses and lonely-voiced news vendors. The neon signs over the cheap saloons were lit, but the hour was at that terminal stage when the lights seemed muted in the last gasp of daylight. Christmas tinsel, green and silver in giant wreaths, whispered on the street poles in the wind. People moved by, dark and shapeless in heavy winter coats. Coins jingled in passing pockets. Stores took in money with cash registers ringing. Self pity flooded through Eddie.

Merry Christmas.

No job.

Shafted.

"Watch where you're goin'," a dollar voice rasped.

Eddie glanced, shrugged at the man, stood on the corner. What could he say to Zara? To Kathy? He knew that jobs were tight right now, that his chances would be punk for at least two or three months. Could he carry his debts for that long? And what about Christmas? House payments? Food? What about....

The first bar he turned into was a small dump named The Zodiak Plaza....

10 (THURSDAY, DECEMBER 18th)

The Christmas tree was up, set before the main windows behind the TV. It was a sad, droopy affair with a bent crown, too fat on one side, too thin on the other. There was the faint, sweet scent of pine in the room. Under the tree, on the split bedsheet that represented a snow drift, there were only a few packages: red and gold and green and white; stickered with reindeer and church-tower stamps; fuzzy with bows and ribbons.

The TV was on but no sound came from the mesh-faced speaker. Eddie had fooled with it for an hour, became more disgusted as time passed. As far as he could tell, the volume was dead. Kathy had cried, whimpered really, for fifteen minutes, wanting to watch the cowboys. Eddie's nerves were raw, and, for the first time, he had snapped at his daughter and ignored the shocked stare of his wife.

He turned the picture off, sat moodily in the front room. In the kitchen, Zara was feeding Kathy, soothing her. Eddie snorted, poured himself a small bowl of tea and vodka, lit a cigarette. It was eight o'clock. Zara had waited dinner for Eddie. All day, as well as yesterday and the day before that, he had gone to the union hall, had played checkers, watched the chalk board, read copies of *Time* and the *National Geographic*, had listened to the complaints of the "brothuh's," had stared at the crowded morning buses of commuters. He had gone to the employment offices, stood in the shabby lines, read the open jobs that not a living soul could possibly qualify for, bought dixie cups of coffee, read the want ads and tramped the streets. He had hung around the docks, drank beer in sawdust joints, drifted into the Tenderloin, avoided a few ex-cons he had seen standing on the corners near waterhold bars, cafeterias, "under new management" hotels. He had chewed his teeth, looked at movie stills under theater marquees, stared at the banks, thought of Walter and Jimmy Sargatanas, of Zara and Kathy. Door after door had been closed. Employment office after employment office had smiled, expressed their well-fed sorrow, riffled papers, fingered paperclips, sighed ... but nothing.

"You're a thief," Wadsworth had said.

Eddie finished his drink, poured another, going light on the tea. He paced the room, holding his drinking bowl, walking the room as if in a cell, moving from the sad Christmas tree to the green shaded lamp. The rats of despair and self-pity gnawed at his guts.

He had never really noticed it before, but his house was a dump. Just as Sargatanas had said. The ceiling was cracked, like a daddy long legs mashed on paper. The front windows needed putty. The carpets were thin, worn, ratty looking. The wallpaper in Kathy's room was sour and peeling, and where the rain seeped from the broken water gutter on the roof there were long dark stains, as if the house, aware of its ugliness, had cried great tears of passion. And the front yard was grassless, weedless, cluttered with broken toys, pepper tree leaves and brown pods.

It was true. Now that he thought about it, the house was a crummy Mission District dump. How could he have ever thought himself contented in a dump such as this? If it wasn't so pitiful it would be amusing. In the old days he used to walk tall, ride first class, rustle thick sheaves of bills that smelled faintly of purses, cosmetics, and bought drinks, cars, thick American steaks.

He poured another drink. It was his twelfth. He was drinking too much, he knew, but he wasn't becoming visibly drunk. It had been the same way last Monday, after he had left the stinking loan office. He had gone to the nearest bar and had tried to get drunk, but hadn't been able to; he had succeeded only in blowing fifteen bucks, had returned home in cold fury, and for the first time he had curled up on the couch in the front room and had slept alone, without Zara, without explanation.

Nothing was the same anymore. He doubted if it would ever be good again. Why should he get another job, break his neck, keep himself straight, just to have Drago come along and tear it down again? Why? What was the profit in getting another job just to lose it again? Why should he be Drago-bait all his life?

He made another drink, his thirteenth, and walked coldly to the window, eyes flat, mouth turned down, ears ringing. Strange voices sounded in his inner depths.

"Try and see my point of it, Pesak.... You're a whiner."

"You tried to assassinate me many years ago. I'm not going to forget it. You're a thief. Thieves should be punished. And I'm going to punish you."

"One hundred thousand dollars cash. For you. For one night's work."

"Still the tough guy."

"Did I ever tell you—I mean really tell you—that I love you, Eddie...."

He flicked on the volume switch of the TV, the picture came on. Nothing else. With sudden violence he slammed his fist on top of the set. The sound returned.

"So for a thrill, this kit, along with the magic—"

He turned the volume down, sneered in triumph, turned the set off completely. That was the way to fix something if it went wrong—slam it with your fist.

He went to the hall closet, grabbed his scarf, hat, and topcoat. Zara came from the kitchen, moving hesitantly, probably frightened of his ugly mood. She was wearing the skintight white trousers, a peach colored blouse, looking lovely and concerned.

"Where are you going, Eddie?"

"Out."

"But—"

"Can't I even go out?" Eddie snapped. "I'm going out. That's all."

"If you're going to see Cody ask him if he's coming here Christmas Eve. We'll have a small party. The Nicholsons next door are—"

"The hell with the Nicholsons," Eddie said. "Don't tell me about the Nicholsons. I'll see Cody and give him your message. Anything else?"

She took a slow, deep breath, touched her cheek, brushed the dark-blonde hair. Her blue eyes avoided his stare. "Yes," she whispered. "There's something else. Us, Eddie. You and I. And Kathy. I want to know about us. About your mood. Don't shut us out, honey. Please. It's—it's not like you."

"Isn't it? What *is* like me?"

She shook her head, as if unable to play straight-man to his sarcasm. She looked at him, almost pleadingly, and he saw, for the first time since he had known her, that her eyes were moist, blinking rapidly, appearing black in the dim hallway light.

"Eddie, are you that worried about getting a job? About the money? Cody will—"

"I don't need to crawl to Cody," Eddie snapped. "I don't need to crawl to nobody for my money. I can support my family without standing on the corners and begging."

"I didn't mean—"

"What did you mean?"

"Please. Don't shout. Kathy can hear!"

"All right," he whispered tightly.

"You'll find a job and—"

"And what? Drago'll come and hustle me into the slammer again. Sure. Every year for five years. Every year for the next fifteen. Sure, I could pull out, go to another town. But why? I live here. I was born here, right out on McAllister Street. Why should I have to run? Because a fat cop doesn't like me? Hell no. Eddie Pesak runs from no one. Eddie Pesak doesn't beg for his beans, either. And right now, Eddie Pesak's going out." He opened the front door. "No arguments. No cocker spaniel looks. I'm going out."

He shut the door behind him, pulled on his gloves, buttoned his overcoat and crawled behind the wheel. He started the motor, looked back at the dreary house and saw Zara sadly watching him from the window by the Christmas tree.

For a brief moment he felt a twinge, almost turned back, but then remembered the futility of living the way he had been living; he backed into the street with a roar.

It started to rain. A slow, fat drop hit the windshield, then another. In a minute the hood was splattered with drops and the tires hissed on the asphalt.

Rhenny's restaurant was situated on Chestnut Street, a block west of the usual business district, near the Palace of Fine Arts. The front had been built to resemble a huge Conestoga wagon, the canvas hoop serving as an awning, the rear wheels as entrance lures. Inside to the left was the dining area: muted lights; soft carpeting; gilt-framed oils; carriage lanterns; the odors of food; cosmetics; cigars. To the right, the Olde West Taproom: a large room with cowhide seats and stools; booths resembling miniature Conestoga wagons; jazz combo in the far corner; horseshoe bar in the center.

Eddie ignored the headwaiter with the three foot menu, turned into the bar and slid onto the nearest stool, which was at the head of the horseshoe. He ordered vodka and soda, settled down to stare at himself in the mirror fixed to the post in the center of the horseshoe.

An ugly face, not really handsome, too far out of line to be handsome. A caricature. Slavic face. Thief's eyes. He drank to Inspector Mihaly Dragoman, thought of another toast, ordered another drink. His thumb was twitching.

"This has been taken care of, sir," the bartender said.

Eddie picked up his drink. "Yeah? By who?"

"The lady at the end."

The bartender drifted off. Eddie turned on his cowhide stool and saw Carol Hewitt. He nodded, turned back to face the mirror.

Carol had been with Walter for the past nine years. They had never married. Theirs was an arrangement that had always seemed to satisfy them. Eddie had never had much to do with her because she had been Walter's. She, in turn, had never stepped out of bounds as far as Eddie knew. At least not with any of Walter's boys.

She was a pale blonde, almost silver, rather tall with wide shoulders, heart shaped face, pouting underlip. A strikingly beautiful woman. She was probably thirty now.

The bartender brought a glass toward Eddie, set it before the stool beside him. "The lady's going to join you," he said quietly.

Eddie nodded.

When Carol slid onto the next stool the first thing she did was put her cigarette in a horseshoe shaped tray and pick up her drink. Eddie looked at her, studied her closely. He was mildly surprised. Even though the bar was, as usual, dim and flatteringly gold and amber, Carol showed her age. Her hand shook on her glass. Her heavy-lidded eyes had fine crow's-feet and too much makeup.

Seeing Carol, not even saying a word to her, demonstrated to Eddie more than anything else the gulf that had existed between his present life and the old one. And, in a strange way, he found himself comfortable, relaxing in the silence, in a familiar night life of glasses and bare shoulders and smiling thieving bartenders and thick carpets. He felt almost as though he had returned home.

He bought a round of drinks. Carol still said nothing. Eddie was beginning to feel uncomfortable.

"I'm sorry," Carol said.

She seemed a little drunk. "About what?" Eddie asked.

"My silence. I took the opportunity to study you in the mirror ... Wanted to see if you've changed much."

"Have I?"

"No. Hello, Eddie."

"Hello, Carol."

She nodded. "Aren't I the same, Eddie?" she whispered.

"Sure," he lied casually.

"No, I'm not. I drink too much. Don't I look it? The black roots show, sweetie. Have you thought about me?"

"No."

"Ah." She picked up her glass, drained it. "Now you're being Eddieish. Buy me another drink, Eddieish."

He ordered a double. "Where's Walter, Carol?"

"You don't want to see him."

"Where is he?"

She shook her head, touched her bare shoulder, moved her silver painted nails down to her exposed upper-half breasts. "I have a little wrinkle, Eddie. Down here. An ugly little thing. I love Walter. Isn't that funny? I mean, how I could still be in love with your rotten brother?"

Eddie smiled and shrugged.

"I should've married him, then I could hate him." She looked wistful. "You've been away a long time, Eddie. The last I saw of you was right here, in Rhenny's, two nights before they nailed you and sent you away. When you got out and told Walter no more dice I could hardly believe it."

"Why not?"

She blinked, looked at her glass. "I didn't know you were that smart."

Eddie finished his drink, ordered another. "Where's my brother?" he asked again.

"He's out with Jimmy. Back in about—oh, maybe two more minutes. See, he never lets little Carol sit here too long. Afraid I'll get drunk. When I get drunk, Eddie, I embarrass Walter. Did you know how much he loves you, Eddie? Wait—" She touched her forehead and frowned. "—my conversation is becoming drunkish, isn't it? Sorry, Eddie. I hear you're married."

"That's right."

"Is she good?"

"She's good."

"Can I give you some advice?"

"Sure, Carol."

"See that thing over there? That's called a door. I'd like to see you walk out through it. Be good, like your wife."

Eddie shook his head. "Not until I see Walter."

"You're still a sucker, aren't you, Eddie?"

"How do you mean?"

"You've always been a sucker for Walter. It's your only weakness. When Walter whistles, you come. That's why you came tonight. Because Walter whistled. A hundred grand is an awful lot of money, Eddie." Her eyes narrowed and she smiled thinly. "But that door over there's an awful lot bigger. And so are the good people at home."

"Shut up," Eddie said.

"Conscience? Do you hurt, Eddie? How can an old friend hurt a tough guy like you? Sargatanas can hurt you, but—"

She suddenly stopped talking. Eddie followed her gaze, saw Jimmy Sargatanas and Walter entering the bar. Walter looked at Carol, then at Eddie, his face going from a frown to a wide, toothy smile.

"Eddie!"

"Hi, Walter."

Walter clapped him on the back, and, with his typical sense of organization, pulled Eddie to a booth, ordered drinks, told Carol to buzz off, winked at Sargatanas, removed his topcoat and hat with a proud flourish and shook Eddie's hand with a hearty salesman's grip.

"A sight for sore eyes, Eddie. My eyes. Jimmy, too. He said you'd change your mind and damned if you didn't. I think Jimmy's part swami, like a gypsy down in the San Joaquin. Eddie, it's like old times, old, old times. How's your wife? Here let's make a toast to Carol and your wife."

Walter was happy, Sargatanas his usual cautious self: not drinking, eyeing everything, everybody, with cold flat round eyes, pure white face. He sat in the covered wagon booth with his charcoal gray hat on, his overcoat buttoned, hiding the .45 automatic strapped under his arm.

"Eddie, old Walter feels good. Just seeing you, my son. You've made my day warm."

Eddie nodded. "Sure, Walter."

Walter passed a hand over his white hair, looked at the bar with dark eyes.

"How do you like the decorating job, kid? I picked out the trappings myself. The carriage lanterns in the dining room cost twenty-five clams apiece.
Can you imagine that? Twenty-five. Money's scarce. Right?"

Eddie nodded, his face expressionless, his dark eyes hooded and his
mouth turned down. The overhead lamp turned the gray in his hair to gold,
created dark pools under his brows and prominent cheekbones. He felt at
home now, vaguely drunk, but through with the rat race, with Drago, with
carrying the lunch bucket for an annual trip to the slammer. He owed
something to Zara and Kathy, to himself, and he owed something to *them*:
all the shafters, the dragons lurking in the corridors.

"Is that hundred grand still open, Walter?"

Walter's smile faded. He nodded.

Eddie picked up his glass. "Am I still wanted?"

Sargatanas said, purring, cold, "It couldn't go without you, tough mouth."

"Am I in?"

Walter nodded. "You're in, Eddie."

"About what Jimmy just said. Why couldn't it go without me?"

"You know the layout, the operation. We don't."

"What is it?"

Walter glanced toward the bar, maintaining a casual expression. "It's simple. We're going to hit Steffman's Industrial Metals for nearly six hundred
thousand dollars!"

11 (MONDAY, DECEMBER 22nd)

It was still raining—a cold black rain, wet, beaded curtain rushing in the
gutters, drumming on the pavements. Eddie parked in the lot next to
Rhenny's and walked to the corner, stood waiting under a dripping awning.
Christmas shoppers scurried by, galoshes smacking the sidewalks. Eddie
watched the slow traffic with tired, heavy-lidded eyes. Lenahan and Shoenstein were to pick him up at eight; it was almost time. He had finished the
Steffman's plans and had them with him, wrapped in plastic sheets and carrying them as he would a loaf of French bread, tucked under his arm.

When he spotted the tomato-colored Volkswagen, he crossed the street
and waved the car to the curb. He crawled into the front, nodded to Lenahan, who was behind the wheel, and to Cleve Shoenstein, who was sitting
hunched in the rear. No one spoke. The windshield wipers whirped, rain
tapped on the roof.

Shoenstein was tall and thin, with kinky, red hair, seamy face, lumpy nose
and waxy-looking, jug ears. He and Lenahan had joined Walter nine years
ago, just before the L'Agneau job. Shoenstein, Eddie remembered, was un-
communicative and vicious. And Lenahan was the opposite. A small, ane-
mic looking man with owlish, gray eyes, short graying hair, moon face, yellowish false teeth. He looked more like a high school teacher than a crook.
"We about ready to hear the details?" Lenahan asked.
"Yeah. Unless we find something wrong with it tonight."
They crossed Van Ness Avenue. Walter's Pesak Appliances warehouse
was six block further, east on North Point, then north toward Fisherman's
Wharf. The car bounced on rail tracks, swerved left, then turned into a wide
lot before a brick building. Walter's black Lincoln was parked near a loading ramp before a long shed. They left the car by the gate and crossed the
rain-puddled yard, walking toward the building. As Eddie passed the Lincoln he saw a silver blur from the corner of his eye. It was Carol Hewitt. He
continued walking alongside of Lenahan, then he heard her voice call his
name. Lenahan and Shoenstein waited while he went back to the car. Carol
was drunk, the same as the other night, watching him with half-closed eyes.
"Hello, Eddie. Hello again."
"What can I do for you, Carol?"
"Do? You can buy me a drink if you'd like. See?" She held up a plastic flask
with leather trim. "I'm fresh out."
"Some other time."
"Because of Walter?" She pouted. "The boss? Isn't that cute? The boss....
Don't you want to talk to me, Eddie? It's been a long time."
"I talked to you the other night," Eddie said.
"Eddie! Please don't go ... yet. I have something to tell you. It's about—"
"Some other time," Eddie said.
Her mouth grew tight, a frown pulled her dark brows together. "I don't
know why I bothered to tell you.... You're like Walter. Cold. Did you know
that? Cold. That's why I—All right, cold Eddie Pesak. You're like black ice.
I wanted to tell you, but I'm afraid. I'm afraid of everything." She pushed
a gloved hand to her mouth, biting the leather knuckle, her eyes filling with
tears of pain.
"Take it easy," Eddie said softly.
He turned and went back to the entrance of the warehouse. Shoenstein
opened the door with a key and he followed him in. The office was in the
far rear. Eddie could see just enough to follow Lenahan and Shoenstein
through the shiny maze of refrigerators and stoves, washers and air condi-
tioners. The frosted glass door was marked "Private." Lenahan pushed it

open.

Walter was behind the desk. Sargatanas stood by the filing cabinets, still wearing his hat, smiling lazily when Eddie entered.

"Everything okay?" Walter asked.

"Sure. It's fine."

Walter looked relieved, but not too much. There was a certain tightness around his eyes and mouth. Eddie glanced at Sargatanas, then back at his brother. Tension was in the air, cold tight lines just now being relaxed. Eddie sat by the desk, pushed the plastic roll toward his brother. He gave him a look, saying that he was ready, that everything looked good. Walter returned the look, but there was an uncomfortable light behind his eyes, as if he weren't fully convinced.

For the past few days Eddie had been nervous, possibly because he and Zara weren't talking much now. He knew that she suspected something and he had been trying to appear normal—too normal—which only led to further strain. He hadn't liked the look of hurt in Zara's eyes, the occasional guilty winces that he had had. But, in spite of Walter's discomfort, he was feeling better now. Everything had gone well so far. It was going to remain that way.

Lenahan asked: "So? What do we go for?"

"Platinum," Eddie answered.

Sargatanas and Shoenstein moved closer to the desk. Lenahan nodded, licked his thin lips, fingered the knot of his tie.

"Steffman's deals in common and uncommon metals for industrial use," Walter explained. "It used to be small spuds, but it's come up in the world. I'll give you the general idea and Eddie can fill in when he wants."

With the increase in rocketry along the peninsula, and with television and jewelry manufacturing, Steffman's had had to expand their annual purchases of pure platinum. The platinum came from the mines in heavily-guarded, staggered shipments and remained in the Steffman's warehouse for only one week of the year, then was moved to the individual manufacturers in small loads. The one week at Steffman's was from the last part of December to early January. That time was the outfit's custom because their early dealings with precious metals had been mainly with the jewelry houses that had customarily replenished their supplies directly after Christmas. The week was still observed by the company. There was no reason to change it.

But now, because of the advance in TV and rocketry, they handled approximately six hundred thousand dollars' worth of platinum, silver and gold during that week. And their methods of protection hadn't changed too much. Aside from the huge new safe and alarm system they hired only one extra guard during that week.

"The safe," Eddie said quietly, "would take six or seven shots. And our time'll be too valuable for that."

"Juice is tricky anyway," Shoenstein said.

"It'll be burned," Eddie said. "Like L'Agneau. Cleve? You know the new Normand-Würzburg safe?"

"Sure. It isn't as bad as a Diebold but it's bad enough. It can still be burned. Has it got a bar? It'll take heat and plenty of it."

"We'll get the heat," Eddie said. "And like L'Agneau the Steffman safe has a bomber; the moment the doors jar—poof it goes off and triggers an additional alarm. But I think I got that figured, too."

"Okay," Walter said briskly, "let's go over it and see how good we are."

"When do we take it?" Sargatanas asked.

"The twenty-sixth if it's okay."

"It'll be okay," Eddie said. He unwrapped the sheets and spread them out on the desk. "The grounds, containing the two storage buildings, melting-cutting house, and main warehouse, are surrounded by cyclone fencing. You can see here where Carlyle Street faces south and runs east and west. The two entrances are here: one at Carlyle where the day-guard post is, and the other off Third where the spur-line runs direct through the south lot to the ramp."

Three hours later they were finished, having gone over the entire plan seven times. Eddie was to be first gun, Shoenstein burning the safe, Walter and Lenahan loading, and Sargatanas acting as second gun as well as loading. Lenahan doubled as the telephone re-routeman. It was all down pat. It looked perfect.

When they broke up, Eddie left the plans with Walter to burn. Sargatanas and Shoenstein left without a word or a nod. Lenahan said that he would wait out in the car for Eddie, offering him a lift back to Rhenny's. Eddie thanked him. When Lenahan was gone Walter took the plans to a metal sink near the filing cabinets and set fire to them. Eddie watched his brother, waiting for an explanation for the tension between them. Walter said nothing. He finished burning the papers and returned to the desk.

"Okay, Walter. What's up?"

Walter shrugged, avoiding Eddie's gaze. "Up? What do you mean what's up?"

"You know what I mean, Walter. Something seems to be missing. I can smell it."

Walter shrugged again, not too convincingly. "Everything's okay, kid. I'm just nervous, that's all. Hell, can you blame me? Six hundred grand's a lot of money!"

"Is that all that bothers you?" Eddie asked in Hungarian.

"Yeah, sure. That's all."

Eddie stood up, put on his overcoat.

"Wait a bit, Eddie. When we make the hit let's do a switch. Why don't *you* take the truck with the stuff. I'll take your car to the car-switch with the others."

"How come?"

"It's better."

"You want to keep your eye on Sargatanas?"

Walter started to answer, then sighed. He nodded.

"Okay. You contact me at the Zodiak hotel."

Walter seemed relieved. He reached into his pocket and pushed a manila envelope across the desk. "Here, kid. Christmas money. No, don't tell me you can't use it. I know you can."

Eddie thought of Zara. "Sure," he said softly. "Thanks, Walter."

He left his brother and met Vic Lenahan by the gate. They piled into the car, Lenahan driving.

"Buy you a drink?" Vic asked.

"Sure. I can use it."

It had stopped raining and the neon seemed brighter, reflecting on the wet, black top; the air smelled of wet pavements; a few bright stars showed overhead. Eddie felt moody, thinking of Walter's suspicions toward Sargatanas, of Zara, the Steffman's robbery. December twenty-sixth. It wasn't very far off. Six hundred grand.... He thought again of his wife, of the hurt in her eyes and of the growing guilt and apprehensions inside him.

"Eddie?"

"Yeah."

"Have you given this a lotta thought? I don't mean the plans, I mean the rest of it."

"Such as?"

Vic narrowed his eyes thoughtfully. "You're an ex-con Eddie. You been inside. And you're an ex-employee of Steffman's. You know you're gonna be the first guy they grab don't you?"

"This's a funny time for you to bring that up, Vic. Sure I've thought about it, but I'm not planning on being around long enough to get busted."

"You running, Eddie?"

"Yeah."

"What about your family? You told your wife yet?"

"No."

"I hope you know what you're doing. For myself, I'm running, too."

"It might be best if everyone ran."

"Yeah. This's gonna be the biggest job the west coast has seen in a long time, and I don't wanna be around when the heat comes. I want out. I've never talked about this, Eddie, but I've been wanting out for a long time. Know what I mean?"

"Well, with a hundred grand you can dig a pretty deer hole, Vic."

"That's just what I been thinking."

Rhenny's was crowded. They found two stools at the bar, ordered vodka martinis. Eddie drank too fast. He knew that he couldn't bury his questions in drink but he kept at it anyway. When Walter and Carol came in half an hour later Eddie was working on his fifth drink. Walter ushered Carol, who was slightly staggering, into one of the rear booths.

"Feel like joining them?" Lenahan asked.

"No. I'd better get going home."

"Sure, Eddie. I'll see you tomorrow."

Eddie looked at Vic over the rim of his glass. "You look worried."

"Me?" Vic smiled nervously. "I feel okay. It's just at—"

Eddie nodded, feeling a bit high. "I know. It's Sargatanas, isn't it? I can smell it, too."

"I thought you could, Eddie. He's got me jumpy. He doesn't say anything, it's the way he looks. He's too damn quiet for one thing."

"I'll keep my eyes open," Eddie said.

"Sure, Eddie. Sure. Keep your eyes open."

12 (WEDNESDAY, DECEMBER 24th)

Zara was making an effort not to start an argument with Eddie for Kathy's sake. It was obvious. And Eddie was sullenly grateful for the diversion of Santa Claus and the toy department of the Empire Department Store.

Every day, since his contact with Walter, Eddie had been leaving the house, telling Zara he had a job parking cars during the Christmas rush, and every evening he would return home to make up hollow little lies about the job. It was obvious Zara didn't believe him. Eddie didn't want to think about it, didn't even bother to lie any more. It was too much trouble.

And at night, more and more, he was sleeping on the couch in the front room. Zara rarely spoke. Except, like tonight, when Kathy was with them. It was as if they were living with a bomb, both waiting for it to explode— waiting for it to complete the shattering of their marriage.

The tension was telling on Zara. There was a dark-eyed, almost haggard look about her. Eddie's signs were in his sullen moods and his snappishness and drinking. He couldn't seem to work up any interest in his surroundings.

Like now, standing in the area that led to Santa's Domain in the toyland of the store. He looked at things almost without registering them. And, as if to awaken him, he felt Zara's elbow jab into his side and he blinked. He turned, looked at her and saw what seemed to be a stranger. What was happening to them? Weren't they the same persons of a month ago? How was it possible that two people who loved each other could become such hated strangers in such a short time?

"Maybe you're sick of Christmas and shopping and your family, Eddie. But Kathy isn't. She's calling for you."

He looked at the line of nervous children waiting to see Santa. Kathy was next in line. She was waving at Eddie, trying to show him that she wasn't afraid as she had been last year. Eddie forced a smile, waved back at her and nodded encouragement.

Santa was seated on a golden throne in a cavern with tinsel stalactites. Pretty girls led the children to Santa's lap and held the mike up. When it was Kathy's turn she froze, the same as last year, and she stared at the mike. She looked as if she were about to break into tears.

"I want Daddy," Kathy whispered into the mike.

Eddie left the waiting section, stepped over the velvet cord, went to Kathy's side. She looked at him and smiled sheepishly. "Daddy," she whispered. "I *wasn't* scared. Then I sat on him and I got scared."

"That's okay, honey. Now you tell Santa what you want, and then we'll go have a soda. Okay?"

She nodded, wide-eyed, no longer afraid. "Can I ask for anything?"

"Sure."

"That's right," Santa purred. "You tell me what you want and I'll bring it on my reindeer."

"I want a robber set," Kathy said. "Like Timmy's, with rubber bands, the kind you shoot the robbers with and knock 'em down...." She rattled on for a minute, then Eddie led her back to the waiting area. Kathy broke from his hand and ran to Zara. "Mommy! Santa's going to get me a robber set like Timmy's. Did you see him, Mommy? Daddy came to see me on Santa's lap."

Zara looked at Eddie. "Thanks, Eddie," she said.

While Zara took Kathy to the lunch counter for the promised soda, Eddie went to the liquor department and bought a half pint of vodka. He joined Zara and Kathy in a rear booth, ordered coffee, and while Kathy was occupied with her treat he laced his coffee with the liquor. Zara looked his way, saw the bottle, and again turned cold. It was the same as before. The hell with it. The hell with everything, Eddie thought.

They drove home in silence. Eddie felt bitter, annoyed by Zara's air of righteousness. Perhaps he shouldn't have bought a bottle in the store, but that couldn't be helped now. Why didn't she just forget it? Why didn't she leave him alone? Didn't she realize that the Steffman job was for her, for Kathy? Didn't she realize how many times Eddie had been shafted? Olden, Drago, loan offices, traffic cops, everybody! Didn't she know how sick and tired he was of living like a goddamned worm?

He wanted out, wanted that hundred grand, and he was damned if he was going to let family arguments get in the way.... Still, he felt rotten inside. When he let Kathy and Zara off at the house he excused himself lamely and drove down to the Budapest for a few drinks to help settle himself.

The bar was full. Cody was drunk, waddling behind the bar and singing songs in Hungarian. The neighborhood old men—red-nosed, rosy-cheeked—clapped their hands and smiled through Magyar mustaches. Eddie ordered a Scotch and soda.

"What, Eddie? No vodka? Huh?"

"No. Scotch and soda."

"An American drink for my brother," Cody said. He made the drink, sloshing it on the bar. "Brother, I've bought Kathy a three-wheeled bicycle for Christmas. Will she like that?"

"Sure, Cody."

"Well! Cheer up, Eddie! Christmas Eve. Not a mouse is stirring, hah?"

Eddie sat morosely at the end of the bar, thinking of his brother's fears of Sargatanas, of what Carol had tried to say, of what Lenahan had said. Why hadn't he listened to Carol? At first he had shrugged her talk off, but now.... He could smell the double cross. But why did Walter ask him to take the load of platinum? It didn't make sense. He finished his drink, ordered another, sat brooding doubtfully over the way the robbery was building up....

13 (THURSDAY, DECEMBER 25th)

Christmas day was cloudless and cold. They opened their gifts early, be-fore breakfast. Eddie felt lousy, he couldn't even force himself to pretend to be happy for Kathy's sake. He was hungover, grateful when the packages were finally all unwrapped. Zara was openly hostile, Kathy confused but mollified once she opened her gifts. When Eddie ignored breakfast and opened a cold beer Zara had hissed: "Drink it in the kitchen! Don't ruin *this* day along with the others!"

"I didn't—"

"Don't make excuses!" Zara snapped.

He shrugged. He had no idea what he was going to say anyway. What could he say? There was nothing else for him to say—or do. He left the room with what he hoped was a proud air. He stood in the kitchen, staring at his reflection in the mirror. What the hell did he have to be proud about? "You are a dog," he said in Hungarian. "A soon-to-be wealthy dog, but a dog nevertheless."

He put on his jacket and left the house by the rear door, taking his beer with him, feeling, briefly, like a sneak thief. He walked to the Budapest, curs-ing himself, cursing Walter, cursing Zara.

He drank two draft beers in the Budapest, talking idly with Cody's re-placement behind the bar. There was no one else around. He played a few numbers on the jukebox, then left. Walking home he felt a terrific urge to tell Zara the whole story, then an urge to keep quiet about it. The need to tell and the fear to tell argued in him, so he was too absorbed to notice the car parked in front of his house. He wasn't aware of the visitor until he heard a booming, male laugh coming from the front room.

Kathy had set up the robbers game against the wall and was showing Mike Drago how to load the rubber bands into the gun. Eddie froze at the door-way, shocked, disgusted, resentful, confused; he stared at Drago. Drago glanced up, rose to his feet. Zara was on the couch, flushed, hands folded on her lap. Eddie glared at her. What had she been saying to Drago? What the hell was—

"Hello, Eddie," Drago said, offering his hand.

"Get out of here," Eddie said.

Zara pressed her fists to her temples, as if she were going to lose control. "Please, Eddie! Not in front of Kathy!" Kathy put her toy gun down and

went to her mother, pressing her head into her lap, hiding from her father.
Zara caressed her head, soothing her with small words, meanwhile glaring
hatefully at Eddie. Eddie shrugged helplessly. What else could he do? He
jerked his head toward the kitchen and angrily stalked down the hall with
Drago directly after him. At the cupboard he deliberately took out the bottle and poured himself a drink. He sat at the table and Drago joined him.
He lit a cigarette, watching the big policeman with narrowed eyes. "Got a
warrant, Drago?"

"No."

"Okay, then get out of my house."

Drago didn't move. Without his hat he didn't look much like a cop, but
more like a big, aging dockworker, smiling in a friendly, tolerant way.

"Didn't you hear me, Drago? Out."

"Settle down, Eddie. This's a social visit."

"I don't socialize with cops. If you want to bust me again, why don't you
wait until I've got a job! Do it the usual way." A bitter smile twisted his lips
and his eyes looked hollow, deadly. "You deliberately picked this day, did-
n't you, you bastard!"

Drago shrugged, watched Eddie with patient eyes. "Listen, Pesak," he
said quietly. "Each roust was legit, no matter what you think. Each investigation was on the level. Get that through your head."

"Sure. Drago. Like the armored car roust. You had proof of my being in
it!"

Drago backed down on that. "No, not positive proof. Suspicion. I suspected you had something to do with it." He evaded Eddie's gaze by lighting a cigar, then he watched him through the blue veil of smoke. "All right,
Pesak. I've rousted you once or twice when you didn't deserve it." He smiled
grimly. "See? I'm leveling with you."

Eddie nodded. "Thanks. I believe you, Drago."

"I'd like to talk with you. Can I have a minute?"

Eddie was wavering. He hadn't expected Drago to admit he had hounded
Eddie in the past. He was feeling his drinks now, the shock of Drago being
in his house wearing off as the effects of the liquor caught up to him. He
poured another drink, shrugged as if he couldn't care less, then nodded.
"Okay, Drago. Help yourself to the coffee."

"Thank you, Bela," Drago said in Hungarian.

"Forget the goofball talk."

Drago poured coffee, chuckling softly. "You got a right to be angry, Eddie. I've never said you didn't." He puffed on his cigar, tasted the coffee,
sighed quietly. "The last roust," Drago said, almost tiredly, "I really thought

I had you nailed. The facts were strong—too strong—too good for me to overlook. Think about it, Eddie. A tall man wearing a leather jacket, driving a Model A the same color as yours. After the shooting his accomplice stupidly says the killer's name. Eddie. It's my job. I feel I got you cold. I order you picked up and I execute that order."

Eddie watched him suspiciously, waiting for some trick, a kicker that would throw it back at him. But Drago shook his head as if saddened; his eyes appeared guileless, his manner affable.

"I goofed," Drago admitted. "It wasn't you. McCrea either backed down or he was telling the truth."

"He was telling the truth. I never shot anyone and you know it."

A curious light came into Drago's eyes: shrewd; glittering. "I believe *part* of that, Eddie. You didn't shoot McCrea's brother. But you *did* shoot someone." Drago's smile tightened. "You know who I mean. Me. Nine years ago. L'Agneau. I was the cute hero thinking it was only two or three men. I rush in and a figure jumps me. I step back. The figure drops and his mask slips. Just before the bullet gets me I see a pair of eyes. Guess whose eyes I saw, Eddie?"

It was eerie. Drago was looking directly into Eddie's eyes. Eddie tried to look away but couldn't, he was held fascinated by Drago's gaze.

"Your eyes," Drago said softly, without anger. "It was you and you know it and I know it."

"I didn't—"

Drago broke him off with a tired wave of his hand. "Don't deny it, Pesak. Admit it. To me." He paused, frowned, puffed on his cigar. "You know what an obsession is, Eddie? Sure, you know. Well, just about everyone's got some kind of obsession. One guy wants to fly to the moon, another wants to sleep with a movie star, another wants to have a million bucks cash. I don't want none of them things, Eddie. I got a different obsession. I want to make Edward Bela Pesak admit that he shot me nine years ago during the L'Agneau holdup. When he admits it then I am satisfied. No roust, no jail, no publicity. Nothing. All I want is to have this guy confess it to me. In private. Just between him and me. That's my obsession."

Eddie sipped his drink, smiled wryly. "Is that why you came here today? To get this guy to tell you something he didn't do?"

Drago sighed, weary, deep, patient. "No. That's not the reason." He drew out a sheet of onionskin paper, passed it across the table. "Read it. I marked the spot."

Puzzled, Eddie glanced at the sheet. It was a stolen vehicle report.

Drago said, "A 1930 Model A Ford, the same color as yours, was reported stolen by the Marin County Sheriff's office one day after the McCrea shooting. The car was reported on Tuesday, the ninth. The owner had parked it on Sunday, the seventh."

Eddie handed back the sheet. "So?"

"When I saw this I investigated."

"Why?"

"Because a car of this type was identified in a robbery homicide. It's my job. Maybe you don't think so, but I'm a pretty good cop."

"So someone stole a car and used it in a holdup. You still think it was me, is that it?"

"No. But think a little further. A car like yours, a shooting in your neighborhood, a tall guy with graying hair and a leather jacket, answering to the name of Eddie. Big coincidence? I think you were framed. Someone wanted you in the gas chamber in a pretty bad way."

Eddie swallowed his drink without tasting it. No, he thought, not in the gas chamber. Just picked up, resulting in another lost job, then released. No one wanted him in the gas chamber, just wanted him out, disillusioned, ready to fall for the Steffman offer. After all, Steffman's needed an inside man, the answer to the layout, didn't it? Sure, and Eddie was the pigeon. And Walter Pesak was the frame artist. Eddie's own brother!

"Who was it, Eddie?" Drago asked.

Eddie shrugged, keeping his face calm. "I don't know."

"You'd better level with me!"

"Don't you think I would if I could? What kind of sucker do you take me for anyway? You think I'd sit back and let someone try and frame me for murder in the first? Believe me, if I knew I'd tell."

Drago sighed disgustedly. "Don't insult me. You know who it was—"

"Why should I shield a killer, Drago? Jesus, do you think that I'd lie about a thing like this?"

Drago regarded him with narrow eyes. He didn't speak. He rose wearily, shaking his head, puffing his cigar. "Okay, Eddie. Okay. I take your word for it. Maybe you know. Maybe you don't. But I take your word for it. Not because I like you. But because I don't think you're a big enough fool to hold back something like that."

Eddie mumbled thanks.

"Thanks for your time, Eddie."

"Sure."

"If you think of any—"

"I'll let you know, Lieutenant."

Drago left; Eddie remained at the table, slowly pouring himself another drink. Everything was rushing in at once, hurting him, confusing him. Framed! But he hadn't been able to tell Drago. Eddie was a lot of things, but he wasn't an informer. And besides, there was still six hundred thousand dollars to consider. Even if he was framed he was still broke. His position didn't change just because he learned that he had been suckered into the job. And, also, Eddie could never inform against his own brother, no matter what.

It was quiet in the kitchen. He could hear Kathy playing in the front room. Eddie shivered and slowly closed his eyes against the light in the room. He pressed his fingers against his eyelids, pushing hard, shutting everything out, trying to forget. But it kept coming back in.

14 (FRIDAY, DECEMBER 26th)

It was raining hard. Eddie waited behind the large black van marked *Steffman's Industrial Metals*. His hands and face were numb from the cold. His body perspired under the black and yellow slicker. The thick uniform shirt clung to him. He was dressed in heavy rubber boots, rain slicker, and an Atlas Protection Agency uniform hat with a plastic headpiece that showed the brass shield over the visor. Under the slicker he wore his own clothes except for the uniform shirt and necktie.

It was fifteen after ten. Above him, at the top of the lead-in Pole to Steffman's, Lenahan was working at the telephone re-route connection. A spool of wire lay at Eddie's feet.

It was a good night: poor visibility; deep puddles everywhere; rain drumming steadily on the warehouse roofs; splashing from gutter spouts, gurgling in drains. The streets were deserted; everything was quiet. The van was parked some fifty yards from the main gate, but was hidden from view by the high brick wall under the lead-in pole. When Lenahan finished he crawled down, tool belt clinking, nodded an okay to Eddie, then ran the wire spool to the rear of the van. They crawled inside, Eddie closing the doors and squatting by the acetylene tanks and big dolly. Lenahan made the wire connection to the portable phone set in a canvas field bag. The rain drummed on the van roof, echoing in the dark interior. Shoenstein drew the portable typewriter across his knees.

Walter moved from the driver's seat, pressed his lips tightly and looked at the time on his wristwatch. "Okay. Eddie, you've got ten minutes. Don't forget the wine jug. Shoenstein, remember as soon as the guard at Steffman's

calls the Protective Agency you start hitting that typewriter. Not too fast;
not too slow. And keep up a soft chatter with me, as if we were a couple guys
in an office. Lenahan, you answer the phone on the first ring. Nasal voice—
like we rehearsed. Tell the guard—the guy's name is Artie if he sounds
young, and Jack if it's soft and old—tell him George'll be right out to investigate." Walter looked at them. "I guess we got everything. Okay, Eddie. Make it look real good."

"Sure," Eddie said. "I'm three delinquents out on a spree. Don't worry."

He opened the van doors, swung down, checked his pockets for the
equipment: hacksaw; gloves; lengths of wire; tape; gun; empty wine bottle.
He moved carefully in the rain, following the track to the gate. Peering into
the yard he saw the silent boxcars on the tracks, stacked crates of metal
spools, two black vans, identical to the one Walter was driving, parked near
the melting-cutting house. The only light was a square of yellow in the second story of the main building. That was the office overlooking the loading ramp and yard front.

He drew out the hacksaw and worked on the thin chain that wound
through the gate lock and cleat. It took five minutes. He pocketed the saw,
pulled out the empty wine bottle, slipped quickly through the gate. He
ducked behind the first boxcar, waited a second, then worked his way
across the inky blackness of the yard, ducking from one car to another. He
stopped at the closest pyramid of stacked crates near the loading ramp of the
main building.

A long structure, dark-red brick, with no windows save the upper offices.
No more waiting. Rain. He thought of Zara, Drago, the money, the others
waiting. Why wait? He took a deep breath, hurled the empty wine bottle at
the warehouse doors. The bottle sounded loud in the stillness, glass tinkling.
Eddie cupped his hands to his mouth and shouted in a highpitched voice:

"*Hey, Benny! Whadda ya think you're doin'? Whad you do that faw?
Goddammit!*"

He snickered loudly, Then: "*Yah! Yer drunk, daddy!*"

Grabbing a handful of gravel he jumped up and threw it at the office window. A window cracked.

"*Yah, stupid mothuh! Gimme that other bottle! Let's break into the joint!*"

Laughing loudly, he threw more gravel, then whooped and laughed
again. He turned, raced back to the nearest boxcar, boots splashing in
deep, rain pools. He made for the brick wall, leaped, scrambled over and
dropped to Carlyle Street, only a few yards from the parked and waiting van.

The two guards, Eddie knew, wouldn't chase the "kids" away. They
couldn't open the doors for that. Instead they would follow their instruc-

tions and report minor commotions to the Atlas Agency.

Eddie moved to the van. Walter rolled down the window. "Like a charm, kid," he whispered excitedly. "They called for George. Report of kids or hoodlums raising a ruckus in the yard."

Eddie grinned. "Okay, I'll give it two minutes. Wait for my flash."

He left, walked up Carlyle to the next corner, slid behind the wheel of the parked black Ford sedan. He waited, checking the fake microphone, the visor light, sidelight. Then, when three minutes passed, he kicked the motor to life and spun out into the street. He screeched to a halt at the gate, pretended to open the chain, swung the gate wide, drove quickly into the yard, the red visor light flashing. He flicked on the spotlight and swung the beam along the row of boxcars and piled goods. The rain was easing off now. He drove twice around the yard, poking the beam in nooks and dark corners, making it look good. He knew that the two Atlas guards were watching him. He stopped the Ford, which was identical to the Atlas cars, parked near the ramp. He swung his flashlight to the ground, waved up to the office windows, saw a blur of a return wave, then he trudged off toward the boxcars in the yard, swinging his flashlight.

The door at the head of the ramp, Eddie knew, had an alarm fixed and could only be turned off from the inside. The problem was to get inside without the alarm being triggered. He waited a moment, then returned to the Ford. He faked a return call on the dummy mike, then moved up to the ramp. Artie and Jack were watching him. It had stopped raining.

Eddie rapped on the metal door with the heel of his flash. A minute later he heard the footsteps inside moving toward the door. "Open up," he growled, "It's old George, Artie. Soaked to the skin."

A muffled voice answered, "Just a sec, dad."

The lock rattled. Eddie drew on his white silk gloves, drew out his .38, turned his back to the door as if casually watching the yard. When the door finally opened Artie's voice greeted him: "I suppose you wanna mooch a little coffee, huh, George?"

Eddie turned. "Inside, Artie! Or you're a dead man."

Artie looked once at Eddie, then the gun, and he backed up with wide terror in his gray eyes. His blond pencil mustache quickered on his sullen mouth. Eddie stepped into the warehouse, closed the door after him. "Don't make a sound, kid," he whispered tightly. "Turn around."

Artie turned. Eddie jerked the service revolver from the holster and nudged the guard toward the stairs. "Move up to the office. No stalling."

"Look, Mister, I—"

"Shut up. Keep moving."

Artie dragged himself up the steps, moving stiffly, being prodded from behind. When they reached the office Eddie shoved him into the room and covered the older guard, Jack, with his gun. The old guard blinked, turned white, looked to Artie for an explanation, then slowly raised his shaking hands. Without a word Eddie disarmed him and motioned him away from the window.

"What—what's this all about?"

"What does it look like? Turn around. Both of you. Now lay on your bellies. Make it quick."

He bound their hands and feet with the lengths of wire, then gagged them with four strips of tape, being careful to leave breathing space.

He returned to the warehouse proper, swung open the ramp doors and flashed his light several times. A few seconds later the Steffman's van driven by Walter rumbled through the gate and backed up against the ramp. Eddie swung the rear doors open and dropped the gate onto the platform. No one spoke. Shoenstein grabbed the handcart and fitted the lift-blade under the acetylene tanks. Lenahan carried the hose, torch and tools. Eddie followed with the gas masks, and Walter wheeled out the big dolly. They moved through the warehouse in single file, not making a sound, then through the far, rear passageway that led to the iron door which opened into the safe room. Eddie opened the door and the others entered the room. From the dim flashlight beams reflecting from the concrete floor, the safe looked like a solid sheet of circular steel with a drawbar and ship's wheel on its gleaming face.

Eddie dropped the masks and returned to the ramp. He checked the time on his wristwatch. Everything was going fine. He was feeling a little shaky, reaction setting in, but he expected that. He held the grip of the revolver free in his right hand and paced the platform. Minutes dragged by. A cold sharp wind rose, riffling the slick, black pools of rain in the yard. He left the ramp only once, to check the trussed up guards in the office. Then he waited by the staircase, listening for Sargatanas's signal.

When it came he returned to the office and undid the tape from Artie's mouth. He whispered: "Listen, and listen good. I'm only going to say this once. I'm calling Atlas for you. You got that?"

Artie's eyes shone, his head jerked in a tense nod.

Eddie continued: "You're going to tell them that a gas main blew and that everything is fine otherwise. Tell them that you've already notified the fire department and the cops. Got that, kid?"

Artie nodded. Eddie dragged him to the desk, propped him in the chair, then dialed the Atlas number, leaving out the last digit. Seconds dragged by,

Eddie strained to hear the blast, then a moment later he felt rather than heard a muffled explosion. He dialed the last digit and held the phone to Artie's face. Artie did exactly as he was told and when Eddie hung up he replaced the tape over the kid's mouth and shoved him again to the floor near the other guard.

Moving quickly he went out onto the loft balcony, raced down the stairs. In the long passage in the rear, through the spider-webbing of the tear gas, he could see the others loading the platinum boxes onto the dolly. Each box was bound with black metal bands and marked platinum. Eddie returned to the ramp.

His heart was hammering in his chest now, his vision was bright, sharp, and time seemed to drag by. He checked his watch. Three minutes since the call. Why didn't they—?

The door behind him swung open and the heavy dolly emerged onto the ramp. Shoenstein and Walter were pushing. Sargatanas was nowhere to be seen. Walter shoved the dolly, groaning under the mountain of boxes, into the truck. Eddie slammed the doors.

"Time?" Walter snapped.

"Four minutes since it went off."

Walter nodded, pressed the truck key into Eddie's hand and remained that way for a brief moment, his eyes studying his brother's, as if he were trying to tell him something. Then, softly, "Okay, kid, call me first thing in the morning. I'll take the Ford."

Eddie jumped from the ramp and piled into the cab of the van. The motor caught without trouble, and, as he was pulling away, he heard Shoenstein's voice arguing with Walter. As Eddie passed through the gate he heard the Ford growling after him. Everything seemed okay, but feeling the first panic of flight, he ground the truck into gear and raced down Carlyle to Third. Just beyond the Islais Channel drawbridge he heard the high, thin wail of the sirens.

Steady. Drive to the second bridge near the train yards. Take it easy, Eddie. Back the truck against the second truck. Push the dolly into the second bed and make the transfer, close the door, drop the canvas and chain door, steady, steady. In the second truck he changed his clothes, then he drove to Mission Street and pulled into an all night truck station.

He was supposed to leave the truck there, but the moment he saw the squad car squeal into the station he changed his plans. Without pause he drove straight through the truck yard, slowed as he passed between two diesel rigs, then added speed once he was behind the station and out of view of the squad car. His mouth was dry, knees quivering, and he could think

88

of nothing. No Zara, no Kathy, no Walter. More sirens. Jesus. Dang-a-dang and the hunt was on. For the first time since he agreed to do the job he regretted it. He drove aimlessly, the gun resting on the seat beside him.

He found another truck yard on Bayshore Highway going south. He parked on the wide, graveled circle, killed the motor. A cigarette. What he needed was a drink. He had six hundred grand worth of platinum in the back of the truck. What he needed was two, three drinks—big ones.

He still hadn't called Zara. He left the truck, crossed the yard to a roadside cafe near the gas station. What the hell was the matter with him? He paused before the cafe windows, peering in with suspicion. He was afraid. Something had gone wrong—but what? It smelled of double cross—somewhere, somehow, Sargatanas had double-crossed him. But how? Eddie had the platinum. And if Walter had been in on the first frame why had he executed the truck-Ford switch? It didn't make sense. It all spun around in fear, puzzlement.

It was warm in the cafe. Rock'n'roll on the jukebox. No one looked up at him when he entered.

"Coffee." he said to the waitress.

15 (SATURDAY, DECEMBER 27th)

He had checked the truck at the Bayshore yard, then had caught a Greyhound and returned to the city. He decided against going to the Zodiak Hotel and holed up in a cheap off-Mission hotel near Valencia Street instead. He dreamt that night. Of Zara and Kathy in a silver cavern—Santa's domain—with tinsel stalactites, and Kathy frozen on the red velvet knee; Eddie ran to soothe her, only to discover that Santa was Mihaly Dragoman. Mihaly's voice boomed, promising Kathy to bring her a game that shot rubber bands at the crooks. And Eddie awoke in a sweat, his finger squeezing the trigger of his gun. The safety had been on. He sat up. It was raining again. The room smelled like sour library paste.

He hung around the lobby, watching the seventeen inch TV set, calling Walter's home number every hour. So far there had been no answer, not even at the appliance warehouse.

Two o'clock—the big clock on the wall ticked the seconds. What had happened? Why didn't Walter answer? The lobby window was steamy, blurring the faces of the passersby. Time dragged. No one else in the lobby. If Eddie was a cheap thief he could very easily walk off with the TV set. He chain smoked on an empty stomach, chewed his underlip, jumping at Western gunshots on the TV. Half-past two. He called Walter. And this time there was an answer. No voice, just the receiver being taken off the hook.

"Walter? Hello? Walter?"

Police? No, that didn't seem likely. The cops always answered the phone—at least they always did in the movies. Eddie hung up, puzzled, standing in the booth, chewing his thumb, trying to think it out. Eddie had platinum, sure, but it was a worthless pile of junk without the name of the fence. And, as far as Eddie knew, only Walter knew who the outlet was. He was certain that Sargatanas didn't know it and that Walter would never tell him. Walter had always kept an ace-in-the-hole, and in this case it was the name of the fence.

Something up. Something wrong. It stunk. After all, Walter had framed Eddie for the job. But was he also planning to make Eddie the fall guy for the Steffman job, too? If that was so, then why did Eddie's brother want the truck switch?

Eddie left the hotel, walked hurriedly down to Mission Street, caught a jitney and rode it as far as the Coca Cola plant near Van Ness Avenue. He stood on the corner, bundled in his topcoat, his hat dripping rain. The neon was lit and the sky was dark. Half-past three in the afternoon. Cars whished past. A squad car cruised. Eddie started walking, feet squishing on wet pavements, heart hammering in his chest. Mike Drago was somewhere in the city, tracking him, wondering about him. Did anyone know how it felt to have half a million in platinum? Did anyone know what Eddie felt, what he was supposed to do?

He caught a cab at the Fox Theater on Market Street.

"Take me to Fisherman's Wharf."

He settled back, deciding to try the appliance warehouse before going to Walter's apartment. He worried in a black mood, remembering Walter's look of the night before. A warning? About Sargatanas? So why didn't Walter stay in one place long enough to make the arrangements for the fence?

"Where on the Wharf did you want, buddy?"

"This is fine. Right here."

He left the cab and walked south, away from the Wharf and toward the industrial yards. He crossed a weed-grown lot and approached the Pesak warehouse from the rear, moving cautiously, waiting for the first sign of trouble. The sky grew darker, the rain heavier. He moved onto the loading ramp, the rain drumming on the corrugated tin overhead. The yard was empty, silent, the gate closed. There was no one about, nothing, just the rain, the dark sky, the suspicion in Eddie's heart. It was too quiet. Eddie's guts were tight, warning him, and he moved more slowly. He stopped at the front door. It was unlocked. He pushed it aside, holding his breath, pressed against the building, waiting, listening, watching. Nothing. He counted to three and dove into the door, raced into the gloom and crouched behind a pastel pink refrigerator.

The only sound was the sharp rasp of his breathing, the hammering of his heart. Nothing else. He worked his way to the rear of the warehouse. He pulled the hammer of his gun back, the chamber movement sounding too loud; he opened the office door. Then he froze, lowered his gun.

Vic Lenahan was behind the executive desk, his gray eyes looking directly at Eddie, his gray false teeth smiling at him, unreal, pasted there. Eddie felt a sickening turn in the pit of his stomach. He closed the door behind him and crossed the room. Lenahan was dead, and when Eddie touched his face he felt only the cold waxiness under his fingers, like a crushed dixie cup—stiff, cold. Lenahan had been shot four times in the chest. Blood was smeared everywhere.

Eddie turned his back to the dead man, picked up the phone and dialed his brother's number. The line was busy. Eddie dropped the phone on the hook and closed his eyes. It didn't seem like something Walter would do. It didn't seem possible. And yet.... He stepped to the door, moving as if a great weight were on his shoulders. He looked back at Lenahan. "See you later, Vic. The dogs have started to bite ..."

Walter lived in an apartment on Pacific Heights, a six-story structure with small balconies and green window awnings. A doorman stood under the lobby canopy; a fountain was set in the court. Eddie left his cab one block around the corner off Pacific Avenue. He walked back to the garage side, slipped into the tradesmen's entrance and crossed the dark basement garage. The stairs were beyond the elevator, near the furnace room.

Walter's apartment was on the fifth floor. Eddie paused outside his door, dripping rain from his hat and topcoat, listening for sounds while a dark puddle formed at his feet. He could hear nothing. He moved quietly to the fire escape French door at the end of the passage, stepped out onto the narrow balcony and made his way to Walter's window. He saw nothing. Just vague furniture shapes. There were no electric lights on in the living room. Back outside Walter's door he listened again; then, holding his breath, he slowly tried the knob, and when it turned free he pushed. He slipped into the foyer, revolver ready. There was still no sound.

There was no need for caution, for holding the gun. He felt like the actor who stepped out onto the stage only to find the theater empty. He dropped the gun to the carpet and staggered to the bathroom. There he bent his head into the bowl, heaving and racking with painful sobs. It was a long while before he could return to the foyer and retrieve his gun. The sickness had passed, a cold fury overtook him. He had had too much shock. Nothing more could hurt him now.

Walter was there, crumpled in the living room; his white naked body a horrible map of bruises and deep, bloody gashes. Before they had cut his throat they had worked him over, using the knife. Walter's eyes spoke the terror. His hands were tied behind his back, his knees pulled close to his chest as if to deny the knife. Blood soaked into the carpet, smeared the white body.

But Walter wasn't the only one. Carol Hewitt was lying on the carpet near the phone stand. The phone dangled from its base by the curled wire. It must have been Carol who had grabbed at the phone when Eddie had called. Sargatanas must have left her for dead.

Eddie replaced the receiver, turned Carol's body over with his toe. She moaned. He bent quickly and held her head, his hands touching a warm, sticky knot of torn flesh by her ear. Her eyes fluttered long enough for her to see who it was. Her voice was a bare whisper.

"You're late."

"It was Sargatanas?"

"Yeah . . ."

"Shoenstein with him?"

She didn't answer.

"Carol!"

"What?"

"Who's the fence?"

"Sargatanas killed Walter ..."

"Listen! Who's the—"

It was no good. She sagged. Eddie stood, closed his eyes, breathed deeply for a moment, trying to clear his thoughts. But nothing came. Just the fury, the sight of Walter, and another scene—a memory of two boys standing on a doorstep, watching the sunshine in an alley. *"So, what'll we do, Walter?"* And the other boy smiled, *"We'll play King Of The Mountain, Eddie."* The youngest frowned, *"Yeah, but you always win, Walter. You're always King Of The Mountain. I never even get a chance ..."*

Eddie left the apartment without looking back. He returned the street through the garage and walked down Pacific Avenue toward the Marina. The rain splashed all around him, but he felt nothing. The cold within grew, blotting out everything. Walter hadn't framed Eddie for the job, hadn't killed McCrea to force Eddie's hand. It had been Sargatanas and Cleve Shoenstein. Jimmy Sargatanas, the cold white frog with the bowtie, the only thing with life about him. Sargatanas was as good as dead now. As dead as Walter.

He turned into a bar, found a stool, sat staring at his face in the mirror. His eyes looked like black pebbles, his face dark with beard.

"What'll it be?"

"Vodka. Double."

16

The cab melted into the traffic flow on Lombard Street going east. Eddie sat slumped in the rear, watching the motel neon, gas stations, restaurants, bars. Saturday night, traffic heavy, rain thinning. The Christmas decorations were still out. Eddie had the cab wait outside a bar while he slipped into the phone booth. He picked up the phone directory, looked up Mihaly Dragoman's address on impulse, wrote it down on an envelope. Then he dialed his own home number.

"Hello?"

Zara's voice sounded pale, strained, and Eddie winced slightly. "This's Eddie," he whispered.

"Eddie! How did—"

"Is anyone there?"

"No, but—"

"Are you okay?"

"Yes, but—"

"Has Drago been there?"

"Yes, Eddie, he—"

"He fingers me for Steffman's? Well, he's right, honey."

A silence; painful; long; paced by her breathing which sounded more like sobs to Eddie. Jesus. He closed his eyes, cursing himself now for having brought the pain, the needless pain.

"Zara? Listen.... Walter, my brother, is dead!"

"Dead? Walter? But—"

"I'll get in touch. Zara, I love you. I—"

There wasn't anything else to say now. He hung up, had a fourth vodka at the bar, and returned to the waiting cab.

"Where to now, Mac?"

Eddie frowned. That was a good question. Where to now? Eddie had the platinum; Sargatanas wanted it, obviously knew the name of the fence now. The only thing Eddie could do is work for a deal, get the word.

"Take me to twenty-fourth and Mission."

The cab swerved into the traffic. Eddie smiled to himself. He pictured Sargatanas' panic when he had gone to the Mission truck yard and saw that the truck wasn't there. Then he had probably tried the Zodiak. And no Eddie. It was almost funny. Cross. Double cross. Cross again. It was Jimmy's move now. Eddie had the loot and if they wanted it they would have to deal on Eddie's terms.

He left the cab at twenty-fourth, walked two blocks to the Garfield Theater. The marquee lights winked, reflected on the streets. The stills outside showed Steve Reeves cracking temples, throwing his enemies around like cordwood. Saul, the blind man, the see-all and know-all, stood at his usual post near the newsstand. Eddie sided next to him, pretended to read the papers. It was all over the front page now. Bela Edward Pesak hunted for questioning in the million dollar robbery of ... and so on. Of course, the papers had to say it was a million. And who knows, perhaps it had been.

"Hello, Saul."

"Reading your notices, kid?"

Eddie smiled thinly. "Yeah, sure. I want to know how the critics liked me."

"They loved you," Saul said. "They're looking for you."

"Jimmy Sargatanas?"

"Yeah."

"The word is that you crossed them."

"The word's wrong, Saul. Walter and Lenahan are scratched."

"Sargatanas?"

"Yes," Eddie said. "Where is he?"

The blind man shrugged. "I don't know, kid. That's the truth. Try Rhenny's. If Walter's gone, Sargatanas is on top."

Eddie nodded, a spare gesture, then he dropped a five-dollar bill into Saul's box. He bought a ticket at the box-office. In the lobby he entered the phone booth and called Rhenny's. The bartender was cagy, but finally Eddie was connected with the manager.

"Give me Sargatanas," Eddie said.

"Who? No one here by that—"

"Tell him Pesak wants business."

Silence. Eddie waited. Another voice, purring. "Hello."

"I hear you're looking for me, Jimmy."

"I am, Eddie. I am."

"I've been to the warehouse, Jimmy. I saw Vic."

"I see…"

"And I've been to the apartment."

Sargatanas was quiet. Eddie could hear tense whispers in the background, muffled as if Jimmy had his hand over the mouthpiece. Then again, "I see …"

"I'm glad you understand, Jimmy," Eddie said tightly.

"Where are you at?"

"I'm still in town."

"All right, Eddie. I'll set a meet and we'll swap."

"No. We'll swap, but I'll set the meet."

"Fifty-fifty?"

"No. You'll get what you worked for. One hundred grand. That's all. No more deal. No other way."

A pause, then, "All right, Eddie. If that's the way it has to be, I suppose I've no choice. I'll meet wherever you say."

"Just you. No Shoenstein. Tomorrow at nine o'clock in the morning. The Marina Green. In the center of it."

The line went dead. Eddie hung up, walked out into the lobby. He bought a bag of popcorn and found a seat in the rear of the theater. Darkness, safety, people, voices on the huge flickering screen. An hour later he left, not being able to follow the story on the screen. He caught a cab and returned to the motel strip on Lombard. He bought a shaving kit and a hamburger to go. Once in a rear unit off Lombard he shaved and ate, turned on the TV and flopped fully clothed on the bed.

His thoughts churned. It had gone easy, too easy. He had one purpose now—to get the name of the fence and kill Sargatanas and Shoenstein. What else mattered? Right was right and Jimmy had to get his for Walter. There was no other way to look at it. Zara and Kathy were now lost to Eddie. He couldn't allow himself to think about them. He had to push them from his mind. Maybe later, if the heat cooled off, but not now. He loved them, wanted and needed them, but to think he could have them now was stupid. It was dead. He couldn't turn back time; he couldn't ignore Walter's death, the six hundred grand in platinum, the fact that Drago had him fingered for the job.

He tried to concentrate on the TV. A handsome detective was pointing to a luscious blonde, a smile on his lips. "You thought you were clever, baby. But you made one little mistake."

Eddie turned the set off and doused the lights. He fell across the bed, still clothed, and slept fitfully. He dreamt again. Of bowties, frogs, Zara and Kathy, of two boys playing King Of The Mountain.... When he awoke the sun was pouring into the room through the blinds. It was eight o'clock. He scrambled out of bed, looking tired, drawn, rumpled, haunted. He felt terrible. His picture had been in the paper last night. His nerves were tight, his stomach rumbling. He jammed his hat on his head, left the motel, and had coffee in a diner while he waited for a cab.

The Marina Green was empty, a grand sweep of lawn, blocks long at the edge of the bay. The sky was cloudless, the hills of Marin incredibly clear and seeming close, Alcatraz a gloomy ship in the center of the bay, gulls wheeling white and lazy overhead. It was half-past eight. He started pacing the lawn. A few children came onto the Green, passing a grass-stained, white football back and forth. Yachts churned out on the bay, more gulls moving overhead. Nine o'clock.

When the cab came he watched it suspiciously. The driver parked near the harbor, left the cab and started across the lawn, moving hesitantly, looking over his shoulder, pushing his yellow hat on the back of his head. When he came up to Eddie he frowned, as if he were a little confused.

"Is your—your name Eddie?"

"Yeah."

The driver nodded, seemed to make up his mind about something. "Well, I don't know if this's a gag or not, but a guy paid me to give you a message."

"What's the message?"

"It's funny. He said for me to spell it out for you."

"Okay," Eddie said. "Spell it out."

"K-a-t-h-y."

The blood drained from his face and the violent jerk of his thumb was almost painful. He barely heard the words of the driver. His insides crumpled like ice, like fire, and his eyes blurred. What little food was in his stomach turned to cold lump in the pit of his gut. He started walking toward the cab, moving with leaden feet.

"You okay, Mister? Is it bad news, or somethin'? See, this guy came to me right off Powell Street, told me what to do. Said to say 'Kathy' and spell it out for you. Is that—"

Eddie nodded dully. "It's spelled out. I got the message."

He piled into the cab.

"Where to?"

Eddie closed his eyes wearily. "A phone. Just take me to a phone."

17 (SUNDAY, DECEMBER 28th)

He wanted to see Zara but he knew that Drago would surely have a stakeout on the house. If he tried to get to her, to comfort her, he would undoubtedly be picked up, and, if that happened, Sargatanas' chances to get the loot would be slim. Eddie had no doubt that Kathy would then suffer the consequences. Sargatanas, Eddie knew, had little or no regard for others.

Eddie left the cab on Chestnut Street, not too far from Rhenny's, and went into a nearby drugstore. He dialed his home number with a shaky hand, almost reluctantly, fearing the worst. When Zara answered he immediately caught the evenness of her shock, the lifeless, weak whisper: "Yes? Hello?"

"This is Eddie—is anyone there?"

"No." Zara's voice was strange, distant, as if she were acting out a dream. "There's no one here. No one at all. No one."

"Is—is Kathy—"

"She's gone, Eddie. She's not here anymore. She's gone—with Sargatanas. There's no one left here but me."

"Zara, listen, I—"

The phone went dead. Eddie quickly dialed the Budapest Bar. Cody answered. Speaking in Hungarian Eddie briefly described Zara's state of mind to her brother, he told Cody to rush right over to the house, stay with Zara, see what he could do, call a doctor if necessary. Cody agreed, asking no questions. Half-relieved Eddie hung up and hurriedly left the store. From the street he could see the covered wagon awning of Rhenny's two blocks away.

Questions crowded him as he walked. How had Sargatanas managed to snatch Kathy while Drago had a watch on the house? How was Sargatanas planning on connecting with Eddie without showing himself? Eddie quickened his step. Kathy had been snatched; that was all that mattered. He no longer cared about himself, the platinum, Drago—nothing. He wanted only to get Kathy back to Zara and avenge Walter and his family. Nothing else mattered.

Rhenny's was closed to business, but the service entrance to the kitchen was open. Eddie passed through the kitchen and stepped out into the thickly carpeted restaurant. From somewhere up front, near the foyer off the bar, a vacuum cleaner hummed. The carpet muffled his steps. He walked up the flight of steps to the office, drew out his .38, listened for a long moment. When he heard a muffled cough behind the door he kicked it open with violent impatience and stepped into the room.

The manager spun around on his desk chair and gaped at him. No one else was in the room. The manager was a whitefaced spare young man, wearing tuxedo trousers, house slippers, and open, white shirt. His eyes flicked fearfully from the gun to Eddie.

"Pesak ..."

"Where's Jimmy Sargatanas?" Eddie asked.

"He—he's been expecting you—to call here," the manager stammered. His tongue darted nervously over his lips, his hands held halfway up and in clear view. "I—he said that if you phoned here I was supposed to get your number—that he'd call you right back. I'm just the middleman, Pesak—honest."

"How often has he called in?"

"Every—about every five minutes."

Eddie closed the office door. "I'll wait."

The manager tried to relax during the next five minutes, but the constant threat of the gun kept his hands up, his face in a pale sweat, his eyes transfixed. Eddie said nothing more. He sat on a leather chair near the phone, his gun ready, his eyes watching the manager. When the phone rang the manager started, but Eddie remained perfectly calm. He picked up the receiver, still watching the manager.

"Has he called yet?" Shoenstein's voice wanted to know.

"You're talking to him right now," Eddie said softly. "This is Eddie. Put Jimmy on the line."

Surprisingly, Eddie's voice was even, almost seemed to lack emotion. He sounded tired, indifferent, as if he couldn't care either way what happened now. And when Jimmy's purring evil voice came on the line Eddie didn't seem to mind it at all. Nothing seemed to be able to break his cold shell — his curtain of single purpose and hate.

"Hello, Eddie boy ..."

"You have Kathy." It hadn't been a question, simply a statement. "You have her with you."

"That's right."

"And you want the platinum with no strings attached."

"That's what I had in mind," Sargatanas said. "But I'm not a hog, Eddie. I said fifty-fifty last night, and I still say fifty-fifty. I'm a reasonable person. There's more than enough for all of us."

"Including Walter," Eddie said.

"I'm not going to bother to explain myself to you, Eddie. I've got the outlet and you've got the stuff. That's the basis for the perfect swap. But I've also got a little girl. That changes everything, doesn't it? Makes it kind of one-sided."

"She's all right." Still it wasn't a question, or a threat.

"Sure. She's fine. She's having breakfast right now. You remember—" the voice smiled—"I once said how I liked little girls. I take care of them. I'm Uncle Jimmy."

"Let me speak to my little girl, Jimmy."

A pause, whispers, then Kathy. "Daddy? Daddy, I'm having corn flakes with bananas on them."

"Fine, honey," Eddie said, half choking. "Honey, the men you're with— they're friends of mine ..."

"I know, Daddy. They tol' me. And Jimmy says I can have more bananas if I want."

"Fine, Kathy, that's real fine. You be nice to Jimmy. In a little while he might take you to see me and—"

Sargatanas' voice cut in. "Okay, Daddy. No more talk. You meet me at five o'clock."

"Where?"

"Castro and Market. Five o'clock."

"Listen—"

"I don't have to listen," Sargatanas interrupted. "I've got the ace-in-the-hole, and if you want her to be okay then you do as I say. You come alone. Alone. You got that? I'll have the kid with me. You take us to the stuff, and we let you and the kid go free. Understand?"

"Yes. But I—"

The connection broke. Eddie hung up and sat staring at the manager with dull, hating eyes. The manager's attitude, during the phone conversation, had changed from one of fear to something like compassion. He was watching Eddie now, his eyes thoughtful, brow wrinkled.

"They took your kid, Pesak?"

Eddie nodded.

"Look, I'm sorry about it. I didn't know. That's the truth, Pesak."

"Sure."

"What're you going to do?"

"Do? I'll have to deal."

The manager thought that over, then nodded. "Maybe you could call the—"

"The law?"

The manager seemed to hate to say it, so he nodded slowly, almost shamefully. He muttered, "Yeah. It's kidnapping. I don't like it, that's all." He shrugged his thin shoulders.

Eddie rose and left the office without a word. Out in the street he caught another cab, not knowing what else to do. He told the driver to start driving—anywhere—and he settled back in the seat. It was a full five blocks before he surrendered to himself. He sighed, resigned now, directed the driver to take him to Noe Street near the Twin Peaks' tunnel.

Sure, there was a slim chance of his getting Kathy out and making the deal, but not much of a chance. He was tired, drawn down with guilt and pain, his thoughts were dark, unselfish thoughts. The things that he truly wanted he knew he could never have now—Zara and Kathy; a chance to turn back the time.

It was as if he had known all along that he would come to this house. He was drawn to it now, a strange feeling within, as if he were returning to his own home in the past.

It was an old house, high on Noe Street hill, three stories of pre-earthquake gingerbread, tall dusty windows; dark gray with elaborate, white trimming. He stood in the front alcove, rang the bell twice, and waited with his hand gripping the checkered butt of his revolver; concealed but ready in his topcoat pocket. The woman that answered the ring was tiny, about seventy, with small, gray eyes, thinning white hair, bent, little shoulders.

Eddie spoke in Hungarian. "Good afternoon, Mrs. Dragoman. I've come to visit with your son. Is he at home?"

"No. He's due to be here very soon. Come into my house. You are welcome."

"Thank you."

The house smelled of camphor, cooking spices, tobacco, sour velvet and thin, worn carpets. The foyer walls were paneled in dark rosewood; the furnishings were very old but remarkably well kept. Eddie was led into the front room, the formal visitor's room, and he removed his hat. He sat gingerly on the edge of a damask couch that faced the hallway.

"You are Hungarian, sir?"

"Yes. My name is Bela."

Her little eyes sparkled, wrinkled hands, held before her, folded across her tiny waist. "Have you known Mihaly for many years?"

"Yes. Many years. But I'm certain he hasn't mentioned me to you. Our relations have always been conducted on a business level. He has called but once socially at my home, and I'm taking this opportunity to repay him."

Mrs. Dragoman smiled, her face wrinkling like a soft, white walnut. She offered Eddie a cup of tea while he waited; Eddie accepted. She disappeared down the hall toward what Eddie imagined was the kitchen. He lit a cigarette, drew out his revolver, held it in his right hand and placed his hat over it.

The living room was much the same as the one he had lived in as a child. Even the odors were familiar. The portrait wedding picture on the wall, the carved, serving table, elaborate brass samovar no longer in use, the stained-glass lamps, damask couch—all had deep associations in Eddie's thoughts. He lit a cigarette, and when Mrs. Dragoman returned with the tea he neglected to rise from the couch. He kept the gun in place.

"A pleasant tongue, Hungarian. Mihaly speaks it, but not as well as some."

This was a compliment and Eddie gave her a short bow. The tea was hot and sweet without being sugary, sharp and biting without being acrid. Mrs. Dragoman went on to say that she found English a difficult language, thick with synonyms and local references that tended to confuse. She had never bothered to learn and she rarely used what few words she knew.

They talked for twenty minutes, and as Eddie was pouring himself a second cup of tea he heard the lock rattle on the front door. He tensed. Drago's mother rose slowly to greet her son.

Drago came into the hall whistling an aimless little tune. He smiled at his mother, turned, and the tune died suddenly on his lips when he saw Eddie sitting calmly in his living room, a cup of tea before him, a cigarette hanging from his lips.

"Don't go for it, Mike," Eddie said in hurried English. "I've got mine right under my hat, looking right at you."

"Your friend," Mrs. Dragoman explained with complete innocence, "has come to repay a social visit, Mihaly. I've made him welcome in our name."

Mike Drago stood frozen, gaping at his mother, then at Eddie. It was obvious that he wanted to try for his gun but he seemed to think better of it, glancing knowingly at the hat covering Eddie's right hand. He smiled nervously, bringing himself about, kissed his mother lightly on the forehead, then asked if he could talk to the visitor in private. The old woman thanked Eddie for the pleasure of his company, then bowed her way out of the room. It was silent. Drago stood with his hands at his sides his jaw set grimly, his eyes burning at Eddie. No one spoke.

Eddie lifted the hat from his hand. "Open your coat, Mike. Put your gun on the table. Use your left hand, just the thumb and first finger. Move very slowly."

Drago did as he was ordered, then stood aside, watching, waiting. Eddie scooped the gun up and dropped it into his topcoat pocket. "All right now, Mike, now we talk. Sit down."

Drago sat opposite him. "Can I have a cup of tea?"

"No. You'd probably throw it in my face, like they do on TV."

Drago smiled thinly, without warmth. "I suppose I'm supposed to admire your gall. What's it all about?"

"We talk," Eddie said. "I don't have too much time. When are you due back on duty?"

"Tonight."

"Good. How far along are you on the Steffman job?"

"Pretty far. We've got almost everyone."

"You haven't got me."

"Perhaps."

"Who do you have?"

"Carol Hewitt. Vic Lenahan. Walter Pesak. All on ice."

"You've got three more to go, Drago."

Drago nodded slowly, his eyes narrowed. "We'll get the others. Including you." He smiled. "It looks as if the thieves are falling out, eh, Eddie?"

"Yeah, it looks that way."

"Can I ask a few questions, Eddie?"

"If you want."

"Who planned the Steffman job?"

"I did."

"I thought so." Drago pointed to Eddie's pack of cigarettes. "May I have one?"

"I'll light it and hand it to you." He lit a cigarette, tossed it to the serving table. Drago retrieved it, smoked in silence, watching Eddie suspiciously. Two old friends having a nice civilized chat over cigarettes. It was almost funny. Eddie said, "I didn't do the Lenahan kill. And I don't have to tell you that I didn't slice my brother's throat."

"I know that," Drago answered quietly.

"Do you?"

"The doorman at Walter's apartment fingered Shoenstein and Sargatanas. Lenahan's bullets match the ones in Carol's body."

"Sargatanas did them all," Eddie said.

"As well as McCrea? That's how they got you to finger the Steffman job, isn't it?"

Eddie nodded. "Shoenstein probably did the actual shooting, but Sargatanas planned it."

"Did you know that when I asked you before?"

"No. I thought it was my brother."

Drago dragged deeply on his cigarette, keeping his hands in plain view. His brow knitted thoughtfully, and he blew smoke at the ceiling. "All right, I'll rise to the bait. Why the confession? You worried you're next, Eddie? Do you want to make a deal?"

"Not quite."

"Revenge? For Walter?"

"Partly."

"An honorable gesture," Drago said wryly.

"I said partly, Drago, I want to see Sargatanas fry, but that's not all of it. I came here for your help."

"My help? Don't make me laugh, Eddie. I can't make a deal and you know it. I tried to get to you Christmas morning but you weren't in the mood. You could've saved yourself a helluva lot of trouble then, but not now. You're in it up to your neck."

"You haven't heard me out."

"All right. I'm listening. You've got the gun."

Eddie said, "I've got the platinum. All of it. No one can touch it but me. And you know I'm willing to rot in prison before I give it up."

Drago pursed his lips. "You've got all of it?" He smiled softly, almost gently. "I guess you've got a right to be worried about Sargatanas and Shoenstein."

"Not for myself. Jimmy Sargatanas kidnapped my little girl this morning. They have her now."

Drago stiffened and his eyes narrowed, regarding Eddie as if to gauge his honesty; then, apparently satisfied, he sighed and shook his head. "Have they made contact yet?"

"I'm supposed to meet them. Alone. They said they'll have Kathy with them."

Drago stabbed out his cigarette. Some of the arrogance seemed to have left him, and the heavy lines under his eyes seemed deeper. He looked as tired as Eddie.

"Want to help me, Drago?"

"I can't make a deal, kid."

"I'm not asking you to, goddammit. I'm asking you to help me get Sargatanas. That's all. No deals. I'll turn the Steffman platinum over to you, take my punishment, anything; but I can't very well go into a deal with Sargatanas without another gun to back me up."

"I don't know ..."

"He's not expecting anyone to be with me, especially a cop. He's a cocky little bastard and as long as he holds Kathy he's got me. He knows that. But before I go down I want to know that he's going with me, that Kathy'll be all right."

"And you want police prot—"

"No. No other cops, Drago. Just you." Eddie's jaw muscles worked, his feelings lost in him. "I trust you. Don't ask me why. I just do."

Drago nodded, as if he understood Eddie's reasons. He said, "I get the Steffman loot, get to nail you, Shoenstein, Sargatanas, and clear up the McCrea kill as well. Right? And all you want is your kid back safe."

"That and Sargatanas. That's all. I didn't come here to beg favors. I don't beg favors from no one, ever. I just want another gun I can trust. You're the only guy in this town that I could think of."

"All right. I'll agree, but on one condition."

"Shoot."

"The L'Agneau job. Confess it to me. Here, in private."

Eddie saw the strange gleam in Drago's eyes, the hard line of his jaw, the tensed muscles of his shoulders. He sighed and nodded. "All right. It was me."

"Who planned it?"

"Walter. Lenahan drove. Shoenstein hit the safe and Sargatanas and me were guns. I was front guard."

"You shot me."

"Yeah, but it was a lousy mistake, Drago. The gun went off when I hit the floor."

Drago was quiet, alone with himself, his eyes deep, his face slowly relaxing. "All right, Eddie, it's a deal. I'll go along with you."

"I'm supposed to meet them at Castro and Market Streets at five. They didn't say what corner or what direction they'll be coming from. They're supposed to pick me up and follow my directions to the loot. See, only Sargatanas knows the fence—he cut that info out of my brother before he slit his throat—and in the beginning I needed what he had as much as he needed what I had. Taking Kathy changed all that."

"Do you think so?"

Eddie paused, then, "Yeah."

"Perhaps," Drago said quietly. "Maybe you would've done what you're doing right now without their taking Kathy."

Eddie shrugged.

"Where's the stuff, Eddie?"

"Why?"

"Look, you've got to trust me all the way. You've come this far. Sooner or later you've got to hand me back my gun. If I want to shoot it out with you I'll do it. But you don't think I will. So if you trust me that far, with a gun and all, then doesn't it make sense to trust me all the way?"

"Why don't you just follow me to the—"

Drago interrupted with a shake of his head. "Too many things can go wrong. For instance, what if Shoenstein shows up for the meet without Sargatanas and Kathy? What if no one shows up at all."

"All right, all right. I'll go all the way. It's the Allrin's truck yard on Bayshore. A silver and white truck."

Drago nodded briskly, held out his hand. "Give me my gun now."

Eddie drew out the gun, looked at it a minute, then handed it to Drago. Drago took it, put it in his holster, stood up. He smiled. "I'm playing it straight with you, Eddie. If this thing goes off—and there's no reason why it shouldn't—I'll be *Captain* Drago before the week is out." He pointed at the tea pot. "Can I have my cup of tea now?"

Eddie shrugged, made a compliant gesture. "Sure. Be my guest."

18

Five o'clock in the winter evening. The corner of Castro and Market Streets. The sun dipping yellowly toward Twin Peaks. A chill wind rising. Eddie Pesak bought an evening paper from the corner stand and leaned nervously against a concrete light stanchion, the paper opened in front of him. His mug shot was still on the front page, along with sensational photos of Walter and Carol in the apartment, Lenahan on a morgue slab with Drago in the background. The new angle of the text was that Lieutenant Drago promised to have Pesak in custody shortly. Eddie smiled. Drago would no doubt be keeping his word.

Eddie dropped the paper into the trash can, paced the corner, watched the five o'clock traffic. Streetcars, bells clanging, trucks rumbling. One block north of the corner, parked and facing east, was Drago's unmarked Ford sedan.

Had Eddie done right? What would happen if Drago fumbled? If Eddie fumbled? Thinking of Kathy eating bananas, chatting with "Uncle Jimmy" sent a cold shudder through him. He wondered how Zara was taking it now. He had called Cody a second time. Cody had talked briefly in Hungarian, most likely because the cops had the line bugged; he said that Zara was good, that a doctor was with her right now. Eddie had thanked him and hung up.

He had made the call from Drago's house, had remarked with a tired smile: "If they traced the number and found out it was yours, what do you think would happen, Drago?"

The cop had made a sour face. "I don't even like to think about it."

A blue cab wheeled to the curb. The driver looked at the passengers waiting for the bus, spotted Eddie, waved. Eddie should have thought of their using the cab trick again. He stepped to the open door. "You looking for me?"

The driver frowned. "Is your name Kathy, mister?"

Eddie nodded and piled into the cab.

"Your friend's paid me already."

"Where to we go?"

The driver jerked the car into gear and started west on Market. "I'm supposed to take you to the Embarcadero."

"Okay. Don't go too fast."

Through the rear window he saw Drago's Ford sedan make a U-turn on Market, barely missing a streetcar. Eddie tried to relax. He tried smoking a cigarette but it was dry, flat, scorching his mouth; he stumped it out. He was carrying two revolvers: one that he had borrowed from Drago, taped now to his left calf; and his own .38 which he carried in his topcoat pocket. He had no idea how Sargatanas intended to make his play, so he and Drago had decided to work it by ear.

Drago, had again attempted to convince Eddie that they should bring in the department, hut Eddie had scotched the suggestion. No more cops. He didn't want cops in on it. It wasn't the kind of thing he could bring himself to do. He would never work with cops. Never.

"I'm a cop," Drago had reminded him.

"I know."

"Don't I count?"

"No."

"Why not?"

"Because you are Mihaly," Eddie had answered in Hungarian. "You've been involved in my life for many years."

The cab made a left turn onto Folsom Street. When they reached the Embarcadero it was half-past five. The overhead freeway was jammed with honking cars, but the underpass was fairly clear. The cab headed north along the piers, past the Ferry building, then pulled up to the curb. Eddie looked back but saw no sign of Drago.

"This is the place, Mac," the driver said.

Eddie stepped out, watched the cab drive off. He was at a pier opening.

It was growing darker. Still no sign of Drago's Ford. The back of Eddie's legs became suddenly weak and his heart shivered under his topcoat.

Another cab, red and white, pulled up. Cleve Shoenstein was in the rear. His thin, lined ginger-haired face broke into a self-assured grin. He leaned over, opened the rear door. Eddie took another look for the Ford, saw nothing, and with a sinking sensation he piled into the cab. He curled his hand around his .38, shut the door after him.

"Hello, Cleve."

"Hiya, Eddie. Have a nice day?"

"Where's Kathy?"

"Kathy? Oh, you mean little Kathy? Why, man, she's fine. She's with her Uncle Jimmy." He leaned forward, tapped the driver. "Make a U-turn here, buddy."

As the cab turned Shoenstein watched through the rear window, smiling all the while. "Okay. Go three blocks, turn right."

The cab swerved and Shoenstein continued giving him patternless directions, still watching the rear window. Then, apparently satisfied, he swung around, settled back.

"Satisfied?" Eddie asked.

"Why not?"

"Where're we going?" the driver asked, irritated.

Shoenstein grinned. "Castro and Market. Make it fast."

Eddie cursed silently, conscious of the gun taped to his leg, itching to take Shoenstein now, holding himself back.

Shoenstein lit a cigarette, threw the match to the floor, then, moving quickly, he clamped his hand on Eddie's right wrist. His voice was a hard whisper. "Pass it over. Don't be cute."

Eddie shrugged, handed him the gun. Shoenstein pocketed it, but kept it aimed at Eddie through his coat.

Fifteen minutes later they left the cab on the same corner where Eddie had started. Shoenstein directed him, following right behind. They walked through a neon-lit drive-in restaurant and turned the corner. Halfway up the block, in a short deadened alley Eddie saw Walter's black Lincoln sedan. When he entered the alley ahead of Cleve he saw Sargatanas and Kathy sitting in the front seat. Kathy spotted him and her face brightened. She waved to him.

What now? He couldn't very well make a play here in the alley. He kept walking, his legs quivering. Was the gun slipping from the tape? He moved awkwardly, trying to smile at his daughter. When he was close enough to see Sargatanas' cheese-colored heavy-lidded eyes, he sensed a quickening movement behind him. He saw Sargatanas lift his thin, white hand.

Eddie stepped to one side just as Shoenstein was bringing his gun down to club him on the head. He grabbed for Cleve's wrist, caught the gun just as it hit the street. Shoenstein fell forward and, when he gathered himself up scrambling to his feet, he froze. Eddie had the gun trained on him. He turned, looked at Sargatanas. Kathy was crying now. It was no longer a fun game. Sargatanas had his knife next to Kathy's throat.

Eddie didn't move. Sargatanas watched him with bulging, dead eyes: cruel; uncaring; expressionless.

"Stalemate," Shoenstein said nervously.

"Right," Sargatanas said, raising his voice.

"The deal still stands," Eddie said.

Sargatanas smiled, "Does it?"

"You let the kid go, let her walk to the mouth of the alley and you've still got me."

Sargatanas showed his small, pointed teeth. "Two things, Pesak! First, I don't give a goddam if you do shoot Cleve. I've still got the kid! Go ahead! Shoot Shoenstein!"

Shoenstein's eyes popped, "For Chrissake, Jimmy!"

Sargatanas ignored him. "Go on, Eddie. Scratch Cleveland, and I still sit where I am with the kid."

Eddie hesitated. Shoenstein's face was gray, shining with sweat, the lips twitching. No one moved, no one spoke, the only sounds were Kathy's small whimpering. Each waiting second tightened the screws on Eddie.

"I can't do that, Jimmy! This is what I say. Go ahead! Slit the kid's throat! The second you do I start shooting! And once I pull this trigger I don't stop until it's empty!" He smiled coldly, eyes glittering, finger visibly tightening on the trigger. "Go on, goddammit! Quit fooling around, Sargatanas! It's a question of how much you value your life. You value it as much as I value the kid's? Think it out!"

He waited: his stomach in knots; his heart hammering; his hand quivering on the gun. He could see the knife faltering at Kathy's throat, Jimmy's expression arguing with himself.

"Jimmy!" Shoenstein screeched. "Let the kid go! She walks out and we still got him. If he tries to walk out shoot him. But let the goddam kid go ..."

The knife came away. The Lincoln's door swung open and Sargatanas disgustedly shoved Kathy out into the alley. Then he drew his automatic and aimed it directly at Eddie. Eddie didn't move. The stalemate continued, but Kathy started walking out of the alley, shaking with sobs.

When she passed Eddie he said, "Go to the drive-in on the corner and tell the waitress what happened. Just tell her you want to go home to your mother."

Kathy nodded, still crying, and left the alley.

"All right, Pesak. Hand the gun back to Cleve."

Eddie hesitated, chewing his underlip. No matter how he tried it he wouldn't make it. Sargatanas was protected by the Lincoln. He was exposed. He couldn't use Cleve as a shield because he was seven or eight feet away from him.

"Drop it and step back!" Sargatanas ordered.

Eddie set the safety catch and dropped the gun. Shoenstein scooped it up and prodded Eddie into the back of the Lincoln. Shoenstein drove, Sargantanas sat next to him with his automatic covering Eddie. When the car wheeled past the drive-in, Eddie was relieved to see Kathy through the front window, talking to one of the waitresses. That part of it was over. The rest was Eddie's plan to finish with his brother's murderer.

"Where do we go from here?" Shoenstein asked.

"To the end of the rainbow, buddy," Sargatanas purred. He turned and faced Eddie. "Okay, Pesak, tell us where we go."

Eddie twisted to one side, scrambling for the gun taped to his leg.

The explosion from Sargatanas' gun seemed ten times louder in the close confines of the Lincoln. The red-hot hammer blow slammed into his leg just under his knee. Great waves of pain swept over him, electric shock, quicksilver lightning, flashed to his brain—nausea, fire, death.... Eddie started to pass out, fought desperately against it, squirming, gasping for breath. His leg throbbed, blood oozed down into a puddle on the white rug of the Lincoln's floor.

Sargatanas shouted, "Keep driving!" He leaned across the seat, yanked Eddie up and swept the end of his gun into his face. Eddie felt the flesh tear, the hot streams of blood gush down his cheek. More pain, blinding, visions of his dreams of King Of The Mountain, of Walter mutilated and dead.

"Come out of it, Pesak. I can go back to that drive-in and get the kid! Or I can go where you tell me. Take your choice!"

Eddie nodded, spoke in short gasps. "Bayshore."

"Where on Bayshore?"

"South. Straight down. I'll tell you where to turn."

He could say nothing more, and curiously his leg didn't pain him now as much as it had a minute ago. He slumped down on the seat, raging inside, his hand reaching for his leg. He found the tape, the gun, and his fingers froze. His stomach sank. The gun! When Sargatanas had fired to punch the leg he had hit the revolving chamber of Drago's .38 instead of flesh. With frantic fingers he investigated the damage. The chamber was smashed, the firing pin no longer there. Everything was covered with blood. Pieces of metal had splintered and entered the soft muscle of his calf. He moved his toes, found that they moved well enough. He figured that he could walk if he had to.

But he had no gun. His only weapon had been put out of action. There was no sign of Drago. If he had been anywhere near the alley he would have made a play the moment he had seen Kathy leave. But no Drago. Eddie was on his own, without a gun, with nothing. His one chance now was Drago. Eddie figured that he had missed a turn following the first cab and had scooted out to the Bayshore yards, hoping to catch them when and if they arrived. Eddie had no idea what time it was now. It was dark. He could see bright neon blobs whizzing past the window, dizzying highway headlights, street-lights, darkness.

Sargatanas was watching him. "Hurts, doesn't it, Eddie? Yeah, I'll bet it does. How would you like one where I worked on your brother? Would you like that?"

Cleve Shoenstein chuckled.

Sargatanas smiled. "We're going to be fat, buddy. Real fat. Big brown boxes. Platinum. You know how rich platinum is, buddy?"

"Real rich."

"Sure," Jimmy purred. "Better than half a million bucks. That's a lot of money. What'll we do with it, Cleve?"

"We'll get long cars and long broads," Cleve said, chuckling.

Sargatanas shifted uncomfortably, his eyes dull. "I don't like broads," he said tightly. "I hate them."

"Well, everyone to his own taste," Shoenstein said.

They were moving south now on Bayshore. They were almost to Allrin's truck yard. Eddie was recognizing a few of the buildings.

"Where now?"

"We're almost there," Eddie said.

He pressed himself against the window, watching. When Allrin's came into view he saw no sign of Drago's Ford. He cupped his hands against the glass, peering frantically. Sargatanas watched him.

"Is that it?"

"Unh? No, no that's not the place."

Sargatanas backhanded him across the face, his face twitching violently, his dull eyes narrowed. "You're lying! Cleve. Stop the car and back up into that place."

Shoenstein pulled to the shoulder of the road, shoved the gears into reverse, and backed up to Allrin's yard. The Lincoln swerved, jerked to a stop at the vacant southern end. A hundred feet across the yard Eddie saw the silver and white truck sitting exactly where he had left it. There were a few other trucks nearby, all silent. The gas station was brightly lit; a faint echo from the jukebox came from the all-night truckers cafe at the northern end. There was no one else in sight.

Sargatanas opened his door, looked out at the dark, empty yard. "Cleve. That's the truck there. The switch truck."

Eddie swung open his door and lunged for Sargatanas. Shoenstein tripped him, clubbed him with his revolver.

"Finish him," Sargatanas purred.

Eddie shook his head, tried to fight the yawning black ocean of unconsciousness. He looked up and with blurred eyes saw Cleve fitting a rolled-wire silencer on the end of his gun. It looked unreal, in slow motion.

Eddie tried another lunge.

Phhht! The first bullet slammed into his thigh. He tried rolling aside to pull himself under the Lincoln. Bright lights: sudden; sweeping; crazy yellow-white patterns. The gun cracked a second time, but this time without the silencer. Eddie rolled partly under the car, his thigh biting painfully, his leg throbbing. He saw Shoenstein, outlined in the lights, fall to his knees and gape wonderingly at Eddie. Then he coughed, smiled once, and fell over on his face, his nose cracking on the black top. The silenced revolver fell near Eddie's hand. He grabbed it and swung completely under the car.

Drago was moving quickly across the yard. Another shot was fired and Drago stumbled. More shots answered and Eddie saw the squad car squeal into position near the station. Spotlights flashed. More shots whacked into the Lincoln.

Drago was writhing on the ground, holding his shoulder and cursing. Sargatanas was crouched at the front of the Lincoln, panicking now, watching and waiting for a chance to break. Eddie could see his feet, his knees.

"You lousy fink, Drago!" Eddie roared from under the Lincoln. "You fink cop bastard! You and your cops!"

Sargatanas heard the shouting and bent to peer under the car. Eddie shot him four times in the face with the silenced revolver.

19 (MONDAY, DECEMBER 29th)

First there was the light: dim; somewhere to the left; like a fuzzy glob of orange with something spiky and curly in front of it. Flowers? Was he dead?

There were the deathly, mingled odors of flowers and floor wax. He moved. His thigh shot pain to his brain and he sank back, moaning.

"I see you're back in the world, Mr. Pesak."

It was a nurse: heavy-set; dark-eyed; crisp white uniform. Eddie nodded, closed his eyes. He heard the door opening and closing. A gruff voice talking with the nurse. Eddie tried to turn on his side. He felt the perspiration streamers tickle the small of his back. He looked about the room: a white cloth screen folded in one corner; a wash stand; a closed closet; another stand with a small light and a cut-glass vase of red and white flowers. Flowers! Jesus. He looked to the blinds, saw that it was dark outside. He wondered why there were no bars on the windows.

Drago came into the room, his arm in a black-silk sling, his back facing Eddie. He was arguing with male voices out in the hall. "No, not right now. You can talk to him after his wife sees him. Sure, I promise. You know me, boys. I keep my word, don't I?"

When the door was closed again Drago turned and faced Eddie's bed. "How're you feeling, kid?"

"Fine. Ducky. How're you, Captain?"

Drago shrugged. "I'm still a lieutenant."

Eddie smiled dryly. "Yeah, what happened? Didn't they let you cop all the credit for catching all the bad guys?"

"Don't be tough with me, Pesak. I didn't cop all the credit. I shared part of it and got chewed out for doing it." His eyes narrowed and he glowered. "You'd better not cross me, Pesak."

"Cross you, Drago? Cross you with what?"

"I made a report. Said you were my bait. I didn't finger you for Steffman's."

Eddie stared at him. "Drago, you're out of your mind. You won't get away with it."

"I already have. The papers make you for a cop's private bait. You fingered Sargatanas and drew him out because he murdered your dear brother."

"That doesn't make sense and you know it."

"It does. See, Walter called you the night of the robbery. He was suspicious of Sargatanas, figuring a cross, so he told you where the Steffman's loot was. Sargatanas knocked him off and kidnapped your kid to get you to turn the stuff over to him. Instead, you came direct to me and we worked out a connection together."

"It stinks."

"Sure it does. They bought it though, And you'd better not cross my story."

"Why're you being gallant, Drago?"

"Look, you helped me, so now I help you."

"And that ends that, huh? I walk free?"

"Don't sound ungrateful, you thief bastard. When you plugged Sargatanas you probably saved my skin. That's the way I see it. You aren't going to give me no more trouble. You've had it. You'll work your ass off until you're an old man and you'll keep clean. I know that, and you know it. I'm giving you a break, you sonofabitch, so don't get tough with me."

Eddie closed his eyes. "Sure, Drago."

"I ought to punch your mouth."

He opened his eyes. "Try it."

Drago's fists clenched and he started for the bed. Eddie pulled himself up and glowered at him. Drago turned suddenly and went to the door. "You cross me, thief, and I'll hound you for every penny-ante job in this town. I'll see you get twenty years and the day you get out I'll see you get twenty more!"

Eddie shrugged. "Get out of my sick room, Drago. Send in my wife."

"You going to cross me?"

"No. Send Zara in here."

"Your fatso brother-in-law's with her. Shall I send them both in?"

"Yeah."

A minute later Cody and Zara came into the room. Drago left them alone, shooting Eddie another warning glance. Eddie smiled at him. Cody shut the door after Drago and stood, wheezing, at the foot of Eddie's bed, looking uncomfortable in a necktie and sports jacket. His parrot's eyes watched his sister, then Eddie.

Zara was wearing a gray suit, black gloves, her hair combed back in a pony tail. She looked young, in spite of the faintly puffed effect of her eyes. She moved to Eddie's side, touched his hand. They looked at one another for a long minute. Then, to break the silence, she asked, "Can I—is there anything you want, honey?"

Eddie nodded, feeling suddenly embarrassed. He looked about the small room, gestured toward the stand with the light on it. "Yeah. Get rid of them flowers."

The End

House of Evil
by John Trinian

For Stefan Marko

CHAPTER ONE

Ralakin stood by the high arched window. He watched until the girl, slim, beautiful, dark-haired, crossed the wide apron before the window and moved out of sight. Then, slowly, he turned away and thoughtfully stroked the thin gray point of his beard.

A lovely girl, he was thinking. Absolutely lovely.

The sun glinted on the glass spires of the temple. Thin rays of light, angling steeply from the towers, spilled into the vast foyer. Hot lemon-colored puddles reflected from the polished marble floor.

Walking slowly, Ralakin entered a narrow hallway off the foyer which led, after a dark and confusing warren of corridors and arches, to the deep inner chambers of the temple. His sandals squeaked softly on the floor and his long black robes fluttered at his bare ankles.

When he came to Kozma's brass door he hesitated, then, making up his mind, he pressed the concealed button and watched as the door slid noiselessly to one side.

He stepped into the room.

"Are you busy?"

Kozma was alone in the room. He looked up when Ralakin spoke.

"I just saw the girl," Ralakin said with affected nonchalance.

"The girl? What girl?"

"Anne Woodbridge."

Kozma's eyes narrowed. His interest was obvious. He waved a gloved hand, gesturing Ralakin to continue.

"She was walking from the publishing house, going toward the south side of the canyon. Probably going to visit her father's grave."

Kozma nodded, pursed his lips, gazed thoughtfully at the top of his desk.

"She's a beautiful girl," Ralakin offered.

"Yes. Very beautiful." He snorted softly, amused by his thoughts. "Her father was such an ugly old fool. Do you know, when I first saw that girl she was only thirteen. Skinny, all elbows and knees, like a newborn colt. But now, so lovely...."

The room was large, rectangular, high-ceilinged, and, since it was windowless and illuminated with but a single green lamp, was always in deep shadow. There were few furnishings. An elaborately carved desk, a big bishop's chair with a plum-colored awning, and a high rosewood throne which was inlaid with mother-of-pearl plating and intricate silver scroll. The throne was behind the desk and directly under the light.

There was, even at this early hour of the day, the sharp, smoky flavor of incense in the air.

Ralakin asked, "Do you want me to contact the girl again?"

Kozma's voice was deep, black, purring. "No, I don't think so, Rolly. We don't want to rush this. Give her a bit more time. Let her think that the decision was hers. I'm sure she'll come around. The true believers always do."

"How much time?"

"Entirely up to you. You handle it."

Ralakin smiled, his foxy face looking devilish in the green light. The shadow from his sharp-pointed nose seemed to blend with the shadow of his beard.

"Have you made the arrangements for tomorrow night?"

"Yes."

"The usual crowd coming?"

"I think so. Except for the new one."

"Have you told Sarah yet?"

"I haven't seen her yet."

Kozma nodded. "MacLean likes Sarah."

"She's worth her weight in gold."

"Quite true." Kozma smiled, this time showing the tips of his white teeth. "You see, Rolly, once you know what it is that a man desires...."

Ralakin stroked his beard.

Kozma settled back on his throne and closed his eyes. The usual crowd for tomorrow night.... That meant, of course, the camera would have to be set up and readied, that Sarah would have to be instructed to be particularly attentive to MacLean. It wouldn't do to have MacLean become bored.... The usual crowd. The ten or twelve that had been carefully chosen and primed by Mrs. Bosco. There would be Jesse Kincaid, television western star, with his opium habit. Edmund Tobias, motion-picture producer, sex. Irving A. MacLean, private-aircraft tycoon, with his childish obsession with sex and religion. Lilly Winter, society woman, narcotics. And so forth. A sophisticated selection of screwballs. Big money and power people letting down their hair and their morals.

The monthly parties, or Rites as they were called, had been the brainstorm of Mrs. Dolly Bosco, a once-wealthy, now scheming, confidante of upper society. Her assistant was a confidence man, Lemuel Toomey, an old-time acquaintance of Zedek Kozma and Charles Ralakin.

"Getting back to the question of that girl," Kozma whispered, "Anne Woodbridge. I want her. I want her here, in the temple, with me. So don't fail me, Rolly."

"I haven't yet, have I?"

Kozma smiled, shaking his head.

Ralakin studied him out of the corner of his eye. It was, he realized, one of Kozma's better moments. He was being pretty much as he used to be, calm, self-assured, cautious. But more and more lately, to Ralakin's growing concern, Kozma had been having terrible moods of depression. It was as if the man was terrified of something. And what it could possibly be, Ralakin had no idea. He knew better than to come right out and ask him what was bothering him. He had to content himself so far with standing anxiously on the emotional sidelines and propping him up whenever he felt it necessary.

Ralakin's motive, concern, aside from the fierce, near fanatic love and loyalty he felt toward Kozma, was a simple one: if Zedek Kozma failed now the entire movement was sure to collapse....

He stepped close to the desk. "How're you feeling?"

"Feeling?" Kozma regarded the little man with narrowed, suspicious eyes. "How am I feeling? I'm feeling fine, excellent in fact. Why do you ask? Don't I look all right to you?"

"Sure," Ralakin assured him. He was aware of how little it took these days to trigger him into one of his moods. "You look great. Real great. I just thought I'd ask, that's all."

Kozma settled back again, suspicions mollified, mumbling sullenly, stroking his forehead. "I'm perfectly well," he insisted to the green darkness. "Everything's going perfectly. Why shouldn't I feel all right?"

"I didn't say that you—"

"Then don't say it!"

He rose from the throne, and slowly lighting a long thin cigar with a gold lighter, he moved to the center of the room. He smiled, blew smoke at the ceiling.

He was a tall man, unusually so, powerfully built, with thick shoulders, deep chest. His expression and bearing were of regal arrogance, the air of a man long accustomed to having absolute authority. He wore his thick black hair brushed straight back from his broad forehead. A theatrically handsome man, he had heavy, voluptuous lips, black Arabic beard, thick eyebrows over his proud, patrician nose. His eyes were large, intensely black, like wet olives, cold, insolent, penetrating, heavy-lidded.

To thousands he was a living Saint.

He had proclaimed himself a savior, the true reincarnation of St. Willibald, and by the sheer force of his personality he had managed to convince nearly

all who had come into direct contact with him that this was true. It had been
with this curious talent, this magnetic power, that he had been able to lead
his new religion, Kozmanism, to the heights that it now enjoyed.

He looked at his gloved hands, at the six thickly jeweled rings worn over
the velvet fingers. He smoothed his robes. He turned one ring, then another,
a satisfied smile playing on his lips. He loved jewels, loved to watch them
sparkle. Carefully, almost tenderly, he touched one after another....

"You mentioned a new one, Rolly. Someone new from Mrs. Bosco."

"That's right. Martha Mason. She's pretty big in motion-pictures."

"Has she been prepared?"

"Yes. She knows that we only provide the entertainment and the accom-
modations, that we are discreet, and that we expect only a cash donation to
the movement."

"The usual."

"Right. Lemuel hasn't met her personally yet. He's been working on her
through Mrs. Bosco. Mrs. Bosco has been, as usual, very helpful."

Kozma continued to admire his jewels.

Mrs. Bosco, he was thinking, was a greedy little pig. Certainly she was
helpful. Why not? The fat bitch raked off twenty percent of everything that
Ralakin collected from her little group of perverted suckers. Mrs. Bosco! A
faded old dragon. A bleached, corseted, giggly, powdered, rouged, bloated,
nearsighted old hag with a thousand and one highly important connections.

Kozma had always suspected the old bitch of being a blackmailer.

So, to safeguard his racket, since it had grown far beyond his earlier
dreams and was now a million-dollar-a-year business, he had, with the
clever Ralakin's urging, set up a hidden motion-picture camera to record
Mrs. Bosco and her carefree group during their more wild moments at the
Rites. This, too, could be considered blackmail. But since no one, other than
Ralakin or himself, was aware of the existence of the films, it would be more
fair to call it a form of insurance. Just in case Mrs. Bosco harbored any ideas
of blackmailing Kozma, too.

"Will that be all, Carey?" Ralakin asked.

Kozma glared, the muscles of his jaw working angrily. "I've told you,
Rolly, a thousand times! Don't call me Carey!"

"I'm sorry,"

"All right. You can go now."

"I'll be getting back to work. I'll be in the accounting room if you need—
want—me for anything."

"Get me the figures from last week the first chance you get."

"They'll be ready some time this evening," Ralakin said, then he stepped quietly from the room, closing the huge brass door after him.

Kozma returned to his throne. He closed his eyes, lazily turned his thoughts.... Then, as if he had been asleep, he opened his eyes. He suddenly realized that he was alone, that there was no one else in the room.

Had Rolly been there?

Of course he had!

But he was gone now. Kozma looked at the darkness, forgetting the jewels on his fingers, forgetting the cigar burning between his fingers. Alone. He didn't like being alone. Not now. In the dark. Without an audience. He could feel the light of his personality growing dimmer. He sagged in his robes. There was no need for the pretense now. He looked tired, older....

He was, in fact, fifty-nine years old. The proud black mane of his hair was carefully dyed once each week. He had added two inches to his height with the aid of elevated shoes. His teeth, so white and strong looking, were false. And on public occasions he wore a fine pancake make-up, lending a ruddy, healthy color to his otherwise pallid features....

He peered suspiciously into the gloom. He believed, no, he was convinced, that he had heard a sound. There! In the dark. Was someone breathing? He began to quiver. It was as if he knew it was coming, creeping up on him. The suspicions, the fears again. He was a magician, wasn't he? He could conjure demons, couldn't he? He was an expert at exorcising devils, wasn't he?

Then why didn't he say a magic formula? Why didn't he drive that ... that thing away? He was St. Willibald! He had no fear of any ...

He was moving into the shadows again. Blackness descending. He gazed intently at the darkness, as if he suspected someone, or something, to be lurking there, watching him....

CHAPTER TWO

The old man came shuffling forward, holding his patched robe clear of the dusty path. When he saw the young, dark-haired girl standing under the pine tree, in the pool of blue shadow, he bent his head and smiled hesitantly.

"Seeing after your father, Anne?"

The girl looked up. "Yes. I see you've planted some flowers."

"No. They're wild. Lupine. I didn't plant them." He looked down at the grave. "They're nice little things though. Blue. So fresh looking."

The girl nodded and said nothing. She was thinking about her father.

The old man gestured away from the tree, toward another row of headstones. His voice was gentle. "They're growing over Isaac's grave, too."

The girl started to move away.

"Wait, Anne," the old man said. "Wouldn't you care to look?"

She shook her head, not unkindly. "No, thank you, Ben. I remember my father. But ... I don't really remember Isaac."

The old man shuffled after her. "But," he protested, "he was your husband."

Anne Woodbridge paused at the edge of the shadow. She didn't look at the gravekeeper. "I know," she said quietly. "But, you see, I only knew him for three months. Three short, sweet months. And then ... he died. It's as if he had never really existed. He existed a year ago, but not now. Not now."

The gravekeeper was silent.

The girl turned and looked at him curiously. "What did you do before you came here, Ben?"

"Do? What did I do?"

"Yes."

"I was a—" He frowned, pressing his eyes with a gnarled thumb and forefinger. "I'd been in prison, you see, and ..." His voice played out and he blinked his eyes rapidly.

"Do you like it here?" Anne asked.

"Like it? Why, of course, I—it's peaceful, a good way of life."

She nodded, her brown eyes troubled and distant. "Yes," she half-whispered, "I guess that for some it is a peaceful place."

She left the old man standing in the shade of the tree, a puzzled expression on his weathered face, his tired old eyes following after her until she took the downhill path and disappeared out of sight.

The path, beaten down and dusty, led from the gentle slope of the graveyard away from the administration and factory buildings that were grouped near the center of the canyon.

The further Anne walked, the thicker grew the trees. At the bank of the brook there were great clusters of willow and pine and fern. Water leaped over rocks. A liquid marimba sound. There was very little breeze and the sun grew uncomfortably warm. Her sandaled feet raised dust along the path, powdering the leaves of the nearby shrubs.

Everything about the place was more than familiar to her. She had been living there for six years, ever since she was thirteen. When she had first arrived, with her father and his brother, there had been nothing there. Just a huge canyon cutting some ten miles deep into the towering mountains. And now there was a bustling community, built as if by magic in the first four years. And it was still growing.

The place was called The Retreat and was situated in the Wide-loop mountain range northwest of Los Angeles. From the mouth of the canyon, at the south rise, the entire spread of the settlement was clearly visible. Residence Halls, Cafeteria, farm buildings, Publishing House, Bread Manufacturing House, administration buildings, and scattered here and there in the groves and fields there were many small tent villages. On the north rise at the canyon head, overlooking the entire retreat, rising like a huge stalagmite of shimmering glass and dazzling white concrete, was the Grand Temple of St. Willibald.

She paused and looked up at the temple, feeling again as though the structure was threatening her, watching her, waiting for her. She turned away and continued walking, avoiding the sight of the temple, looking down at the dry earth.

The Retreat had more than fifteen hundred residents. It had been built by them. The materials had been donated by converts and well-wishers. But the labor had been free. Anne's father and her uncle had been laborers, as well as Anne herself. Everyone, all the converts to Kozmanism, had donated, and were still donating, their all to the furtherance of the new religion, to the growth of Kozma's empire.

Again she paused, looking up at the bright vault of sky, shielding her eyes with her hands. The three walls of the cliffs rose around her. In the deep, permanently shadowed cuts, she saw that there were still traces of snow, toothpowder veins among the black rock and pine.

Peaceful, old Ben had said. A good way of life. She frowned at the sky, at a hawk suspended in a current. Perhaps it was for some. For some ... but for her it was difficult to really imagine any other way of life. She had been but a child at thirteen and her memories of that time were uncertain, indistinct. The Retreat was her home. Before coming there she had never had a home before. She crossed the road and entered the grove. She moved past the tents, past cooking fires, squatting groups of families and friends.

"Afternoon, Anne."

"Hello, Mr. Cummings."

"Have some lunch, Annie?"

"No, thank you, Mrs. Mercer."

When she came to her uncle's tent she raised the netted flap and entered without announcing herself.

"Well, this is a surprise. Come in, Anne dear. Come in."

"Hello, Uncle Edward."

"Sit down, child. You're in time for a bit of lunch. Tea all right by you?"

"Yes, thank you."

She sat on the red ottoman near the serving table.

Edward returned to his cooking fire, feeding twigs and chips of wax to the flames. It was dark, cool, inside the tent. The light glowed alfalfa green and on the pitched roof the shadows of the pines shifted bright gold coins of light. The air smelled dry, sweet, flavored from the fire and the tea. Anne closed her eyes, escaping for a moment.

When she opened her eyes she saw herself reflected in the kettle. Vanity. But the thought never occurred to her. She looked, with idle curiosity, at her smooth, clear complexion, her regular features. An unusual beauty, with thickly lashed brown eyes, sorrowful full lips pale without make-up. Modigliani neck, long smooth hands, black, shoulder-length hair drawn to one side and held there with a plain rubber band. Her figure, concealed as always by the clumsy folds of her robe, was slim, small-breasted, narrow-waisted.

She touched her cheek, watching the face in the kettle. She turned away, looked at her uncle.

He was a little man, bent, shrunken, well over sixty, with the Wood-bridges' brown eyes. His nose was long and thin and tended to run; his thick white beard was matted, ragged, stained. His toenails, which peeked out from his ill-fitting costume, were thick and horny looking, curled and dirty. The skin on his legs was cracked and mottled, the anklebones protruding like big blisters, pale and hairless.

"Anything the matter, dear?"

She looked away from his feet. "No, nothing's the matter," she said.

"Good." He poured the tea and served several cuts of Kozma's gluey bread. "Well, Anne, I haven't seen you for almost a week. Not since, ah, Brother Ralakin, ah, talked with you." His eyes gleamed anxiously. "Have you accepted yet?"

"No, not yet."

"But, you will, of course."

She said nothing.

His tone grew more insistent. "You will, won't you?"

"I'm still thinking about it," she replied.

The question that had been plaguing her all week was a simple one: did she want to go into the temple to serve the Saint or not?

Brother Ralakin, representing the Saint, had asked her. That had been last week, and still she hadn't made up her mind. Edward had pointed out that the offer had been an honor, one of the greater honors that could befall a convert. It wasn't a thing to be taken lightly. She should come to a decision soon

... but there were too many questions, too many suspicions for Anne to ignore.

She'd been avoiding the issue with herself. But now, in Edward's company, she knew that the conversation would inevitably and seriously turn to her state of doubt and apprehension about her hesitancy to serve the beloved Saint. In fact, she had come to see her uncle knowing that he would force the issue for her.

"How was work this morning, Anne?"

"Much the same," she answered. "We're putting out a new cover for one of the old pamphlets. A bright blue cover." She glanced at her hands. "The dyes stay on my fingers and I have to use that pink grease stuff to get it off."

"The pink grease? Have you ever noticed how much it smells like root beer?"

"I've never had any root beer," Anne said. "I wouldn't know about it." Edward gave an embarrassed smile.

"Two thousand pamphlets," Anne said. "Whatever happens to them?"

"Happens to them? How do you mean, dear?"

"The cover says fifty cents. Do they sell them for that?"

"Yes, I suppose they do."

"Where?"

Edward turned away, busying himself with his tea. He looked embarrassed again. "I imagine they sell them in Los Angeles," he said. "Places like that. Big cities."

She wasn't satisfied. "Our bibles go for five dollars apiece."

Edward glared at her. "Just what are you driving at, Anne?"

"I don't know. It's just that when I'm working at the publishing house I see all these printed figures. Seventy-five cents. Fifty cents. Five dollars. Two dollars. I just wonder where the money goes ... that's all."

"Where it goes? Anne, I'm afraid that you don't know very much about the cost of housing, clothing, and feeding almost two thousand people."

She looked at the lumpy bits of food on the table, at the canvas tent, at Edward's patched, ill-fitting robe, the cheap cord sandals. She said nothing.

She looked past the flap, at the cliffs, her eyes grave, reflective. Nearby, yet so distant. Strange. Even to herself she had sounded distant. Not like herself at all. Another Anne Woodbridge. Hidden inside herself, like trick Chinese boxes, separate parts but carved from the same block.

Boredom. An unused word. But she was bored of the sameness of the days, of her four hours at the job. She thought of the rhythm of each day, the humming black machinery rhythm, pamphlet binding rhythm, robes and beards and pious eyes rhythm. The gearclank thunkclank rhythm. A metronome. With a beard. Black and crankly. Tick tick. And praying no longer helped. Prayers were beginning to bore her as well.

Prayers to the Saint hadn't helped her father or her husband. Or herself. The three months with Isaac had awakened Anne had given her, for the first and only period of her life, an understanding of the meaning of happiness. But it had ended. Like that. Isaac had been killed while fighting a brush fire far back in the canyon. She had prayed during the fire, asking for Isaac's safe return. But Isaac had died. Had burned to death. Unfairly. Like a sinner in hell. And Anne had been left with nothing more than a few memories and a handful of ashes.

Edward finished his meal and started his prayers, his thin voice rustling like damp leaves.

"O, I implore thee beloved St. Willibald to protect me and mine with thy ..."

She didn't listen. She knew every prayer by heart. They had no meaning, and, moving her lips automatically, mouthing the words, she looked at the cliffs again, seeing great gashed wounds in the rock ribs of the beast dripping fir and pine blood. Edward's voice fluttered, "Yea, bring forth the Evils so I may struggle alongside thy beloved ..." She touched her cheek, looked at her surroundings with desperation in her eyes, as if seeking a way out.

They walked side by side. The sun was high, bathing the great bowl of the canyon in white and yellow. Waves of heat wriggled from the road.

"Anne, I'm a bit troubled. No, don't interrupt. You don't seem very pleased about being chosen to enter the temple."

She bit her lip, didn't look at Edward. She didn't know what to tell him. How could she explain that lately, ever since Isaac's death, she had been feeling something suspiciously evil about Zedek Kozma? How to explain such outright blasphemy?

"Anne?"

"Yes. I think—I don't know. I suppose, as you say, it's an honor, but—"

Edward drew up, surprised. "You suppose? Why, it *is* an honor. How could you even think otherwise? How could you?"

Yes, how could she? Wasn't it true that Kozma was a saint? What difference did it make if, in the past three years, four girls had entered the temple and had never been heard of again? Such as Sarah Bridge; Isaac's sister? And the others before her? Why should their disappearance bother anyone? After all, the Saint was the holiest of the holies. Wasn't he?

"I'm afraid," Edward went on stiffly, "that the Devil has been talking to you, Anne."

She felt her shoulders stiffen. She couldn't help it. Her environment had been religious. She might suspect Kozma of being not quite as true as he claimed, but she could never bring herself to deny the existence of the Devil. No escaping that.

The Devil. And his black legions. All living under the crust of the earth, exactly as Kozma pictured them in his preachings, hidden in secret white pits, in fiery caverns. Lurking in the recesses of Anne's mind, they were ready to pounce upon her if she weakened.

Perhaps her feelings about the Saint were blasphemous.

Perhaps she was wrong. And if ...

"Yes," Edward said. "The Devil visits the idle, the vain, the selfish."

"I know. But I don't understand—"

"It's hardly your job to understand, child. Your duty is to remain pure, to keep free of Evil, to follow your secret prayers in exorcism, to fight the demons which inhabit every corner of this foul earth."

She listened, oppressed with the familiarity of it all. Edward's words were, as usual, straight from the Book of Kozma, the official bible of The Retreat. The demons. Of course. Black and crawly, winged and sulphuric. All was sin. Kozmanism led the way to the mysteries of black magic, lent the power to mortal man to exorcise Evil, purified the air. Sacrifice led to salvation. The surrender of all wordly possessions was the qualification for everlasting freedom and peace....

"A girl your age should keep as busy as possible. The Devil works over-time because you're at the stage of life where you can be easily swayed. It's easy for you to clown around and not say your prayers—oh yes, I watched you this afternoon—but Kozmanism isn't for clowns. It's sacrifice. And you, perhaps more than others, should know that. Your father, Joseph, and your husband, Isaac, had sacrificed all for their belief in the new and true faith. They gave their lives."

They reached the hard-packed apron before the temple. The Saint's black, gleaming Rolls-Royce was parked near the wide staircase. The sun flashed from the great towers overhead. A few birds hopped on the stairs. A detail of robed gardeners, looking shabby and poorly fed, were march-ing toward the cafeteria, hoes and rakes resting on their shoulders. From somewhere a bluejay racketed.

"Idle time, Anne, is danger time. You start having sinful, rebellious ideas. Rebellion is the child of injustice. Here, in this sacred grounds, there is no injustice. If injustice exists it is bred in your heart. In your heart, stirring re-bellion and sin, lurks the Devil. I recall how last year, right after poor Isaac's death, you grew quiet, morose, so unlike your old self. You spoke sus-piciously of The Retreat and the good life we have here. And now," Edward pursed his lips, frowning, "simply because you've been honored to assist the Saint, you're putting on the same sort of act. I don't understand it, Anne. I just don't."

Every word was true. And she didn't understand it either. Edward's voice creaked pompously, *"Facito aliquid ut semper te Diabolus inveniat occupatum."*

Keep busy at something so that the Devil may always find thee employed. Anne nodded. Her voice was apologetic. "I'm sorry, Uncle Edward. I'll—I'll try and think this out. Really. And I'm sure that you're right...."

That seemed to mollify him a bit and he peacocked his thin shoulders, eyes gleaming, beard clucking approval. "Yes, child, yes. You pray as you've never prayed before. I'm sure the Saint will guide you."

She kissed his forehead respectfully, then left him, not looking back. She passed the spot where the group of gardeners were working in the hot sun. Standing in the warm blue shadow of the huge temple, she looked beyond the rise to the rear of the canyon maze. She saw the long, cultivated fields, saw the long caterpillar-shaped billows of golden dust following the tractors.

She went to the Residence Hall, went up to her room on the third floor, and sat on her hard, narrow bed. The room was, like all the others, spare, poorly ventilated, box-shaped. She had a few books, a portrait of the Saint, and a small yellowing snapshot of her father which had been taken many years ago in Mobile, Alabama.

She lay back, closed her eyes, shutting out the light. Thinking of Edward she became confused again. She was afraid of Kozma, and afraid to deny him. She wanted to leave The Retreat, but knew that she lacked the courage.

What she feared more was that Kozma's five-year hold over her life would eventually pull her into the temple. And, for some inexplicable reason, she feared that if that happened she would be lost forever....

CHAPTER THREE

The big, dark room was silent. The green lamp was out. Incense, exotic, smoky, hung in the darkness. It was ten o'clock. Zedek Kozma, sprawled clumsily in the bishop's chair under the sagging plum-colored awning, dozed fitfully. Now and then his heavy eyelids fluttered and he shifted his weight in the chair, rousing himself just enough to realize where he was. Then, still drugged and sluggish from the effect of his pills, he grew dizzy and closed his eyes, again moving through the disturbing scenes of his dreams.

What was that noise?

Slowly at first, then abruptly, he came awake, opened his eyes and stared fearfully into the dark. He was tense, convinced that he had heard a sound.

It had been soft, sibilant, like the cautious intake of a breath. Inch by inch, careful not to make a sound or a sudden movement, he straightened in his chair. Perspiration broke out on his forehead and his fingers tensed unconsciously, the big fingers closing, painfully squeezing against the many thick bands of his rings. His mouth was dry and sour, his heart hammering in his chest. It was absolutely useless for him to try to convince himself that his fears were simply from an over-active imagination. He had tried that before. His fears had been too great, too terrible and real for his dulled and drugged mind to expel.

There it was again. That cursed sound. Breathing. There. In that corner. No—in *that* one. Or over there, in *that* one.

How many were there? How many? And what did they want?

Fumbling in the pocket of his robe for his gold lighter, he turned in his chair, leaned forward, and rasped the tiny wheel. The flame caught and shadows leaped up, wobbled, orange and flickering. Swinging his arm slowly from side to side he aimed the light from one corner to the other. The corners, shifting and uncertain under the flickering light, were empty. There was no one there. Still clutching the tiny light he made his way to the desk at the far side of the room and frantically stabbed the lamp button. The green bowl glowed reassuringly, picking out the desk, the throne, the thick carpet. The shadows retreated.

Wiping his forehead with his robe sleeve he told himself that he was just being foolish, that there had been nothing, that it had been simply a bad dream. Just a dream. That's all.

Or was it? He cocked his head, watched the corners of the room. He *had* heard breathing. He was sure of it. There was no one there now, but there *had* been something.

Settling uneasily on the throne he cautioned himself to get a hold, to take it easy. If he didn't watch himself he would come apart at the seams. He moaned, clutched the heavy arms of the throne. Sure, that was easier said than done. The demons were becoming real to him. No denying that.

But was he wrong there? What if he was just becoming one of his own suckers, falling for his own guff? If so: goddamn old fool, fifty-nine year old ninny!

He pushed his glove down and fumbled for his pulse, taking the count with pursed lips and closed eyes. Then, satisfied, he slowly lit a cigar with his still-warm lighter and sank back in the luxury of his throne, forcing himself to try and relax...

Another sound!

He jerked upright and hissed, "Who's there? Who's that?"

"It's me. Ralakin."

"Who? Speak up!"

"Ralakin. I'm right here."

"Well, quit sneaking up on me!"

"I wasn't sneaking, Carey. I was just—"

"And stop calling me *Carey!*"

Ralakin stepped to the desk, carrying a thick sheaf of papers, white, blue, yellow, and several maroon ledger books under his arm.

Kozma made a distracted gesture. He disliked being caught whenever he was in one of these moods. He didn't like being seen at a disadvantage.

"You're pretty jumpy," Ralakin said softly.

"So what! So I'm jumpy. I've got problems, you know. Do you think it's a piece of cake to run an organization like this? Do you?"

Ralakin, ignoring his question, set down the books and papers. He recognized this as one of Kozma's bad moments and he wasn't about to add more fuel to the mood by arguing with him. He went about, briskly opening the books, laying out the papers and judiciously remaining silent.

Kozma glared at him. "I'm tired, Rolly," he snapped. "I'm tired right to the bone. I—I've been trying to pep myself up.

It was an opening that Ralakin could hardly ignore. Biting his thin lips and approaching slowly he said, "I know, Carey. I know about Lemuel's slipping you those pills to pick you up...."

Kozma didn't seem surprised; he nodded uneasily.

"And you've been taking another kind of slow you down," Ralakin said. He sighed, sat on one corner of the desk. "Carey, I hate to say this, but you've been worrying me. You're getting dangerously close to climbing on the suckers' merry-go-round by trying to pick yourself up and lay yourself out with those pills. You, of all people should know better than to try that."

Kozma glared at him. He didn't like being criticized.

Ralakin shrugged and went on. "Carey, if you'll take my advice—"

"I thought I just warned you about calling me Carey!" Kozma interrupted loudly. "Don't call me that. I don't like it. My *name* is Zedek Kozma! How many times do I have to tell you, you little bastard!"

Ralakin stepped back, looking surprised and hurt.

Kozma narrowed his eyes, glancing from left to right as if wanting to avoid something directly before him. His voice was harsh and cruel. "Where would you be today if I hadn't picked you up in that Louisiana pokey, Rolly? Have you thought about that? Where would you be? In some broken-down carnival out in the sticks? Barking? 'Step right up, folks and see Little Egypt do her belly dance. Go way little boy ya bother me.' Is that it? Is that all you're good for? Conning hayseeds and gobbies out of their lousy little pokes?"

"Carey—I mean, Kozma, please—"

"*Please*," Kozma mimicked. "I don't like being told what to do. I've built this organization from a one-bible hole-in-the-wall to what it is today. I've made myself from a nothing to a living saint. I've become the very person I call myself. And don't you forget it. I'm St. Willibald. Do you think any two-bit grifter could have built this empire? Do you? Do you think a mortal man could have?" He chuckled insanely. "Well, think again, brother, think again!"

Ralakin swallowed, looking at Kozma with a startled expression.

"I'm surrounded by cheap crooks," Kozma boomed. "Look at yourself, you little carny shyster. Look at Lemuel Toomey. Dolly Bosco. Look at yourselves, goddamit. Then look at me. Without me you'd all starve, every one of you. You'd all be rotting in some crumby state pen for pushing uranium stock. *I'm* the one who made this organization. With *my* power, *my* intellect, *my* magic—yes, my *magic*—I've made all of you rich and myself a true living god!"

Then, suddenly, he was silent.

Kozma's mood, his violent outburst, had spent itself. His words still rang in his ears while deep inside him, for a brief and honest moment, he actually suspected the heights of his own megalomania. Then, just as quickly, the wound closed and the suspicion passed. His words faded in his thoughts and he barely remembered having shouted them. In fact, when he happened to glance at Ralakin, who still stood by the desk, he was a little surprised to see him there.

He looked at the papers spread on his desk.

"What's this?" he muttered.

Ralakin stepped forward again, confused by this reversal, but eager to soothe his master. He spoke hurriedly. "These are the figures that you—you asked for."

Kozma nodded, drawing himself up. "Of course. I remember asking for them. Well, you're very prompt, Rolly. Thank you."

Barely hiding his nervousness Ralakin moved columns of figures to one side, shifting the papers. "We're in good shape," he said. "Last week's talk on the television-radio netted over four thousand in pledges, cash, and check donations. In checks we—"

"Forget the checks. We have to declare those. Just the cash donations. What did we get?"

"Two thousand, seven hundred forty-two."

Kozma nodded, smiling satisfactorily. "All right, Rolly. Sort it all out. Put a thousand aside for the Swiss account and write in one thousand, seven hundred forty-two as being the cash donations. Incidentally, what was the largest?"

"Two hundred. From that old widow in Santa Barbara."

"Good. Initial the accounts."

"Right."

"What does that leave in the straight account for this month?"

"So far, better than three thousand in cash, less than three in checks."

"Good. Leave the thousand aside for the Swiss account. Now about The Retreat. Living off itself as usual?"

"Pretty much. We took in two more families last week. Three singles. Old people."

"Did anyone leave us?"

"No."

Kozma waved his hand. "Okay, Rolly."

Ralakin picked up the ledgers and papers and started for the door. He was still worried about Carey's blow-up a minute ago. It was becoming worse instead of better. He suspected that Lemuel's pills were having a lot to do with it—but not all. Carey had shown signs of going round the bend long before he started taking the pills. It was obvious that he was afraid of something, was still afraid, and Ralakin, in spite of himself, was becoming sympathetically infected with the same fear, even though he had no idea what it was....

"Rolly? Hold on a minute, will you?"

He waited by the brass door.

Kozma asked, "Have you heard from Lemuel about Martha Mason yet?"

"No. He said he'd call tomorrow, after he picks her up."

Kozma thought about that for a moment, then nodded.

"Is that all?" Ralakin asked.

Kozma lit a cigar, stared moodily at the far wall. "No," he said after a bit. "See if you can find Sarah for me, will you. I haven't seen her since we turned her over to MacLean."

Ralakin nodded. "I'll see to it right away."

The door closed after him. Kozma bit on the end of his cigar, thinking that this was more like it. He was just restless, that's all. All keyed up. What he needed was someone to talk to, someone to comfort him. And Sarah, he remembered, was very attractive and very comforting. She believed that he was a saint. She was one of the true believers. Exactly what he needed to soothe him. He was perking up already.

Thinking of women his thoughts drew away from Sarah and turned to the other one, the new one, Anne Woodbridge. He had been impressed with her, more than he had with any other. Her voice, soft, gentle, excited him in a way that he hadn't been in many years. He was almost sixty, true, but his lusts had never dimmed. Thinking of her, remembering the way she moved, the way she looked up at him over her brow, not theatrical or coy, but shy, he could feel the little fires starting deep in his stomach. Shy, gentle girls always made him feel masterful.

Restless. Jumpy. Snapping his fingers. He was hopped up again. Damn that girl. Anne Woodbridge. Eager now, but cautioning himself to wait. No need to push it. He went to his desk, opened a drawer and pulled out his gold box. He took out a small white capsule with a thin yellow band around the center. He swallowed it and returned to the bishop's chair. Smoking his cigar, waiting for Sarah to arrive, he felt the heavy, dulling drowsiness steal over him again. His head started to bob heavily on his chest.

His voice was a vague mumble: "Are there really demons?"

He was afraid that his magic prayers—the very ones he employed during his liturgies—the ones he used to conjure, battle, and expel the demons—would, sooner or later, actually work. He had long been convinced that his power was real, that he was the depossessed magician and saint, Willibald, all powerful, leader of thousands, victor in countless encounters with the lesser devils, the legions of Lucifer.... This was true, wasn't it? Of course it was. He possessed secret powers. He knew every occult trick, every evocative incantation, every formula of expulsion and exorcism. He knew that he could bring the demons forth. His experience in the darkness of his chambers had proven that to him. But, his fears asked, did he actually know how to get rid of them? He hadn't had experience with that yet. Evoking, yes; but expulsion, no. Not yet.

"What then?" he muttered sleepily.

The demons had visited him many times before, had in fact come to him this very evening. He had heard them, breathing, watching him, black, creeping, disgusting, seeking revenge against him because he defied them, because he was Willibald, dedicated to destroying them....

Carey?

He jerked upright, twitching. Who's there?

No one was there. He must be going mad. No! Not mad. He was going sane. Yes, that was it. Going sane.

The light was still burning, casting emerald shadows.

When they came, approached him openly, could he handle them? When Lucifer, or one of his trusted dignitaries, such as Belzébut or Agaliarept or Nebiros, came to challenge him would he be able to dispel them with a few mere chants?

Becoming sleepy again he sank back in the bishop's chair, wondering where Sarah was, asking himself how long it had been since Rolly had left the room. It seemed like hours but he knew that it must have been only a few minutes.

His head dropped forward, the cigar went out between his fingers, and his breathing became even and heavy. In a slow, boiling mist that glowed from underneath he drifted easily, passing through the years, going back to Butte, back to where it had all started, passing like a shadow through the brightly colored mists....

Carey Ledbetter had been born fifty-nine years ago in Butte, Montana, in a small tent. Born indifferently. His father, Albert, had been a carnival pitchman and his mother, Theda, a phony gypsy fortune-teller. Carey had been raised in the atmosphere of the carny, of the traveling life, of sawdust and whirlaways, Ferris wheels in the dark cricket-thick prairie nights, odors of horses and elephants, cotton candy and midways of bright, luring gyp-joints.

At fourteen, wearing patched knickers and a crushed herringbone cap, with no formal education, he left his father's tent and drifted on the road, ending in Oklahoma. There, he joined another carnival and bought his own tent. He felt like a man of the world. He was a tall kid, gangling, dark-eyed, sly, quick, eager, and wise beyond his years. He worked as a ticket-taker on the Ferris wheel, learning how to knock down every dime he could steal, then as a weight-guesser, a ball pitchman, and a barker. He stayed with the outfit for two years, traveling through the Midwest and South, learning the value of the buck on the midway, learning sex on the alfalfa bales behind the big tents in fifteen different states. At eighteen, no longer wearing knickers, he moved on and joined another outfit outside of Ames, Iowa. He apprenticed as a magician's assistant. The magician's name was Zedek Kozma and was a worn-out old drunk who relied on mechanical tricks rather than sleight-of-hand. Carey was immediately fascinated by the intricacies of commercial magic.

"So you wanna be a magician, unh, Carey?"

"Yes, sir."

"You're a smart-looking kid. You'll do all right. You like dames, kid?"

"Sure I like dames. You think I'm a nut?"

"Don't be so touchy, kiddo. See that dame over there? Yeah, the blonde in the silk tights. She's the real goods. Name's Molly. And she happens to be my wife. Get me?"

"Sure, Mr. Kozma, I get you."

"Just so long as we understand each other, kiddo. The pay is eleven bucks a month, room and board tossed in." He applied himself, learning the act, pushing in the rabbits and pigeons on cue, swinging the overhead wires, keeping the machinery in top working order. He stayed with Zedek Kozma for one year. He was saving his money, hoping to try a magic gig of his own. Then, one night outside of Manhattan, Kansas, Kozma caught him near the horse stake-line with Molly.

"You punk! You lousy little punk!"

"Carey, watch out! He's got his sticker!"

Carey had just enough time to sweep up his trousers, swing them like a whip and rap the knife from the enraged magician's hand. Then, in a quick and sure movement, he scooped it up and stepped in, swinging only once. There was a short groan, a hot rush of blood against his wrist, and Kozma pitched forward.

Carey had to punch Molly to silence her. While she subsided into spasms and whimpers he took his own knife and sawed at the length of rope which held one of the horses. Then, leading the animal over to Kozma's body, he stabbed gently at the animal's genitals and jumped aside as the pounding, angered hooves beat down on the magician.

"What—"

"Shut up, baby. It'll look like he was cutting the horse free and got stomped. He fell on his sticker. Neat, unh?"

And that was how it had been judged at the unenthusiastic inquest. Carey hadn't been suspected for a minute. Free, he moved into Kozma's position, taking over the act for himself. Molly stayed as his assistant. Two years later he fired her and replaced her with a younger, more attractive girl.

Leaving the carny and joining a theatrical booking outfit in New York he dropped the name of Kozma and billed himself as Carré the Magician.

The years passed, sawing women in two, breaking chains, firing bullets into his heart, waving cards, silk kerchiefs, skulls, beautiful leggy girls in distracting hose, shiny chromium boxes and bars and stands, wands and silk hats, white tie and tails. He became interested in occult literature. He dabbled in black magic. He suspected that somewhere, some way, there was the key to a real power over human destinies. To improve his act he read Robert-Houdin, Hardeen, Houdini. To improve his suspicions he read Aliester Crowley, Marquis de Paulmy, Robert Fludd, Jacob Boehme. He continued to move through vaudeville, night clubs, and private shows, adding more and more tricks, more and more resembling a caricature of Myrddhin, with robes, peaked cap and long, glowing wand.

Money, liquor, and women flowed through his hands. True to the carny he couldn't quite bring himself to save his money. If he wasn't rolling in money he was flat broke. If he wasn't drinking champagne he was cold sober. If he didn't have five or six women at once he had none at all. He bought jewels, then had to pawn them. He bought high-powered cars, then had to sell them.

He was finally blacklisted from the booking houses as a drunk, a thief and a crackpot. He quit the magic act and drifted. Money grew scarce. He roamed the country, restless, dissatisfied, testing one racket after another. He was deeply convinced that greatness was his destiny. Immeasurable power and wealth was to be his. All he had to do was find the right lever and pull.

In rapid succession he became a bible salesman, con man, manager of a burlesque theatre, con man, armed robber, smuggler, magazine salesman, brake switchman, stock salesman, white slaver, and in Los Angeles, in 1939, a sidewalk pamphlet distributor for Guy Ballard's "I Am" movement.

In '38, before his introduction to the "I Am," he spent one year in the Federal penitentiary for white slaving out of Tia Juana, Mexico. It was there that he met Lemuel Toomey, bunco artist and bootlegger. After Ballard he and Toomey drifted north to San Francisco to try the suckers there.

"A hot town, Carey. You'll like it."

"I hope so. I'm pretty tapped."

"Watch my smoke. We'll put up at the Mark, see, and we'll sign in as New York investors. And from there on all I'll need is a telephone and a fountain pen."

It didn't work out. Lemuel Toomey and Carey ended up in a Mission Street flophouse, nursing their wounds and wondering where to go from there.

"Frisco! A hot town, unh, Lem?"

"It used to be, Carey. It used to be."

"I've been thinking, Lem. The idea came to me while we were down in Los Angeles. I know quite a bit about burlesque shows, carnys, and occult literature. My idea is that we open up a school for theological study. We can feature attractive young ladies, sparsely clad of course, and devils chasing them about. Then, at the right moment, I can step out and drive away the devils and maybe give a short but informative talk on the power of God. Do you follow, Lem? A thing like this can really go over big. We can even print up a corny little pamphlet and sell it between the acts, the way they do Hershey bars and popcorn in burlesque theatres."

"Carey, you're out of your nut. Burlesque and religion is oil and water. Sex, demons, and naked girls and a pep talk on prayer! What've you got in your head? Rocks?"

"Okay, so you don't like it. I think it can work. Whether you want in on this or not I'm going ahead with it. Just give me a straight answer, Lem. Are you in—or are you out?"

"Count me out, Carey. If I want to lose my poke I'll take the next bus to Reno."

Lem drifted to New York but Carey remained in San Francisco.

After renting a rundown hall on Geary Street Carey hired four local strippers and billing himself as Carré he started the Carré School of Theology and Occultism.

Acting as his own press agent he set up an advertising campaign, plugging ads in the papers, printing his own pamphlets, designing the costumes and writing the music for the show. He carefully singled out and lined up several newsmen, letting them know that if his next publicity stunt was exploited properly there would be a few appreciative dollars going in their direction. The newsboys agreed to go along with the gag.

With his cast of four, Carey took a Greyhound to San Mateo in the next county; there he outfitted the girls in scanty medieval-type costumes, himself in a flowing purple robe sewn with yellow stars and moons, and they caught the S.P. train northbound to San Francisco where the newsmen were waiting at the station to cover the arrival of the World-Famous theologian, Zedek Carré. The stunt went over big and a lengthy interview with Carey, as well as several cheesecake shots of the girls, appeared in all four San Francisco papers.

Opening night. Sex. Hoopla. The rented searchlight cut the black sky, swept the face of the old theatre, flashed from the windows. A huge mural-photo of Carey dominated the marquee, spotlit, eyes staring, hands held in hypnotist fashion. Carey was excited. The four girls, hawkers, piano player, and ticket taker were openly astonished. At one-fifty a head the theatre was packed, six hundred and eighty people. And at the end of the first act, which consisted of harmless dancing and singing, the aisle hawkers sold over two hundred pamphlets at a buck a throw.

At the start of the second act Carey stepped out onto the stage to thundering applause. He stood there, smiling, carrying a magic wand and dressed in his robes. When he stepped to the mike and held up his hand the applause continued. Everyone seemed to be having a high old time. So the old showman automatically started clowning it up.

"Welcome, religion lovers."

A nervous titter, then open laughter filled the theatre.

Carey turned, gestured one of the girls waiting in the wings to join him onstage, and a big blonde with saucer blue eyes stepped up to the mike. The crowd started clapping: the old burlesque sound. Carey shrugged. What the hell. Turning to the girl he asked: "What's your name, my dear?"

"Maureen."

"I see. And do you know who I am?"

Maureen blinked. "Sure."

"Who am I?"

"Yer Zedek Carré, aintcha?"

"That's right. Now tell the people here what you did before you became a convert."

"A what?"

"A convert."

She stared at him, frowning. "I've never done nothing like that."

"I didn't say pervert. I said convert. There's nothing wrong with being a convert. That means you've been converted to God, to my religion."

"Oh! Yeah, well, before I was con-verted to religion I was—do you really want me to say it?"

"Go right ahead, my dear."

"I was a stripper."

"You mean you took off your clothes in front of people?"

"Yeah."

"Why did you do that?"

She blinked again. "They paid me to do it. I got a pretty good body."

He put his arm about her waist and nudged her. "Wouldn't you say, Maureen, that you had been a child possessed of the devil?"

"Yeah. I'd say that. I was full of the devil."

"And now?"

"Now I'm full of religion. Con-verted, like you said."

"What would happen if the devil happened to enter your soul again?"

"I guess I'd take off my clothes."

Carey nodded and looked solemn. "All right, my dear, you just stand over there by the magic crystal ball. Now, ladies and gentlemen, let me demonstrate the power of Zedek Carré. I shall, by muttering a few secret words taught me by an ancient Tibeten monk, call forth Satan. Unfortunately you won't be able to see him. But you shall be able to view his evil influence. This poor girl will revert back to her old ways, then, by chanting the right prayers, I shall attempt to cast out Satan and bring Maureen back to us— dressed, that is."

The audience, no longer confused over the intention of the show, cheered and drummed their shoes on the floor.

While the lights dimmed onstage and Carey muttered a string of garbled nonsense the girl started writhing to the jazz music of the battered piano in the pit. She peeled her clothes and draped them across the table holding the crystal ball. The audience clapped with the shedding of each garment. When the girl was down to her sequined halter and silk g she looked questioningly at Carey. Carey gave her the nod and the halter came off. The crowd was silent. Fully naked now, writhing as though caught in the grip of Satan, Maureen slithered around the stage while Carey chased her with his magic wand....

The next morning Carey and his act was run out of town by the police and civic and church leaders. Undaunted he moved on, taking his act on the road, hitting the Midwest, Southwest, South, booking into one dingy theatre after another. He traveled for eighteen months and was arrested seventeen times. It was in the Louisiana jail that he met with his first true disciple, Charles Ralakin.

The act hadn't been quite right. So, sitting on his lumpy bunk and listening to the night bobbery of the Lafayette night, he hashed it over with Rolly.

"One thing's been bothering me and I think I have it figured. Every time I open the show, after the first advertising gimmicks, I always pack the joint. But the second night and the third always turn out to be a flop. And another thing, Rolly, the pamphlet sales always fall off after the first act. Curious, isn't it? What do you think?"

"It's not the burlesque, Carey."

"Right! It's the religion. I always pitch the religion angle to get them inside, then I hit them with the goof act. But that's wrong. People want to be taken on the religion angle alone. Whenever the show degenerates into straight burlesque the marks are willing to go along for the fun, but they don't buy the books and they don't come back a second time. That's where I've been failing, Rolly. I've been underplaying the religion. From here on in I should play it straight."

"Why not? I think it'll work. A straight religion pitch. No more, no less.

No more girlies. Just the pamphlets and the old Elmer Gantry routine."

"Right."

"You need a partner?"

"You?"

"Yep."

"Okay, Rolly, you're in."

After shaking hands Ralakin said: "I think we're going to click it big, Carey. I can feel it."

A week later, after their release, they paid off the girls and moved to New Jersey where they opened another school, trying it again. He dabbled in teaching hypnotism, physical culture and demonism. The effort failed. The big money continued to elude him. He kept plugging. Selling, conning, preaching, he lost one phony show-front after another. In 1941 he taught Crowleyism from a tenement in New York. In 1942 he tried Nazism. Then, finally, in 1943 he proclaimed himself Dr. Zedek Kozma, the true reincarnate of St. Willibald.

He and Ralakin moved to Los Angeles. The ball started to roll. Slowly but surely, as he developed his technique and perfected his bible, the suckers started to trickle in. Carey, now Kozma, adopted the black robes and Arabic beard which were to become his trademark. He entered television and the trickle of suckers became a flood. He had found the lever at last and he was pulling on it with all his might.

Now, years later, the master showman was on top. The power of Kozmanism didn't limit itself to the development of The Retreat. It crept into speculation and investment. With Ralakin's masterminding Kozma owned drive-ins, a television station, a commercial bread manufacturing and distributing organization, and finally, narcotics, stag shows, and blackmail. Every tentacle of action brought in money. Every day his power, his religion, grew. And Zedek Kozma, fat with power and wealth at last, was terrified of the coming of the Devil....

He had been asleep for ten minutes. He turned in his chair, looking at the huge empty room. Where was Sarah? Hadn't she come yet? He thought that he had heard *that* sound again. But he hadn't said any prayers, hadn't mentioned any demons by name. So why should they be there? They couldn't be there. There was too much light.

But they were there. He knew that. Ashtoreth, Nephtalius, Pursan, Alexh, ugly and sinister, these famous demons and their horned, winged, fanged black legions were lurking directly under the earth. He could almost smell them. He felt cold, agitated, and perspiration trickled teasingly down his chest.

"Who's that? Who's that there?"

The brass door had slid open and a pale, white-robed figure had stepped quietly in the green glow of the room. "It's me, St. Willibald. Sarah."

He shuddered, sighed, nodded jerkily. "Of course, Sarah. Of course. Come in, won't you."

"You wanted to see me?"

"Yes."

Sarah's calm blue eyes smiled at him. She crossed the room and knelt at his feet. Her face was flushed a delicate rose color; her soft, brown hair, long and somewhat disorderly, gleamed emerald from the lamp over the throne. Her hands reached for his and she touched them gently to her cheek. Kozma smiled and gazed at the ceiling.

"Are you tired, St. Willibald?"

"Tired? Yes, a little. Rub my hands the way you used to."

Carefully, knowingly, she removed the heavy rings from his gloves and peeled back the velvet at the wrists. Then, rolling and tugging, she removed the gloves until his hands hung naked before her, white, hairy at the heavy knuckles. Sarah lifted them in her hands and parting her lips slightly she kissed them.

He narrowed his eyes.

"I am God," he whispered.

"Yes, St. Willibald," Sarah murmured.

CHAPTER FOUR

Five o'clock in the afternoon. The sun was still high overhead. The roof tiles on the other side of the wide court reflected a bright blood color. The gauze curtains were drawn and in one corner of the cottage the air-conditioner purred.

Lemuel Toomey, whistling softly, finished knotting the white silk necktie and smoothed it against his black shirt. He looked at himself in the mirror and was pleased with what he saw. There was just the right touch of the fascist to his costume. Still whistling contentedly he added a white carnation to his jacket buttonhole and sniffed it.

He turned back to the mirror, carefully brushed his thinning white hair, trimmed his pencil mustache, and, using the little manicure scissors, he cut away the longer nostril hairs from his big lumpy nose. He stepped back, studied his face, then turned away with a sigh. Slowly, with a studied flour-

ish, he took an Egyptian cigarette from a platinum case, lit it and casually
blew a stream of smoke at the ceiling.

Dolly Bosco watched him through puffy eyes.

"You're a self-centered little swine," she said.

"Oh? Is the black shirt too much, Dolly old girl?"

"No. Not on you, you little fox."

Lemuel chuckled.

Dolly rattled the ice in her glass and then looked in it as if she wouldn't
be too surprised to discover an insect there. When she moved, turning to
the silver tray to fill her glass with ginger ale, her heavy corsets creaked and
her breath came in short rasping gasps.

Lemuel held the bottle of soda for her, then built himself a bourbon and
water. He settled in the rattan chair, directly opposite his guest.

Outside in the court, under the palms, there were shouts and splashings
from the palette-shaped pool. Through the gauze curtains Lemuel could see
the white-jacketed Filipino bar-boys moving gracefully between the bikini-
clad bodies and the metal umbrella stands over the tables.

He returned his attention to Dolly Bosco. She was, as usual, wearing a brocade and lace party dress that looked like something from the '20s. A thin
mink stole hung on her fat shoulders. Her huge breasts bulged out of her
corset like silk-encased cannonballs. Her feet, puffy, mapped with heavy
blue veins, looked like monstrous pink sausages. He sat back, making himself comfortable with his drink, and stared at her, fascinated as usual by her
incredible ugliness. Again he wondered how old she was. Sixty? Seventy?
It was hard to tell.

"Did you call Martha Mason?"

Lemuel nodded. "Yes, just before you arrived. I'm to meet her in front of
Chernery's on the Strip. I'm to wear a carnation in my buttonhole and carry
a newspaper under my arm."

"Shades of Eric Ambler."

"Perhaps. But I like to be cautious."

"You just like being dramatic. That's why you're wearing the Hellinger
shirt."

Lemuel laughed softly. "Dolly, you're a gas. A positive gas. Do you know
that?"

"Are you buttering me?"

"No. Why should I?"

Dolly shrugged. She sipped her ginger ale. "God, I wish I could drink
some of the real stuff."

"Why don't you?"

"Doctor's orders."

"Really? What's wrong with you?"

"Old age, sweetie. It has a nasty way of creeping up."

Lemuel leaned forward, giving a leer. "Oh, come now, Dolly. You're not all that old." He reached forward and playfully pinched one steel-ribbed breast. "Why I'll bet there's plenty of pep in the old girl."

Dolly giggled and blinked her puffy eyes. She made a coy gesture. "Don't be that way, you old rake. My days of fun are long over. I'm too old."

"You're never too old."

"I once thought the same way, Lem. Until it was my turn to grow old." She sighed, corsets creaking again, and settled back with a wistful look on her powdered face. "Ah, but when I was young, Lem. When I was young.... Did I ever tell you about my debut? You would have fallen desperately in love with me then. And believe me plenty of dashing young fellows did."

"I'll bet you were a living doll," Lemuel said.

"True. I weighed one hundred six pounds. I was a little sylph in a white Grecian dress, powder blue slippers and blue diamond tiara. There was champagne, bottle after bottle, sticking up from white mountains of shaved ice like gold-necked cannons buried in a snowbank. French, icy and bubbly. I don't recall the brand. But I drank enough to float, Lem. Like a feather. F. Scott once remarked that a debut is simply the first time that the debs are seen drunk in public. How true. I drank tons of champagne, danced all night. The band played ..."

"You're breaking my heart, Dolly. You're beginning to sound like one of those moldy Tennessee Williams women."

"Perhaps," she chuckled. "But it happened just like that. One hundred and six pounds. In those days I was very popular. I lost my virginity thirteen times." She giggled, wriggling her fat fingers and flashing her diamond rings. "It's hard for me to believe now! One hundred and six pounds!"

He made himself another drink. He was thinking how, in spite of Dolly's ugly puss, he had so far enjoyed their association. She had a fantastic business sense, could smell a dollar where he could smell only a two-bit piece. The old girl was a shrewd middleman. Her connections were the best, and these days, what with the scarcity of money, connections were what counted in the business.

Watching her over the rim of his glass he was thinking that she damned well hadn't dropped by simply to recount her gay old days with him. She had something up her sleeve, and he knew that it had to do with money. With Dolly Bosco it would always have to do with money.

He waited, nursing his bourbon and water, listening to the sounds from the pool out in the court, knowing that Dolly would fish around for a while yet.

"Martha Mason," Dolly said slowly, "is a hard drinker. I rarely trust people who drink heavy. They're usually unstable."

"I thought you said she was interested in narcotics and voyeurism."

"I did."

"So?"

"That's her interest. And she'll pay. When I got the line on her through Eddie Tobias I approached her. I'd known her socially for years. So, using my shocked and gossipy voice, I told her in strict confidence that I'd been hearing rumors of a very wicked cult, discreet and exciting. And so forth. You know?"

"And she's set for it?"

"Of course."

"How much was she good for, Dolly?"

She smiled. "That's up to Charley Ralakin, isn't it?"

"I hadn't meant it that way. I meant, how much did *you* get from her?"

"Lemuel!"

"Don't act so shocked, you old racketeer."

Dolly hesitated, then laughed wheezingly. "You're making yours from Carey and Charley. What do you care if I knock down a few extra dollars?"

Lemuel shrugged. "I don't. But is that all, Dolly?"

"Certainly."

"You old bandit, you know that's not what I meant."

"Oh? What did you mean, Lem?"

"I'd like to know why you *really* came here. Surely not because you wanted a glass of ginger ale."

"No. I don't like ginger ale."

"What do you like, Dolly?"

She shrugged, watching him. "I like many things. Money, for instance. I like money."

"I don't have much money, Dolly."

"Others do."

"Mutual acquaintances?"

"Yes." She smiled, asked suddenly, "How long have you known Carey Ledbetter, Lem?"

Down to brass tacks at last. Lemuel grinned wolfishly. "I'm glad to see that we understand one another, Dolly." He set his glass down. "I met Carey in '38. We were in the Federal pen together. As a matter of fact we traveled to Frisco together and he asked me once to start a religion racket with him. I turned him down."

"I'd call that a bonehead play, Lem."

"True. But I had no idea that it would become the success that it is today."

"How much do you know of his operations?"

"Not much. A few investments, public knowledge, things like that. But I'm sure there's more to it than what the public knows."

She nodded. "I don't suppose you have any love for him, do you?"

"Not particularly."

"I want to ask you something. Do you think he's sane, Lem?"

"Carey? No, I don't think so. I saw him only last week and he's pretty much on the edge, about ready to go over. I'm no psychiatrist, of course, but I'd say he was completely insane."

Dolly nodded. "That's what I think. If he goes over, what happens then?"

Lemuel shrugged. "They've probably got several million stashed. Probably in Switzerland. Ralakin would sell out and betray Carey and retire. But, if I detect a glow in your eyes, I might as well tell you that Rolly won't raise one finger as long as Carey can still make sense."

"We've got quite a bit on them, you know. Do you think we could tap them for a larger cut?"

"No. If I know Carey he's got an ace-in-the-hole. I'm sure of it."

Dolly's eyes narrowed. "Films?"

"Most likely. Putting myself in his position I'd have done it. I know Carey and I think I know how his mind works. Especially Rolly. Between the two of them I'm certain they've got films of each and every party that's ever been thrown in the temple."

"If we, you and I," Dolly whispered, "could get our hands on those films—"

Lemuel's eyes glittered. "We'd be in clover, old girl."

"And if we could get hold of his bank statements, his *private* books and organizational set-up? ..."

"We'd be on top. On the very top."

"Do you think we could swing it?"

"We could try. It'd be risky."

"I hadn't thought it'd be easy, Lem. My idea is that the works, films and books, are in that temple somewhere. The gain potential is too great to overlook. The risk will be well worth it."

Lemuel didn't have to think it over for very long. He nodded and held up his glass. "Shall we drink to it?"

"We shall. Here's to you, partner."

They clicked glasses, winked conspiratorially, and drank.

All they needed was an in. And they had that with Martha Mason. Lemuel looked at his wristwatch and saw he had several hours to go before he was to meet her. He made himself another drink. Dolly declined another soda. Then, drawing their chairs closer, the plot thickened as they started exchanging ideas and making their plans. The main idea was to get into the temple during the rites, follow the motion-picture camera and see where it led them. Unfortunately, this week, Dolly hadn't made arrangements to be invited to the party. Lemuel would have to carry it out himself, locating the properties and formulating a follow-up plan. Meanwhile, Martha Mason was their first lever....

CHAPTER FIVE

Deep in the dark theater, which smelled strongly of hot buttered popcorn and dirty velvet, Paul Berko slouched in his lumpy seat and watched himself on the screen. Actually, what he saw at first was just a shadow, a glimpse of something dark that stole across the wall of the crypt where the girl in the filmy negligee stood. His lips drawn tightly across his teeth, Paul watched and listened intently. The thing was fascinating and embarrassing for him. He had never become used to it. No matter how many times he went through it.

Watching the screen now, he remembered how the wind machine had whipped the hem of his black cape, how the crouched men had dropped the crackling autumn leaves before the fan, the leaves swirling from their fingers and fluttering toward the crypt.

Music came from the screen now, soft and spooky. Then the wind died. Leaves settled in crazy gold and bronze piles against the vaults, vaguely resembling a Kenn Davis painting, then, as if on cue, the girl started toward the woods. Paul glued his eyes to the screen, drawn into the action in spite of himself. Up in the balcony, behind and above him, a group of teenagers laughed and started throwing Dixie Cups down to the main floor. Paul ignored them. The scene had changed on the screen. Medium shot. Music muted now. And as the camera trucked back for a full shot the crudely painted backdrop of the medieval castle could be seen through the embroidery of foreground trees.

The negligee clung to the girl's body, molding her high breasts and wide hips in folding stiff smoke. More swirling leaves. The girl's movements were stiff and amateurish, her eyes wide and glassy. Then, oozing like black blood,

a beckoning voice filled the theater, calling the girl to the edge of the woods.
The scene cut. Close-up of the owner of the voice, a dark, aristocratic figure standing tall and gracefully evil in the shadow of the trees. The figure
lifted his cape and stepped into the dim light of the cemetery grounds....
    The figure was Paul Berko.
    Watching himself on the big screen Paul had to bite on the end of his neck-
tie to keep from laughing aloud. As always the whole thing struck him as
being terribly funny. He looked up at his own dark eyes, at his thin, craggy
features, his thick black hair and wide unsmiling mouth.
    Then he saw the so-called Satanist ring on his finger.
    He was still wearing the ring. Having taken a fancy to it during the shoot-
ing of the film he had lifted it from the property department when his part
in the film had ended. He had been wearing it, more or less as a joke, ever
since. He looked at it now, turning it slowly on his finger. It was a large ring,
blood-red with intricate gold inlay, with what seemed to be Latin writing
and various occult-looking symbols on the sides.
    Back on the screen the cloaked figure was drawing the girl to him. Cut.
Fast panning of the handsome hero struggling desperately through the
woods with a hammer and stake clenched in his fists. Paul squirmed. He
knew that, on the screen, he was about to die. He had seen the picture twice
before.
    In this film, *Revenge of The Mad Bat*, which was a year old, he had
played the key role, that of the vampire. He had done the job pretty straight,
had played it in fact pretty much as he had the role of Satan in the off-Broadway original *A Matter of Hell* three years before. For the vampire role he
hadn't had to wear much make-up. As the director had said, he was pretty
spooky looking by himself. So he had played it as himself. Paul Berko. Boy
vampire. Lousy semi-lead in grade-B Hollywood monster movies.
    Revenge of The Mad Bat had been his second picture for Augie Losada
Productions. In his first he had played the Beast in *The Fish-Beast from Another Planet*. And both pictures, because of their summer releases and
teen-market appeal, had done very well, considering their budgets. Kids
thought they were hilarious, and even the critics had panned them with rare
good humor.
    Still, it was a depressing way to make a living as an actor. He was twenty-
nine years old and there he was, running around in a rubber fish-beast costume and playing what he considered to be a third-rate Lugosi in an opera
cape. Slumping deeper in his seat he sighed and closed his eyes. Back in New
York, three years ago, he had had the usual dreams concerning Hollywood. The old story. But it hadn't worked out that way. A story even older

than his childish dreams had interfered. Off-Broadway guy makes fairly good. Low budget producer wants him to come to Hollywood, sign for two films. Monster movies. Type casting. The money trickles out after a while. In the past few years he had had only the two films and three TV parts, and it had proved barely enough to live on. Barely enough to justify the childish New York dream.

The hell with it.

The screen music boomed out. He opened his eyes, saw that this was the climactic scene.

The handsome hero burst into the clearing and the vampire leaped back, releasing the girl from his clutches. The hero then crossed the hammer and stake, making a crucifix, driving the vampire back, back, back until he was pushed against the crypt wall.

Paul almost groaned from his seat.

Hammering feverishly the hero drove the stake into Paul's heart and he turned to dust. Then, in triumph, the hero kissed the heroine, music swinging up, camera pulling back for the usual rising boom shot, and hopeful rays of sunrise crept through the trees. The evil vampire was destroyed at last and all was well with Hollywood and the world....

Paul rose, put on his Riviera sunglasses and left the theater, stepping into the lavender and gold gloom of the California evening. He paused in the courtyard long enough to look at himself in the glossies, then with mixed feelings of disgust and disappointment, he left and started walking. He was hardly aware of his surroundings. Shabby shops, palm trees, gleaming autos, naked legs with high heels clicking drily on the hot pavements. He turned when he came to Hollywood Boulevard, started east toward Highland.

In his pocket he had exactly eleven dollars and twenty-five cents. This was everything he owned in the world, not counting his scrapbook, odds and ends, and the vampire outfit which his landlady was holding in lieu of two months rent.

At Highland he turned again, moving aimlessly, walking down toward Sunset. His feet ached and his shirt clung wetly to his back. Thinking of his low finances he wondered why he should bother eking it out penny by penny. What the hell. He felt like having a beer. Go for broke. Then, seeing a cruising cab he hailed it on impulse and directed the driver to take him up to the Strip. When he came to Shelbourne he stopped the cab and left.

Chernery's was a small cafe that he had frequented two or three times a week when he had been in the chips. It was set high above the pavement. A wide apron led up to a deep apron where tiny umbrella-topped tables were set near the wrought-iron railing, commanding an unbroken view of the vast, cluttered, heat-shimmered sweep of Los Angeles. A beautiful-ugly view, Paul had never tired of hating it. And right now it was particularly vulgar. Streetlights like columns of fireflies. Searchlights. Auto headlights winking. Neon flashing.

He settled in a peacock chair and ordered a dish of pretzels and a mug of beer. It was hot, sultry, the air barely moving. He counted his money, found he had less than seven dollars left.

So far things had been breaking bad. Augie Losada Productions had another monster job lined up but that wouldn't be ready for at least another two months. Thinking it over, nursing his beer, he tried telling himself that back in New York it had been better. At least he could argue that at that time he had had belief in his talents and in his career. In his scrapbook he had lovingly pasted every review of *A Matter of Hell....*

"*Paul Berko, a newcomer, displays a real genius in his portrayal of Satan in this rather drab production of ...*

"*Actor Berko impressed this reviewer; he was, frankly, the only performer in this play worth mentioning ...*"

"*If there is ever a need for Satan, I'm sure Paul Berko can fill the bill. This one will be around for a long time ...*"

Well, he had fooled them. He hadn't been around for a long time. As soon as the run of the play ended he had allowed himself to be lured to lotusland. To the trap. To the monster circuit. To being flat broke, depressed, not knowing what to do and not knowing a soul in spite of having spent three years living and working in the town.

Certainly, he knew his agent, his directors, a few lousy actors and the usual assortment of California nuts and overdressed girls. He knew one person pretty well, the property man on his last film. Jimmy Arketus. Jimmy had lived only five houses from Paul but since his financial difficulties began Paul hadn't bothered to drop by and visit him. He didn't want to borrow from a friend, and he couldn't stomach sympathy.

Turning it all around in his mind he wished he could get out of the city for a while, roam around the mountains and get a fresh slant on himself and his career. He sipped his beer, noticed that it was almost flat, and debated whether he could afford another one or not. He fingered the bills, decided against it and settled back, a cigarette hanging from his lips, his eyes squinting and gazing thoughtfully at the view.

"You're looking pretty moody, Berko."

He turned and smiled awkwardly at Mara January. He hadn't wanted to see her. Last week he had borrowed fifty dollars from her and had been avoiding her ever since.

"Hello, Mara," he said weakly.

"Can I join you?" She didn't wait for an answer but slid into the peacock chair opposite him. She flashed him a cold smile and picked up a pretzel from his dish.

Paul ignored her. She had been his co-star, the heroine in the vampire movie. And she was a terrible actress. She was one of the strange freaks of the film-industry that never ceased to amaze him. She wasn't particularly good looking and she had little or no talent or personality. But still she had managed to parlay nothingness into somethingness. Reeking of ambition, she was young, maybe twenty-two or three, with silver-blonde hair, hard blue eyes, and an incredibly skinny figure. She had that shine though, that ice cold glitter all others just like her had.

"Well, Berko, how are we this evening?"

He smiled tiredly at the "we." He said, "We're just fine, Mara."

She bit into his pretzel, showing him her five hundred dollar capped teeth. "Have you seen the latest issue of *Movieland Stars?*" she asked.

"I never read that crap."

"I've got four shots, two pages," she informed him almost casually. "Shopping in the Farmer's Market. 'A Hollywood Starlet Doing Her Simple Bachelor Girl Chores.' Just like the unwashed." She narrowed her eyes. "Ever been in the Farmer's Market, Berko?"

"No."

"Have you heard from Augie Losada?"

"Do you mean about *The Son of The Mad Bat?*"

"Oh. You've heard."

"Sure. I'm going to be the vampire again."

"I play the same part, too."

"Disappointed, Mara?"

"No. Should I be? Augie said that Sammy and I go into a gangster flick after that."

"I hadn't heard about it. What's it called? *The Mad Bat Meets John Dillinger? Pretty Boy Floyd Versus the Fish-Beast—*"

"Well, that's what Augie told me," Mara snapped. She turned her head, showing him her profile. She watched the cars on the Strip. "Are you working, Berko?"

"Sure."

She looked at him as if suspecting a lie. "Really? Where at?"

"Why? Do you want your fifty bucks back?"

"Of course not, darling. Can't I ask one co-worker what his luck has been lately?"

"A private-eye show," he said. "Hilliard. The eye gets involved with an evil magician."

"And you're the magician? How marvelous, darling. I've always said you looked more like an evil magician than a vampire. I suppose you've signed the contract."

He said yes, which was of course a lie.

"I'm supposed to meet Harvey Crockett here in one or two minutes," she said.

He didn't bat an eye. Harvey Crockett was the producer of the private-eye show.

"Can you buy a girl a drink, Berko? A Rob Roy?"

"No."

"You can't afford it?"

"I don't feel like it."

She shrugged and said nothing. Five minutes later Harvey Crockett showed up, glad-handed Paul, lit a cigar, and snapped his fingers for the waiter. He was a little man about fifty with a bronzed-bald head and Riviera sunglasses. He looked and acted like a burlesque comedian. As he and Mara talked Paul grew more disgusted. He was tired, broke, and sick of playing the game. And paradoxically he had a strong urge to impress them; his stupid pride seemed to demand it.

"Well, Paul, kiddo," Harvey said, "what've you been up to. About that private-eye script. I'm still considering you, you know. I'll let your agent know by next week. You're looking great, kid. Looks like you lost a little weight. Wish I could. What're you doing tonight? Want to trot down to Dino's with us? Glad to have you along, you know."

"I have to meet someone," he lied.

"Anyone I know, kiddo?"

"I doubt it."

While Mara ordered her Rob Roy and Harvey his marguerita Paul sat there, feeling like an ass and nursing his beer. Thinking about the whole thing, about the past three years and the past three days in particular, he wondered if it was worth the trouble. Maybe it would be best to chuck it. The whole thing. Chuck it and go to the mountains for a few weeks.

But he couldn't do that even. To escape he had to have money. And he couldn't very well get very far on what few dollars he had left. He couldn't afford even to go to a movie house and watch one of his own pictures.

He stood up. "I have to be going. Excuse me, Mara, Harvey. I have to meet someone pretty important...." Why did he still lie? He shook Harvey's hand, avoided the mocking look in Mara's icy blue eyes. "Nice seeing you folks."

"Keep in touch, kiddo. I'll let you know about the script."

He went into Chernery's, looked around, then impulsively bought a *New York Times* from the home-town rack. He left and went down the ramp to the sidewalk, knowing that Mara and Harvey were still watching him. Trying to look casual he leaned against a light post and glanced through the paper. Snowing lightly in New York. A saloonkeeper had had a heart attack on Lexington Avenue. Skating in Rockefeller Plaza. Everyone was keying up for Spring. He folded the paper and pushed it under his arm, lit a cigarette and noticed a little old lady coming up the street. When she came up to him he saw that she was a corsage vendor and that she was carrying a cellophane covered cardboard box.

She held out the box and smiled. "Would you like a nice flower for your buttonhole, sir? Add a jaunty touch?"

"No."

"I have some nice carnations for the gentlemen ..."

"Look ma," he said, "you've got the wrong guy. I've got less than five bucks in my pocket and that's it. Kapish?"

She shrugged with her lips. "Sure. You know the score, I guess. Okay, kid. Take it easy."

He grinned at her, thinking she was cute now. "Okay, wait a bit, ma. I'll take a carnation."

Quick as a smile she took his dollar, put the flower in his buttonhole and patted his cheek.

"Bless you, kid."

"Sure, ma. Think nothing of it."

The vendor moved on. Out of the corner of his eye Paul saw that Harvey and Mara were still watching him. For some reason he didn't want to move on. He didn't want to lose professional face so he remained at the curb, watching the string of cars purr by, smoking his cigarette and turning his thoughts around.

When the cream-colored chauffeur-driven Bentley limousine pulled noiselessly to the curb he gazed longingly at it, wondering how much it cost and who the owner might happen to be. Then, when the window slid down, he saw the world-famous, professionally-glamorous face of Martha Mason lean out and look curiously in his direction.

"Hello." Martha Mason said softly. "I'm early."

Paul pulled himself from the light post and glanced over his shoulder to see who the star was addressing.

There was no one there.

"I'm talking to you," she said.

"To me?"

"Yes, of course." Her tone was impatient. "Aren't you going to get in?"

He nodded and stepped forward. Why not? It was a heaven-sent opportunity to show Mara and Harvey. "Yes," he said. "Of course."

The door of the expensive car snapped open and Paul climbed into the rear with Martha Mason. He didn't have time to feel confused or curious. As he shut the door after him he looked up at Mara and Harvey, who were leaning on the wrought-iron rail of Chernery's and gaping at him with creased foreheads and open mouths.

He gave them a casual wave.

"All right, Jacob," Martha Mason said to the chauffeur, "start driving. Stick to Sunset, I guess." She turned to Paul. "Is that right by you?"

"Unh? Yeah, that's fine. Just fine."

The car whispered away and blended into the Beverly Hills traffic.

At the time Paul was buying his copy of the *New York Times*, Lemuel Toomey was stepping jauntily from his cab two blocks from Chernery's. He paid the driver, tipping a dollar, and turned into The Careless Spot, a small bar and grill where he was friendly with the owner. He slid onto a stool, asked for his friend and was told that he wouldn't be in tonight. He started to leave, then noticing by the neon-lit clock behind the bar that he was still early for his appointment with Martha Mason, he sat back on the stool and ordered a bourbon and water.

The bar was long and dark, air-conditioned, smartly appointed, and the bourbon was good. He lingered, smoking an Egyptian cigarette and studying an attractive young couple who were seated two booths from the bar. The man was fairly typical, with white teeth and wavy hair. But the girl was something else again. A touch of the Oriental, dark-haired, almond-eyed, with an amazing bust and the sexiest pair of legs Lemuel had seen in many a year. He remained on his stool, keeping one eye on the bar clock and the other on the girl. She was wearing a low-cut dress, white silk with tiny silver and blue flowers. When she moved, bending toward her wavy-haired escort, Lemuel saw the creamy tops of her breasts.

Finally, reluctantly, he noticed that it was time. He finished his drink, placed two dollars on the bar, and strolled out onto the Strip. Checking the time he saw that he still had ten minutes. He walked quickly anyway. A flower vendor shuffled by him, looking tough and forlorn. It was a warm night, heavy with traffic, bright with neon. He stopped at a news-rack and bought a *Los Angeles Mirror*, pushed it under his arm and continued walking.

What he saw next he could hardly believe. A huge Bentley pulled to the curb in front of Chernery's and he caught a glimpse of Martha Mason's profile. Lemuel started hurrying, having some fifty yards to go. Then, moving purposefully, a strange figure stepped toward the car and the door swung open to admit him.

Lemuel gasped.

The man was wearing a carnation in his buttonhole! And he was carrying a newspaper under his arm!

Sprinting to the car Lemuel was just in time to catch a quick glimpse of the stranger's face; then the Bentley pulled away from the curb and headed toward Beverly Hills.

Lemuel just stood there, his mouth hanging open, unable to think. The newspaper dropped from under his arm and fell unnoticed into the gutter. He felt the blood drain from his face, then slowly return. The shock of what he had seen began to wear off and he clenched his fists angrily. His first thought was that he had just been double-crossed by that old bitch Dolly Bosco! Only three people had known the carnation-newspaper arrangement. Himself. Martha Mason. And Dolly. Shades of Eric Ambler, indeed! The dirty, scheming, fat old double-crosser.

Then, thinking it over, he realized how little sense that made. No, it couldn't have been Dolly. And it made even less sense if it had been Martha Mason. So, it had to be a ringer.

A *ringer!* Lemuel Toomey, the con-man's con-man had just been taken! Had his cottage been wiretapped? How big was the ringer's organization? How had they managed to get a line on him? Who? What? How? Questions tumbled into his brain. Either way, the fact remained—someone had just stolen Martha Mason out from under his nose. He had to work fast. He turned and raced up the ramp to Chernery's.

He had to get to a telephone. First, to talk to Dolly, and second, to warn Carey and Ralakin that a ringer was on the way....

CHAPTER SIX

In the dark grove of pine trees near the brook a tiny red light flickered in a small wooden box where a votive cup and candle burned before a colored lithograph of St. Willibald. Anne, still troubled and unsure, had been sitting on a bench before the crude shrine for the past two hours, doing her best to follow Edward's advice.

Crickets made the only sounds heard over the whisper of the creek. The crowns of the trees moved with the soft, warm breeze. A piece of the moon, white and waxy, was peering over the black rim of the canyon cliffs.

It was useless to continue praying. Her thoughts were wandering and her good intentions were floundering. She could no longer concentrate on her words.

Another five minutes passed before she decided to give it up. When she rose from the bench she heard a distant sound, detached from the usual sounds of the forest. It was the unmistakable muffled throb of an automobile being carried to her on the breeze.

Curious and restless she started following the path toward the temple. Darkness closed in tight. Branches whipped at her legs. Minutes passed before she saw the temple lights through the trees. Then the path became easier to see. She stepped from the shadows of the bushes at the south side of the building, toward the rear where the cars were parked.

She went to the nearest car, an innocent and awed expression on her face. It was long and black and shiny. The motor block was cooling, popping softly under the hood. She touched the tri-pointed emblem over the grille and sighed. Then, seeing that the window on one side was down, she leaned into the dark interior and gazed wonderingly at the glittering chromium dials and buttons and the glass-faced instruments. There were rich smells of pipe tobacco and auto leather.

She wondered what it would be like to ride in such a machine. She had ridden in many of the farm trucks and even on the tractors, but there was no comparison.

She heard sounds. Footsteps were crunching behind her. Turning, half-guiltily, she stepped away from the car. The near bushes quickly closed around her again and she stopped. Normally she would have continued down the path, but now her curiosity got the better of her. She stayed, concealed in the leafy dark, and watched as the two familiar figures approached the car-park clearing.

Brother Ralakin stopped by the car she had been looking at. St. Willibald walked a few feet past him then turned and made a short angry gesture.

Anne held her breath, not making a sound.

"After all these years—now this!" St. Willibald snapped. "The vultures are moving in!"

"We can handle it," Brother Ralakin said.

"I hope so, Rolly. I hope so. And listen, do you think we can speed up the services tonight?"

"Well, I can give a quick introduction to get the ball rolling. Then let Sarah and the other girls take over. They'll probably like it better that way anyway. They're a pretty conditioned crowd. They don't need the religious angle to let themselves go any more."

The Saint bit his lip, frowning and wringing his black-gloved hands. "We'll have to play it by ear, Rolly. I want Martha Mason in there tonight! I want to get that camera on her."

"I'll handle it, Carey."

The Saint waved his hand, obviously worried and impatient over something. "I don't like it," he hissed. "I don't like it one goddamn bit!"

"The ringer?"

"Who the hell else do you think I mean? Lem was right on the telephone; we can't take this thing lightly. We've got to nip it in the bud or play it out to see how much the guy knows and how much he merely suspects."

Ralakin nodded, looked down at his feet. "I've been thinking," he said slowly, "maybe there *isn't* another outfit trying to horn in..."

The Saint's eyes grew wide and his voice was a mere gasp.

"What—what do you mean? ... You mean—Lucifer...."

Ralakin looked perplexed. "Lucifer? What're you talking about, Carey?"

The Saint looked pale, haunted. He glanced nervously over his shoulder, looked once, intently at the bushes where Anne was standing with a horror-stricken look in her eyes.

The Saint finally shuddered and said, "Forget it! Go on. What were you driving at?"

Ralakin shrugged and elaborated, "I meant that maybe this ringer is a phony. I'm not saying that he doesn't exist. I'm sure that he does. But how are we to know that he isn't simply the first in a series of steps. A gesture, or some kind of trick. Knowing Lemuel I wouldn't put it past him. And with Dolly Bosco mixed up in it...."

The Saint nodded. "I hadn't thought of it that way." His expression grew thoughtful and suspicious. "Maybe you've got something there. Maybe. But there's an argument against it. Don't forget that I've known Lem ever since our days in the Federal pen in '38, and I think I know him as well as I know anyone. I'm sure that if he had anything up his sleeve he'd handle it himself. He wouldn't toss in a ringer to deliberately put us on our toes. That's not the way he works. And don't forget the way he'd sounded on the phone. He's not that much of an actor, believe me. He sounded really disturbed. But don't worry, Rolly. I'll keep both questions open in my mind when the ringer gets here."

Brother Ralakin started walking, his sandals munching over the gravel. The Saint walked at his side. Their conversation drifted back to Anne in fading snatches.

"Take care of him, Carey ... up in the hills ... near by ... where we buried ..."
The Saint's voice rumbled. "... make sure first ... never know until ..."
The night took them. It was silent again.

Anne turned and started to race back to the garden, terrified, confused, panicked, back to the tiny flickering votive light, unmindful of the black branches that sprung at her and lashed smartly against her face and robe.

It was hard for Paul to keep a straight face. Try as he might he couldn't figure out what it was all about. Martha Mason offered no clue. She sat back in the luxurious seat and calmly smoked her cigarette, not saying a word.

Maybe he should be used to it. But he wasn't. Screwy things had been happening ever since he came to Hollywood. Once he had been mobbed at an autograph session by crazy kids who had absolutely no idea what or who he was. He had even been slugged at a cocktail party by a big-name singer who he had never met before.

Another time he had been baptized by a modern messiah with a chartreuse water-pistol shaped like a German Luger. And only last week he had been accosted by a young girl with a southern accent. She had asked him to sign her book and when he had complied she had looked at the signature with unconcealed disgust. "Ah thawt y'all was Jawn Cassyvettes." Then she had torn out the page and threw it at his feet.

Now, here he was in a Bentley with Martha Mason, going off to God knows where. Perhaps he should just take it in his stride and play it out. But it was hard to do. He was burning with curiosity.

Martha Mason suddenly remarked, "I believe I would have recognized you even without the carnation and the newspaper."

"Oh? Thank you, Miss Mason." He smiled to himself. Mystery number one was cleared up. "I'm flattered," he went on lamely. "But of course, your—"

She looked at him then. "You sound different off the phone."
"I do?"
"What's your name again?"
"It's Berko. Paul Berko."
She shrugged. "I thought it was Lemuel."
"Ah—Lemuel couldn't come."
"I see. I don't suppose it makes much difference."
He could think of nothing more to say. He was excited and quite im-

pressed in spite of himself. Martha Mason was one of the Hollywood elite. She had won the Academy Award for her portrayal of a Southern-belle-tycoon in *The Red Hills of Love*. She was, as Paul figured, in her late thirties or early forties. He had seen her in five or six films, all of which had been produced by her own company and had been pretty lousy, even though they had been successful at the box-office.

She was a beautiful woman, severely featured, full-lipped, dark-eyed, platinum-haired, well-groomed, and slender. Smaller than he had imagined. She was dressed in a lime green gabardine suit, gold shoes, and gold scarf.

"I'm glad to see, as Dolly told me, that Dr. Kozma is being ... ah, careful." She smiled nervously, twisting the filtered end of her cigarette. "I've never done this sort of ..."

Paul said nothing. The mysteries were clearing up. He sat back, thinking it over and unconsciously fingering his property-department ring.

The Bentley purred through Beverly Hills and entered Bel Air. Lights slid past the window. The chauffeur drove close to the limit. The University grounds whipped by. It was obvious now that they were heading for Sepulveda Boulevard.

He had, like nearly everyone else within earshot and eyeshot of Los Angeles, heard a great deal about Dr. Zedek Kozma and his crackpot group northwest of the county line.

He crossed his legs and tried to look bored. Thinking it over, turning it around this way and that, it became obvious to him that she had made arrangements with a man named Samuel—or was it Lemuel?—to meet him in front of Chernery's. The man was supposed to wear a flower and carry a paper—quite cloak and daggerish—and take her to Kozma's place for some reason or other. And she had mistaken him for that man. And now he was supposed to bring her to Kozma's place.

That part, it would seem, was going to be easy. The chauffeur obviously knew the way and was in on the game.

While he was still thinking along these lines, Martha Mason turned to him and smiled curiously. "You don't look much like a Kozmanite to me."

"Really? What had you expected?"

"I suppose someone with a beard. Or with one of those cloaks."

"I don't look very well in a beard."

"I don't like beards," Martha Mason said.

What was she so nervous about? He noticed that she was working on the filter of another cigarette.

"Do you attend the meetings, too?"

"Rarely," he answered.

"A pity." A tic moved her upper lip. "You're nice looking."

"Thank you."

"Have you ... seen many of my pictures?"

"Most of them."

"Was I—were they good?"

"You were great, Miss Mason."

She seemed relieved by that. "Very kind of you," she said.

He gave her a sincere look. "I saw *The Red Hills of Love* five times," he lied intensely.

"Why—how flattering!"

"I hadn't said it to flatter you, Miss Mason."

She moved on the seat, turning a bit closer to him. He became aware of her perfume, her personality, her flattery as she gazed at him. "Ah, Mr. Berko—would you care for a drink? Or don't you drink?"

"I drink. And I'll have one if you've a jug handy."

"In that cabinet."

He opened the cabinet, poured two stiff Scotches, and after clicking glasses they drank. Martha Mason gulped hers, as if it were a medicine, using both hands on the glass. He could see that she had really needed it, so after a proper minute he offered another and refilled her glass.

They passed through Sherman Oaks, heading toward San Fernando. Paul was relaxed, sipping the excellent Scotch, enjoying the smooth ride along the moonlit highway. He wasn't too worried yet about what his reception might be at Kozma's mountain home. Kozma must be an understanding sort; after all, the man claimed to be some sort of a saint, and saints were supposed to be understanding, weren't they? He half-decided that when he arrived there he would simply make a clean breast of the matter and explain to them that he was just a victim in a merry mix-up. Which, of course, he was.

He would try to get Dr. Kozma aside, of course, to explain his being there. He didn't relish the idea of disturbing his short acquaintance with Martha Mason. She could be very valuable to his career. She had been already. He recalled the looks of astonishment on Mara's and Harvey's faces back at Chernery's. Yes, she had been very valuable. And if he played his hand right she could be even more valuable. He hoped that he would have a chance of explaining his intrusion to Kozma in private.

And, as for Miss Mason, if she wanted to become mixed up in such an obviously phony group like the Kozmanites, then it was no business of Paul's to try and discourage her.

He sighed, sipped his Scotch, and smiled softly to himself.

Someone had once remarked that God must have lifted three corners of the United States, like a huge handkerchief, and that all the loose pieces rolled down to settle in Los Angeles.

Paul didn't doubt it.

Where else could crackpot religious movements thrive? Salvation was peddled there as legitimate merchandise. Secrets of destiny hawked like underarm deodorants; poof there goes sin. Wear Jesus ... because ... Jesus is my copilot, my buddy, my savior. God and me are just like that. All it needed was a jingle. Sung to "Beautiful Dreamer"....

> *I love sal-va-tion*
> *Good sav-ing prayers*
> *Hard rocky high-ways to rich golden stairs*
> *Take me to hea-ven*
> *Make me de-vine*
> *Call Zedek Kozma—it costs but a dime....*

It was amazing—the number of people, rich and poor alike, who could fall for a charlatan such as Kozma. And, so it would seem, Martha Mason was no exception.

First, in order to pave the way for his excuses and his plans, he decided to stop and telephone Dr. Kozma before he took her to his place in the hills.

"Would you stop somewhere for me, Miss Mason? I have to make a call."

She nodded. "Certainly, no trouble at all. Meanwhile, would you care to make me another, Paul? Is it all right if I call you Paul?"

"Please do. And may I call you Martha?"

She cast him an amused look. "I'd be delighted."

He made two more drinks. He was beginning to feel mellow and very sure of himself.

"May I ask you, Paul? ... Have you ever seen any of the Doctor's shows?"

He made a noncommittal gesture.

Her voice was a little sharper. "Don't you approve?"

"I didn't mean that," he said hurriedly. "Of course I approve. I wouldn't be taking you there if I didn't."

She seemed mollified and her expression softened again. He fell into silence, brooding, thinking again. He had a fourth drink and when he settled back again he discovered that the liquor was already beginning to affect him. And, also, that a cold hard lump was forming in the pit of his stomach.

CHAPTER SEVEN

They sat in thoughtful silence in the drawing-room of Dolly's suite in the Beverly-Hanton hotel. Dolly, bundled in a red quilted house-jacket, had said very little since Lemuel had arrived and had once again described how he had been beaten out of his mark by the stranger. Between them, on a little lacquered tray, a selection of bottles and glasses remained untouched.

Lemuel sat on the edge of the divan, chain-smoking Egyptian cigarettes, nervously dancing the points of his shoes on the thick gray carpet.

"Describe him to me," Dolly said. "Maybe he'll ring a bell for me."

Lemuel made a hopeless little gesture. He was still embarrassed by it all. "I don't know, Dolly," he said. "He wasn't anyone I know. And believe me, if he'd done any work around here before I would have heard of him. He's probably a dark-horse from out of town or a complete amateur—"

"He didn't act like an amateur, Lem. He pulled it pretty damn smooth if you ask me."

Lemuel nodded reluctantly. "Yeah. It *was* pretty smooth—"

"Was he tall? Thin? Fat? Redheaded? He must have some kind of description."

"Well, I only saw him for a second. Once on the sidewalk just as he was entering Martha Mason's car, and then when I ran up to him I caught a glimpse of his phiz through the window. That's all."

"Don't apologize."

"He wasn't an average type," Lemuel said slowly, "but then he wasn't *un*-average either. Know what I mean? He was on the tall side, slender, with dark hair, possibly black. He had dark eyes—I think. A rugged face. Not the Marlboro type. More haggard or worn down than rugged. He had no mustache or beard. Well-cut clothes, black, looked like a good quality of rough silk. White button-down shirt and dark necktie." He puffed on his cigarette and rubbed his chin. "And that's about all there was. I didn't see anything more."

Dolly thought for a long moment, then shook her head, chins quivering. "Nothing else? Are you sure?"

Lemuel looked indignant. "Aside from that damned white carnation and the newspaper, no, nothing else."

"Sorry, Lem. Don't be touchy." She lifted a pudgy hand as if to make another point, then she sighed and dropped the hand. She looked at the lacquered tray. "Help yourself to a drink, Lem. I'm being a bad hostess tonight."

While he built a triple bourbon over ice he noticed, to his surprise, that his hand was shaking a little. He gulped at his drink.

"Any ideas, old girl?"

"None whatever, aside from the very obvious."

"Do you think I'm being wiretapped?"

"I've no idea. Have you checked your place out?"

"No."

"Do that first thing. And, just to be on the safe side, use outside lines when you have to make calls."

"Right."

"And another thing, you'd better contact Carey and Ralakin and ask them when it'll be best for us to come up there. We've got to speed this thing up. Our ringer friend is going to put them on their guard. They might bury their films and books. I'd like us to be up there while the ringer's still nosing around. We'll have to play it cautiously from here on in. First, we don't know how much the guy knows or who's backing him. Second, we'll have to find out if he's willing to make some kind of a deal. If not, then we'll have to step up our action and try to beat him out."

Lemuel agreed, again admiring how cool the old buzzard was. Nothing seemed to shake her. He looked at his hand, saw that it was steady now, and he poured more liquor over his melting cubes.

The dining table was filled from end to end with elaborately prepared foods and various pitchers and bottles of wines and liquors. The air was thick with incense, with a hint of hashish burning through it. The lighting was dim, red and gold and emerald green.

Fifteen or twenty people were moving in the dark. Their voices mingled together, rising over the piped-in music. Here and there alcove rooms with gauze-like curtains over the entrances showed a candle. Like a firefly in a mist.

Kozma had decided, for the sake of maintaining ritual, to put in an appearance. He sat at the head of the table, like a medieval baron, and gazed disinterestedly at a flickering oil lamp set in a bronze skull. Irving MacLean, bronzed, gray-haired, dressed in corny silk robes, sat on his left, Sarah at his side. On his right, drunk, stringy, muttering incoherently, was Jesse Kincaid, television western star.

"Then, Doctor," MacLean was saying thickly, "eudaemons and kakodaemons? Were they simply 'nother way of saying good 'n evil? Emh?"

Kozma, coming to attention, looked at the man as though he were insane.

He hadn't been paying the least attention to what was being said. The problem cast him by Lem's phone call was still torturing him. "What was that, Mr. MacLean? Eudaemons? Kakodaemons? Yes, of course. Certainly. Quite right."

MacLean looked puzzled. "I'm afraid I don't follow you, Doctor."

That was all right. Kozma couldn't follow either.

Sarah excused herself from the table and walked unsteadily to one of the alcoves on the far side of the room. Then, a moment later, MacLean excused himself and followed her. Jesse Kincaid moved two chairs down, found Edmund Tobias there, and started to talk to him. The party was beginning to break up. Couples were moving into their alcoves. The night was settling down.

Kozma poured himself wine, drained it, poured another. He wasn't being his usual self but he couldn't help it. The party lacked its usual wild air, but he could do nothing to help it. Tonight everything was upsetting to him.

At the far side of the room, carved into the thick pillars, there were representative demons. Asmodeus, fat and crowned, many-headed. Belphegor, naked and bearded and horned. Baal, tri-headed, spider-legged, frog and cat and man. Ashtoreth, riding the back of the familiar dragon-beast, winged, naked, holding a writhing snake in one hooked talon. Ugly statues. He felt like hurling his cup of wine at them. What had ever possessed him to have them put there? Had he been out of his mind? Why build statues to honor his sworn enemies? Madness. They were evil, foul, wretched things. And, looking at them with suspicion, he felt now as though he could smell them, hear them....

Carlo, a dim-witted but trusted monster of a man, padded up to the table. He had been with Kozma for six years. An ex-wrestler with a petty criminal record, he had a thick bald head, bushy red beard, and huge hands with fingers like bananas. His voice was like wet sandpaper.

"Brudder Ralakin wants to see you, Saint."

"Oh? Where's he at?"

"Outside. In the hall."

"Thank you, Carlo. Stay here for a while; make sure that our guests get anything they ask for."

He excused himself and made his way to the front door. Outside in the hall he saw no one and heard nothing. He looked cautiously left and right, then touched the side of a panel in the wall, twisting a tiny lock. The panel slid to one side, then closed after him.

Ralakin was there, standing in the dark, narrow passage, watching the party through a small two-way mirror. In the rear of each alcove there was a similar mirror.

"What's the matter," Kozma whispered anxiously. "Did they show up here already?"

Ralakin shook his head. "No. But the ringer is on the phone. I just talked to him. He's holding on."

Kozma was somewhat startled. "The phone? *Our* phone? Now? He's called *us*?"

"Yes. And I don't get it any more than you do, Carey."

Kozma didn't hesitate. Ralakin was directly behind him as he rushed through the narrow passage and mounted the stairs which led to his chambers. Another button was pressed and they entered his darkened office. Kozma flicked on the lamp, punched the outside button on his phone, held the instrument to his ear. He waited, collecting himself, then said slowly and carefully, "Hello. This is Dr. Zedek Kozma."

The answering voice was deep and well spaced.

Kozma frowned. "Yes? Miss Martha Mason? Yes, I am expecting her. I see, Mr. Polberko. And why have you called? Oh. I see. But of course you'll be welcome! I'm looking forward to meeting you, Mr. Polberko. No, think nothing of it. My pleasure. Yes. The Retreat is open to you. Yes. Good-bye."

He hung up and stared at Ralakin.

"Well?" Ralakin prompted.

Kozma pressed his hands together, as if in angry prayer. "I don't know, Rolly. Hard to figure. He's either very naïve or very clever. Whatever he's got up his sleeve escapes me. It doesn't make sense for him to call here! I just don't get it."

"What did he say?"

"He announced himself. Big as life. Said his name is Polberko. Does that mean anything to you? No? Not to me either. Next he said that my man Lemuel couldn't make it and that he was taking it upon himself to escort Miss Mason to our Retreat. Can you imagine that, Rolly? The gall! My man Lemuel! What kind of a fool does he think I am?"

"I've been thinking. Do you think he might be a reporter?"

"I doubt it. The press knows that I've nothing to hide. And, if they did suspect that I did, they wouldn't go about getting a snoop in here with such a clumsy front."

"How about the cops? Or the T-boys?"

"No. That idea stinks as bad as the reporter angle. And for the same reasons."

"All right. We'll settle on his being a ringer. Either way we'll have to have some sort of plan."

Kozma agreed. "We can do several things, Rolly. First, we can run them both off, Mason *and* this guy Polberko. Second, we can try to find out what the guy wants, how much he knows, and who's backing him, if anybody."

"I don't like the idea of running them off."

"Neither do I. If we run them off we don't solve the problem. It'll be just like kicking them under the carpet and out of view. The only way to solve a problem like this is to remove it completely. Not to ignore it."

"Such as we—ah, discussed?"

"I think that may prove necessary, Rolly. If this is a shakedown then we'll have to take him up into the hills. And make sure that he doesn't come back."

Ralakin nodded. He was a bit pale and when he licked his thin lips he found that his tongue was dry.

"Go back to the party, check on how it's coming along, then come back here for further instructions. Bring Carlo with you. He's an idiot but he might come in handy."

Ralakin nodded and left.

Kozma remained at his desk, deep in thought, lighting a cigar. Murder. The idea wasn't distasteful to him. It wasn't anything new. But he still didn't like it. To knock off a shakedowner was all right by itself, but it might prove tricky later on. If the ringer had an organization behind him it could possibly blow his racket sky high. He hesitated to murder, but still he could think of no other solution if it *was* a shakedown. Why in hell did Polberko phone? What sense did that make? A con-man never puts you on your guard that way.

The man was either a fool or he had an ace-in-the-hole that was ironclad.

"We'll see," he muttered. "We'll see...."

CHAPTER EIGHT

Paul was holding his glass, sipping now and then, enjoying himself immensely. Since telephoning Dr. Kozma he had been exchanging corny old jokes with Martha Mason.

"So, this ventriloquist became a medium. He threw his voice here and there. Voices of the dear departed came from horns, from floating, phosphorescent skulls. He was a tremendous success. One day this old woman was praising him, telling him what a wonderful medium he was and how

fine it was to hear from her husband again. So the ventriloquist puffed up
with pride and told her 'When you come back tomorrow, not only will you
hear the voice of your husband, but I'll drink a glass of water and smoke a
cigarette at the same time!'

Martha Mason laughed, placing her hand on his and giving little squeeze.
"Let's have another drink, Paul."

"Good idea. Wonderful idea."

Her hand remained on his and she smiled.

The chauffeur pushed the limit and the big car swerved on the twisting
hill roads. They had no trouble finding the place. All along the way, once
they left the main highway, there were little white signs and arrows to
guide them. The road grew rough. When they came to the gate that led to
the canyon Paul was working on his seventh drink of Scotch. Outside
everything looked wild and barren. Great crops of rock glowed in the
moonlight. The ground was rough, empty of shrubbery, rolling away in
crusted waves. The headlights washed yellow circles on the cut embankment
as the Bentley bounced from rut to pothole.

Finally, as the road wound uphill toward the mouth of the great canyon,
trees appeared, thin at first, then becoming thicker. The ground became
shadowed and the crowns of the trees scraped the waxen face of the moon.

"So this is The Retreat."

Paul nodded abstractedly. "Yes. This is it."

On either side of the road, through the timber, he saw an occasional
light, indistinct and greenish-gold, as though burning behind the canvas
walls of camping tents. The Bentley gathered speed as the road smoothed
and the lights dropped behind them. When they came to the wide hard-
packed apron before the grand temple Paul stiffened and caught his breath.
The nightmarish building before him was the last thing that he had expected. It was as if some Siamese monstrosity had been plopped down on
an old John Ford location. *The King and I* incongruously overlapping with
Fort Apache. For a long moment he was completely dumbstruck, his eyes
following the spiky glass towers, dunce-capped domes, rococo arches,
multi walls and tall arched windows.

"What—what is it?" Martha Mason whispered.

"It's—a temple ..." He almost added: I think.

He stepped out, helping Martha Mason after him, and they stood side by
side, weaving a little drunkenly, looking down into the canyon beyond the
temple, seeing the blocks of light which indicated more buildings and
sheds. The operation was on a grander scale than Paul had imagined. He felt
vaguely threatened by the temple, the buildings beyond, the quiet of the

night. Suppressing a shudder he guided Miss Mason away from the parked Bentley and toward the staircase of the temple.

Jacob, the chauffeur, remained where he was; a cigarette was planted between his lips, his gloved hands resting on the steering wheel.

"Well, what do we do now, Paul?"

"Do? Oh yes, what do we do—"

Leading her up the stairs he noticed how stiffly he was moving. Some people, when they were high, sagged or wobbled, but Paul moved with stiff, careful steps, as though he were trying to appear regal or arrogant.

The huge door ahead of them swung open and a small bearded man wearing long black robes stepped out to meet them. Behind him, and to one side, stood a thick figure with a bushy red beard and totally bald head. The little man, who seemed the more important of the two, stepped forward and held out a small pale hand.

"Mr. Polberko?"

Paul nodded, feeling a bit awed and confused by the beards and costumes, and shook the little man's hand.

Then, for some reason he decided it best to put on his act. Perhaps the liquor had prompted him, or the obviously theatrical trappings of The Retreat. At any rate he bowed stiffly at the waist—exactly as he had when he had played Satan and the Mad Vampire. His voice became dark and smooth, carrying just a touch of what he had always imagined was a Transylvania-Lugosi accent.

"Yes," he purred suavely, "I've brought Miss Mason to you."

The little man's brows jumped up a quarter inch, then his eyes shifted hurriedly to Miss Mason. He took her hand, saying, "My name is Brother Ralakin, Dr. Kozma's assistant." Then his eyes flicked back to Paul. "If you'll follow me, Mr. Polberko."

The red-bearded chap tugged at Ralakin's sleeve and looked confused.

Ralakin frowned. "You wait here, Brother Carlo. I'll be back in a minute or two."

"Yuh, sir. I'll wait right here."

Ralakin led the way. Paul and Martha Mason followed him into the temple. The first thing that impressed him was the curious odor, incense and flowers, like an Oriental funeral parlor; then vast white halls, brocade panels and paintings, plum-colored awnings with yellow and gold patterns, Persian carpets, wooden totem things and tall pillars with ugly carvings.

Going deeper into the building, following Ralakin through a confusing warren of corridors, Paul was struck with the elaborate murals of demons and saints, scenes after Brueghel the elder, Bosch, Quevardo, then vast tapestries depicting mythical landscapes of Hell, a weaving after Goya's Transformation of Sorcerers, others from Spanger, Francken, Baldung. The air of the fourteenth century. Long marble halls, magic symbols, pyramids of votive lights casting brass and ruby illuminations on thick carved panels and grotesque statuary. The place was a museum of occult horrors. Paul's mouth felt dry, his senses blurred by the constant inhalation of the pungent incense. His eyes watered. Each step seemed to become heavier. His decision to match the insane stage-setting of Kozma's palace with his own brand of theatrical deception was strengthened. He could be just as spooky as the next man.

Ralakin stopped before a round brass door. Paul saw no bell or knob and, half-humorously, he wondered if to open the door the little man had to strike it with a mallet, like in the J. Arthur Rank movies.

The door slid open and Ralakin ushered them into a huge room that glowed a mysterious green. At the far end, behind a massive desk, stood Dr. Zedek Kozma.

He was, Paul decided, just the figure to top off the insanity of his temple. He was more impressive than his newspaper photos. A big man, deep-voiced, with eyes like big black pearls.

"Good evening, Miss Mason, Mr. Polberko."

Paul shivered slightly. The Doctor's performance was a definite challenge to him. One actor versus another. Paul, assuming his Vampire stance, bowed very slightly, unconsciously clicking his heels and smiling fiendishly.

Kozma watched him as if he were sizing him up, then he quickly turned to Martha Mason. He stepped from behind the desk and took her hand in his. "How nice to see you, Miss Mason. I trust you had a nice trip."

"Yes. Your man here was very entertaining, Doctor."

"So? My man? You mean, of course, Mr. Polberko?"

Martha Mason gave him a curious look. "Of course. Who else, Doctor?"

Kozma made no answer. He pointed to a chair and said, "My dear, do sit down. And, if you'll excuse me, I'd like to have a word with—ah, my man, Mr. Polberko."

"Of course, Doctor."

Shrugging mentally, Paul followed Kozma to the brass door and stepped out into the hallway. So this was it, he was telling himself. They were going to cuss him out and throw him out on his ear. Ah well, he had a ball....

The corridor, wide and well-lit at this point, was empty. The incense wasn't quite as strong as it had been in the room where Martha Mason waited. Directly across from where he stood, where Kozma took his position, there was an ugly old tapestry from the Tarot, depicting the Hanged Man, after

Gringonneur, and beside that, a pair of fat candles burned.

An embarrassing silence grew between them.

Kozma studied him in complete silence and Paul grew increasingly nervous. With forced casualness he reached for a cigarette, placed it in the exact center of his lips and lit it with his Zippo. As the flame burst out Paul's property-department ring flashed and Dr. Kozma's eyes narrowed and his sensual lips seemed to tighten.

Something about the ring? Paul put the Zippo in his jacket pocket and deliberately smoked with his ring hand, giving Kozma an opportunity to study it. He was thinking that since the good Doctor was such an avid collector of such things he might make him a decent offer for it. That is, of course, if he could find room for another ring on his thickly jeweled fingers.

Thinking of possible profit he smiled and suppressed a liquor hiccup.

"You seem pleased, Mr. Polberko," Kozma said after a minute.

Paul smiled stupidly. "I do?"

Kozma glanced at the ring again, then wet his lips nervously.

"Nebiros," he whispered.

Paul frowned. Nebiros? What was Nebiros? What was the old charlatan talking about? Suddenly he wished he were more sober. He still felt a bit dizzy and threatened by the scene. He blinked once or twice, dragged deeply from his cigarette. Why wasn't he being tossed out? What was Kozma being so suspicious and nervous about? Nebiros? Why fool around? Deciding to make a clean breast of the entire mess he dropped his cigarette and stepped forward, intending to explain.

But Kozma moved back, his face twitching, a strange look in his dark, heavy-lidded eyes.

"Doctor, I'd like to explain about the Lemuel business."

"Lem? Yes, about Lem."

"You see, I'd never met the man, Doctor. In fact, to be honest, I don't even know what he looks like. But there I was, losing face. In my business it's bad to lose face. Do you follow me?"

"Yes, of course," Kozma rumbled. "Do you plan to remain here long, Mr. Polberko?"

"Remain here? I don't—"

"Be my guest. I'm sure I can find room for you. We've some comfortable guest cottages. Right behind the temple in fact."

Paul stared at the man. "I don't think I've made myself clear, Doctor...." How drunk was he? His head was reeling and he suspected, just for a second, that he was caught in a dream. He blinked, tried again. "About this ring, you see?" He held it up. Kozma gritted his jaw and nodded stiffly. Paul went on, "Arketus, the prop man, gave it to me. This Nebiros—"

"I assure you, Mr. Polberko, I'll respect the ring. And, I repeat, I'd feel honored if you'll be my guest. I've been expecting your visit for some time. I confess that now this has come about I am at peace. I think you understand."

"Yes, but—"

"Remain here at least until our Great Sunday Rites. I think then that our powers will reveal themselves. Meanwhile, allow me to be your host."

"Yes, but—"

Kozma held up a gloved hand. "*Nebiros! O tu Nebiros, Magister invisibilitatis cum Magistris tuis, Lucifer, Belzébut, Lucifugé, mea, Willibald, virtute me involvo!*"

Then he turned and disappeared behind the round brass door.

Paul was alone.

A moment later, Ralakin appeared.

"Mr. Polberko?"

"Yes?"

"I'll lead you out. But will you wait a moment?"

"Certainly."

Ralakin went down the hall and disappeared in the gloom. A moment later Paul could hear the little man's voice, muffled, indistinct, conversing with someone who sounded like Dr. Kozma. Paul shifted his weight, lit another cigarette, studied the ring on his finger, and scratched his head. He was beginning to think that everyone was a trifle nuts around there. Again, he wondered what a Nebiros was, puffing deeply on his cigarette, pacing back and forth, waiting to be led from the place.

What was that business about being a guest until Sunday?

Whatever it was, Paul was willing to accept. He had nothing in Los Angeles to look forward to save for another cheap hotel room and slow starvation until the TV shot with Harvey Crockett came through. And if the old lunatic Kozma wanted to play the host Paul wasn't about to interfere. If Kozma thought he was someone important Paul wasn't going to correct him. Why should he? A free bunk and free meals for a while would be a welcome change.

Ralakin returned, muttering under his breath. He looked at Paul with a puzzled eye, then shrugged and said, "I'm to show you to the guest house, Mr. Polberko."

He sounded disappointed by that.

Paul put out his cigarette and followed the little man. When they were at last out into the fresh air, the nightmare of the narcotic-hazed temple air be-

hind them, Paul felt a little more sober, the air sucking sweetly into his lungs
and his thoughts clearing. As he followed Ralakin to the guest cottage he
glanced over his shoulder and caught a glimpse of a huge shadow following them.

It was the big man with the red beard and bald head.

CHAPTER NINE

The room was small and perfectly square, with tiny casement windows
on either side of the entrance door. A small washroom was set in one corner, closed off by a narrow louvered door. A lamp glowed brightly on a bare
stand beside the steel-frame cot. There were no pictures on the white walls.
The cottage was cold, naked, prison-like.

Paul thanked Ralakin for having accompanied him, then waited until the
little man disappeared along the thin temple path. Then he pulled back the
cheap cotton spread and sat on the cot. He pulled the lamp chain and
plunged the room into darkness.

He waited five minutes, then, hearing nothing, not even the sounds of the
crickets, he opened the door and stepped outside. He saw no one, but he
knew that the red-bearded man who had followed him was still out there,
most likely hiding in the bushes and watching his movements. He lit a cigarette, letting his shadow see his face in the flare of his lighter, then he casually started along the barely visible path which returned him to the apron
before the temple. As he had expected, he heard the cautious tread of
someone following him on the path while he walked along. He didn't
bother looking behind him.

All he was after was another drink. He was the type of person who, once
he was wound up alcoholically, didn't like to stop. Besides, all the cheap
mysteries and bogeyman Latin curses—or whatever they were—were beginning to disgust him. A couple of shots from that bottle of Scotch would
help dispel his confusions. A good belt of liquor would put him back on that
weird wonderland plane where he couldn't care less what the Kozmanites
and their beloved Saint were talking about.

He came up to the Bentley, still walking stiffly, looking forward to a
nightcap. Jacob, the chauffeur, rolled down his side window and smiled
nervously.

"Ah, don't mean nothing disrespectful, sir, but I'm glad you came back."

"Why's that, Jacob?"

"This place, sir. Not knowing how you feel about it, but to me it's kind of spooky. I'm still not sure what this is. But it's mighty spooky."

"It's a retreat," Paul explained. "The people who live here think they're riddled with sin. I remember reading about it. They have big fights with the demons up in the hills. At least, that's what I think they do."

The chauffeur was a short, thick-set man with a flushed face, lumpy knobby nose, and bright blue eyes. He seemed about fifty years old.

"Is that true?" he asked.

"Sure," Paul said. "Then I guess old Kozma chases all the evils away with his big magic and everyone's pure until the next session."

The chauffeur chuckled and rubbed his jaw, squinting at the temple building and nodding his head as if he had finally understood the punch-line of a good gag.

Paul turned and looked down the path he had come on. He thought he saw a quick blurred movement near the trees. Was it his guard? He clenched his jaw, resentment boiling in him, not bothering to puzzle why he should need a guard. Then he remembered the teak bar in the rear of the Bentley and he turned back to Jacob.

"Care for a nip, Jacob?"

"Why, sir, now do you think—"

"Sure. Have a drink with me. I won't tell Miss Mason. I'm staying up here for a while so I probably won't be seeing her before she goes back anyway."

"Well ... if you think so, then right you are."

The moon had pushed higher now and the grounds were brightly patterned. The wind was gentle, warm, mountain-scented. There was the sough of the branches, the sounds of crickets and, in the far background, the chuckle of a creek.

"Meaning no disrespect, sir, but are you with these people here?"

"Hell no. I'm just a friend of Miss Mason's. And, even at that, I hardly know her. Jacob, my friend, I don't even know what I'm doing up here. Do you? Perhaps I'm getting a bit too drunk. Think so?"

"You look fine to me," Jacob assured him.

"Thank you. But when I act dignified that means that I'm half-boiled."

"Here's the bottle, sir. I'll just have a little one. Just to keep the chill off, so to speak."

"Don't apologize, Jacob. Have all you want. I don't like drinking alone." He hoisted the bottle of Cutty-Sark, swigged deep and passed it to the little chauffeur. "Here you go, my friend. And you can call me Paul. That's my name. Paul Berko. And not Nebiros. Incidentally, do you know what Nebiros is?"

"I'm afraid not," Jacob said. "'Well, here's to the Devil," he saluted. "Mm, that's good. Mind if I stretch my legs?"

"Course not. Join me."

Jacob stepped from the car, passing the bottle. The Scotch was warm, turning him around and around. His eyes no longer burned and he wondered again what they had been burning back there in the temple. It had smelled like hashish and the effect had been pretty much like it; as though the floor had been tipped a little, everything becoming terribly unreal.

He was becoming drunker. He knew it. But he was at that the-hell-with-it stage. He noticed that the bottle of Cutty-Sark wasn't the same one he had been drinking from before. This one was still pretty full.

"I'm a hard drinker I am," Jacob said wistfully.

"Are you Irish?"

"I am."

"An Irishman named Jacob?"

"Ah, call me, Jake. You're an all right fellow. I can tell."

"Sure. I'm all right. Have another snort, Jake."

"Thank you. Martha Mason always drinks the best. Say, do you think the people up here are nuts?"

"Do you?"

"Why not? Wearing robes and beards like they do, and like you say, fighting devils and such. I think they're as nuts as people can get. Know what I mean?"

"Sure, Jake. Pass me the grog."

"Are you in show business?"

"I used to be," Paul said thickly, sadly.

"So was I," Jake said. "I had a bit in Martha Mason's first picture. Did you ever see it? *This Is Molly Wanderer.* I was the stage manager in the scene where Molly Wanderer gets her first big break. Did you happen to see that?"

"No. How many pictures did you do, Jake?"

"Only six. Six bit parts. You see, I'm a singer. Irish tenor. And, if I may say, I've still a nice voice. I played in London during the war, entertaining the boys overseas. I was too old for the real scrap, you see. And that, the time in England, was my last engagement. Since then I've been Miss Mason's chauffeur and gardener."

"Whatever made you try Hollywood, Jake?"

"Dennis Morgan did, sir. He's a great voice. I loved that man's voice. Have you ever heard Bill Frawley?"

"Yes."

"Another voice, Bill is. He's kept his voice up, you know."

They had left the car some minutes ago and were now walking down another path, lit by moonlight, weaving, talking, stopping now and then to sip
the Cutty-Sark. Jake was taking small drops, but Paul was drinking more
heavily.

"Maybe I'm a prisoner here, Jake," Paul said, slurring his words. "Feel
like a prisoner, any rate. You should see that cottage. Like a cell. Maybe their
guests're all monks, unh? Look here, Jake, do I look like a vampire?"

"Absolutely not!"

"Good. Tell it to m'agent, Jake. Tell him that. Tell him that old Paul Berko
looks like a combination of Rock Hudson and John Carradine." He giggled.
"Sing me a song, Jake. Sing me a nice old tune from Ireland."

"Would you really care to hear?"

"Course."

"Here? I mean, here in the woods like this?"

"Why not? Here's a bench. Lemme sit down, then you can sing me a
song."

With bottle in hand, pressed to his thick chest, face lifted solemnly to the
moon, the chauffeur started to sing with all the flair and lilted timing of an
old pro. Paul settled back with a big smile on his face and hummed along
with him. Jake sang two numbers from the stock tenor repertoire, then
swung into a fine old number from World War One. *Tipperary*. Then, with
grand comic gestures:

> *Standin' on the bridge at midnight*
> *Throwin' snowballs at the moon*
> *She said, George I've never 'ad it*
> *But she spoke too bloody soon....*

The chauffeur's voice filled the air, sharp and sweet, as clear as gin. Paul
laughed and applauded loudly.

"Great, Jake. Just great."

More Cutty-Sark. The trees spun around a little now. He was aware of the
brook sounds again, off to his left, deeper in the forest. How nice if he could
go down there and plunge his stuffy head in the cold mountain water....

"Well, sir, while I'm still sober enough to drive, I think I'd better be getting along. It's been swell."

"Jake. Ditto. You've got a wonderful voice."

"Thank you."

They shook hands and promised to look one another up when they were
both back in town. They made some half honest vows about getting together

over a bottle of Bushmill's to sing a few more of the good old songs. Then Jacob left, returning up the path. Paul turned and, just in time, plunged through the timber toward the creek. He was sick, but still giggling and enjoying himself.

The water, sloshed on his neck and face, revived him. He sat on a rock, swaying, humming Irish tunes, and tried to light a cigarette. The cigarette fell into the water and was carried away.

He rose and wandered on a strange path, dripping water on his shirt front, in love with the night, the spring night with the ice cream moon and the damp pine-needled floor. What was that crazy line from Jake's song? Oh yes. Throwin' snowballs at the moon. A great image that. Like Paul's screwy career.

Throwin' snowballs at the moon.

He stopped, leaned on a tree, looked at his feet, then up at the trees. He was only vaguely aware of where he was, then, remembering the name Nebiros, he chuckled softly and started on the path again.

CHAPTER TEN

"You stupid clod!" Kozma screeched. "Ralakin asks you a simple favor! Follow that man and keep your eye on him! And what do you do? You lose him! You are a moron, Carlo. An incompetent moron!"

He gasped for breath and started to pace back and forth, his eyes blazing and his mouth working furiously. Carlo looked stunned and confused. Neither he nor Ralakin, who was standing stiffly by the bishop's chair, had ever seen Kozma so worked up. Neither one spoke. The air was tight with the tension. Kozma puffed angrily on his cigar, looking from one to the other, his built-up shoes thumping on the carpet.

"All right, Carlo! Tell it to me again. You say he went to the cottage and turned out the light."

"I thought he was goin' to sleep, Saint—"

"I don't give a merry hoot what you *thought*, nitwit! Tell me what you saw."

"Yes, Saint. I was there, watching just like Ralakin tor me. Two, maybe three minutes go by, then he leaves and I stay right behind him. He goes to the car. Miss Mason's car. He talks with the driver and they go off together. Then they start singin' chants and things. But like no chants I ever heard."

Kozma's eyes narrowed and his nostrils flared with his heavy breathing.

"Go on," he said tightly. "Tell me what Polberko chanted."

Ralakin stepped in. "Carey, I don't see what's so damned important about what the ringer sang—"

"You don't see? You don't see! You're a fool, Rolly! Am I surrounded by fools? Don't you know *who* the ringer is yet? Don't you know *who* sent him? Are you all so blind that you can't see that? That ringer is Nebiros! Nebiros! He's from Lucifer, you ass! Now get out of here! Out! Get out of here and leave me alone!"

Ralakin stepped back in open fear, turned, and fled from the room. Carlo, close to tears now, started after him.

"Not you!" Kozma roared. "You stay here!"

Carlo froze.

"Now tell me what Polberko chanted!"

"Like—like I said, Saint, it was—was about midnight and snowballs and something about bloody something. Something like that..."

"*Something* like that!" He wound up for another violent outburst, but his fury dwindled and he made a hopeless little sob deep in his throat. He didn't trust his own anger. He sighed, shoulders slumping under his robes. "All right, Carlo," he said softly. "All right. Get out. Go into the forest down there and see if you can find him. And when you do—*if* you do—*gently* lead him back to the guest cottage. Do you understand that, Carlo?"

Carlo brightened a little. "Yes, Saint. I unnerstan'."

"I hope you do. Now get out of here and leave me be."

Anne was still sitting on the bench, still looking at the little votive light burning in the shrine. After her first flight of panic from the car-park she had become calm. She wasn't really sure why she had been frightened. She hadn't been able to understand everything that Brother Ralakin and St. Willibald had talked about. But, as before, she had been made aware of the evil about the Saint and that, connected with the night, had terrified her. The evil of Kozma, like a huge shadow, still hovered over her. She was afraid to even think about it. And now, before the protective little glow from the candle, she fixed her thoughts on other things, escaping from the revulsion she felt for the man who was her father-figure, her saviour, Kozma.

A while back, perhaps ten minutes ago, she had heard what she thought was singing. A sweet, heavenly voice, singing a song that was completely unfamiliar to her. It had been a touching thing, making her feel oddly restless. Tipperary. And she had asked herself what or who a Tipperary was. A new saint? A magic word she hadn't heard before?

Then the song had ended, the wind had shifted, and she had heard noth-

ing more. She had no reason to investigate so she remained on the bench,
her hands resting on her lap. But the song lingered and when she heard the
humming, along with the softly approaching footsteps, she looked up curiously and started to rise. Then, startling her, a stranger entered the clearing.

He wasn't wearing the Kozma robes and he was clean shaven. He was
humming, smiling in a strange way, walking even more strangely, as though
the ground was rocking gently under his feet.

"Hello," she said.

The man stopped and looked at her for a long moment.

"Were you singing a few minutes ago?" she asked.

"Me? Singing?"

His voice was deep but faintly slurred. She watched him with a puzzled
expression in her brown eyes, wondering if he had difficulty in seeing—for
he screwed up his eyes as he watched her.

"No," the man said. "That was Jake. And now, honey, don't go asking me
who Jake is. He's my Mr. O'Malley. Little Irish guy with pink wings and
a cigar for a magic wand. Wisecracking, you see, like Pat O'Brien."

He had moved closer to the bench, talking more to himself than to her.
Anne said nothing. She was feeling uncomfortable now, a little afraid of him;
he was the first non-Kozmanite she had talked to in several years.

"I'm afraid I don't understand," she said.

"Forget it," Paul said. "I'm a little gassed still. Stream of Joyce talk.
Don't pay any attention to me. About Jake. He's a chauffeur. He just sang
a few songs for me."

His smile was nice. But, she wondered, why hadn't he seemed surprised
to see her sitting in the woods? She had certainly been surprised to see him.
Why was he so relaxed, his manner so easy?

He was very nice looking, if a bit thin, and his eyes were large and seemed
to understand.

"You see, my dear, I'm one of those guys that always manage to drop into
one weird scene after another. You follow? I just drift along, like old Shane,
coming into one strange circumstance after another. A child, you might say,
of others' destinies. For instance, I'd like a drink, so I leave Kozma's cottage—it's too much like a cell, you see—so I look up Jake and, naturally, he
turns out to be an Irish tenor who likes to sing songs, even at his age. So we
do. Sing songs, I mean. *Tipperary. When Irish Eyes Are Smiling.* That sort
of thing."

He turned and faced her. "Now I ask you who, I say *who* else could this
sort of thing happen to except Paul Berko?" He grinned and held out his

hand. "That's me, incidentally. Paul Berko."

"I—I—My name is Anne Woodbridge."

They shook hands.

"You'll have to excuse me," Paul said. "I've got a terrible head. They're shooting billiards up there and I don't want to tip their table."

"I'm sorry."

"Don't be. The wages of sin and all that. I'm not much of a drinker but once I start—look out. You don't know who Paul Berko is, do you?"

"No."

"Well, let me introduce myself. Sometimes I'm known as the Mad Vampire. Other times I'm the Fish-Beast. But, considering all, my best role to date has been that of Satan. You know, The Prince of Darkness. That was in *A Matter Of Hell*. They loved me. I'm a great old Satan. Is there something the matter?"

She had turned pale, her eyes wide and staring, her lips parted slightly.

"What're you afraid of? Don't you like actors? Is that it? If so, then I'm sorry."

"Actors?"

"Sure. I'm an actor. I just told you. I played Satan and the Vampire and the Fish-Beast. See, I have to tell this now and then because I'm ashamed. You follow me? Ashamed. I can't even stand to look at my own pictures. In the last one they pounded a wooden stake in my heart. Wham wham. Ah well." He chuckled softly. "Don't mind me. Joyce is still in me. Don't mind my rambling. It'll wind down in a minute."

Anne was watching him. An actor! She had never known an actor before. She had never seen a play or a film and, listening to Paul Berko and his rambling, she found herself reacting in a strange, new way.

"Are you smiling?" he asked suddenly. "Yes, you are. Good. Actors don't bite. Maybe Sonny Tufts. But not Paul Berko. I'm a little stiff. Shall I sing for you? Would you like to hear a song? What was your name again?"

"Anne. Anne Woodbridge."

"Ah, yes. And I gather you're a Kozmanite. That is, unless you're a Ku Klux Klanner who just happened by."

"No, I'm a Kozmanite."

He talked so strange. But there was nothing shady or suspicious in his manner. She was relaxed now, curious about him, wondering how he happened to be there.

"Enjoying this, Anne Woodbridge?"

"What."

"My talk?"

"Yes. Very much. I—may I ask you something?"

"Shoot."

"Pardon?"

"Go ahead. Ask me anything you want."

"Is your name really Paul Berko?"

"Yep. You see, if I wanted to really click big I would have changed my name to Rocky Strong, or Windy Hill, or Bat Guano. But I'm old-fashioned. I don't even have capped teeth. I wanted to be the Dana Andrews type but they thought differently. To them, I'm more the Lugosi type. I can't even be a Joseph Wiseman. I'd gladly settle for a Wiseman. Or a Jack Elam. But they don't let me. Strictly monsters, that's me. But then, I don't give up easily. Did you know that Jim Arness started as a monster? Sure he did. He was that vegetable in *The Thing*. But I don't want to be Arness. I cite him as precedent. All I want is to pay my back rent, get my scrapbook back and my white tie and tails and get enough extra to jet back to New York. Back to my good brother Bernie and Octobers that smell and act like Octobers."

She had tried to follow what he had been saying but it meant nothing to her. She apologized, "I'm sorry, Mr. Berko, but I don't understand—"

"I suppose not."

He yawned, shuddered, lit a cigarette and blew smoke toward the votive light. "Sorry. Talk cleans me out. I'm sobering now, I think. How do I sound? More sane?"

"You sound fine. I mean, you sound very good to me."

He looked at her again. "You seem pleased, Anne Woodbridge. Do I please you?"

"I—I think you do." She smiled nervously, not really knowing what to think. She was too puzzled by all this.

Paul Berko continued. "I want to do something without a script. Just once. I'd like to do *something*."

"Have you joined, Mr. Berko? I mean, The Retreat? Have you become a member?"

He laughed loudly. "Me? Hell no! I wore a robe only once in my life. A high-school production of *King Lear*. Never again." He squinted at her, shifting his weight on the bench and moving closer toward her. There was a warm, curious look in his eyes. "Let me ask you a question. How long have you been up here?"

"Since I was thirteen. I'm nineteen now."

"Six years? Jesus Christ on a broom, old girl. Where'd you come from? Originally, I mean. Where was your home?"

"I don't know," she answered. "Not really. You see, we traveled most of the time. My father was a preacher. I was born in Rifle, Texas. Do you know where that is?"

"No. But I know where Texas is. Edna Ferber wrote a book about it once, I think."

"Where were you born? Do you mind my asking?"

"Nope. I was born in Danbury, Connecticut. Raised in Manhattan. I lived with my brother Bernie and his wife."

The votive light sputtered once and then died. They took no notice of it. The moon was past the opposite canyon rim but there was still enough light to see by. From somewhere close by an owl hooted. Paul loosened his tie and lit another cigarette, his eyes remaining on the girl.

Anne didn't know how it started but she was soon telling him about herself. He said nothing, not interrupting her, but watching her with his strange eyes.

She told of her life with her father, how he had led her to one odd religion after another, sack dresses, bibles, writhing tongue-darting snakes on the pages, firewalkers, penitentés, one Ism after another. She relived it in her heart, relived the warped little pieces and pictures that she had for so long kept buried within.

It had been a strange life. She believed in demons so much that she could taste them. The cure of evil had absorbed old Joseph's life and he had dragged Anne along with him and his obsessive search for the pure path.

Be pure, baby. Cleanse thyself. Cast out that old devil. Rock 'em, sock 'em. Go get 'em for Jesus. The Atom Bomb is the devil. Motion-pictures are the devil. Cosmetics are the devil. Watch out! Here comes that old devil now!

Which way was the right way?

At six she could remember being in the desert. They had been following Joe Smith's idea, digging in the sun-baked Utah earth for buried messages from the Prophet. "I got the word, Annie," Joseph had said. So they dug, one senseless hole after another, looking for the lost or forgotten parchments of Moses.

She could remember breaking her nails in the dirt, burning her face and hands under the blazing sun. Oh Lawdy. Moses ten feet down. Dig a bit more, honey. Bound to be there. Dig. And of course they found nothing. Not one page. Not one word or dropped comma. Nothing at all. And old Joseph had wailed at the campfire, his great voice rusted with anguish. "Moses, he says for sure that it's not time for us, honey. Not time yet, that's all."

"Yes, Daddy."

"But soon, Annie. Cuz I got the call. Got it strong, I have. Same's you, Annie. You'n me, honey. Sure's there's God in heaven and sin right here on earth. We gone find it for sure, you bet. Yeah. And one of these days, like a great chariot fire whamming down from the skies, the Prophet's going to point his big old finger at me and give me the word. Yeah. Give me the big word. Just like that, Annie. Joseph, he'll say, them's the Devils over there and here's your weapons. Now go and get 'em. Give 'em thunder, Joseph. Yeah!"

"Daddy! I know. I can feel it, too!"

"Sure! And you know what? Once I got the word you just watch my smoke. I got these mighty arms not for the plow, but for to deliver that blow against the Devil himself. Wham! And down goes old Devil. Wham wham! And he stays down. Yessir!"

"Yes, Daddy. Oh, yes!"

They had continued searching, attending a hundred meetings in theaters, in tents, in camps, in churches. Houston. Savannah. St. Louis. Dallas. Salt Lake. Jacksonville. Mobile. All they needed was a true leader to point out the way to them.

So after years had passed they found the leader in a theater in Los Angeles, California. Dr. Zedek Kozma was the one man Joseph had found who had the personality and the power of the fire of truth, who knew the black mysteries of demonism, who knew the way to conjure and deal and could give complete instructions to his faithfuls on how to combat and defeat them. His philosophy was much the same as many others, but his presentation was more spectacular, his speaking voice and theatrical command more convincing. Joseph was hooked. He attended meetings, distributed pamphlets, grew a beard and adopted the robes. He and Anne canvassed the suburbs selling tracts and lithographed pictures of the Saint.

Along with the first few hundred converts they moved to the canyon northwest of the city, bringing with them their few possessions, their hopes, their new-found faith.

"Look at this place, Annie. This is our *home* ... home at last. This's where we belong and this's where we gone stay. Sure, I agree it don't look like much right now. But you just wait. The Saint says we're going to build. You heard his plans, honey. A city's going to rise from this empty ground. A city where folks can come and live in peace, under the protection of St. Willibald. This's going to be a place free of sin, free of the Devil. A city of God."

And so Anne had stood by helplessly while her father killed himself, working ten to twelve hours a day, praying, building, living in a filthy tent and living on black bread and weak tea. He worked himself to death for Kozmanism and they buried him in the canyon, under the pine on the slope above the creek....

Paul sat in thoughtful silence, hunched forward, his elbows resting heavily on his knees, an unlit cigarette dangling from his dry lips. The girl had stopped talking and was quiet now as though embarrassed by having revealed herself to him. He looked at her profile, the dark, shoulder-length sweep of her hair, the pale lips slightly open. He was more fascinated now than before. The pathos of her story had genuinely affected him. He couldn't take his eyes off her.

She sat with her hands resting on her lap, her thick-lashed brown eyes on the sooty lip of the votive light in the darkened shrine. When she finally spoke she sounded faraway. "And, as I told you, my husband died, too. They're both buried back there. And sometimes, when I've been alone for a long time, I begin to feel cursed, as if no matter who I love he will soon die." Her lips moved in a small, plaintive smile. "I suppose that sounds silly, doesn't it, Mr. Berko?"

He said nothing. He shook his head and, concealing his thoughts, lit his cigarette with his Zippo. He felt uncomfortable, as if he had somehow insulted her, was still insulting her. He couldn't explain himself. The girl was too real for him. He had been too long familiar with the selfish and the phony to honestly answer her.

Misinterpreting his sudden silence Anne rose slowly from the bench and started toward the path. Paul jumped up, touched the sleeve of her robe, and stood hesitantly before her. She gazed up into his face, waiting, looking troubled.

"Yes?"

"Why are you leaving? Where're you off to?"

"I—I talked too much, I think."

"No. No, you didn't."

He didn't want to let her go. He felt that for some reason if he allowed her to leave now the moment would be lost, that it would somehow prove itself to have been nothing more than a dream. And he stood there, foolish, wanting something, looking at her neck, at the tiny hollow where the thick square cut of the robe crossed her chest.

"Do you come here often, Anne Woodbridge?"

"Not too often."

She started to step away and again he detained her with a touch to her robe. She paused, not looking at him now, her eyes cast down to the pine-needled ground.

"Will you meet me here tomorrow? Say at eight o'clock in the evening?"

Without a word she nodded and turned down the path. Then she was gone, the night folding after her. Paul stood there for a long minute, dragging deeply on his cigarette, his hands thrust in his pockets. Then, slowly, his thoughts turned inward, he started back in the direction of the temple. Branches whipped unnoticed at his jacket, his feet brushed silently along the spongy track. He didn't notice the bulky figure in black robes until he was but a few feet from him.

"Mr. Polberko? Where you been? I'm s'posed to see you get to bed."

It was the bald, red-bearded giant who had followed him earlier.

"That's just where I'm going," Paul said.

"Gently," Carlo repeated.

"Of course. Gently. I rarely go to bed violently. How about you? Are you supposed to creep along behind me?"

"Unh?"

"Look, let's simplify your job. Walk alongside me. I promise I won't try to run away. Okay?"

They started up the path. Carlo looked confused. His thick face was gleaming with sweat, his breath coming in quick rasping gasps.

"Been running?" Paul asked.

"Yuh. I been lookin' for you. The Saint says I should see you should get to bed gently."

"That's nice of the Saint." He dropped his cigarette and stepped on it, making doubly sure it was out before he resumed walking. "Answer me a question, friend?"

"Sure, Mr. Polberko. What you wanna know, unh?"

"What's Nebiros?"

Carlo frowned, stroked his beard with his banana fingers.

"Nebiros? Gee. I think he's one of Lucifer's guys. There's all kinds of guys what work for Lucifer. Maybe seven or eight. Nebiros is one of them. Yeah, I'm pretty sure."

"One of Lucifer's guys?"

"Yeah, sure."

"That's interesting. And one more question. What's the Great Sunday?"

"You don't know? Gee. Well, that's when the Saint takes everyone up to the cliffs and chases out Lucifer and all his guys."

"Chases them out? That's amazing. Really amazing."

When they came to the cottage Paul thanked Carlo and closed the door behind him. He waited by the louvered window and watched as his guard retreated into the bushes near the temple, paused, ducked down in the shadows to continue his watch. Paul smiled drily and moved to the iron-frame cot, after pushing the bolt on the front door and checking the windows. He peeled off his jacket and trousers, kicked off his shoes and flopped down.

He closed his eyes and the girl, Anne Woodbridge, entered his thoughts again. He couldn't stop thinking about her. He had been profoundly disturbed by their encounter. He could see her lovely face in the brassy dark behind his squeezed lids, could hear her shy, halting voice in the dull red throb of his pulse against the cold stiff pillow. It was a half hour before he finally dropped off to sleep.

CHAPTER ELEVEN

Since the arrival of Polberko-Nebiros two days before, the fear within Zedek Kozma, the terrible awareness of the possible outcome, was becoming more noticeable. He was going mad, helplessly, inexorably, drawing into the dark waters of inner-life, tossed on the unrelenting waves of his growing megalomania. His movements and gestures were erratic and compulsive, his speech rambling and at times incoherent. His robes were wrinkled, his beard uncombed, his pancake makeup sloppily applied. He was finally beginning to look his age.

Obsession fired him. He had to prepare himself for the great battle that was surely to come unless he could discover some lever to use against Polberko, a gimmick he could use to worm free. Meanwhile, he had to know exactly how powerful this Polberko-Nebiros really was. There was a slim chance that he was simply an observer, an agent without specific instructions.

He spent the first day buried in his candle-lit study, poring over heavy volumes of philtres and death-spells, books of sorcerers, macrocosmic tracts, and in a fit of desperation, chiromancy and talismans and demon spells. He found nothing. Found no trace of the name Polberko.

He re-read the ancient literatures on Nebiros, the descriptions from *Le Grand Grimoire*, and learned nothing further. He knew that Polberko was Nebiros, or at the very least a close associate. And he was just as sure that the man had been sent to The Retreat to investigate ... but for what? He wasn't sure yet.

He had only one thing to truly rely on. His magic. His powers. He would face the problem of driving away the Evils, if and when they actually erupted from the earth, when it happened. Meanwhile he didn't even want to think about it. He continued with his books, feverishly assuring his shaky convictions that victory would be his if he was properly prepared for it.

The candles sputtered. One died and another flickered, threatening to go out. He replaced them, bringing light back to the room.

He had taken three pills and he was sitting on his huge four-poster bed, holding his aching head in his gloved hands, trying to get a hold of himself.

Who the hell was he? He wasn't too sure now. The name of Carré Bedder, or Carey Ledhead, or something like that, kept pushing into his thoughts, persistent, teasing, repeating itself like a chant. Who was *he*? Ledhead? Kozma? Then with the latter, from somewhere deep within, the odor of horses and sawdust and warm grass came to him. Kozma. The name was associated with a knife, with streaming blood, with a girl sobbing. So curious. What was it? Had anything like that happened?

The pills worked on him, firing his blood, drugging his thoughts. His pulse eased and the brilliant colors of exhaustion no longer swam before his eyes. He breathed deeply, rose stiffly from the bed and gazed indifferently at his figure reflected in the full-length mirror before him. He was a stranger to himself. He had no idea where he began or how he had arrived. He was aware only of being St. Willibald, a living god to adoring thousands, the saviour of the entire world....

Ralakin moved noiselessly across the room, pushing the girl before him. She was moving stiffly, her arms held fearfully at her breast. Ralakin ignored her and stopped at the desk. Kozma smiled, rose from his throne and stared at the girl as if she were standing there naked.

"A little present, Rolly?"

Ralakin nodded, obviously pleased. "She didn't want to come, but I—ah, persuaded her." He chuckled drily. "She was with Polberko yesterday after the dinner hour and she admits to having been with him the night before that."

"What's her name, Rolly?"

"You know. It's Anne Woodbridge."

Kozma's eyes glittered and he smiled again. "Anne Woodbridge? Really?"

"Sure."

"Do I know her?"

Ralakin frowned, then glanced nervously from the girl to Kozma. "Certainly you know her! Remember? Don't you—Carey, you okay? I mean, do you feel all right?"

"Feel? I feel fine. What about the girl?"

Ralakin shook his head doubtfully, then resumed with a slow voice. "She's been with Polberko. She says that he's very friendly with her. I tried to press her but she clammed up. So I brought her here, knowing you could get it out of her. And besides, I knew you wanted her here anyway."

Kozma thought a moment, then waved a hand. "All right, Rolly. You can leave us alone now. As you say, I'll handle it. There won't be any problem."

Ralakin left, glancing at Kozma over his shoulder, looking suspicions and concerned. Then the door slid shut and Kozma advanced toward the girl, watching her carefully. She appeared frightened of him. He found a cigar, bit the end off and lit it with his gold lighter, taking his pleasure, not looking away from the girl.

"Do you know who I am?" he asked.

She jerked her head up and down. "Yes. You're St. Willibald."

"That's right. And your name is Anne Woodbridge."

"Yes." She was retreating from him, taking one small step after another, her voice showing her fear. "Brother Ralakin came to me this—this afternoon, St. Willibald. I've been thinking over your—your offer, and I—"

"My what?"

"Your offer. Don't you remember—"

"Not particularly. But go ahead. Tell me about it."

"You wanted me to come here—to the temple, and my uncle, that's Edward Woodbridge, said that I should. But—" She kept looking at the brass door. "But I don't think I want to accept. You see—"

"What about Polberko?" Kozma interrupted.

"Paul Berko? I don't see what—"

"You don't see?" Kozma stopped advancing and pointed his cigar at her. She shrunk back. "You don't see? You've been with him, haven't you?"

"Yes, St. Willibald. He's been very—nice to me. We've had talks—"

"What about?"

"Nothing. Honest. We just chatted about this and that. I can't think of anything important. Just—this and that."

"Don't you know *who* he is?"

"Yes. Paul Berko. He's an act—"

"Don't play *me* for a fool, young lady! You know damn well who that beast is. He's *Nebiros!* Lucifer's agent! He's been using you. Don't you realize that as long as this man stays here every man, woman, and child is in peril? Don't you know that? And furthermore, don't you understand that I, St. Willibald, am trying to protect you from Nebiros?"

He started to pace the huge room, ignoring Anne completely, his speech rambling, his thick hair tumbling wildly over his brow. The shadows were closing in again.

"*Yahwe!* I am the Saint and I shall lead the way. I am the saviour. I shall bring evils to you in conjury and I shall expel them from your soul. I shall wield the sword of truth, of St. Willibald, shall slash through the cancers of sin. I shall purify ..."

He looked like a desperate man now, a trapped animal, pacing the room, his eyes glittering with madness. His voice rumbled, thick, black, sepulchral. He could hear voices in his mind, cheering voices louder than the moans of the damned. The dark waves were crashing. His hands were waving compulsively.

"I'm not a wizard! I'm a saint. But I know the powers of wizardry, of sorcery, of black magic, and I possess that power. What do they say? Those old fools of sorcery? That the devils that creep into the depths of man's soul to destroy cannot be beaten but must be sopped off, must be pacified with adoration and prayer and sacrifice? There's no worship to appease the evils, no way to solicit their good will. I know that! I'd fought them and beaten them! I ..."

Had he really? He couldn't remember. He stopped pacing, breathing hard, licking his voluptuous lips with short snakelike motions. He saw the girl before him, her eyes wide with terror, her mouth agape.

What was this all about? Where had he been? Why couldn't he collect his thoughts?

Then he suddenly remembered who the girl was. Anne Woodbridge. Of course. A slow smile spread across his face, not reaching his eyes, and he quickly snatched at a raven-black fold of her hair, twisting it cruelly and yanking her to his side. She made no sound. He twisted harder, pushing down until she was forced to her knees. She crumpled, her shoulders quivering with inaudible sobs.

"I remember you," he whispered. "Your father was an ugly man. A fool. And you're the true believer who didn't want to serve your beloved Saint. Your father's dead, isn't he? Ha?" He jerked her head viciously, yanking it back and forth. "What did Nebiros tell you? What have you told him about me? What's he up to? Enh? Answer me!"

He released her hair and she pitched forward. She had fainted. With a disgusted curse he went to his bed chamber and searched through the drawer in his study desk. Pushing aside an odd assortment of pamphlets, notebooks, boxes of narcotic pills and experimental philtres and potions, he drew out the small redwood box and opened the lid.

The beautifully compact hypodermic needle and glass capsules gleamed in the candlelight. He chuckled deep in his throat and carried the box back to the girl. He touched her wrist, lifted one eyelid. She was still out. Working quickly, he cracked a capsule end, plunged the needle through the rubber stop, filled the hypo. He had difficulty working the vein up. Finally, holding the vein fast with his pressed thumb, he stabbed the needle and pushed the whisky-colored liquid into her arm.

"We'll find out," he muttered softly. "Soon we'll know all about Polberko."

He replaced the kit in the drawer and locked it, then he returned to the girl and lifted her easily in his arms. He carried her into the bedroom. She fell like a limp doll across the four-poster. He lit a pile of incense in the huge bronze burner, then lit two more candles along the walls.

He stood at the foot of the bed, watching the girl, remembering his wanting her, but not being able to recall when that had been, how long ago. He went to the side of the bed, lit his gold lighter and held it in front of her face. No reaction. He slapped her cheek softly. Her eyelids fluttered. He slapped her harder and a moan escaped her lips. She tossed her head to one side, away from the light, and he hit her again. Harder.

Her eyes came open and she looked at him without recognition.

"Anne?"

Her voice was a bare whisper. "Yes?"

"Do you know me, Anne?"

"The—the Saint?"

"Yes. That's right. May I ask you a few harmless questions?"

"Yes."

"Do you know a man named Polberko?"

The eyelids fluttered again, slowly closing over the dilated pupils.

"Wake up, my dear. Force yourself. That's right." He kept his voice a persuasive purr, reassuring her, coaxing her without being pushy. His hands carefully stroked her pale cheeks. "That's it, dear. Open your eyes. You *do* want to talk, don't you?"

The voice, if possible, was even fainter. "Yes."

"Do you know a man named Polberko?"

"Yes."

"And where did you meet Polberko, Anne?"

"In the—the woods."

"The woods? That's right, Anne. You're doing very well. Now ... what was Polberko doing there?"

"He ... singing ... hair was wet."

"His head was wet?" Kozma lifted his brows. "Go on, dear."

"He was very ... funny ... he said he was a—a Fish-Beast."

Kozma pressed toward her impatiently, convinced that he was getting someplace finally. The flame from the lighter cast an orange circle over his face. "Go on. Go on, Anne! What else did he say to you?"

"That—that he was—Satan."

Kozma's mouth fell open.

Anne's lids fell and her nose twitched.

The incense was burning close to the bed, the plumes of spiced smoke gathering under the overhead canopy, clouding in thick blue layers.

"Anne? You're doing *very* well. Don't stop now, my dear. Open your eyes once more. That's it. Now look directly into the flame. Do you see it burning? Yes, you do. That's fine, very good. Keep watching the flame. Red, bright, burning into you. You can't close your eyes, can't look away from the flame. See, it moves its fiery mouth, flickering lips. The flame wants to know what Polberko said to you. He said that he was a Fish-Beast, that he was Satan. Now what else did he say, Anne? Try to remember, my dear. The flame *must* know."

"He said—that—Mr. O'Malley—that he had pink wings—a cigar—magic wand ... he said—he said—" Her words came more quickly as she recalled their first strange encounter. "He said that he was a—a child of others' destinies that he left Kozma's cottage because it was a cell that he sang Tipperary and missed Octobers that Octobers didn't act that Anne had been in The Retreat for six years ... that on a broom ... yes, that Jesus Christ was on a broom ... Anne was so pleased, more than with Isaac dead under the pine with Father lupines are wild ... Edward said!"

Tears formed in her eyes and streaked down her cheeks. She sucked in a quick, deep breath and squeezed her eyes shut. Then, letting air out slowly, the painful grimace fading, she turned on her side and said nothing more.

It was five minutes before she was breathing normally. She was out again and Kozma knew that to try again this soon would be useless. She would make even less sense if he forced her back now. He was going to have to keep her in his chambers, keep her doped up and on ice for a while until he decided what he should do with her.

He sat there, stunned. He still hadn't recovered. The word of The Fish-Beast, of Satan, of magic wings and blood, had shocked him deeply. It didn't entirely clear up the mystery of Polberko-Nebiros but it gave him a pretty good idea of what he was going to have to come against. He shuddered and the merciful shadows closed in; he remained on the bed for several long minutes, not seeing, not feeling.

Then, as he had before, he came back abruptly, almost painfully, and he jumped from the bed, a thin screech coming from his throat. His limbs shook, his eyes flashed, and with a violent swing he hurled his cigarette lighter at the full length mirror.

His image cracked, split, spun and twinkled. Glass starred in frosty slow-motion, shattered and collapsed in a hundred bright quicksilvered shards. Mirrored triangles, squares, and jagged splinters, winked, flashed, reflected a hundred leering Kozmas and scattered on the black carpet near the opened doorway.

CHAPTER TWELVE

The room was filled with blue smoke.

When Anne came to she opened her eyes and rolled to one side. For a slow second she didn't know where she was. Then she remembered. She had fainted when that madman had grabbed her hair. She tried to sit up now but she couldn't move. Her lungs were raw and aching, her senses dulled and unreliable, her head throbbing. The entire length of her right arm was sore and stiff. When she drew her legs in, attempting to sit again, twisting on the hot damp sheets, she realized that she was naked, her body wet with perspiration. Her robe was hanging on a statue at the far side of the room.

"You're very sick, Anne. You'd better lie still and try to go back to sleep."

A young girl was standing quietly at the side of the bed. Anne hadn't noticed her at first because the girl was standing behind a pale blue veil which was draped from the overhead canopy. It took Anne a minute before she recognized her. It was Isaac's sister, Sarah.

"Sarah!"

"Rest easy, Anne. Don't try to move."

She nodded obediently, a wave of relief sweeping over her. She felt sure that everything was going to be all right now. Sarah would help her. She tried to reach for her old friend, her hand brushing against the veil, but the effort proved too great and she sank back against the pillow.

Sarah's expression didn't change. Anne closed her eyes, blacking out again, exhausted, uncaring. Her breath sawed like fire in her breast and her limbs felt leaden and useless. Sudden nausea overcame her. Her vision blurred as if wet fur had been pressed over her eyes and she floated into the dark once more....

She had no way of telling how long she had been out this time. The room hadn't changed. The smoke was still there. She vacillated between her dream and the eerie reality of Kozma's private chambers.

A curious dream. She was walking up a gradual hill. The sky was overcast. Walking beside her, dressed in long gray robes, was a silent figure without a face. In the distance she saw another figure, dressed in black, walking slowly down the rugged track toward her.

She couldn't recognize the approaching figure and she experienced a moment of terrible panic. She wanted to run but she was afraid that she might insult the gray-robed, faceless figure with her. The lack of sky upset her. And further ahead there was fog, great bleak wisps of gray strung along the empty fields and rolling hills, whirling mist intestines. The sky grew darker. Lightning flashed overhead. Hot jagged needles in the black cauliflower clouds. She stopped when the black figure drew up to her. The gray figure said nothing. The black figure said, "Anne, the sky is falling. A piece of it just fell on my head."

Paul Berko! She moved into his arms and lifted her mouth to his, kissing him in a way she had never kissed before.

The gray figure started walking away. "That's okay, Annie honey, that's okay."

Her father.

"Let's find that nut Kozma," Paul said. "We've got to tell him that the sky is falling...."

Then she had opened her eyes, saw the hovering layers of incense smoke, and remembered Sarah Bridger. She wondered if that, too, had been but a part of her dream. Why hadn't Sarah helped her? Didn't she know that Anne had been drugged somehow by Kozma? Didn't she know that she was in trouble?

She turned expectantly but saw no one beyond the canopy veil. Her robe was gone from the statue. She moved her fingers slowly under the sheet and found that she was still naked. Inch by painful inch she managed to pull herself to a sitting position. She moved her tongue against her teeth, trying to work a little moisture to her parched lips. The sockets of her eyes burned cruelly and her arms ached as if they had been repeatedly struck with clubs. She had no idea of the nature of the drug that obviously had been administered to her. She didn't know why Kozma had done it or what he wanted from her.

She crawled from the bed, breathing heavily. It took more than ten minutes for her to make it to the far side of the room. There, great stone statues leered at her nakedness, reached out for her with taloned hands, laughed with merry fangs and forked dragon tongues. Candles swam before her. Something cold and sharp pierced the bottoms of her bare feet. She looked down. Broken glass was scattered on the carpet all about her. Her feet were bleeding, dropping bright little drops like liquid rose petals on the jagged pieces of mirror. She felt no pain.

She stepped as carefully as she could, avoiding the shards, and made it to the carved oaken door that led to Kozma's office. The ornate brass handle didn't budge. She started to slap on the panel, feebly, desperately pounding, trying to arouse someone in the office.

Minutes passed. The rhythmic hammering action of her fists grew weaker, arousing a small tingling recovery in her sense of touch. A thousand needles tatooed in her fingers, slowly working painful life back into her arms and shoulders. She sobbed, pounded harder, throwing her weight against the door.

An eternity later the lock clicked and the door swung open. Anne sagged against the wall, salty tears blotting her eyes, numb hands hanging limply at her sides.

"Go to bed," Sarah said softly, but insistently.

"I—I can't," Anne stammered. "I want to go. I don't want to be here."

Sarah's hand was firm, leading her back across the carpet of glass to the huge four-poster. "You have to sleep, Anne. You're very tired. Here. Now lie down."

"No, I—"

Sarah looked at her indifferently. Her voice was cold. "If you don't do as I say, Anne, I'll have to call the Saint."

Anne fell on the bed, too tired and resigned to argue further. The sheets became spotted with blood from her feet. She started to laugh with defeated hysteria. "The Saint! Sarah, how can you be such a fool? Sarah ... where have you been?"

"I've been here," Sarah answered. "With the Saint."

"You don't understand. He's mad. You've got to help me, Sarah. Please! I want to get away from here."

"Hush now! Hush, Anne."

It was useless. Sarah was probably drugged too. Anne shut her eyes and almost immediately felt herself drawing away. She half-heartedly tried to resist but it was no use. The last thing she remembered was Sarah's cool and gentle hands swabbing and bandaging her wounded feet. Then it was dark again.

CHAPTER THIRTEEN

"I think you'd better tell us what's been going on around here," Dolly said. "We've got a stake in this thing, too. The way I see it is that, so far, we've stood together while profiting so we may as well stand together if there's going to be a little trouble." She paused deliberately, watching Ralakin. "Why can't we see Carey? Why the hell isn't he here?"

Ralakin looked pained. He shrugged, ran his hand distractedly through his hair. He said nothing.

They were in Ralakin's office, just off the grand foyer. The sun was bright, reflecting from the polished floor and desk. It was a bright, sensibly furnished room, with typewriter, cabinets, guest chairs and IBM machines. Dolly was sitting in one of the larger chrome and leather chairs. Lemuel was too upset to take a chair. He was standing in the center of the room.

Lemuel didn't like it. Something was wrong. Ralakin was being too evasive, answering their questions reluctantly, not looking at them. Lemuel was worried. There was always the chance that Ralakin may have already crossed Carey and had made a deal with the ringer on his own. If that was true then Lemuel would have to try and make a counter-deal. There was too much at stake to quit.

"Let's quit running around, Rolly," Lem said. "What's been going on since I called? What's with this Polberko guy? Who is he? What's he after? And, like Dolly asked, why hasn't Carey shown up?"

It was a moment before Ralakin said that he didn't know, that, believe him, he was just as confused as they.

"Come off it. You're not dealing with aluminum-siding salesmen. Have you seen this Polberko or haven't you?"

"Of course I've seen him. But only once. And that was the first night."

"The first night?"

"Yes. He's still here."

"For two days? Goddammit, man, you'd better—"

Ralakin made a lame gesture, explaining, "He's here as Carey's ... special guest."

Dolly moved uncomfortably and cast Lem a look.

Lemuel regarded Ralakin with open suspicion. If he was going to play it this stupidly then Lem had no other choice. He decided to take a chance and throw up a little dirt to see which way the wind was blowing. After a moment, he said, slowly, "I don't believe you, kid. I'll lay my cards face up for you, Rolly. I think the ringer came up here and impressed you with what he knew and how much power and juice he had behind him. It's a shake-down, pure and simple. And you threw in with him because you know damn well that with Carey's present mental shape he won't be lasting much longer. You're in league with Polberko. I think that you're both go-ing to try and crack Carey, force him to puppet for you guys and divvy the take a little more evenly." He gave Ralakin a reassuring smile. "Come on. Level with me, kid. That's it, isn't it?"

Ralakin looked pained. "Lem," he sighed, "you've got a terribly dirty mind. I'm ashamed of you. How the hell can you think I'd do anything like that? It's preposterous. Why, I've been with Carey for—"

"You're breaking my heart," Dolly snorted.

"No, no," Ralakin protested. "It's not like that at all. I swear. I told you I don't know a damn thing about the ringer. I don't know *who* or *what* he is. I just don't know. Carey simply told me that *he* knew who the guy was and that he'd handle it his way."

"I don't believe you."

"But it's the truth. Jesus, Lem, why should I lie? If I wanted to squeeze Carey I sure wouldn't need the ringer, would I? Think about it a minute. I've got plenty on Carey. I admit it. I've never used it, have I? Why should I start now and split with a total stranger? Hell, if I wanted to cross Carey I'd probably come to ... well, you for instance, or Dolly here. I wouldn't need a stranger, would I?"

"How do I know he's a stranger to you?" Lem asked. "How do I know *you* didn't ring him in yourself?"

"Lem, you're horrible! You yourself said that only three people knew about your cloak and dagger routine with Martha Mason. Mason, Dolly, and yourself. I certainly didn't know about it. I hadn't seen you for weeks."

"Maybe you had my phone tapped."

Ralakin looked indignant. "Are you accusing me, Lem? Or are you just fishing?"

"I'm fishing," Lemuel confessed.

"Then you'd better pull in your line. I didn't tap your phone. I don't even know *how* to tap a phone. How do you tap a goddamn phone? Look, I've leveled with you. I don't know Polberko. I'm not crossing my boss. Not for the ringer, for you, or for myself. And you know that I'm speaking gospel, Lem. You know me well enough."

"You might be," Lem admitted. "Tell me then, Rolly, *why* is the guy still here?"

"I've told you. I-don't-know. I asked Carey how long he's going to be here and he said until Great Sunday. That's this Sunday. He said he's going to straighten it all out once and for all this Sunday. Now don't bother asking what he meant by that, because I don't know."

"All right," Dolly interrupted. "We'll take that at face value. Meanwhile, where's Carey?"

"I'm not sure. I think he's in his rooms. He's got a new girl with him, working her over. She was getting kind of cozy with Polberko and Carey wanted to get some new angle on the guy through her."

Lemuel thought about that for a minute. He asked a few more questions, learning a little about the girl, that she was a Kozmanite, that she had been seen fairly often with Polberko. He wasn't sure but it seemed to be an important piece of information and he filed it away. Then, casually, he asked after Carey's health. He was rewarded with a definite reaction. Just as he had figured. Ralakin grew evasive again.

"Quit lying, Rolly. Cards face up. Remember?"

Ralakin bit his lip, looked guilty. "Okay. Okay. I admit he's been acting strange."

"Explain it."

"Well ... it's the same as before, Lem. Only worse. But don't get me wrong," he added quickly. "He'll snap out of it. He's done it before. And he'll do it again. Don't go getting any ideas that the ship is sinking. Just because this guy Polberko comes up here and Carey asks him to be his guest. I'm sure he knows what he's doing. Right now it's tricky, but don't worry; he'll straighten out and we'll still be at the old stand, selling the same old bill of goods. Don't worry about it."

"Has he been coherent?"

"Partly."

"And you say he'll snap out of it."

"I'm sure of it," Ralakin said. "It'll all blow over."

Lemuel wasn't sure of it. Ralakin was scared. And Lem suspected that Ralakin felt the ship was sinking but, wanting to cover his bets, was holding on as long as possible in case the ship somehow righted itself. Lemuel, personally, doubted if it would. The smell of disaster was too strong about the place.

"Can you take Dolly to see Carey, Rolly?"

"I don't know how he'll act. He might blow up, and he might not."

"Give it a try, will you?"

Ralakin sighed. "I don't suppose you'll be satisfied until I do. All right. I'll give a try."

Lemuel looked pleased. "I'll wait outside. Both of us might upset him if he's in a seesaw mood."

Ralakin rose from behind the desk and opened the door to the foyer. Lem stayed behind to help Dolly from the big chair.

Her voice was quick and urgent, barely whispering. "Find him, Lem baby. Whatever lever he's got it's a dandy. He's got the whole joint rocking. Make a deal as fast as you can. Nothing under thirty-three percent. But start the haggle at fifty-fifty."

"Right."

"Are you coming?" Ralakin called from the foyer.

"I'm coming. Be patient with an old woman."

Lemuel waited at the main door until the two of them were out of sight. Then, moving quickly, he swung the door open, stepped outside and hurried down the stairs to the apron.

CHAPTER FOURTEEN

Paul lay back, exhausted, on the hard narrow cot, fully dressed, eyes closed, and tried to tell himself that just because Anne hadn't showed for their meeting that morning was no reason to be worried. But he wasn't being too successful. He sensed trouble in the air and it was too strong to ignore. Maybe he was making a fool of himself but he couldn't help it. He felt certain that if Anne could have met him she would have. But she hadn't. And the last time anyone had seen her was at ten that morning, heading toward the woods at the foot of the temple where their rendezvous bench was located.

At first he hadn't been too worried. After waiting in the woods for more than an hour he had gone to the cafeteria building near the tin-roofed farm sheds. He had been anxious and a little curious. It had been the first session of the lunch hour and there had been about three hundred people there, eating their sparse meals in absolute silence. The air had been heavy with food and farm smells—boiled meat and tea, damp earth and manure. He had drawn curious and hostile stares while he had strolled down the aisles, looking at the white-robed women and girls and black-robed men. He hadn't found Anne.

Returning to the woods he had followed the many winding footpaths, crossed the log bridges over the rushing brook, and had waited with growing concern and suspicion at the rendezvous bench. He had chain-smoked, hot, sticky, brushing away silvery insects, ignoring strolling Kozmanites who glowered at his suit and beardless face. The minutes had dragged by. Nothing. No sign. No one at her residence house had seen her. The foreman at the Publishing House had been the one who had told him that he had last seen her at ten, heading toward the woods.

He sat up now, found his cigarettes, and stretched out again on the cot. He couldn't stop wondering about what may have happened to prevent her from seeing him. He had thought that she had been enjoying their times together as much as he. Maybe she hadn't. Maybe she was just fooling around, amused by him for a while, and was no longer. But that didn't make sense, he argued. He was certain that she had been genuinely looking forward to seeing him for the third time.

It was quiet. The air in the cottage was muggy and unmoving. He was keyed up, his thoughts turned inward, and he didn't hear the door when it opened. Instead, he felt the faint breath of fresh air when it moved across his face. He opened his eyes and sat up.

A slight, sharp-looking little man was casually leaning against the door frame, regarding him with curious eyes. He was wearing a gray silk suit, black shirt, white necktie, and a smile like a used-car salesman.

Paul came up from the cot.

"Hello, chum. The name is Toomey. Lemuel J. Toomey."

"You going to sell me a car?"

The smile shifted uncertainly. "Beg your pardon?"

"Nothing. Forget it." Then he remembered where he had heard the name before. Lemuel Toomey. Kozma's contact man. More strange doings. But this time he might find out what was going on. After all he still wanted to learn about Martha Mason and possibly help his career. Wasn't that why he had become involved in the first place? He smiled affably and invited Lem into the room. "Anything I can do for you, Mr. Toomey?"

Lemuel winked. "Well, yes. You just *might* be able to help me, Mr. Polberko. There. You see, I knew your name. Honesty is always the best policy. Ha ha. And, speaking about helping one another, I *might* be able to help you as well."

Paul lit a cigarette, gestured Lemuel to the only chair in the room, then he filled the toothbrush glass with cold tap water and held it out to his guest. "Like a drink?" Lemuel shook his head. Paul drank the water, sat on the edge of the cot and faced the little man who was lighting an Egyptian cigarette and studying him with veiled eyes.

"So, Mr. Polberko, you think you can be some help to me."

"You're leading me. I didn't say that. You did. And where did you learn my name? From Kozma?"

"Nope. From Rolly. We were just discussing you."

"I don't know anyone named Rolly."

"Charley Ralakin," Lem explained.

"Ralakin? Yes, I know him. Sorry."

"No need to apologize. Why'd you ask?"

"Because my name isn't Polberko."

Lemuel's interest sharpened at that and he leaned forward, tugging on his white tie and smiling smugly. "It isn't? And what would your *real* name be, sir?"

"It's Paul Berko. Two names. Paul like in Muni, and Berko like in Berko."

Lem's smile faded and he appeared confused and disappointed. "Oh? Ah. Fine. Two names, enh? Yes, I see. My mistake."

Paul smiled. "You seem let down, Mr. Toomey. Were you expecting an alias?"

"Enh? No. Nothing like that." He sat straighter in the chair and assumed a brisk, business-like air. "I'm a man what likes the truth, Mr. Berko. I don't like haggling. I think you're being unnecessarily cagey."

"You do?"

"Now look, I asked you if you could help me. That's a decent lead, isn't it? We both know what we're talking about so why not be straight with each other. What do you say?"

"I'm willing. Get to the point."

Lemuel started to say something, then seemed to check himself. He shrugged, crossed his legs, and puffed slowly on his cigarette. "You ever work L.A. before, Berko?"

"Work it?"

"Why act dumb, kid?"

"Don't get tough."

"Sorry."

"You said we both know what we're talking about. I asked you to come to the point. What do we both know?"

Lem smiled nervously. "Well, we're ... ah, in the same racket. Right? I mean..." He held up an empty hand and winked.

"Are you a demon, too?"

"A D-Man? I don't get the phrase. You from New York?"

"Yes. Are you?"

"No. I'm from Seattle originally, you see I—wait a minute, Berko! Goddammit, quit giving me the runaround. Let's say we get down to business. I'll start. Why are you here?"

"Because I'm a guest. Why are you here?"

"Because. Because—because—"

"Okay. Forget it. No need to get red in the face."

Lem made an exasperated face and looked at the ceiling, sighing heavily. "Listen, Berko, I'm not here to kid around. I know you think you're in a good position and I grant you that. But there's always other wrinkles and maybe you don't know them all. I'm an old-timer. I know my way around and I've got the perfect cover once the crack in the wall shows. I quit selling the Brooklyn Bridge years before you were a glitter in your father's eye. You follow me?"

"So far."

"Good. How big is your outfit?"

"How big is yours?"

"What're you a psychiatrist, for chrissake? Do you always answer a question by asking another one?" He looked angry enough to spit at Paul. He bit his cigarette and glowered.

Enough of the sparring. Paul was becoming impatient "Make your pitch," he said.

Lem brightened. "Down to brass tacks, enh? No more ying-yang, Berko?"

"No more ying-yang, Toomey. You give me your pitch and I'll consider it."

"Fifty-fifty," Lemuel said quickly. "Right down the middle. Charley McCarthy. We fuse the two outfits and we crack it."

"Who's backing you? Kozma?"

"Unh? What're you talking about. It's Kozma we're cracking. Now look, don't let's get cagey again. We both understand each other. We're both after the same thing. We've made that clear so let's not backslide. I'm laying my cards down. Like I said, honesty pays. Now, me and Dolly have the connections. We have the in to lean on every sucker on those films. Right? Now you and your group have the lever to lean on Kozma, squeeze Rolly out, and take over the Kozmanism racket. So we work it together. Even Steven. You have the In, and we have the Out."

Paul sat, impassive, using the empty toothbrush glass for an ashtray. Lemuel was using his trouser cuff. Paul was getting the picture now. Toomey and someone named Dolly were trying to horn in on Kozma but they had no easy way to lay their hands on whatever it was they needed. They had to have a way to get Kozma in the middle of their palms. And they thought that he, Paul, knew of that way.

"You mentioned the films," Paul prompted.

"Yes. There's that and the books as well."

"Who did you say was with you?"

"Dolly Bosco."

Paul was surprised. He knew of the woman. She was one of those "friend of the stars," a party-goer and party-giver, one of those semi-legendary old bitches who had, for some inexplicable reason, fantastic power and influence over the powerful and influential. Dolly Bosco? Why the hell not. The whole thing reeked of names. And Paul had stumbled right into the middle of it.

After a moment he said, "Fifty-fifty seems pretty steep. Do you think you and Dolly could act without my help? I *know* I can get what I want without your help. So what makes you two so indispensable?"

"I don't think you understand the greater picture, Berko. Of course we can act without you. The same as you without us. Don't let your position go to your head. We can try and squeeze you out, make our own play, but if we do it the way I offered it'll make it easier on all of us in the long run. There's plenty to go around and there's no sense in making hogs of ourselves."

"I can blow the whistle," Paul suggested.

"To Kozma? You wouldn't do that, kid. You're smarter than that or I'm a bad judge of my characters. What would be the profit? You'd screw yourself by giving away your cover. You see my point? Your lever here would be kicked out and we'd all be out in the cold."

"My lever, enh?" Paul smiled at that. Too bad that during his varied summer-stock and drama-school days he hadn't played a con-man. He could use the dialogue right now. As it was he had to content himself with talking a little like Sheldon Leonard. "You don't know what my lever is, Toomey. Maybe that, and my cover here, is the kind that can't get kicked out. Maybe I've got Kozma too well."

"Okay. That might be. Although I doubt it. But that isn't my whole argument. Do you have the cover and contact set-up that we do for the films? How can you approach millionaires like Ed Tobias, Kincaid, Iry MacLean, Martha Mason? Take Tobias or MacLean for instance. If you don't have the cover then guys like those two would simply hire a couple of close-mouthed goons to squeeze you hard until every bit of information and film footage came spurting out of you like so much toothpaste. Believe me, chum, it wouldn't be the first time that something like that happened to an ill-prepared blackmailer. I know what I'm talking about. I've known a couple of good boys who were never heard of again after they tried to lean on people like Tobias or MacLean."

Paul had difficulty in following it all. He nodded, "All right. So what are *your* outlets? Your cover?"

"Dolly Bosco. Quite simple, enh? And you'll have to admit that she's the perfect middleman for a set-up as delicate as this. She can contact those people as their close friend, saying that she's acting as Kozma's agent, even though she's horrified, *absolutely* horrified. Old Dolly would be a confidante and helper, not a blackmailer. Follow me?"

"Yes. But fifty-fifty still seems high. Come down a bit and I'll think it over."

"I won't come down one percent, Berko. And I'll tell you why. You're strapped without us, and you know it. If you weren't you would have thrown me out on my first offer ten minutes ago. But you didn't. So you need us. Just like we can use you. I see it this way. You can crack the Kozmanism racket. Carey's got maybe a million stashed out of Federal eyes, but a million isn't the real pay-off. The films are. If we get the books we get only the Kozmanism angle. But with the films we also control some of the richest perverts in the state. You're shooting for Kozma and the racket because you can handle it. We're shooting for the films because we know we can handle them. But we need the Kozma front. And I know you'd like to share in the dough, too. Why reach for peanuts, enh, Berko?"

"You make it sound pretty good."

"Fifty percent of the blackmail pay-off alone will match the Kozmanism pay-off."

Paul nodded. "I'll think it over."

"Swell. You ask your outfit and if they like it—"

"I don't have an outfit. I'm all by myself."

Lemuel stared at him. "You kidding me? What about your inside girl?"

"What inside girl?"

Lemuel shrugged. "I was told that you'd been using an insider. A girl."

A suspicion nudged him and he had difficulty keeping his voice calm. "What else did you hear about the girl? Did you happen to hear her name, anything like that?"

"It was Anne something."

Paul stared at him.

Lemuel grinned. "So you *were* working with the chick."

"What else did you hear!"

"Don't be impatient, Berko. She's in the temple. All I heard was that Carey wanted to get a line on you through—"

"Who's Carey!"

"Carey Ledbetter. That's Zedek Kozma to you."

Paul stood up. His eyes were like wet pebbles. His hands were shaking. Lemuel jumped up, bouncing like a jerked puppet, and hurriedly laid a restraining hand on his shoulder.

"Wait a minute. Don't be heroic. I gather you dig the frail, Berko. All right. But I wouldn't go running into the temple to pull an errolflynn until Carey's high on his pills and the place is a little more quiet. There isn't any profit in getting caught in there. You act hasty now and you might blow the whole deal. The girl's all right. I know Carey and I know how far he'll go. So relax. Take it easy."

"You know your way around in there?" Paul asked flatly.

"Pretty much. Now listen, Rolly's throwing a small dinner tonight and I think you're supposed to be there. Okay. When it's the *right* time you can scoop up the frail and meet me and Dolly back here."

The little man was right. He would have to wait until it was dark.

"Sit down, Berko. Carey'll just ask her a few questions for the time being. That's all."

Paul sat, feeling hollow inside.

Lemuel tried to change the subject. "Let me ask you a question, Berko. How did you know about the carnation and newspaper bit? I was there, right in front of Chernery's when you stepped up and nosed me out."

Toomey's question rattled around in his brain. He answered almost automatically, "Martha Mason."

"You had her phone tapped?"

"Yeah."

"You were getting a line on her junk habit, unh?"

"Sure."

Lemuel rubbed his hands together. "Okay, what's your lever here?"

"I haven't agreed to the deal yet. I'd said I'll think it over. I'll let you know as soon as I can. And then I'll let you know my lever."

"Well, you have only until Great Sunday, you know."

"Why's that?"

"According to Rolly that's when Carey says he's going to straighten you out once and for all. He also says he's onto you, knows who you are and all that. But I know that Rolly was lying through his teeth when he said that. He's scared and he's hanging onto the ropes. Carey's going whacky and he knows it. And once Carey's completely nuts the whole racket withers and dies. Carey's the heart and soul of it. I've seen things like this blow up before. And each time it was because the hypnotizer either dies or he goes Dixie with the kitty. That's one reason why the books alone aren't as important as the films. The racket here can flop any minute. But the films have that sweet smell of everlasting coin. Follow me?"

Paul nodded. He was still thinking of Anne. They sat there for a few min-

utes longer, telling each other O. Henry type anecdotes, then Toomey
rose, shook Paul's hand warmly, and said, "You're a clever guy, Berko. Glad
to have done business with you. Glad to have you on our side. Well, back
to the old temple. See you at dinner." He winked again. "We'll make our
play tonight, pal. Don't worry about a thing. You handle Carey and we'll
handle the books and films."

Paul stood by the window and watched as the little con-man left, whistling
and striding jauntily up the pine-shaded footpath.

Things were, to put it mildly, growing complicated. It was big. The patterns emerging on either side of him seemed to be totally unaware of each
other. There was Toomey and his mistaking Paul for a fellow con-man. And
there was Kozma and his mistaking him for Nebiros, an agent of Lucifer
who was, Paul had decided, supposedly there to war with St. Willibald.

It was too much. All of it.

Martha Mason was a junkie. Kozma had blackmail films of big-shot millionaires. Dolly and Toomey, the bunco-steerers of the racket, had had
Martha Mason as their last victim. And enter Paul Berko. Kozma was going off his rocker. And Paul, or Nebiros, or a con-man, was caught in the
middle.

Meanwhile, all he gave a damn about was Anne Woodbridge and a decent
part in a picture.

Anne was there, caught deep inside him. He could taste her, see her, feel
her there. Warm and gentle, beautiful and very real. She was the third one
to be there. The first had been a girl named Ballinger (he couldn't remember her first name) and she had been fifteen to his sixteen. Then, when he
had been twenty-four, there had been Tina, an actress who had been able
to speak nine languages. Now Anne Woodbridge was there. Strong. Along
with the rest of the gay confusion of the past few days. Kozma, Ralakin,
Lemuel, Bosco, Mason, and of course ... Nebiros.

CHAPTER FIFTEEN

Dinner that evening, though it was small and without occasion, was a
dressy affair. Carlo came to the cottage with a black velvet robe for Paul. He
explained, in his halting, sand-papery way, that the other guests, Lemuel,
Dolly Bosco, Ralakin, and a girl named Sarah, would be similarly dressed.
"And the Saint, he seems to be in a kind of nice mood," Carlo added.

"Isn't he always?"

"No, not always." He sounded sad. "You know, lately he shouts pretty much."

"I suppose he has his little everyday problems just like everyone else."

Dusk was gathering when they left the cottage. It was a warm night. The great canyon was gradually filling with long purple shadows, and the sky, above the black cliff outline, was deepening from shrimp to boiled lobster.

"Are you sure everyone's going to be rigged out in robes like this, Carlo?"

"Yeah, Mr. Polberko. When the Saint has people eat with him he always gets 'em dressed up. Every time. You look kinda good."

"Thanks. That's very reassuring."

The dining room was a vast baronial hall, half demonist, half religious. There were statues and a large walk-in fireplace. Wall chandeliers were spaced here and there, the bulbs turned low. Glass shrubbery full of lightning bugs. On the long table there were candles. A medieval scene. The largest chair, Kozma's, which was at the head of the table, was conspicuously empty. Ralakin looked unhappy. When he saw Paul he greeted him only half-heartedly and quickly placed him at the far end of the table, between Lemuel Toomey and a glassy-eyed girl Paul assumed was the Sarah that Carlo had mentioned.

"Where's our host?" he asked Lemuel.

"Search me. That is if you can find any pockets in this robe. Try the wine, Berko. I think they spiked it with vodka."

Ralakin rose and clapped his hands lightly. All heads turned to hear him.

"I guess that Car—the Saint is—will be late. Accept my apologies in his place. Later, maybe, we'll be—ah, graced with his presence. Right now he's not feeling—too well."

No one said anything to that and Ralakin sat down edgily, looking none too well himself. The dinner started on that curious note, the atmosphere artificial and stiff. However, when the wine pitchers were filled again, the talk resumed.

Lemuel nudged Paul.

"What do you make of it, chum?"

Paul shrugged. "Maybe a demon gobbled him up. I don't know. And I don't care. I think you're right, Toomey. The wine is spiked with vodka."

A pair of young boys came into the hall and settled in one of the dark corners. Then, during the entire meal, they played an eerie duet on a harp and reed flute. And again Paul was impressed by the obvious display of fantasy. If, at the moment, someone were to charge breathlessly into the room and shout, "My Liege, Robin Hood is attacking!" he wouldn't be surprised in the slightest. The entire scene was, like most of the goings on in the temple, childishly incredible.

While he was working on his egg and abalone soup Dolly Bosco caught his eye and treated him with what seemed to be a conspiratorial wink. It looked like two white snails kissing. He smiled back and playfully wriggled his fingers at her.

There was little talk then. With Kozma's absence the occasion of the get-together seemed pointless. Ralakin looked more unhappy. Carlo kept serving the dishes. Duck, roast beef, salmon, salads, and heaping bowls of iced shell fishes. There was, however, no roast pig with apple. Paul felt a bit let down. There were no jugglers either, or minstrels, or Afghan hounds on chains. The glassy-eyed girl didn't eat. She only drank and occasionally blinked her big vacant eyes.

"You see that back door there," Lemuel whispered. "When we break up and sneak back that's the one we'll take. You go get your girl Friday back and I'll go snoop around and see what I can find. Where you get your bearings is by the big centaur tapestry. Once you see it you can't miss it. You turn left at the tapestry, then take a half right. As I recall, just across from Carey's door there's a big painting of some character hanging upside down."

"I remember the painting," Paul said. "But there seemed to be about fifty twists and turns before you get to it."

"Illusion, Berko. Sheer Carey Ledbetter carnival trickery. You find that tapestry, turn left, then half right. Bear toward the center of the building to find the tapestry. But don't get lost or you'll be in there for hours trying to find your way out."

Ralakin was busy talking to Dolly at the other end of the long table. He seemed to be unloading his worries onto her and she was leading him on. Paul pulled his chair closer to Lem.

"Where will you be?"

"Downstairs. There's a party room I want to give the once over to."

The harp and reed flute fluttered and whistled in the gloomy room, the candles flickered on the table, Carlo came and filled the wine pitchers for a third time. There was no further mention of Kozma's strange absence.

It was easier than he had imagined. Ralakin had asked Carlo to see that Lemuel and Paul were escorted back to their respective cottages. But once outside Lemuel told him that it wouldn't be necessary. "Hell, Carlo, we'll find our way all right. And listen, don't forget to tell Rolly that it was really a great meal. Best food I've had in years."

Carlo nodded and lumbered off, looking pleased. Paul and Lemuel waited until he was out of sight then crept back up the stairs to the temple. From the front window they saw the square of yellowish light from Ralakin's office where Dolly was keeping him busy with more wine and sympathy. She had told Lem that she would remain there for at least twenty minutes more, then would return to her cottage and wait for them there.

The door opened before them and they slipped quietly inside. Lemuel's robes fluttered before Paul as they glided across the marble floor to the dining hall. They saw nothing and heard nothing. The rich food odors still lingered in the darkness of the hall. And as they moved past the now empty table Paul remarked to himself how fantastic his being there was. He wasn't nervous at all. It was, in fact, just like being in a B-movie.

He moved on, passing through the black door and entering a long, dimly lit corridor. Lemuel led the way, his shoes barely sounding on the flooring. Moving cautiously still, staying close to the wall, their backs brushed against heavy picture frames, candle stands, and hanging tapestries. When they came to a fork in the hall Lemuel stopped, quickly pressed his hand on Paul's arm and winked. Paul smiled a smile he hoped said good luck. Toomey took to the right and a moment later Paul was alone.

He stood there pressed against the wall and listening for Lemuel's footsteps. He heard nothing. For a brief, nagging moment he had an urge to turn around and chuck the whole ridiculous affair. Then he thought of Kozma and Anne and the thought quickly left him. He wouldn't leave a mad dog with that old charlatan, much less a young girl, much less a young girl that he suspected he cared for more than the someone Ballinger and the linguistic actress.

Continuing down the hall, he passed one closed door after another. Finally, he paused and investigated one of them, running his hands along the frame. He was surprised to discover that the door wasn't a door at all but a cleverly carved fake. The handle was stationary and when he pressed his face close to the crack between the panel and frame he felt no passing of air on his lips. Further down he found more fake doors, then arches that led to dead-ends, awnings that protected nothing, and arched windows that looked out at bare walls.

He thought he found the tapestry but the lead-off corridor proved a dead end. He backtracked and came out on the corridor again. It was like moving through a house of mirrors—only without the mirrors. Occasionally there was a candle burning on a stand, or a rack of votive lights. After five minutes more of searching each frustrating false passage, he came to the centaur tapestry and found the right passage.

At the same time, almost directly under Kozma's rooms, Lemuel was entering the party room.

The room was pitch dark and he had to light one of the alcove candles and carry it with him. Moving across the floor he felt the back of his neck suddenly tingle. A warning. He had that unnerving sensation that he was being watched. He stopped and stood perfectly still. The suspicion grew stronger and he felt cold all over. Slowly, stiffly, he held the candle high and gazed all about him. He saw nothing. Just the moody shadows, alcove curtains, and huge rosewood statues of demons. He shuddered, reprimanded himself for being childish, and forced the feeling away from him. He relaxed a little, but he wished now that he had had enough sense to have brought a pistol with him. He doubted if he could ever shoot it, since he had never handled a gun in his life, but just having it, he felt, would help his nerves considerably. He found a heavy bronze candlestick, thickly encrusted with wax droppings, and carried that with him instead.

He entered one of the alcoves. Carefully, missing nothing, he went over the entire room. Nothing. He moved to the next alcove, then to the next. He was sure that there was some way to make films in the rooms, so there had to be something each and every alcove had in common. So far there was only the carvings on the rear walls. He fixed his candle on the wall and ran his fingers carefully over the leering faces, flowers, tendrils, stars, and half moons. Nothing. He pressed them, pulled on them, pushed at them. It wasn't until he shook the protruding pieces that he finally found what he was looking for. The lumpy nose on one of the faces shifted very slightly.

Jamming the heel of his palm against the nose he put his weight to it and pushed. A moment later there was a snicking noise and the nose broke away from the tiny steel hinges. He bent, peering into the three-inch hole, lowering his candle for a better look.

A cold, dark eye stared back at him.

He shrieked, jumped back and dropped the candle. His heart fluttered wildly and his entire body broke into a cold sweat. He grabbed for the candle and bronze stick and pushed free of the gauzy curtain. It wasn't until he was halfway across the length of the floor that he remembered himself and chuckled.

Certainly that eye had been familiar. And why not? It had been his own! There was a mirror there, most likely a two-way. He returned to the alcove, still shaky but chuckling edgily over his unreasonable flight, and investigated the mirror a second time. Then it was obvious. An infra-red camera and two-way mirror. A perfect set-up. He tried two more alcoves and in the nose of each face he found a mirror.

Smiling his satisfaction he proceeded to systematically search for the door which would lead him to the secret passage. He was excited. The films,

the books, and quite possibly a large cache of cash, were probably somewhere in the passages beyond the walls.

He went over the whole place, quickly but not missing a thing. He no
longer had that feeling of being watched. He held the flame to each con-
ceivable place where a passage could be concealed. The flame didn't flicker
once. Swearing softly, he left the party room and tried the panels in the corridor. It took him ten minutes of patient searching before he saw the flame
quiver. There was a draft. He stroked the wood until he found a tiny irreg-
ularity in the frame. He pressed it, then turned it, and a panel slid open. He
slipped through and closed the door after him.

The air was close, dry smelling. Fifty-fifty, he kept thinking. For more
than a half century Lemuel J. Toomey had been seeking the end of the rainbow. Once, when he had been a boy, someone had asked him what he
wanted out of life, and he had promptly answered, "I want to be everything
that the rest of you ain't!" He smiled to himself, moved through the passages, turned corners, and finally came upon a flight of stone steps that led
up to the next floor.

The end of the rainbow. He found it. A chain hanging from the ceiling
turned on a small naked bulb and bathed the room in an unhealthy yellow
glow. He blew out the candle and knelt before the stack of round film cans.
He ran his fingers over them lovingly. For some queer reason he remembered, for a fleeting moment, the dark-haired, almond-eyed, Oriental-
looking girl with the amazing bust. Then he started to look at the cans. He
saw that they were not only marked by date and reel footage but with the
participants. There was also a desk, a common oak affair, against the far wall.
He moved to it and hurriedly tried the drawers. They were locked. He pried
them open with his candlestick head. There were books, hundreds of them,
statements, checks, entries into an account in Switzerland under the name
of Albert Z. Carré.

Jackpot. Rainbow. He set the books aside and started for another drawer.
Then, without hearing a sound or seeing a shadow, he knew that someone
was standing behind him, watching him. The back of his neck tightened and
his mouth went suddenly dry. He didn't turn. Moving jerkily, he pretended to reach into the next drawer, then he lunged for the bronze candlestick.

He didn't make it.

Hands whipped out and locked around his throat. Powerful hands, black,
with fingers like steel. Lemuel jerked and was forced to his knees. He could
feel his tongue stiffening in his throat, the blood hammering frantically in
his temples. He tried to shout, to squirm around, to wrench the hands from

his throat, but he was powerless. His eyes bulged, his vision swam crazily.
Not Lemuel J. Toomey! It couldn't be! He screamed silently, kicked
wildly out with his feet, striking the tripod of the camera.

When the camera fell and struck the stack of metal film cans he didn't hear
the terrible noise they made. The pounding blood in his ears was too great.

It took a few seconds more. Then he was dead. His body, looking much
smaller now in death, sagged to the floor. A voice whispered in the now
quiet room.

"Faber est quisque fortune suae...."

CHAPTER SIXTEEN

Anne had been awake for the past hour.

When she first tried to move, testing herself, she found that, this time, she
had sufficient strength to stagger from the bed, rummage Kozma's closet,
clothe herself in a large black robe and tie it at the waist with a sash from the
four-poster. Then she had to rest. She was pale and trembling, still terribly
weak. But her thoughts were clearer and when she moved she no longer
ached as before. She took a few steps, fought down a wave of nausea and an
urge to go back to bed, then started walking, determined to wear away the
effects of the drug by pacing the length of the room, back and forth.

For the first twenty minutes she was foggy and plodding but gradually she
felt herself becoming stronger. Clumsily, one foot would follow another,
then the wall, turn about, then more steps. She started to count in time with
herself. She hummed snatches from old Biblical songs, quoted prayers
aloud, and started to plan. She felt that once she was normal again an opportunity of escape would somehow present itself. She had to be ready for
it. She went on, walking away the minutes from one wall to another, avoiding the broken pieces of mirror, growing more confident with each step.

When she first heard the sound she jumped back as if someone had suddenly touched her.

Curious. There had been a crash, followed by a muffled clattering, then
silence. She stared curiously at the panel where the mirror had been. The
sound had seemed to come from behind the panel. She moved closer. Putting her cheek to the wood she listened, hearing vague, thumping noises, ac-
tive at first, then becoming slower, then complete silence. She waited a few
minutes, barely breathing, straining to hear more. She pressed herself
closer.

The panel squeaked and shifted slightly on a center hinge. Then it swung open, revealing a square of darkness, a passage, a slow waft of dry, stale air. She made no move. Then, after waiting five full minutes, hearing nothing more, positive that the passage was now empty, desperate enough to try anything that could possibly lead her from Kozma's room, she entered the passage and silently, slowly, moved into the darkness. There seemed to be a gradual slope to the floor and she ran her hands lightly on the rough sides of the wall as a guide. She went about five yards. Then her left hand sunk into an opening and she stopped. Feeling along the one side she decided that the entrance was either to a room or another passage. Moving blindly, arms held before her, she passed through the entrance and groped in the dark. She wished now that she had brought a candle from the room. The air was cooler now but the darkness was like a weight pressing on her. She moved a little further in, scuffling her feet. Then her fingers brushed a chain. A light. She pulled the chain and the overhead bulb bathed the room in a sickly yellow glow.

Then she screamed. Froze. Sucked in her breath.

The grotesque mask of the strangled man gaped up at her from the bare concrete floor. His ugly popped eyes were filmed, looking like fat, peeled grapes. His purplish tongue was projecting from his lips, which were twisted in a horrible smile. His neck was blotched with deep red marks.

Anne moved back a step, mechanical, stiff, cold, then another. The shock took a long minute to be pushed aside by blind panic. She shuddered and that seemed to bring her back to life. She was mesmerized, unable to look away from the face of the dead man. She kept backing away.

Then the hands reached from behind her and she screamed again.

A hell of a note, Paul was thinking. He had been hammering on the brass door, with no success, for the past fifteen minutes. He hammered with his fists, kicked with his shoes. He no longer cared about the noise he was making, no longer cared if they did hear him. The girl was in there somewhere, probably being pushed around, certainly being questioned, and all because she had talked to him. A lousy reason to be hung up for. He had a vague idea of finding her, slugging Kozma, and leaving the place. He hammered again, gave a final, angry kick, then stood back and glared at the door.

He started for the other corridor again, thinking that he may have overlooked something before, that possibly the phony door there wasn't phony.

He turned the corner and stopped a few feet in the passage.

"May I help you, Polberko?"

Kozma was in the center of the corridor, looking haggard, terribly aged.

His brunette pompadour was a dusty tangle over his brow. His shoulders seemed bent. His breath was heavy, his black olive eyes unmoving, dull, and curiously detached.

He was also holding a .45 automatic in his velvet gloved hand, and it was aimed directly at Paul's stomach.

"Were you going somewhere, Polberko?"

He couldn't take his eyes away from the gun. His smile felt phony on his lips and his voice seemed, even to him, unnatural and squeaky. "I was just looking for one of your guests, Doctor. Lemuel Toomey. You see we were drinking pretty heavy at dinner and he must have wandered off. I just thought I'd take a quick look for him. And I must have got a little lost...."

Kozma continued to gaze dully at him. His eyes admitted neither belief nor disbelief. And the gun didn't waver. "I understand, Polberko," he said. "Very kind of you to be so concerned. But you can turn around and leave now." A brief flutter on his full lips. "I'm sure that both of us have much to prepare before our final encounter this Great Sunday. Good night."

"But—"

"Good night, Mr. Polberko. You can quit worrying. I've already seen to Mr. Toomey."

He could think of nothing else to say. He had never had a gun pointed at him before. He had had his turn at barroom brawling, using bottles and an occasional stool; once a drunken kid had threatened him with a hunting knife. But no guns. Guns were something else. In the Army he had been the lousiest shot in the outfit. Guns, banging, aiming, the whole routine, left him cold. And right now he felt like ice. He gave Kozma his best smile and did as he was ordered. He turned and started walking, aware all the while of the .45 trained on his back.

Coming upon the first turn in the corridor he quickened his step as much as he could without feeling ashamed of himself and he hurried out of the temple. The cold night air hit him and he became aware of how great a sweat he was in. He stood for a while on the apron, the failure of his mission nagging him. The stars were bright overhead, the moon like wax, the trees blacker than the sky. The honeymoon, it seemed, was over. Kozma was no longer playing games. From here on in the party was going to get rough.

Cursing, he thought of Anne still back there. What was she to him? Why should he stick his neck in Kozma's damn cannon for her? It was stupid. He had only talked to her a few times. That was all. And now he couldn't even pull a decent errolflynn without bungling it. He felt like an ass, standing on the apron, looking at the stars and trees, and thinking about Kozma's .45 and

Anne Woodbridge's soft voice. He was angry. He didn't like being pushed around. And, his voices deep inside reminded him, when a girl, a toy, just about anything, was denied him it made the game all the more interesting. He would be going back in the temple sooner or later. He knew it. And the hell with the guns and the blackmail and the cheap mysteries.

And Anne wasn't all of it. What about Lemuel Toomey? What the devil had Kozma meant when he had said that he had already taken care of Mr. Toomey?

He kicked at the gravel, made a frustrated scowl, then turned down the path to Dolly Bosco's cottage.

Dolly was worried.

"What the hell happened in there? It took you guys long—where's Lem? Isn't he with you?"

"No. I don't know where he is."

"But—"

He flopped in an overstuffed chair and quickly reviewed what had happened. She clucked sympathy for his "girl Friday," widened her eyes at Kozma's behavior, then worried some more over Lem. Seeing her now, watching her, Paul could feel no revulsion, knowing that she was a black-mailer and seducer. He saw her as a beat-up little old lady worrying about a friend. There was something sad about her.

"Don't worry, Miss Bosco. I'm sure Lem's okay. If anyone can take care of himself it's that little character."

That seemed to help some; she sniffed and said, "Isn't that the truth? Lem's very resourceful. You've got to get to know him better. He's not really a crook, at least not in the way that most people think of crooks. Pushing grapefruit in girls' faces, things like that. No, Lem's really nice. You know, in my day I've known many bunco boys but there's no one, not one mind you, that plays it as straight with a friend as Lem. And he's sweet, too. He's always very sweet to me." She bit her lip and looked at her lap. Paul wondered if the old girl wasn't, in some weird way, in love with the little con man. She made a distraught face and sighed. "I hope he's all right. If anything happened to him I'd—I'd never be able to forgive myself."

"He'll be all right," Paul repeated. He was feeling a little foolish. "It's my girl Friday that I'm worried about."

Dolly shook her head. "Don't be. If Carey thinks he can get a line on you through her then he won't lay a finger on her. He'll just hold her for a while and then let her go."

"I hope you're right."

She went to her suitcase and opened it. "I brought a few bottles of liquor with me, Mr. Berko. Would you be so kind as to pour me a little ginger ale? There's an opener in that little pocket with the toothbrush sticking out of it."

"Sure."

"There's a bottle of bourbon there, too. Lem always drinks bourbon. Help yourself to a drink if you want. We might as well sit here and be the cheery little lights in the window until Lem gets back."

Paul made the drinks and they sat, making themselves as comfortable as possible. The bourbon was pretty good and he drank it with only a little water. They sat for a half hour, speaking very little, both deep in their studies, concentrating on their drinks and their problems. Paul was still feeling bad about having goofed his rescue scene in the temple. He was beginning to feel ashamed of himself. He should have given Kozma the Alan Ladd, the old one two punch. The bourbon warmed him and he propped his legs up on Dolly's suitcase.

Dolly finally broke the silence.

"I don't think he'll be coming."

"He'll come," Paul said. He didn't believe that but he couldn't think of any way of saying it. "He'll be bouncing in here with a big tale to tell us."

"I hope so. I don't like just sitting here and worrying. I keep thinking of what you told me. About Kozma saying he had taken care of Mr. Toomey. It had an ominous sound to it. As though he had knocked him out and tied him up."

"He might have meant that. But I wouldn't worry about it. We'll get him out of there before Sunday."

She bit her lip again, not liking the idea of keeping Lem in there for so long. She filled her glass with ginger ale, then poured Paul another drink.

"I've been meaning to ask you, Miss Bosco. What do you know of this Great Sunday thing? Have you ever seen one?"

"I saw the last one. Why?"

"Tell me about it."

"Haven't you ever read about them? For a while, oh, maybe two or three years ago, the reporters used to write them up. For the Sunday supplements. Like the La Brea tarpits or the cement rituals at Grauman's. No? Well it's pretty simple. Carey's always been a good one for putting on a show. Great Sunday is his pet idea, a kind of hangover from his burlyque days in Frisco."

"What does he do? Show naked chicks?"

"No. Not any more. He leads his followers up into the hills, to the top of the cliffs. He has a platform up there, sort of like a stage, built out of stone.

There's a lovely view of the whole canyon from up there. Like being on Mount Olympus, or something. I think that was what he had in mind. It would be just like him.

"Anyway, all the Kozmanites gather up there and they sing and pray. It's impressive. They carry candles in little cups and the whole hillside looks like a church or something. Thousands of people with their little lights. Carey, Rolly, Carlo, and a couple of the regular Kozmanites, holy people I guess he calls them, sit up on the platform and lead the prayers. Carey gets all dressed up in his fanciest robes and gives long talks and prayers. They have a microphone outfit up there so everyone can hear him.

"He's supposed to be calling the devil, or something like that. They light flares and big pots of things that make smoke. It's like a religious fourth of July."

Paul nodded. "And of course the devil doesn't show up."

Dolly chuckled. "That's part of his hustle. Carey asks the devil to come and take him away. He's supposed to be so good that the devil can never get him. And naturally the devil never shows up and Carey never gets caught. You should hear the Kozmanites talk about that! It's funny about people. It's so easy to hustle them. The world is the hustler's oyster. That's what Lem always says."

They had another drink. It took time in coming, but when the thought first occurred to him he almost laughed aloud, then, the more he thought of it, the sounder it seemed. Kozma had been right. There was a great deal for him to prepare before their encounter on Great Sunday. A tremendous joke. The idea took shape and he started to mentally elaborate on it. There were a few kinks but he would work those out as he came to them. He started to chuckle and when Dolly gave him a funny look he shrugged and subsided to a self-satisfied smile.

CHAPTER SEVENTEEN

They slept until noon the next day. Dolly woke, half sprawled on the hard cot, and squinted at the light. Outside the leaves of the trees were shining like green coins and there were great sprawling shadows along the mulchy ground. A pair of chipmunks were on the window sill, chattering and waving their feathery tails. Paul roused himself from the overstuffed chair and the half full bottle of bourbon rolled from his lap. His black velvet robe was badly wrinkled. He moved slowly, carefully, remembering the all night vigil

with Dolly. Lem hadn't showed and they had finally dozed off. He went to
the corner basin and splashed water on his face and neck. His mouth tasted
of stale bourbon and his eyes, when he peered into the small mirror, were
grainy and reddish. When he finished washing he sank back in the chair and
made a sour face. Dolly came to life and looked around her as though she
half-expected to find Lem hiding in one of the corners of the room.

Her voice was husky, cracked. "Maybe he's in his cottage," she offered.
"It was kind of late and maybe ..."

"I'll go check and see."

"Yes, please—"

He didn't hear the rest of it. Like a drugged man he went down the path
to Lemuel's cabin, which was several yards from his own. He pounded on
the door. No answer. He turned the knob and entered. The cot hadn't been
used; Lem's one piece of luggage was still sitting near the pillow. Paul tried
his own cottage, found no note or any sign of anyone having been there, then
he plodded back up the slope to Dolly's cottage.

She was out of her Kozma robe now and wearing a flowery wrap-around
with a feather boa collar. She looked at him anxiously, frowning, holding the
wrap closed at her waist.

"Nothing," Paul reported glumly.

"Jesus," she swore softly. She sagged down on the edge of the cot and
stared at her lap, her voice coming in sad little gasps. "I know something is
terribly wrong. I can feel it. He's in there, all tied up like a kidnapped kid.
I'll bet he was hit on the head and he's bleeding. Jesus. Poor Lem. So sweet
to everybody. Maybe—" her eyes grew wild, "—maybe Carey shot him! Do
you think he'd do that?"

"No, I don't. Take it easy. I told you that Lem's okay. If he'd been shot I
would have heard it. A .45 makes a lot of noise, you know."

It took a while but she finally calmed down. She looked as if she wanted
to leave The Retreat, wanted to chuck the whole thing and go back to L.A.
But Paul knew that she would never bring the idea up herself. She kept looking at him as if she wanted him to suggest it and coax her into it. "I should
have talked him out of it," she said. "But no, not Dolly Bosco. Avarice, Mr.
Berko. Just plain old avarice. But then, there's nothing really plain about it,
is there? I feel terrible. Why don't they invent a damn pill that turns back
time."

He sat beside her, moved, and put a comforting arm around her soft fat
shoulders. She was a nice old gal. "Look, Dolly, let me make a suggestion.
I think it'd be better if I took you back to the city. You could lay low and let
me take care of things up here. I can bring Lem's car back up and keep in

touch with you. As soon as I get Lem out I'll bring him right back into the city. How does that sound?"

"I don't know. Maybe."

"Look, you can't do much good up here the way things are now. How do we know that Kozma won't grab you too? We don't know what's going on in that maniac's mind."

She was weakening. Finally, she nodded and started sniffling again.

"Maybe you and Lem should forget the whole idea. You're clean. Pretty clean at any rate. Maybe it'd be better if we all pulled out while the getting's good. I think Kozma's going to pull one bonehead play too many and when he does the cops will move in. It won't be too wise for us to be there with our fingers sticking in the pie when that happens." He gave her a little squeeze. "What do you say, Dolly?"

She looked accusingly. "Avarice again, Mr. Berko? Are you trying to scare us out so you can hog the whole thing for yourself? Is that it? Maybe you slugged poor Lem yourself and made up the whole story just to scare me out of it."

He stood up. "For Christ's sake, Dolly! Don't you trust *anyone?* What kind of vaudeville act do you and Lem have anyway? No matter what I say you twist it around. Can't you get the hustle out of your system long enough to see the truth?"

She sounded tired. "The truth? What is the truth, Berko?"

"If you let me I'll tell you a funny story."

"A traveling salesman story?"

"Don't get cute."

"I'm sorry. I suppose, like you say, that I'm clean enough to get out. But what about Lem? He won't want to pull out. What'll I do if he scores and wants to split with me? Do I just throw it away because I've traded in my horns for the halo? You tell me."

"Lem will pull out. If he doesn't then I won't give a damn what either of you do. The only reason I'm caring now is because I want to get the girl out of the temple. And if you're still around, stirring up trouble, it might jeopardize her. I don't know. But I'm not going to take any chances. Now do you want to hear my story or don't you?"

She made a resigned gesture. "Fire away. But it better be good."

"I guarantee it." He sat down in the overstuffed chair and told it to her, the whole story, taking his time. The mad vampire part, the Fish-Beast, his success in New York. He skipped over the lousy breaks in Hollywood, filled in a little about Mara January and Harvey Crockett and why he had stepped into the car with Martha Mason in front of Chernery's. He showed her his ring and explained how he had lifted it from Jimmy Arketus in the prop department. Then he described his meeting with Kozma, Ralakin, and Anne Woodbridge, and the merry doings since that time. When he finished he was holding his glass from the night before, having unconsciously poured himself a bit of the hair while he had been talking it out.

Dolly looked at him, a silly smile on her wrinkled face. All she had said during the recital was, "I'll be damned!" She stood up now and clapped her hands to her stomach. "Berko, you're a classic. Do you know that? Do you know that I, *me* of all people, *saw* you as this Fish-Beast? It's true. I was in Santa Barbara during the sneak preview with Augie Losada and Colin Butler. I just hadn't paid any attention to your name. And of course I didn't see your face because you were wearing that ugly rubber suit with the big eyes and fangs." She shook her cheeks. "Priceless! Egad, an actor! Of all things a monster actor from teen-age movies!"

Paul didn't think it funny. No matter how he earned his living, or how silly the situation was, nothing had changed. Lem was still missing, Anne was still in the temple, and Kozma was still packing a .45 automatic. And he still had to get Dolly away from Willibald Canyon. Her presence would just add to his worries, and, too, he rather liked her and wanted her to get out before the whole place blew up.

"Don't look so glum, Berko," Dolly said. "I'll take you up on your offer. You take me back to the city. I'll go—but on one condition—that you try like mad to get Lem to pull out too. I'm going because I don't like it here, because I'm scared, and because I think Lem *will* change his mind. If Carey hurt him, even a little just to scare him, then I know he'll want to pull out. It doesn't take much to scare Lem."

"Okay. Pack your things. I'll be back for you in two shakes of a lamb's tail."

Paul returned to Lem's cabin, picked up his suitcase, then took it to his own room. There, he sponge-bathed as best he could, shaved with Lem's razor and shaving soap, and dressed in Lem's shorts and socks. He put on his suit, packed the case again, and left. He was feeling human again. Dolly was waiting for him in front of her cottage. Carrying both bags he led her up the path to Lem's Ford station wagon, which was parked at the head of the canyon road near the temple. The keys were under the driver's floormat in a metal hide-a-lock box.

"I feel something like a traitor," Dolly said. "I hate to sneak off like this and leave Lem back there."

He spun the wheel, stepped hard on the throttle. He shared Dolly's traitorous feelings, but not over Lemuel. He drove quickly, spraying yellow dust behind him. It was almost two o'clock by the dash clock. The sun was high. The traffic, when they reached the main highway south to San Fernando, was light and fast.

CHAPTER EIGHTEEN

The city was a terrible let down after being in the mountains. There wasn't a breath of air moving anywhere and the smog seemed unusually thick. Traffic was heavy and irritating. The streets looked dirty. It had been hard for him to realize just how wretched the city really was. It hit him now. The smog burned his eyes, his lungs ached for a breath of fresh air. His shirt was clinging to him and he felt tired and dirty.

"Turn here, Paul. It's the Beverly-Hanton. Ah me, for a cool shower, a tall glass of ice cold ginger ale, and a stack of Ray Charles on the hi-fi. Ray Charles relaxes me."

He turned into the impressive grounds, curving under tall palms, and stopped before the canopied walkway to the entrance.

"Thanks, monster man." Her hand rested on his for a moment. "You've been swell."

"I'll keep in touch, Dolly. I'll take the cavalry up there and get Lem back for you."

She smiled sadly and opened the door. "You do that. I won't forget you, Paul. Thanks again. For everything."

He watched her as she waddled to the hotel entrance. A hustling bellhop carried her suitcase and when they came to the big glass doors the doorman saluted, snapped to attention, and swung the doors open. Then she was gone. Paul didn't start the motor. He had a little time and he wanted to think it out. He needed a few things, such as powder, a wide bottle, and road flares. He also had to get gas for the Ford and food for himself. He needed money. He checked his pockets. One dollar and thirty cents and three Oasis cigarettes. He lit one and slumped behind the wheel.

He would have to see Jimmy Arketus. Not only for a small loan but also for the costume.

A pair of blondes strolled by, wearing matching shorts and halters, sunglasses, carrying beach junk; blankets, cigarettes, transistor, magazines. Their legs were long, bronzed, hips moving under the skin tight shorts. Ah life. Smoggy air, bright green lawns, tall palms, and lush blonde girlies with cigarettes and *Time* magazine.

He would have stayed a minute longer—a nice brunette was angling up the path—but the doorman came down the canopied walk, sneered once at the dusty Ford, and jerked his head toward the street.

Paul gave him his toughest Richard Conte look, then left the driveway with a little squelp of his tires. Lousy doorman. Comes on like Doug MacArthur. Big shot. He turned into the northeast traffic on Santa Monica and followed it into Hollywood. When he came to the ancient pillars of the studio gates he stopped at the guard shack and identified himself. It took a few minutes while the guard connected with Losada's private secretary and got an okay for him.

He left his car in the lot, and with pass in hand started along the little path which led through the trim gardens in front of the administration buildings. A little blonde fairy, swishing along and carrying a sheaf of papers under his wing, flattered and irritated him by calling him by his name. "Good afternoon, Mr. Berko." Paul nodded back. Tra la la. Hollywood. Once, when he had been a kid, he had seen a photo of Alan Ladd riding a Schwinn. It had been an ad on the back of a comic book. Captain America, in fact. Alan had been pointed out as a great Schwinn rider. Two years ago, while on the Warner lot in Burbank, he had seen Alan Ladd. He hadn't been riding his Schwinn. He had been standing by a big Caddie limousine with William Demerest. He hadn't been sure why at that time, but he had broken up, giggling uncontrollably. No Schwinn. He found the sound stage that Arketus was on and waited on the cool concrete steps until the red light went out.

Inside, it was dark and cool. The floor was cluttered with cables and canvas chairs. The set was a section of a police station. Like monsters closing in there were huge lights, boom, camera, booths, portable sound and make-up rigs. Paul skirted the set and found the costume booth in the far rear. He took off the Satan ring, slipped it into his pocket, and called for Arketus.

"Jimmy? Hey, Jimmy?"

Someone from the set behind him blew a little tin whistle and told him to shut up. He stepped into the booth, closed the door, rang the little buzzer. Jimmy Arketus told him to keep his shirt on and came into the room from somewhere in back.

He was a stocky little man, part Eskimo, with a flat, freckled face, thick black hair, and two gold teeth in the front. He was wearing a chartreuse sport shirt and pale gold sunglasses.

"Hey, Paul!" He grabbed his hand, shook it, winked for no reason. "What's happening, keedo. No long time see, baby."

"I've been in the country, Jimmy. You know. Thoreau. Trees. Brooks. New values. That sort of thing."

Jimmy nodded. "Yeah, I heard that you've been keeping pretty busy these days."

"Lay off, Jimbo."

He chuckled and sat on the corner of the cluttered desk. His expression was half-serious. "I went out to your place the other night, baby. I was getting kind of worried. You haven't called me in a long time. Why didn't you tell me you were having it rough? When I got out there I was surprised as hell. Your bitch landlady told me that you were two months behind in your rent."

Paul shrugged.

Jimmy picked up a calendar, looked at the nude girl, then rolled it into a telescope. He looked at Paul through the roll, one eye squinted. "I'll tell you what I did, but you better not flip your cap. I paid the back months for you and one in advance. Now don't get mushy, baby. I did it as a friend. I know you'd do the same for me. So no arguments."

He wasn't going to argue. What Jimmy said was true. He would do the same for him any time. "Thanks, Jimbo. Did she say I can have my vampire costume back? And my scrapbook?"

"It's in your pad. I put everything on the bed. I even opened your patio window a few inches. The air was getting stuffy in there."

Paul accepted one of his cigarettes and lit it. He was waiting for a chance to hit him for the costume and loan. Jimmy had already done more than he had expected from him. It was hard for him now to put the hustle to him.

Jimmy shook his head. "Keedo, why didn't you come to me? Unh? You ashamed or something?"

"I didn't want to bug you."

"You bug me more if you don't treat me like a pal. You could have called me at least."

"Sorry. I've got the kind of pride that gets in my way. You know that."

"Balls. It's not pride, baby. It's stubbornness. And maybe even a little self pity."

"Okay. You want me to hit you for a few bucks? That's why I came."

Jimmy laughed, throwing back his head. "That's more like it. I've got fifty-three bucks on me. Look. Here's forty. Will that hold you?"

Paul looked at the offered bills, then at Jimmy. He said that it would do just fine. He took the money. "One more favor. Do you keep the costumes from the old pictures?"

"Some of them. Why? Are you going to a costume party?"

"Something like that. What I wanted to find out is whether you still have my old Fish-Beast outfit."

"I think so. If it's anywhere it would be over in the other building. You want to go with me and take a look-see?"

"Sure."

They picked their way around the police station set, which was now being pushed around and opened for a new angle. They stepped out into the narrow street, started back toward the front gardens. A young brunette with a striped sweater came swinging by. She gave them a bright hello and swung even harder.

"Listen, Paul, if you want to borrow the property you'd better give me your word you'll take care of it. I'll have to sign the damn thing out and it'll be my Eskimo ass if anything happens to it."

"I'll take care of it," Paul promised.

He waited outside the building, smoking his last cigarette, while Jimmy went into the building. He spotted Mara January walking on the opposite side of the court with a freckle-faced photographer. He leaned against the stucco wall, his face warming in the sun, and he thought again of Anne Woodbridge.

He found that he couldn't be indifferent to the girl. He felt he owed her something. There were other considerations; she was very beautiful and naive and this excited him. He once knew of a man who had married a girl because he detested the touch of her skin. And there was his own brother, Bernie, who married because the girl hadn't been able to speak English. Bernie had thought that was pretty cute. It seemed that there had to be that difference, that hint of perversion, and in Paul's case it was the girl's spiritual confusion and social naiveté. He couldn't get her out of his mind.

Jimmy came out with the costume wrapped in thick, mottled pink butcher paper and tied with white cord. Paul thanked him again, promised to keep in touch, and left. At the end of the path he happened to look back. Jimmy was still there. They waved good bye to each other.

Paul was feeling good now. Watch out Zedek Kozma, here comes Nebiros. Nebiros on Sunday. The cavalry was on its way. He waved cheerily at the guard as he wheeled the Ford out into the street. It was growing late. Traffic was becoming heavier, pedestrians were hustling along the walks, jaywalking, shouting, looking stupid and mean. He headed for La Brea, then turned north to Sunset Boulevard.

After having the car serviced and having a club sandwich and a bottle of beer, he drove slowly around, going east toward Western, until he found a hardware store. He bought a plastic bucket with a screw-down lid, a roll of scotch tape, five highway flares, a small tin of sulphur, and a can of lighter fluid. As he was leaving he spotted a folding GI shovel and bought that as well. He carried the packages back to the car and tossed them in the rear. Then he found a phone booth and looked in the yellow pages for a nearby sporting-goods store. There was one listed on Western near Beverly.

The store was done in shiny knotty-pine. There were outboard motors, tents, fishing gear, gun racks, footballs, and skin-diving equipment. A sign pointed the way to the "hunting room." The clerk there was a pale young man with a fringed leather jacket.

"Do you sell plain gunpowder?"

"Yes, in the kegs. I suppose you make your own, sir?"

"Yes."

The clerk showed him a display of empty brass casings, a weighing machine, and a press-rig that fitted the slugs. There were also several black kegs of gunpowder there, some marked "smokeless."

He bought a keg of black powder and a small hunting knife. He walked back to the car, threw the packages into the rear with his other purchases, then drove to his old apartment.

It was growing dark, the sun hidden behind the hills, the sky a dull gold. Quickly ascending the steps to his apartment he smelled honeysuckle and damp grass; off to one side a sprinkler was whirling silvery sprays of water; the steps were wet.

"Hello, Mr. Berko."

It was his landlady, fat, haughty, painted, smirking horsey teeth and clutching the daily horoscope. She was standing on the first landing.

"Hello, Mrs. Cartier. Can I have my key back?"

"I have it right here. I hope you're not angry with me, Mr. Berko. After all, I'm a business-woman, and I—"

"Shut up. I'm tired."

"Why—"

He grabbed the key from her and went up to his unit. He found his shabby straw case, scrapbook, and vampire outfit on the bed. Silently thanking Jimmy again he laid out clean linen and a razor. He showered, shaved, and brushed his teeth three times, gargling mint-flavored water. In his shorts and socks he went out onto his patio and pulled in his twenty-five foot garden hose. He coiled it and tied it and set it by the door. Then, taking his time, he packed his white tie, tails, and opera cape in his straw case. He found a pair of blue jeans and a chambray shirt, put them on, picked up the hose and case and left the apartment.

He was as ready as he would ever be.

CHAPTER NINETEEN

Time. It meant nothing to Anne. For, lying in the great bed in the gloom, there was no way to measure time, no sound, no daylight, just the dark, closed room. Of course, she was no longer bothered by the incense. But the candles were going out. The only one still burning, red wax and heavy with a curled lip, was in the brass wreath bracket on the wall near the door.

When she had been caught with the dead man in the cold yellow room in the passage, Kozma had dragged her back into the bedroom, locking the panel after him, and then, in a wild-eyed act of choking her, he quoted long streams of Latin gibberish. Then she vaguely remembered that he had again taken a needle and injected fluid into her arm. But this time, when she came to, she had experienced no after-sickness. Her mind had been surprisingly clear. She had been alone. The only proof of her having been drugged was an empty phial that she had found on the floor. The blue label attached to the rubber stop had told her that the drug had been Amytal.

She sat up now and looked at the empty, locked mirror panel.

"How awful," she whispered. That poor old man in the passage. She could still see his bulging eyes, protruding tongue, horribly twisted face. She shuddered. Would she never be free from this place? Would she be a prisoner of that homicidal maniac forever? Or was he planning to murder her like he had that man in the passage?

She sagged back on the pillow and for a long while her imagination spun sonsied pictures of escape, grabbing at all the little omens and memories, ranging from sunny fields thick with spring flowers, to the strange man called Paul Berko sitting on the bench in the woods, his hair still wet from the brook. She wasn't sure why she thought of him. Surely he was gone now. But she found it nice to remember how, in her dream, she had pressed herself to him, raised her mouth to his and kissed him, her lips parted, moist and warm ...

The door suddenly swung open and Kozma stood, outlined against the strange green light of the office behind him, hard against the frame, a bottle of gin in his hand.

"It is almost time," he said thickly, slowly. "Did you hear me, young lady? It is almost time. Almost time."

Her body grew heavy, her eyelids fluttered. Somnolent. Falling into spinning black depths. His voice echoed in her ears. His voice was everything, the only true and real thing; the rest of it was meaningless. All of it. His voice was the most beautiful thing she had ever heard.

"It is *time*. Now, come here to me, young lady. That's it. You're doing very well. Come right to me. Now. Do you know who I am, young lady?"

Her voice was flat, lifeless.

"Yes. I know."

"I am God."

"You are God."

"Come into this room. All right now, sit in that bishop's chair. Yes, that's the one. Now remain still."

She obeyed.

He sat on the high throne and started drinking gin. When he asked her questions she answered in dull monosyllables. He grew irritated. It was like talking to the wall. He stared at her for a long moment, vaguely wondering who she was. When twenty minutes passed in silence he cursed loudly and spat on the carpet. "Dead," he muttered. "A dead girl." After taking another drink he laughed like a child discovering a new toy; he clapped his hands three times, watching her intently. "I remember now! Wake up. Wake *up*. Come out of it."

She jerked in her chair, temples throbbing, vision suddenly, painfully, clearing. What now? Was she losing her mind? She had lost a slice of time, like a magic wink, and saw that she was in Kozma's office, in the emerald green light, in a canopied carved chair with a kneeling stool and tiny rail.

She didn't move, afraid that if she drew attention to herself he would send her into that wink of time again. He had power over her now. Amytal. Certainly it had been that drug. She had to take it easy; she couldn't afford to upset him. She wanted to remain in reality no matter how ugly it was.

Kozma muttered darkly to himself, becoming confused again, the voice of someone proclaiming him God whispering in his ear. He had no idea where he was, who he was, or what he was doing. Perhaps he was in heaven. He could hear singing, the voices of children, sweet, soft, muted in the billowing clouds.

He found that he was holding a bottle in his hand and he took a cautious sip. Gin. Gin was all right. Juniper. He took a deeper drink. Then the return to darkness, where he stood in the center of a large circle etched in the dark ashes of a partially burned house. People crouched all about him, dressed in filthy rags, peaked caps, soft leather boots. He crossed himself and, with the toe of his shoe, stroked the letters KIS in the circle. "*Kadosh Ieve Saboath*. Holy the God of the Septenary."

In the half light, not dawn nor evening, he saw an old woman, magnificently dressed in white silk embroidered with seed pearls. In her left hand she held a broken crucifix upside down, and in her right the skull of a human foetus. She smiled at him and tossed the skull at his feet. The ragged crowd oohed and ahed.... Then there was a swimming green light above him. His arms were resting on an elaborately carved throne. He remembered the Sabbath. Great Sunday. Nebiros. He could hear a girl crying somewhere.... And the little skull rolled in the ashes, breaking the design of the circle. A black cauldron beside the old woman whispered, bubbled, glowed red and white and yellow. The woman reached into the glittering folds of her dress and drew out a fat pouch made of silk. Diamonds, rubies, emeralds, sapphires, poured into the cauldron. Red garnet flashes, beryl droplets, flakes of blue diamonds, thin ropes of pearls, kunzite, topaz, huge red rubies, pink and blue sapphires, sparkled, flashed, winked in the cauldron light. The crowd gasped. Kozma threw back his proud head and laughed.

Raising his hands high over his head he screamed and roared and howled. The sky darkened. The only light came from the jewel-fed cauldron. The splendid costume of the old woman was suddenly ripped from her body by a black wind. Her face was aged, like a gray prune pierced with bright birdlike eyes. But her body was that of a lovely young girl. Her waist was narrow, hips smoothly curved, flesh the color of cream. But there were no nipples on her firm breasts. There were ugly black cockroaches instead. The woman tried to grab a long fork beside the cauldron, but with a horrible screech she was swept up into the night.

Kozma's voice shouted after her:

> *Beim Schmause*
> *Aus dem Haus*
> *Zum Schornstein hinaus!*

She could no longer ignore him. Every time he grunted, growled, or swigged loudly from the second bottle of gin her eyes reluctantly moved to the throne. She was more disgusted than frightened. She had never seen anything so vile.

He was naked except for a pair of bright silk shorts. He was drunk, had been drinking steadily for the past two hours. His skin was a sickly white, oyster-colored, and the heavy folds of his belly hung over the tight elastic band of the shorts. She could see the thin, rubbery breasts, matted with limp gray hair, jiggle disgustingly every time he laughed. His legs were lumpy, hairless, flabby, and marked with ugly purple veins. He sat, ignoring every-thing, with the bottle clutched to his breast. His false teeth, which he had removed, grinned back at him from the polished top of the desk.

He looked almost a hundred years old. Filthy, dirty old man. Like a big gray spider. She closed her eyes and turned her head. Kozma growled like a beast and slobbered incoherently through his gums.

She looked at him.

"I said, c'mere, you!"

She didn't move.

He peered at his teeth. "Y'know who I'm?"

"Yes," she whispered.

"You know who who I'm? Unh? God, tha's *who!* I'm Saint God! Thousenz worsh'p me. Thousenz. God, tha's who."

He belched and grinned, his chin almost reaching the tip of his nose. Gin dribbled on his chest.

She couldn't stand it any more. She knew that if she remained in the room for another minute she would be sick. She crept from the chair and made it to the bedroom. He didn't call her. She closed the door, carefully, quietly, and pushed a stone statue—St. Jerome—under the door handle. Then, ex-hausted, sick, she sat on the edge of the four-poster and started to cry.

CHAPTER TWENTY

Paul parked the station wagon beside a stand of eucalypti and doused the lights. He had stopped at a truck stop on highway 99 and had bought a large canvas sack and a flashlight. Using the light he quickly unwrapped the pack-ages and filled the sack. It made quite a load.

He started across the field on his left. The south cliffs of Willibald Canyon loomed a quarter of a mile before him, where the field, broken here and there with groups of trees, gently rose into them. The night was deep, chilled, filled with the tender odors of spring grasses and wild flowers. Crickets whispered all around him. Passing through the first line of trees he shifted the weight of his pack and dug in his toes as the field rose sharply. The ground became rough, scarred with shallow ruts, the flowers less frequent, the night wind stronger.

Perspiring freely, the muscles in his legs quivering from the unaccustomed exercise, he made the top, set his load down, and paused to catch his breath.

A greater field stretched before him, gently sloping from his far left and ending at the edge of the cliffs at his right. The view was magnificent. Far below, perhaps three hundred feet, he saw the tiny lights of the great temple and the other, smaller, buildings. Picking up his sack he continued, following a rough track up the slope. A minute later he came upon the stone stage that Dolly had described. He pushed his load onto the platform, pulled himself after it, and stood for a long minute, studying the layout.

The platform was some fifteen feet long and ten feet deep. A double row of logs set on stone cairns acted as a rail on three sides. From the back rail it was a sheer drop to the canyon floor. He lit a cigarette, imagining the scene. The loudspeaker system was up already, the microphone and cable connections hooded with plastic to protect them from the night. Facing the stage and resembling huge coliseum bleachers, the field swept up for perhaps a half-mile. Directly before the stage, thirty feet out, there was another rail. Obviously there to keep the Kozmanites from pressing too closely to the stage during the performance.

"This is insane," he said softly. "Augie Losada should see this damn place."

He had already noticed the clump of rocks to his right, and, taking a closer look now, he saw that nothing else nearby could serve his purposes as well.

There were six large rocks, the boss stone being some seven feet high and pushing up from the ground like a monstrous half loaf of gray bread. He climbed one of the smaller rocks near the stage and peered over the edge. There was a shelf between the rocks and the cliff. It was approximately six feet at the widest point and twelve feet in length.

"Better than I expected."

He slid over the rock, carefully lowered himself to the shelf, then froze. Pressing himself against the rock he peered down into the darkness, then closed his eyes, his head swimming giddily with vertigo. He inched himself back up the rock, fingers scrambling carefully from handhold to handhold. He returned to the stage, nervously lit a cigarette, and glared at the boulder, cursing himself for his fears.

It was going to be tough, but if he was going to go through with it he had no other choice. The rest of the grounds offered nothing. It would have to be the shelf hidden behind the rocks or nothing at all.

He removed the Fish-Beast costume from the sack, tore away the butcher paper, and climbed the rock again. He lowered the suit to the shelf, returned to the stage, dumped out everything in the sack. When he finished sorting the pile he sat down and started to make the bomb.

He broke open the highway flares first, set them on a rock, and beat them to a crumbly pulp with the flat of the GI shovel. It came to quite a pile. He opened the soft plastic bucket, pried the lid from the heavy keg of gun-powder, and poured an inch of the black grainy powder into the bucket. He opened his sack of sulphur. Then, alternately, he filled the bucket with flare powder, gunpowder, sulphur, and more gunpowder. After each layer he doused the bucket with lighter fluid.

The mess was beginning to stink already.

He was, frankly, ignorant about the makings of bombs, explosive powders, and the like, so he was exaggerating his preparations, wanting to make dou-bly sure. When the bucket was filled he punched a hole in the lid with his hunting knife and secured the whole thing with the scotch tape.

He paced ten feet from the foot of the stage, keeping well away from the crowd rail, then dug a hole approximately four feet deep. He dropped in the bomb. Then, using the sharp point of the shovel, he carefully dug a two inch trench from the bomb hole to the boulders.

"So far so good," he said. He checked his watch and saw that he was mak-ing good time. He smoked a cigarette, then returned to work. Using the knife again he uncoiled the plastic garden hose and sliced it evenly along the top for about fifteen feet. Then, back at the bucket bomb, he put one end into the hole in the lid, then paid out the remainder of the hose, tapping it into the narrow trench until it reached the rocks. He had a little better than ten feet left over and he worked it between the rocks until it rested on the shelf.

Holding the gunpowder keg in one hand and prying open the top of the garden hose with the other, he carefully laid a black trail in the hollow tube from the bomb to the shelf. Then, backtracking, he buried the hose with dirt and filled in the bomb hole.

He sprinkled the area with dry dirt and stepped back to survey his work. It looked pretty good. The hose-fuse and bomb were completely con-cealed. Not one trace of tampering or digging.

"Hell, I should have been a spy. I'm a natural."

The plan was shaping up. Once he touched off the powder at the shelf end of the hose it would burn through the underground tube, taking two or three seconds until it contacted the bomb. Then when it went off—which, he fig-ured, would be little more than a scaring explosion—he would be ready, poised atop the boss rock and dressed in his Fish-Beast costume. From there he could easily leap through the confusing smoke clouds to the hole where the bomb had been. Then, growling fiercely and ugly in his scaly cos-tume, he would emerge from the sulphuric bowels of the earth as the Prince of Darkness, the Great Beast.

"Hee hee, Berko, you've got an evil mind."

He collected his tools and empty cartons and stuffed them into the sack. Then he left and hurried down the hill, following the same route to the distant line of eucalypti at the far end of the lower field.

CHAPTER TWENTY-ONE

He had to find Lemuel and get him out of the temple before he even considered approaching Kozma. Meanwhile, if he was caught snooping, he planned to bluff his way. He would simply explain that he was Nebiros and that he had a message to deliver from his boss, Lucifer.

It was, frankly, a silly idea, but he was counting on Kozma's really being as crazy as everyone said he was. If he wasn't, he would never swallow such obvious nonsense. Instead, he would simply haul out his .45 and start banging away.

It was perfectly simple. Either Kozma was truly insane and terrified of the presence of devils—or Paul was a dead man.

More than an hour had passed since he had finished his work on the mountain. And now, cleaned and smartly costumed in his long opera cape, white tie and tails, he silently crept up the wide stone steps to the temple and slipped into the darkened foyer. No light showed anywhere. Ralakin's office door was closed. The huge statues, queer arches, canopies and candle stands, were merely darker areas in the overall darkness.

When he passed through the dining hall, then through the black door, he was relieved to see that here, in the rear corridor maze, there were a few poorly spaced candles, burning dimly, casting uneasy, but protective, shadows.

He made no wrong turns this time and easily found the spot where he had left Lemuel the night before. He listened a moment, watching the restless shadows. There was a dry, gritty taste in his mouth and his heart felt as if it were jammed up into the base of his throat. Calm nerves, Berko. The place is too silent, that's all. He moved on, following an off hall, and found the ramp. Descending, he found himself in what seemed to be another corridor. It was too dark to see. He flicked on his faithful Zippo and, following the flickering light, came to a large oaken door. This led him into an enormous, low-ceilinged room where the air was close, unmoving, and smelled of incense.

He accepted a candle from an outstretched hand, lit it and proceeded to investigate.

An outstretched hand?

He turned, held the candle toward the hand, found that it was attached to the nude figure of a woman carved from white marble. He chuckled, softly, nervously, and continued to look about the room.

There were more statues, bright silk pillows, comfortable rooms in alcoves with curtains before them, and, to one side, a long table with leather chairs. A stone statue was near the head of the table; a man and woman, naked, making love in an almost impossible position.

He searched the rooms, but it wasn't until he came to the last one that he found anything unusual. When he put the candle on a low table a tiny pool of light appeared on the floor at his feet. Reaching down he placed his hand in the light and followed it until he found himself peering into the opened nose of a carved face on the rear wall. A small mirror showed him his own eye staring back at him. The candle must have caught the mirror and thrown the reflection to the floor.

He immediately thought of a two-way mirror. It explained the presence of the blackmailing films. There must be a secret passage behind the wall. And then what? Bela Lugosi stalking the passages? It was a strange way for a reincarnated saint to be running his business.

He retrieved his candle and searched for a secret door in every wall and panel in the alcoves. Then he tried the floors, looking for an unusually large separation in the wooden inlays.

He drew a blank. His watch told him that he had been inside the temple for more than an hour. Disregarding caution he sat at the table and lit a cigarette. He stared at the love-position of the stone figures. It might be possible at that.

He decided to give the outside hall a try. He brought the candle and played it quickly along the panels and frames. Then he saw it flicker. He found the side key, twisted it down, and stepped back as the panel slid open. Okay, here comes old Nebiros with the cavalry. He drew in a deep breath, closed the panel after him and started along the narrow passage, the huge shadows dancing all around him.

Small frames roughly shaped like open cigar boxes were set in the walls and he stopped to look at one of them. He noticed a small switch device on the side of the frame and he pulled on it, squeezing it like a shotgun trigger, first one click, then another. It unhinged whatever movable piece there was on the other side of the wall. Peeping through the two-way Paul found himself looking into the corridor at Kozma's round brass door, the upside down tapestry, and the ornate candle stand.

The next frame revealed a section of Kozma's office, which appeared to be empty. Another frame, further down, showed another corridor, which Paul recognized as the one in which he had encountered Kozma the night before, the one which had no visible exit or entrance. He searched for and found a sliding door that opened onto the passage..:. Paul remembered the dust on Kozma's hair the night before. Lemuel, if he was in the temple, probably would be close by....

Paul found a steep passage and followed it until he came to an open doorway half way up the slope. When he stepped inside and played the light over the floor he found what he had been looking for.

"Jesus," he whispered, "poor Lem...."

There was no need for him to bother feeling for Lem's pulse; he was obviously dead. And besides he doubted if he could find it anyway; he had never been able to find his own.

He knelt and carefully pushed the stiff body to one side. He couldn't bare to look at Lem's face. Setting the candle in a heavy stick which had fallen near the body Paul picked up one of the light aluminum cans and read the taped label. *Irving MacLean/Sarah Bridger.* He unscrewed the lid and held up two feet of film to the flickering candle. Nothing. Each frame seemed murky. He unrolled a bit more and saw a naked girl standing beside MacLean. Paul recognized the man from his newspaper photos. He fed out a few more feet and found himself looking at the girl and MacLean sitting on the edge of a bed, both naked, laughing about something, and holding between them a brass pot of flickering light. He replaced the reel to the can, picked up the candle and moved to the center of the room. At the far side, near a camera and tripod dolly, an editing machine had been set against the wall near a large metal sink. Paul counted the cans near the body, checked the camera in case another reel had been left in the magazine, then went through the desk, counting the books and accordion envelopes of banking records. There were twenty-one cans of pornographic film and thirteen books and envelopes. Quite a haul.

He went to the editing machine, found an empty film can on the bench, then looked for the missing reel. He found it still in the machine. He flicked a switch and the viewing screen flashed on. Another switch started the film through the viewer. Paul smiled thinly. It was a film involving Jesse Kincaid and a lovely young blonde girl. Again, both were naked, lying on a huge swan bed which had been placed but a few feet from where the camera had been set. Paul chuckled, squinting into the viewer. Kincaid never looked like this on his television show.

Obviously the girl had had her instructions because she kept moving her position on the bed to include as many full face shots of Kincaid as possible. But this was a little difficult because it obviously had been Jesse's feeding time. An opium pipe, or what looked like an opium pipe, was propped in an ash tray beside the bed. The film ground on. The girl was holding Kincaid's face in her hands and her knees were locked against his ribs. Kincaid was smiling. So was Paul.

When the reel ended he rewound the film, watching Jesse undo all the weird things he had been doing with the girl, and stopped at the same frame he had started with, then he turned the machine off, picked up his candle and returned to the body.

Lem's death changed everything now.

Paul could do nothing now about the films and books. He would have to return tomorrow evening, after Kozma led his followers up onto the mountain. Then, if he worked fast, he could grab everything, stash it in the station wagon, and make it back to the hidden shelf behind the rocks before it was too late.

Meanwhile he had to check the two-way mirrors in the passages; he had to find out where Kozma had holed up; if he didn't then he would have no way of being sure the girl would be on the mountain tomorrow night.

Now comes the tricky part—facing Kozma in his vampire get-up. He grabbed the candle, took a last look at Lemuel, and hurried from the room, his long black cape fluttering after him.

Bela Berko rides again.

Kozma had put his teeth in his mouth again and had put on his robe. His naked feet pattered softly down the empty corridor.

The dining room was dark and empty, which was strange because he distinctly remembered having invited Polberko, Lemuel, and Dolly to dinner.

He went into the kitchen but there was no sign of anyone having been there. In the walk-in refrigerator he found a turkey wrapped in tinfoil. Staggering, weak and aching all over, he tore off a drumstick and returned to the dining hall. He sat at the head of the table, chewing noisily, and watched as the ghostly figures of Lemuel and Dolly smiled up into his face.

Then he remembered something. It surprised him, almost shocked him. He dropped the drumstick and the ghosts vanished.

Lemuel was dead! Why hadn't he thought of it before? And why was he so tired, so tired? Hadn't he slept? He left and returned to his office.

Pacing back and forth in the green light he remembered something else. There was a girl in his bedroom ... but who she was, or why she was there, he had no clear idea. She was important to him for some reason. He went to his desk. When he found his box of pills he jiggled them in his palm, debating whether to take two or three of them. He decided three would be best, swallowed them, and left the room.

In the hall, just outside his door, he heard a sound. He turned, stared, wide-eyed, at the walls. Had that been a click, a chuckle, a whisper? He frowned. What the devil was that name Carey Leadhead all about anyway? He went back into the room and shut the brass door after him.

"Just let them try it," he whispered. "Just you let them!"

He started to shiver and he sank into his throne, holding his robe close to him. It was, as usual, dark in the room, but why was it so damned cold? He had to be prepared for Great Sunday. He remembered that easily. He also remembered something about a young woman—or was she old?—who had had no nipples. Just cockroaches. He shuddered again, uncontrollably, and his false teeth clicked against his lips. Where had that young—old—woman been? And, also, hadn't there been something about jewels, melting in some kind of a pot?

Christ, he wasn't sure of anything any more. He was being tricked, that's what. Sure, Lucifer was tricking him. Lucifer and Nebiros, casting their evil spells over him. *"Dominus adjutor meus."* Fish-Beast, indeed! His eyes widened and he sat upright on the throne. A new question occurred to him. Fish-Beast? What was that? Where had he heard....

There was a sound behind him. A sliding, slithering sound. He chuckled loudly. He wasn't going to be fool enough to turn, to fall into a Lucifer trap. He was wise to their game now. They were trying to trick him all the time. They were trying to make him doubt his own powers. *They* were afraid of *him!* Their tricks and spells proved that.

"Dominus adjutor meus," he whispered.

A figure appeared before him. He was tall and slender, dark, evil, aristocratic in long black cape, white tie and tails. A blood-red ring gleamed on his finger. His black, piercing eyes were watching him intently. A thin smile played on his lips.

Kozma made no move. For a long moment he mistrusted the presence of the figure. Lately there had been so many strange inexplicable happenings that he was no longer certain what was real and what wasn't.

He finally waved a tired hand and closed his eyes. "Go away, Nebiros. Leave me alone until tomorrow. I don't want to see anyone."

"Zedek Kozma."

Paul's voice sliced into him.

He opened his eyes. Polberko-Nebiros, still smiling calmly, raised his hand and pointed the ring at him. His strangely accented voice filled the room.

"I have a message for you, Zedek Kozma...."

"For me? A message?"

"Yes. From Lucifer, Prince of Darkness, the Great Fish-Beast, the ruler of us all. You are to bring Anne Woodbridge to the mountain with you. You are to obey. It is a simple request. I am sure, Doc-tor, that you will comply."

Kozma frowned. "Anne—who?"

Paul's eyebrows jerked up. "Why, the girl here in the temple with you."

"Oh. That one."

Paul worked himself back into character and went on. "You see, Doc-tor, *all*, every Kozmanite, must be present tomorrow. Those who are sick, of course, are to be ex-cused. That is my message from my lord, Lucifer, the Rightful Ruler of the Universe."

He smiled. The last expletive, the rightful ruler of the universe, was a line he had just remembered from Dr. Sivana, a mad scientist in the pre-war comic books, the nemesis of Captain Marvel.

Paul had to force himself to keep a straight face. The whole thing was hysterically funny. He was even looking forward to tomorrow night's performance.

It had been ridiculously simple. He had spotted Kozma through one of the two-ways, found the sliding panel directly behind the throne, and had stepped into the room.

It was almost too easy. But he could see that Kozma wasn't pretending. The guy *was* as screwy as everyone said. And Paul felt a little guilty, like hustling a child, until he remembered Lem's body back in the passageway....

"About tomorrow, Nebiros. I *have* to know. Will—will Lucifer come?"

"I don't know, Doc-tor. I am merely an agent. If you truly have the power to evoke, then he will be there."

Kozma smiled thinly. "And if I have the power to evoke, then I have the power to banish."

Paul shrugged. "I wouldn't know about that. As I say, I'm only an agent."

Kozma narrowed his eyes, addressed himself, whispering half aloud. "Yes, the power to banish. Ardenal." He waved his hand slowly, thumb and forefinger joined, his eyes closed. "Go, jinnee; return unto the places destined for thee, and be thou always ready to come—"

Paul didn't hear the rest of it. He quickly stepped to the panel, shut the door, and raced down the passage, returning to the downstairs hallway.

When Kozma completed the command of dismissal he looked all around the room, even under the desk. He chuckled contentedly. Their spells and tricks meant nothing to him. Nothing at all. His power was unlimited.

Satisfied that he had made the demon vanish, he carefully prepared a needle for his much needed sleep.

"Dominus adjutor meus," he whispered softly.

CHAPTER TWENTY-TWO

In the morning Ralakin and Carlo drove the jeep up the rough track through the west fields to the mountain. They checked the grounds surrounding the stage, tested the loudspeakers, and laid out the various objects for the night's show. Everything appeared to be in perfect order.

During the day the minor Kozmanite leaders put up posters, gave small talks, and enthused the residents, reminding them that tonight was the night of the evocations of the demons, the night of Great Sunday.

Toward noon a stiff breeze swept in from the west, but by five o'clock it had died down completely. The evening grew soft, coral-colored and cloudless, with faint stars showing in the east. It promised to be a perfect night.

Ralakin kept busy. He presided over the special meals and prayers in the cafeteria, then helped the residence hall leaders and storekeepers pass out the red glass cups and stubby candles. When he learned they had handed out more than nine hundred lights, Ralakin became enthusiastic and excited. It was going to be the best turn-out ever.

Finally, in the gathering darkness, in the lavender shadows, the Kozmanites lit their candles and whispered excitedly. They began to move in long, uneven lines of black and white robes to the mountain.

Ever since his minor victory over Polberko-Nebiros the night before, Kozma's thoughts had been surprisingly peaceful. He was pleased with himself. The victory had acted like a tonic to his soul. It had been just what he had needed. A little shaking up, a testing of his powers, an affirmation. Of course, there were many dark areas left in his mind, such as how he happened to be St. Willibald, but he considered them unimportant, harmless, and best left alone.

In his pink-tiled shower room he laid out his white silk high-priest robe, long, red velvet gloves, and peaked red hat. He took his time in the shower, relaxing under the warm, soapy spray. Then he shaved, trimmed his beard, and carefully went through his hair with the blue-black rinse. He went over his face with a light pancake make-up and meticulously plucked his eyebrows. Then he fished his teeth from the jar of mint-flavored cleaning solution and slipped them into his mouth. He sprayed his throat and squeezed glycerine drops into his eyes.

Whistling contentedly, he put on his waist girdle, gay silk underwear, and high heeled boots.

Anne Woodbridge was waiting in the bedroom. She was dressed in her white robe, staring glumly at the floor, only vaguely aware of the activity around her. Her mind was having difficulty focusing.

Ralakin entered the office as Kozma was adjusting his robes.

"How are you feeling?"

Kozma's eyes were bright. "Fine, Brother Ralakin."

Ralakin smiled. He liked the way Carey sounded, clear, full of pep, the old familiar Carey. Ralakin was feeling good. The holy men were up on the mountain getting the show under way and Ralakin had a few minutes to spare. Lighting a cigarette he sat on a corner of the big desk and watched Carey brush his hair before the mirror.

As Carey stroked the brush, his white silk sleeve slid down to his soft bicep and Ralakin noticed the fresh pink marks over the line of his veins. He started to say something, then thought better of it. He bit his lip and remained silent.

Kozma pulled on his red gloves, slid the many glittering rings over his fingers, then, careful not to muss the arrangement of his hair, he put on the peaked red hat. He stood back and smiled broadly at his image in the glass.

"How do I look?"

Ralakin smiled distractedly. "What? Oh, you look real fine. Are you ready? I've got the jeep right outside. We'd better hustle, because I left the ceremony singing up to old Edward Woodbridge, and you know how he is."

"Woodbridge?" Kozma frowned. It had almost slipped his mind. "That reminds me, we have to bring the girl with us. Anne Woodbridge. You'll find her in my bedroom."

Ralakin gave him a curious look. "Why's that?"

Kozma answered lightly, "Lucifer wants it that way."

"Oh." Ralakin started for the bedroom, then stopped. "Who did you say?"

"Lucifer," Kozma said innocently. "He asked me to bring the girl."

"Lucifer?"

"Of course. Are you deaf?"

Ralakin looked incredulous, then crestfallen. So, Carey hadn't snapped out of it. Maybe Lem had been right after all. Carey was sinking. No doubting that. He no longer suspected the reality of devils, he *saw* them now. One of the coolest rackets ever dreamed up, being threatened by a man who carries on conversations with Lucifer....

"Is there anything the matter? You look sick. Are you all right?"

"Sure, Carey. I'm fine. Listen, we'd better—"

Kozma paled under his make-up and his lips twitched crazily. "What? What was that you just called me?"

"Nothing. I'm sorry. I know you've told me a hundred times, but—"

Veins stood on Kozma's brow. *"What did you call me?"* he screeched.

Ralakin was scared now. "I just called you Carey. Look, I'm sorry if—"

Kozma grabbed the front of his robe and jerked him closer, his eyes blazing.

"All right. Explain it! I've heard that name before and don't think I haven't. You're not kidding me, whoever you are. Nobody kids me any more. I'm wise to your game, see. Now, you little scum, tell me what that name means!"

"I—"

"Who is Carey? What is Carey? If you don't speak I'll break your scrawny neck!"

Ralakin turned to cream inside. He tried to pacify him. "Carey means—it's another word for—for St. Willibald. Don't you remember, Saint? It's a term of endearment. People use it to let you know how much they love you...."

The iron grip relaxed and Ralakin staggered back. Kozma's expression grew sly, pleased, proud. "Of course," he purred. "I knew that all along. Because they love me. Certainly. Because they love and adore me." He gave Ralakin a curious look, his face impassive, eyes hooded with quiet madness. His voice was far away. "By the way, who are you? What's your name?"

Tears had formed in Ralakin's eyes. "It's Charley. Charley Ralakin. But most people call me Rolly."

Kozma nodded. "I remember you now," he said. But did he really? He wasn't sure. He was becoming mixed up again. Patches of darkness. Damn! But it no longer mattered. Just as long as he had the great white light in him, the secret knowledge, the power, guiding him.

Another name, a phrase, a jumbled sequence, occurred to him and he turned to Ralakin. "Do you know someone named Samuel? Or Lemuel?"

"Of course. He's—"

"He's dead," Kozma whispered softly. "I found him in a passageway and I put my hands around his throat. His tongue stuck out and his eyes popped. It was like squeezing a pink bull frog. Are you familiar with a place called Montana? No? A strange place, Montana. I was there ... at one time. Did you know that? Yes, it was. Exactly like squeezing a pink bull frog." He held his jeweled hands before him and stared at them. "I strangled him with these hands. He's probably still there, very cold and very stiff now, lying in the passageway......"

Ralakin shuddered. Lemuel, dead... He said, softly, sadly, "They're waiting, St. Willibald. The people on the mountain are waiting."

Kozma said briskly, suddenly attentive, "Of course! We mustn't keep Lucifer waiting. Wait until you see what I can do. With one simple command, *one* mind you, I'll dismiss him just as I dismissed Polberko-Nebiros, his agent."

"You dismissed Polberko?"

"Yes. Last night. He came to me with Lucifer's message. I heard him out, then, as I would a bothersome insect, I simply flicked my wrist and banished him to darkness." He smiled. "My power has at last shown me the way. And tonight, before everyone, I shall evoke the Fish-Beast himself, then with a powerful command I shall send him back to his foul lair. The crowning moment of my life."

What could Ralakin say? He opened the brass door and Kozma joined Carlo, who had been waiting in the hall. Ralakin went to the bedroom and called the girl, Anne. She came, obediently, and when he told her to follow him she did, moving in a strange, lifeless shuffle.

Ralakin, in sadness and resignation, was forming a plan. After tonight's performance, when the show was over, he would try once more to reach Carey. And if that failed, if he saw that it was hopeless, he would call it quits. He loved Carey, loved him more than anyone else, but he had himself to consider, too. If Carey's really washed up then Ralakin would grab the films, the books, the cash, and make a run for it....

CHAPTER TWENTY-THREE

Paul had been watching from the bushes when the jeep left the temple. Then, sure that the building was empty, he hurried to the room, shoved the books and films into his canvas sack, and lugged them out to the station wagon. After emptying the celluloid reels onto the gravel and removing the labels from the cans he tossed a match to the pile.

There was nothing to gain by anyone ever seeing the films. Better to let them burn and forget they ever existed.

The books, however, would have to be turned over to the cops, along with Lem's body.

Now, watching the black strips crackle and writhe in the flames, he heard the distant voices of the thousand followers atop the south cliffs, singing of

Adonai, Eloha, Agla and Elohim, echoing eerily in the vast canyon walls. When the fire died, leaving a gritty pile of shiny ashes, he returned to the wagon, set the books on the seat, and ran up the steps to Ralakin's private office.

He found an extra black robe and slipped it over his jeans and shirt. Returning to the wagon, he cleaned the fingerprints from everything he had touched, then drove down the road with his handkerchief on the wheel.

No sense in leaving prints and advertising himself. Let the cops figure it all out later. If there was a later.

When he parked again in the shadow of the eucalyptus trees and started across the field he saw a group of Kozmanites heading for the upper slopes. He ran and caught up with them.

A female wearing a robe with a hood and carrying a lighted candle regarded his beardless face with undisguised suspicion. He gave her a big smile. "I'm a recent convert," he explained cheerily.

When they reached the top he broke away from the group and moved as close as he could to the rail. All about him the field was alive with the tiny red lights of the cups and candles. A thousand singing voices filled the night. Like some unholy gathering in medieval times, a great conclave of sorcerers and witches on some accursed mountain top. Paul shuddered, impressed with the enormity of Kozma's power, and a cold, unreal feeling rose in the pit of his stomach.

Unlike everyone else, Paul wasn't wearing a hood on his robe. He felt uneasy and horribly conspicuous as he moved among them. All he could see of the people were their hands, which were holding the cups before them, and occasionally the tip of a nose peeping from under a hood.

It took him better than fifteen minutes to work his way through the crowd to the far side of the railing. He was in luck. No one was standing near the group of rocks. They were too far to the left, too close to the stage, and too near the cliff.

The singing came to an end. The night was hushed. Ralakin stepped to the microphone and gazed at the vast audience. His face was illuminated by a small fire in a brass vessel set on a nearby tripod. He took a breath, raised his arms, and his voice boomed over the loudspeakers.

"Kozmanites! Faithful followers of the true reincarnate of St. Willibald!" He paused. "There is no supremacy of evil!"

The crowd murmured, a thousand voices melting together.

"Power. But not supremacy." His gestures and mouth grimacings were reminiscent of Dr. Goebbels. His voice lowered to normal. "We're aware of the evil supremacy in the world beyond our Retreat. We, all of us here in this sacred canyon, under the protection of our beloved Saint, are free from the demonic spells which have been cast over this earth. Here we are free! And here we shall remain free...."

Edging his way to the first rock, which was some five feet high, Paul paused and looked back at the crowd. No way of knowing if he was being watched or not. But from what he could see everyone seemed to be watching Ralakin.

"Through demonology?" Ralakin wanted to know. "Is that how we are to rid ourselves of sin, of demons, of devils? Is it?" He paused. "We know what demonology teaches. It teaches that demons, working toward evil ends, are to be pacified by worship. In the form of prayer and sacrifice. Our beloved protector and teacher, St. Willibald, has told us that there is no form of worship in which to appease Lucifer and his black legions. You can't solicit their good will. They have no good will. Only evil. That is what our beloved Saint has taught us. And we know that to be true! We know beyond a doubt that that is true! We believe it! Yes, we believe every word because ...."

Paul hooked his toe on the rock, paused, then swiftly heaved himself up and over. He tumbled to the shelf, landing on his shoulder, and teetered over the edge. He started to slip, his feet swinging over nothing. He reached out blindly, frantically playing his hands along the surface of the rock. He continued to slide. Half of his body was now over the edge. Then his fingers found a tiny purchase in the rock and dug in. He stopped sliding. His heart was hammering in his chest and his body was soaked with sweat. Slowly, first working his waist along the edge, then his thighs, he finally hoisted himself back to the shelf. He sank to his stomach and lay there, shaking, exhausted, breathing heavily, the cool earth pressing against his damp cheek.

Ralakin's speech ended ten minutes later and the crowd began to follow him in song.

He couldn't waste much more time. Slowly, he crawled to the wide spot behind the larger rock where the Fish-Beast costume was lying, folded and tied. He opened the bundle and spread it before him.

The making of the costume had been a work of imagination and genius. The details had been executed with particular attention so that the suit would pass the criticism of the close-ups on wide screen. From the wide, wrinkled folds of the neck to the webbed, clawed feet the suit was completely covered with tough rubber scales which had been lacquered to appear wet and slimy. Along the spine and at the joints there were crustaceous patches of green, resembling some foul undersea growth.

The hands and head were separate but attached to the body with metal hooks and eyes. The hands were large taloned gloves, the head a hideous part-fish part-human thing, with large, bulbous eyes, heavy lidded and widely spaced, the mouth an ugly splay of gleaming white fangs and purplish gums.

A breeze was rising, becoming stronger. Ralakin was still leading the crowd in song.

Paul removed the black robe and climbed into the body of the suit. Then he pried open the top of the length of hose and checked the gunpowder. Still dry. He put on the gloves and snapped them to the wrists. Then, carrying the fish head, he moved up the side of the boss rock. The rubber suit afforded him a good, adhesive purchase and he made it to the top in less than five seconds. Once he lit the fuse however he knew he would make it in less time than that.

He peered over the top, settled down to watch the show, and waited for the moment when Kozma would call forth Lucifer....

An expectant hush fell over the crowd when Kozma, assuming the role of karcist, finally started the magic pentagram in the center of the stage. He made a large circle, pouring the line with heavy white powder. Ralakin stood at his side. As Kozma worked in the lettering Ralakin dutifully handed him the necessary colored powders. Sitting on the bench near the rail, the holy men of Kozmanism intently watched every gesture of their Saint.

Anne was still bewildered by her surroundings. For a long while everything had seemed unreal to her. But, slowly, painfully, she was coming out of it. The drug-induced state of hypnosis was wearing off.

She remembered everything that had happened to her now. But it was hard for her to believe that it had really happened to her. Memory was like a story she had once heard. She was still feeling dull and uncaring, was still clinging, lethargically, to Kozma's evil but strangely protective spell.

She remained on the bench, a puzzled frown on her brow, and watched Kozma finish the details of the circle.

The pentagram was finished. Ralakin signaled the solemn figures of the holy men. They rose in a body, joined hands, and gathered at the outer edge of the magic circle. The gentle breeze fluttered the flames in the brass vessel. Kozma was smiling, his eyes glittering deliriously, lips working as though talking to himself. Ralakin watched him anxiously.

The holy men began their chant. Kozma took a long white stick and held it ceremoniously over his head. On each side of the stick, in red, there were six-pointed stars, crosses, and strange, ghostly writing. Agla. Zenard. Tetragamaton. Zevoath.

Ralakin moved the tripod and burning vessel to the center of the circle. Then he put the microphone stand beside it. From a small redwood chest Kozma fed the flames with a mixture of charcoal, brandy, willow shavings, and camphor chips. Blue smoke curled from the vessel and slowly tattered in the soft breeze.

"I conjure thee."

Kozma's voice sang through the loudspeakers, deep and powerful.

"I conjure thee in the name of God, thy true Master and mine; I conjure thee by all the might and majesty of the Holy Trinity; I conjure thee by the four sacred words of Agla unto Moses, Io, Zati, Zata, Abbati; I conjure thee by the great teacher Willibald; I conjure thee by the Living God El, Ehome, Etra, Ejel aser, Ejech Adonay Iah...."

Behind the rock, Paul quickly pulled the mask over his face and snapped the hooks on the neck. He was ready. Kozma's voice came to him, slightly muffled. The ear openings in the mask consisted of a few holes concealed by the intricate overlap of the scabs and scales.

Kozma waved the white stick over his head, his eyes searching the skies. His voice rose to a powerful roar:

> *Bagapi laca bachabé*
> *Lamac cahi achababé*
> *Karrelyos*
> *Lamac lamec Bachalyos*
> *Cabahagy sabalyos*
> *Baryolos*
> *Lagoz atha cabyolas*
> *Samahac et famyolas*
> *Harrahya!*

Now.

Paul pried open the hose, flicked the Zippo and touched the flame to the gunpowder. He heard it sizzle, saw it flash, then he scrambled quickly to the peak of the rock, poised, ready to leap.

What he saw next not only surprised him but it almost threw him from the rock and down into the canyon, three hundred feet below.

The earth erupted. The explosion was deafening. A sheet of flame belched up and great clouds of white, sulphuric smoke rose in the air. Showers of sizzling red coals—which were, most likely, the bits and pieces of the highway flares—splattered the ground like hot flakes of lava.

He was on the rock only two seconds after the blast. Then leaped through the cloud of smoke and sparks. Shazam.

But he didn't land quite the way he had planned. For one thing, he had not only misjudged the distance, but the size of the bomb hole as well. What he jumped into was a crater. He pitched straight down into the hole and landed on his head. He was only partly aware of the thousand screaming, shouting voices and the thundering, quaking earth.

The Kozmanites were stampeding.

He shook his head and he stared cross-eyed through the slits of the bulging fish eyes. The complete absurdity of his situation suddenly hit him and he giggled uncontrollably. He was groggy and a little silly.

All right, Berko. Make like the Fish-Beast. Two years ago you were paid for doing it. The reviewer in the *New Yorker* had said you looked like a fancy Halloween figure and that you growled like a third-rate Karloff. All right, let's see if you can do it better this time. Come on, Berko, climb out of that trench and give the hun a couple of licks. Let's go, Cagney. Let's do it for the Fighting 69th. Over the top, kid. Paths Of Glory....

He shook his head a second time, blinked rapidly, and started to struggle out of the smoldering pit.

Behind him, the Kozmanites were running wildly for the lower fields. Many had dropped their candles in their haste and now the hillside was catching fire in a hundred little patches. The holy men had fled the stage. The breeze was blowing stronger and fanning the flames. Kozmanites were fleeing the flames as well as the hideous monster in the pit.

It looked like the end of the world, Armageddon, the field in flames, the sulphuric clouds still clinging to the blasted earth, the brimstone-like pieces of road flares brightly freckling the ground before the stage.

Paul crouched at the edge of the hole, slowly swinging his arms, narrowing his bulging fish eyes and loudly gnashing his great fanged jaws.

Ralakin was frozen stiff. Anne, who had been completely released from all traces of the spell when the explosion occurred, stood near the rail, wide-eyed with terror, unable to scream or move.

Kozma, still in his magic circle, began to wave his stick. His brain had snapped. He started screeching, his voice roaring like thunder over the loudspeakers.

"I did it! I really did it! Look, look, look, it's Lucifer! The Fish-Beast! Goddammit, you stupid clods! I did it! Come back! COME BACK YOU DUMB RUBES! Look at what old Carey Ledbetter did!"

The fire illuminated the stage as if it had been drenched in hot blood. Kozmanites were still racing down the hill.

Kozma's voice exploded, spouted insane gibberish, commanded the beast to disappear. He became frantic, screamed, stamped his feet, wielded his magic stick like a broadsword. He rattled through every order of occult banishment that his fevered mind could recall.

None of them worked. The beast remained, glowering, lifting his jaws, his slimy scales reflecting the flames and turning his body into a thousand bright red and green coins.

The beast moved slowly, ponderously, toward the stage.

Kozma screeched so violently that his false teeth flew from his mouth and clattered to the stage. Ralakin ran to him and grabbed him but Kozma, confused and terrified, started to fight with him. "It can't be," Ralakin shouted. "Carey, come out of it, for God's sake! It can't be!"

"Away from me, you idiot!" He pushed him aside and grabbed Anne. She came to life then and started to squirm free. "Go to him then!" Kozma screamed. "Go to Kozma, Molly! But if I ever hear of you squealing I'll cut you just like I cut him!"

Then he hurled her from the platform. She fell into the outstretched arms of the monster. Screaming, squirming, she tried to run, to escape but the taloned hands drew her roughly toward the gleaming teeth.

"Shut up, Anne," the beast said. "It's me. Paul Berko."

"Paul ... Berko?"

She gasped at the scaly face of the monster and shook her head incredulously. It couldn't be. It was ...

"It's true," the beast insisted. "It's me. Paul. Now get behind me and let's get out of here."

Ralakin was pulling at Kozma, clutching his robe. Kozma didn't want to leave the protection of the magic pentagram. It was the only place where the beast could never enter, could never get to him.

The hillside was a holocaust now. The flames engulfed a large group of oak and madrona trees. The air was hot, suffocating, bitter with blue smoke. Cinders swirled like black confetti.

Paul had to get out of his costume and get to a phone as quickly as possible. Although, by now, he was sure that the fire department and police were already on their way. But someone had to tell them where to find Lem's car, to find the books, and where to find the body.

He jumped up to the platform and pulled Anne after him. The direct exit was blocked by fire now. He remembered a deep draw due east of the stage, beyond the boulders. The draw led to the eastern side of the mountain and away from the flames.

Pulling Anne after him he hurriedly crossed the stage, and accidentally walked through the chalk powder circle. Kozma was too shocked to scream.

He stopped fighting with Ralakin long enough to take a feeble swipe at the Fish-Beast with his magic stick. Paul swung a rubber arm and knocked the stick aside.

Kozma's eyes snapped shut, then opened again, dull and lifeless, his face an expressionless mask.

Defeated ... Carey Ledbetter. Hurry hurry, step right up ladies and gentlemen, let your skill win you a cupie doll. So you wanna be a magician, unh, Carey? Yes sir. You're a smart looking kid. You'll do all right ... Carey, you're out of your mind. Burlesque and religion is oil and water. Sex, demons, and a pep talk on prayer! What've you got in your head? Rocks? ...

Ralakin tried to stop him, but Kozma continued to move woodenly toward the far rail.

Hurry hurry, step right up and let your skill win you a wriggling hula girl....

He stood at the low rail. Ralakin was still tugging at his robe and trying to get through to him. Kozma didn't hear a thing. Slowly, deliberately, he raised his arms out to the sky.

"I hear you, Lord," he whispered softly. "I'm coming, Lord."

Then, like a comic nightmare, Kozma stepped into space and disappeared, with Ralakin still clinging to his robe....

Paul jerked off his mask and stared. He had been mesmerized with horror but now he shuddered. He hadn't even heard them scream on the way down.

Anne stared at the mask in his hand, then at his face.

"It's really me, you ninny," he said tiredly. "Now let's get out of here before we get into more trouble."

She clung to his arm as they skirted the flames and ran along the rough track to the draw. After they had scrambled down the steep slope and were moving safely along the bed of the draw Paul turned and looked at her. She was smiling. He held her hand, hurrying her along. At the end of the draw, half way down the eastern slope of the mountain, in a small group of trees, they stopped while he removed his costume.

Anne said, "I—I don't know what to think...."

He looked at her. "What difference does it make? Kozma's dead and the Kozmanites are still running. I think it's pretty amusing, myself."

She sank down to the embankment and rested against the trunk of a tree. She smiled, deep in her thoughts, and looked at the limp, rubbery mass of lacquered scales, claws, and fangs lying at her feet. Far away, they could hear